The Strange Case of
"The Angels of Mons"

The Strange Case of "The Angels of Mons"

Arthur Machen's World War I Story, the Insistent Believers, and His Refutations

RICHARD J. BLEILER

McFarland & Company, Inc., Publishers
Jefferson, North Carolina

LIBRARY OF CONGRESS CATALOGUING-IN-PUBLICATION DATA

Bleiler, Richard.
　　The strange case of "The Angels of Mons" : Arthur Machen's World War I story, the insistent believers, and his refutations / Richard J. Bleiler.
　　　p.　　cm.
　　Includes bibliographical references and index.

　　ISBN 978-0-7864-9867-3 (softcover : acid free paper) ∞
　　ISBN 978-1-4766-2096-1 (ebook)

　　1. World War, 1914–1918—Religious aspects—Christianity.
2. Nationalism—Religious aspects—Christianity—History—20th century.　3. Nationalism—Great Britain—History—20th century.
4. Mons, 1st Battle of, Mons, Belgium, 1914—Fiction.　5. Machen, Arthur, 1863–1947. Angels of Mons.　6. World War, 1914–1918—Fiction.　7. War stories, English.　8. Paranormal fiction.
9. Apparitions—Fiction. 10. Archers—Fiction.　I. Title.
D639.R4B64 2015
823'.912—dc23　　2015016087

BRITISH LIBRARY CATALOGUING DATA ARE AVAILABLE

© 2015 Richard Bleiler. All rights reserved

No part of this book may be reproduced or transmitted in any form or by any means, electronic or mechanical, including photocopying or recording, or by any information storage and retrieval system, without permission in writing from the publisher.

On the cover: angels © 2015 iStock/Thinkstock; WWI soldiers © 2015 Shutterstock

Printed in the United States of America

McFarland & Company, Inc., Publishers
　Box 611, Jefferson, North Carolina 28640
　　www.mcfarlandpub.com

For Marina

Acknowledgments

This work could not have been accomplished without the generous assistance of others.

I most gratefully acknowledge the assistance of the University of Connecticut's Document Delivery/Interlibrary Loan Department, which is to say, Erika McNeil and her crew of nonpareils: Joe Natale, Steve Bustamante, Stanley Huzarewicz, Robin Lubatkin, and Theresa Palacios-Baughman. These people are not angels but wizards, routinely conjuring up the unobtainable.

Next, I want to acknowledge four lovers of the fantastic (in general) and the writings of Arthur Machen (in particular). I hail and salute in alphabetical order Mr. Douglas Anderson, Mr. Mike Ashley, Mr. Michael Dirda, and Mr. S. T. Joshi.

Next, mere gratitude and acknowledgements are not enough to repay the efforts of Mr. Richard Fidczuk, without whose assistance this book would be so much poorer. A fellow indexer of old magazines, Mr. Fidczuk voluntarily strained his eyes and gave himself writer's cramp transcribing Machen's appearances in the microfilms of *The Evening News* held in the British Library. I hope someday to be able to repay his kindnesses with more than words.

Finally, I wish to acknowledge two very special people. I learned about Arthur Machen from my father, Everett F. Bleiler, who was friendly with Vincent Starrett and had discussed with Starrett his rocky relationship with Arthur Machen. From my father I learned of the story of the Angels of Mons, and his copy of *The Bowmen and Other Legends of the War* led to my becoming interested in this event and its remarkable influence. I regret that he did not live to see this collection.

My wife Marina heard more about World War I, the Battle of Mons, Arthur Machen, and battlefield angels than is good for any person. She offered perceptive advice and consistently challenged me to do my best, all the while making my life warm and welcoming. I could never have accomplished this without her wise assistance.

Table of Contents

Acknowledgments — vi

- ONE • Introduction — 1
- TWO • Arthur Machen and *The Bowmen: The Angels of Mons* — 19
- THREE • Harold Begbie and *On the Side of the Angels: A Reply to Arthur Machen* — 31
- FOUR • Phyllis Campbell and *Back of the Front* — 77
- FIVE • A Churchwoman and *The Chariots of God* — 93
- SIX • T. W. H. Crosland and *Find the Angels: The Showmen: A Legend of War* — 102
- SEVEN • John Garnier and *The Visions of Mons and Ypres: Their Meaning and Purpose* — 128
- EIGHT • W. H. Leathem and "In the Trenches" — 147
- NINE • C. Conway Plumbe and "The Angels of Mons" — 151
- TEN • Ralph Shirley and *The Angel Warriors at Mons: Including Numerous Confirmatory Testimonies, Evidence of the Wounded, and Certain Curious Historical Parallels. An Authentic Record* — 153
- ELEVEN • Isabelle E. Taylor and *Angels, Saints & Bowmen of Mons: An Answer to Mr. Arthur Machen & Mr. Harold Begbie* — 165

| Twelve • Charles Warr and "The Unseen Host" | 190 |
| Thirteen • Arthur Machen and "The Angels of Mons: Absolutely My Last Word on the Subject" | 197 |

Chapter Notes   203
Bibliography   218
Index   225

• One •

Introduction

Much ink has been spilled debating whether or not angels and St. George appeared to protect the beleaguered British troops during their 1914 engagement with the Germans in Mons, Belgium. The results of this debate—the fervent and sometimes cranky pamphlets, testimonies, poems, and parodies—have been uniformly neglected by scholars and anthologists alike. Indeed, owing to their rarity and fragility, many of these responses are not digitally available.

The work that inspired these spirited responses was Arthur Machen's "The Bowmen: The Angels of Mons."[1] A brief and topical piece of fiction, "The Bowmen" evoked in Machen's readers a desire to respond, generally to attest to its veracity, and although Machen at every opportunity claimed that his creation was but fiction, it was generally to no avail. His denials were ignored and disbelieved, and these counter narratives have outlived him. The result of this is a minor myth that endures until now, a century after "The Bowmen" was created merely to fill a column in an English newspaper.

This book collects for the first time Machen's original narrative together with a number of the counter-narratives that appeared in response and reprints for the first time several of Machen's later responses to these. (Although the original texts have been reset for clarity, they reproduce exactly the original variations in spelling and in the ways in which names of periodicals and newspapers were given.) The question that must first be asked is whether any of these documents are still worth reading. Indeed, although Machen was a major writer, what can possibly be gained from reading a number of relatively minor, sometimes pathetic testimonies of faith involving what eventually turned out to be a minor battle in the First World War?

The answer is that they are certainly worth reading. First, these documents are perhaps the first and finest twentieth-century example of a conceptual term used in this, the twenty-first century: going viral. When "going viral" is used today, it is generally in reference to videos distributed through the World Wide Web. But before there were videos, there were books and the printed page, and the memes that these contained could and did go viral. This occurred a number of times during the nineteenth century, and coincidentally, one of the best-known instances was also English and also involved a war with Germany. In May 1871, when George Tomkyns Chesney's *The Battle of Dorking* was published in *Blackwood's Magazine*, its cautionary story rapidly reached an astonishingly large audience:

> An indication of what *The Battle of Dorking* meant abroad can be seen in the editions immediately printed in Australia, Canada, New Zealand and the United States, in the numerous translations, and in the thirty-six pages Charles Yriarte wrote for his preface in the French edition.... From the Carlton it was reported that no one could take up *Blackwood's* for five minutes without a waiter coming to ask if he had finished with it. By June the story had been reprinted as a sixpenny pamphlet, and in a month over 80,000 copies had been sold, mostly to readers for whom it had never been intended.[2]

Like Chesney's *The Battle of Dorking*, Machen's "The Bowmen" became a readily recognizable referent to the culture at large and reached an almost unbelievable array of people through whatever media were available. It is not possible to list all the writers who encountered "The Bowmen" and mentioned it in their writings, but were such a hypothetical list compiled, it would have to begin with such disparate but well-known figures as G. K. Chesterton, C. S. Lewis, and Arthur Conan Doyle. The first alludes to "The Bowmen" somewhat obliquely in 1915, stating in *The Crimes of England* that

> Ghosts were there perhaps, but they were the ghosts of forgotten ancestors ... things were either seen or said among the British which linked them up, in matters deeper than any alliance, with the French.... They were the visions or the inventions of a mediaeval army; and a prose poet was in line with many popular rumors when he told of ghostly archers crying "Array, Array," as in that long-disbanded yeomanry in which I have fancied Cobbett as carrying a bow.[3]

C. S. Lewis explicitly mentions the Angels of Mons in 1915, in a letter to his father. He first describes his readings—"I am still busy with my 'heavy winged Pegasus' as you call Spenser.... I have also been reading in library copies, Schopenhauer's 'Will and Idea' and Swinburne's 'Erectheus' which is another tragedy on Greek lines like 'Atalanta,'" then adds mischievously: "Kirk, I need hardly say, is strong on him, and will talk on the subject for hours—by the way, the real subject to get him on just now is the Mons angels. You should drop him a cue in your next letter: you know—'a man was telling me the other day that he had seen with his own eyes' or something of the kind."[4] Furthermore, Lewis mentions the Angels of Mons again, at the start of the Second World War, in a letter to his brother of 28 January 1940: "did you see that the Finns, like the British at Mons, have been seeing angels?"[5] His question was asked in response to an article of 23 January 1940 that appeared on the front page of *The Daily Mail*, was entitled "Battle Weary Finns See Angels" and presented yet again a discussion of the Angels of Mons.[6]

Although one would anticipate from Arthur Conan Doyle enthusiastic and early endorsement of the Angels of Mons—he seems never to have encountered a spiritualist fad he did not fancy—he is somewhat more circumspect, first mentioning them in the ambivalent endorsement in his 1926 *The History of Spiritualism*:

> This evidence [i.e., an anonymous soldier's anecdotal testimonial] sounds good, and yet it must be admitted that in the stress and tension of the great retreat men's minds were not in the best conditions to weigh evidence. On the other hand, it is at such times of hardship that the psychic powers of man are usually most alive.
>
> A profound aspect of the World War is involved in the consideration that the war on earth is but one aspect of unseen battles on higher planes where the powers of Good and Evil are engaged.[7]

This ambivalence may owe something to the fact that a mere ten years earlier, Conan Doyle had written *The British Campaign in France and Flanders, 1914*, the forty-six pages of its Chapter III describing in gratifyingly precise detail the British campaign in Mons but failing to mention or acknowledge the presence of angelic bowmen.[8]

Chesterton, Lewis, and Conan Doyle are three of the best known writers to reference the Angels of Mons, and the list of the others who also referenced them is lengthy, filled with names now known only to specialists. The minor poet Alfred Dodd, for example, could write the following, knowing that he need not gloss for his readers:

> At Mons I saw, or thought I saw,
> Ghost bowmen fringe the height,
> Smiting with arrow and with sword
> The foe in deadly fight;
> Our quivering, thin-drawn khaki line
> Should have been snapt like burning twine
> Before the Prussian might.[9]

Finally, the Angels of Mons rapidly made appearances in other media. Popular composers Sydney C. Baldock and Paul Paree could write, respectively, a piano solo, the "Angels of Mons (*Rêve Mystique*)"[10] and a waltz, the "Angel of Mons Waltz."[11] If one had access to a gramophone, the Regal Company provided 78 rpm phonograph record offering a sound dramatization of the battle and the advent of the angels.[12] If one had access to a motion picture theatre, the G. B. Samuelson Productions Company released a short feature, now lost, "The Angels of Mons," starring Peggy Hyland and Bertram Burleigh.[13]

Not only do the accounts collected herein provide insight into the cultures that created them, they are primary documents, revealing the sustaining beliefs of those on the margins of these cultures. They expose a side of a culture that is rarely examined and less remarked-upon. The testimonials and statements show clearly a determination to believe and to justify these beliefs to a larger audience. That this is another word for opportunism and occurs at the expense of the truth should not be too surprising. The marginal are often marginalized precisely because their beliefs are perceived as irrational, and anything that can sustain and elevate these beliefs is utilized to do so. One does not often encounter such justifications so baldly presented, opportunities so boldly seized, as they are in the impassioned responses and fervent testimonials of faith involving "The Bowmen." Similarly, knowing that journalist and poet T. W. H. Crosland wrote a lengthy and knowing parody of "The Bowmen" perhaps somewhat humanizes the figure who is now remembered, if remembered he is, solely for being a "fanatical Christian homophobe" and co-authoring Lord Alfred Douglas's *Oscar Wilde and Myself*.[14]

II

Mons—a city in southwest Belgium, the capital of the province of Hainaut—was a thriving place in the early twentieth century and had a not insignificant international reputation. Mons had been occupied since Neolithic times, and a number of its archaeological antiquities had been exported.[15] Mons was also the site of rich coal deposits, and the mining of these and their utilization made the city important to the economic development of the region and noted elsewhere. In 1893 Mons had been the site of a general strike, the Belgian miners wanting better treatment. This strike and its settlement attracted international attention.[16]

Mons was also culturally rich, meriting discussion in a number of English guides to Europe as a place whose sights were worth visiting.[17] In *The Gourmet's Guide to Europe*, Lieutenant-Colonel Newnham-Davis notes approvingly that "at Mons and at Liège, and I think at Charleroi also, there is every year a woodcock feast, just as there is an oyster feast at Colchester. At these festivities a little wax candle is placed on the table beside each guest, so that he can take the head of his *bècasse* and frizzle it in the flame before he attacks its brains."[18]

The 1906 *Black's Shilling Guide to Scotland* references "the *Bomb Battery* and *Mons Meg*, the latter being a gigantic piece of artillery made at Mons, in Belgium, in 1476, according to one story,"[19] a technological note that is in retrospect somewhat ominous, for in 1914 Mons became the location of the first battle fought by the British and German armies, as Mons had both the blessing and misfortune to be strategically located. "Main roads from Brussels, Binche, Charleroi, Valenciennes, and Maubeuge have their meeting-place here, while the railway from Paris to Brussels passes through it. It is also the junction point of the canal from Condé and the Canal du Centre, which connects the former with the Charleroi Canal and the Sambre," wrote Field-Marshal Viscount John French, First Earl of Ypres and leader of the British Expeditionary Force (BEF), in his account of the first year of the Great War, prefacing these statements with the observation that pre-war Mons had a "population of twenty-eight thousand inhabitants, and is situated on a sandhill overlooking the Trovillon."[20]

The British and French forces encountered the German forces on August 23 and 24, 1914. The encounter itself was for neither of the Allies a propitious or an auspicious beginning to the war. The leaderships of the two armies distrusted each others' skills and had failed to communicate, coordinate, and delegate their mutual efforts and intelligences, and on the first day of the battle, the French troops had pulled back without informing their English counterparts, who were left completely exposed. The well-armed and well-led German troops thus split and handily routed the troops of both countries. The English had a long and terrible retreat.

The Battle at Mons made the English newspapers, though the reports were at first vague and uplifting. Through such statements as "the British forces were engaged all day on Sunday and after dark with the enemy in the neighbourhood of Mons, and held their ground,"[21] and "what seems certain, however, is that our Army, doubtless to its disgust and disappointment, must conform with the movements of the French in retreat,"[22] *The Times* claimed that the English retreat was their decision. A day later, *The Times* was to state that, "we know that our little Army, which fought so steadily at Mons, and has had a handsome tribute paid to it by the French, has returned safely from its first incursion into Belgium. It has carried out one of the most difficult of all operations—namely, retirement in face of a superior enemy—with conspicuous coolness and success."[23]

Nevertheless, one can sugarcoat disaster and defeat only so much. Bad news remains inescapable, and on 30 August 1914 *The Times* published an extra, a special Sunday edition. It contained a lengthy telegram, sometimes referred to as the "Amiens Dispatch," sent by Arthur Moore of *The Times*, one of several journalists determined to report the news of the fighting from the front. Headlined "Broken British Regiments Battling Against the Odds, More Men Needed," it offered a terrifying depiction of the battle:

> Amongst all the straggling units that I have seen, flotsam and jetsam in the fiercest fight in history, I saw fear in no man's face. It was a retreating and broken army, but it was not an army of hunted men.
> Since Monday morning last the German advance has been one of almost incredible rapidity. The German attack was withstood to the utmost limits, and a whole division was flung into the fight at the end of a long march and had not even time to dig trenches. Along the Sambre and in the angle of the

Sambre and the Meuse, the French, after days of long and gallant fighting, broke. Naumer fell, and General Joffre was forced to order a retreat along the whole line.

Our losses are very great. I have seen the broken bits of many regiments. Let me repeat that there is no failure in discipline, no panic, no throwing up of the sponge. Every one's temper is sweet, and nerves do not show. The men are battered with marching, and ought to be weak with hunger, but they are steady and cheerful, and wherever they arrive make straight for the proper authority, report themselves, and seek news of their regiment.

To sum up, the first great German effort has succeeded. We have to face the fact that the British Expeditionary Force, which bore the great weight of the blow, has suffered terrible losses and requires immediate and immense reinforcements. The British Expeditionary Force has won indeed imperishable glory, but it needs men, men, and yet more men.[24]

Although the last paragraph of the Amiens Dispatch, rewritten by censors, stimulated English enlistment, the news was not well-received. The House of Commons discussed it at great length, and *The Globe*, which also published the Amiens Dispatch as well as erroneous information, was briefly censored.[25] Nevertheless, there was nothing that could be done, and the general consensus was that expressed by Mr. Hogge in the House of Commons discussions: "everybody round the table was perturbed, and the English people were perturbed, for ... the people were informed that the British Army had been cut to pieces."[26] In addition, the Amiens Dispatch and the phrase "a retreating and broken army" obviously struck a cultural nerve and resonated, for H. G. Wells utilizes them in *Mr. Britling Sees It Through*:

> The British army or a part of it came to light abruptly at Mons. It had been fighting for thirty-eight hours and defeating enormously superior forces of the enemy. That was reassuring until a day or so later "the Cambray—Le Cateau line" made Mr. Britling realise that the victorious British had recoiled five and twenty miles....
>
> And then came the Sunday of *The Times* telegram, which spoke of a "retreating and a broken army."[27]

Some later military historians have attempted to minimize the defeat at Mons, with Moore's telegram being described as inaccurate and overwrought. In his 1951 history of the war, Brigadier-General Sir James E. Edmonds even attempts to impart a positive slant to the retreat, quoting an unattributed German witness who wrote that "the British brilliantly understood how to slip off at the last moment.... The British vanished without leaving a trace," with Edmonds adding on his own that "a few rear-guard actions occurred during the day, but not a gun was lost, and the retreat was not interrupted."[28] Nevertheless, it seems that Mr. Hogge's initial assessment reflects the dominant view, and the recent conclusion of the contemporary military historian

John Mosier echoes Mr. Hogge: "On 23 August, the BEF was routed at Mons by elements of the German First Army."[29]

This was the situation in late September 1914 when Arthur Machen sat down and wrote a short piece of fiction for *The Evening News*, the best-selling newspaper of the day and one whose contents were a bit more popular and accessible than those in *The Times*. *The Evening News* also published fiction, often labeled as such.

III

Arthur Machen was born Arthur Llewellyn Jones on 3 March 1863 to Janet and John Edward Jones in Caerleon-on-Usk, Gwent, Wales. His father was an Anglican clergyman, the vicar at Caerleon and later the vicar of nearby Llanddewi Fach, "a scattered parish of farms, small holdings and remote cottages, and even though it was joined with the neighbouring and similar parish of Llandegveth, the living was always poor."[30] Janet Jones's maiden name was Machen, and in order to receive an inheritance from his wife's family, John Edward added her name to his, the family becoming "Jones-Machen." Arthur Machen rarely ever used this full name, stating in a letter in 1924 that "I don't believe that I have signed myself Arthur Llewellyn Jones Machen since 1880—save in joke, by way of giving people a slight surprise."[31]

Arthur Machen had no siblings and grew up alone, developing a lifelong love of literature and nature. He read his father's library, which contained theology as well as such classics as *The Arabian Nights*, *Don Quixote*, plus the works of Dickens, Tennyson, Borrow, Scott, plus numerous popular periodicals. He was, like many, a youthful autodidact, fascinated by Celtic history, folklore, and mythology as well as Christian history, particularly demonology and the legends surrounding the Holy Grail. As an adult, he corresponded heavily with A. E. Waite, the poet and scholarly mystic, and his letters reveal a profound, formidable, and sustained knowledge of early Christian esoteric beliefs and traditions.[32]

Although Machen spent from eleven to seventeen as a boarder in the Hereford Cathedral School, he does not appear to have been a happy student despite excelling in Classics and Divinity.[33] Following a brief and failed assay at becoming a doctor, he decided he wanted to be a writer, and in 1881, he saw his first significant piece, *Eleusinia*, "by a former Member of H.C.S. [Hereford Cathedral School]," printed in an edition of (at most) 100 copies.[34] He was in later life dismissive of it, stating that "this is a horrible production. The only defence is that it was written when I was seventeen, just after I had left school.... It is a 'poem.' So far as I recollect, it was done by the process of turning the article 'Eleusinia' in Smith's Classical Dictionary into verse, some of it blank, some rhymed, all of it bad."[35]

Machen self-trained as a journalist and moved to London in the hopes of finding employment on a newspaper. He worked for a month at the educational publishers Marcus Ward, tutored children, and "lived on dry bread, green tea and tobacco" in not particularly genteel or uplifting poverty.[36] He continued to read voluminously, and in 1883, "out of tobacco and logic, the two chief solaces of my loneliness," he compiled *The Anatomy of Tobacco*, a companion to Robert Burton's *The Anatomy of Melancholy*. "It was published by an odd accident," stated Machen, explaining that his reading of Hargrave Jenning's *The Rosicrucians* and Herodotus led him to recognize a point in the latter that Jennings might have used. He contacted Jennings, who (presumably out of gratitude) gave Machen's address to his publisher, George Redway. Redway sent Machen a catalogue, and when Machen saw that it contained some books about tobacco, he sent Redway his manuscript, and Redway published it.[37] Machen soon was to translate *The Heptameron* of Marguerite, Queen of Navarre, rendering it into English for the first time.[38] In 1887, in a curious anticipation of the events that came to surround the Battle of Mons, Machen wrote and saw published a work that purported to be something else: *A Chapter from the Book Called The Ingenious Gentleman Don Quijote de la Mancha, Which by Some Mischance Has Not Till Now Been Printed* was, in reality, an extended advertisement for Redway's stock of occult titles.[39]

Machen began publishing fiction in earnest in 1888, with the work known as *The Chronicle of Clemendy*. It too is a bit of a fraud, its subtitle indicating that the volume contains "*the amorous inventions and facetious tales of Master Gervase Perrot, Gent., now for the first time done into English, by Arthur Machen, translator of the Heptameron of Margaret of Navarre.*[40] Written in a deliberately archaic English—"How many a poor author hath had at home but a scurvy bin and piggin, a bare floor and barer trencher, a cup void not only of canary, but even of small ale. How many a scholar, I say, hath passed away the best years of his life, the flower of his age, in some mean cockloft, with scarce enough air (let alone meat and drink) for his sustenance; the which lack of air being by itself well-recognised for a sufficient cause of melancholy"[41]—the stories in *The Chronicle of Clemendy* are described by Machen as a "mingling of an epicurean delight in the table and the tankard and the tobacco bowl, and a relish for improbable yarns."[42] Although praised by some, it is far from Machen's best work, and even the assessment of Mark Valentine, Machen's most sympathetic biographer, reflects this: "it is a pleasant book, a fine curio, and one which will always win the allegiance of connoisseurs in obscure literature, but it is not a significant work even in the Machen canon and it will never be widely read."[43]

Machen's next significant works, however, are those that have sustained his memory. First, his comprehensive translation of *The Memoirs of Jacques Casanova*—began in 1888–1889 but not issued until 1894—was the first complete English edition, proved popular, and was reprinted more than seventeen times.[44] Next, Machen turned to the overtly fantastic for his subject matter. A discussion of *The Great God Pan*,[45] *The Three Imposters*,[46] *The House of Souls*,[47] and *The Hill of Dreams*,[48] is beyond the scope of this introduction, but they are the volumes that "first shocked British sensibilities"[49] and "played a significant role in making the Yellow Nineties so distinctive."[50]

Machen's masterpiece is *The Hill of Dreams*. Originally called "The Garden of Avallaunius," it was intended as "a 'Robinson Crusoe' of the soul; the story of a man who is not lonely because he is on a desert island and has nobody to speak to, but lonely in the midst of millions, because of his mental isolation, because there is a great gulf fixed spiritually between him and all whom he encounters."[51] The book proved difficult to publish—Machen states that before he changed his mind, Grant Richards initially stated that Machen must "never ... publish this dull, futile, unhappy failure"[52]—but in its description of the would-be writer Lucian Taylor, it contains some of Machen's most glorious prose:

> He had tried to sing in words the music that the brook sang, and the sound of the October wind rustling through the brown bracken on the hill. How many pages he had covered in the effort to show a white winter world, a sun without warmth in a grey-blue sky, all the fields, all the land white and shining, and one high summit where the dark pines towered, still in the still afternoon, in the pale violet air.
> To win the secret of words, to make a phrase that would murmur of summer and the bee, to summon the wind into a sentence, to conjure the odour of the night into the surge and fall and harmony of a line; this was the tale of the long evenings, of the candle flame white upon the paper and the eager pen.[53]

Machen had married in 1887, to Amy Hogg, "a bohemian woman some thirteen years his senior,"[54] and although he barely mentions her in his memoirs or letters, their relationship was apparently happy; as has been noted, he composed practically all of his significant works during the span of this marriage, which in 1899 terminated with her death from cancer. Following her death, he briefly became a member of the Golden Dawn, Britain's most prominent occult group, worked intermittently as an actor in Sir Frank Benson's Company, and in June 1903 remarried, to Dorothy Purefoy Hudleston, whose first name was not used.[55] She too was involved with the stage. They had a son, Arthur Hilary, and a daughter, Janet Frances.

In 1907, Machen's journalism came to the attention of Lord Alfred Douglas, whose autobiography contains several recollections:

> Soon after I started editing *The Academy* [25 May 1907] I began to get contributions from Mr. Arthur Machen. It was these contributions of his which first sent me back to Christianity. I gave Mr. Machen a perfectly wonderful show in *The Academy*. I printed columns from him week after week. I even reproduced in the paper, in weekly instalments, a whole book of his, called *The Views and*

Opinions of the Revd. Dr Stiggins, a fiercely ironical attack on Protestantism, and paid him for it (or rather Sir Edward Tennant paid him) at the full rates on the highest scale for contributors.[56]

In 1910, Machen joined the staff of *The Evening News*, then owned by Alfred and Harold Harmsworth. He wrote on all subjects and was justifiably proud of his compositional speed, bragging in a letter that "I have been and am the swiftest 'descriptive' writer on the London Press. My paper is The Evening News [*sic*]. Do not try to watch me describing the Coronation or a Memorial Service at St. Paul's with the naked eye: use leather. Ten minutes after the last organ note my story—2 to 4 columns—is in the hands of our chief sub-editor. People see me writing on buses or trams, on the roofs of pubs in the East End; I have a special recipe for writing in total darkness."[57] Although he occasionally quit to provide copy for such other newspapers as *The Daily Express*, Machen always returned to *The Evening News*. He nevertheless permanently severed relations with it in late 1921, following an obituary he wrote upon learning of the death of Lord Alfred Douglas. Though Machen was to outlive Douglas, Douglas was quite alive and not to die for another 23 years, and he was litigious, particularly when his past relationship with Oscar Wilde was recalled: "Mr. Arthur Machen's way of showing his gratitude for what I did so successfully to bring his name before the public was to write the 'obituary notice' of me in *The Evening News* when that journal published a false report of my death in 1921."[58] Machen departed under the proverbial cloud in November 1921.[59] He nevertheless continued to write, essays and the occasional short novel, and although he stated that he was happy, his financial status was generally precarious.

During the 1920s, Machen's books began to reach an American audience. In 1918 a correspondent, the Toronto-born Chicago-based critic Vincent Starrett, published *Arthur Machen: A Novelist of Ecstasy and Sin*, an enthusiastic appreciation that opens by stating that "Arthur Machen is the outstanding artist of his time, and one of the great masters of all time."[60] This and Starrett's championing of Machen in his columns succeeded in bringing Machen to the attention of a wider audience, and Machen gave Starrett permission to reprint his earlier work, but the friendship did not end well: ever the professional, Machen wanted money for his work, whereas the bibliophile Starrett produced two expensive limited editions that sold poorly and hampered Machen's finding an American publisher. Machen accused Starrett of theft and piracy, and although everything was eventually resolved, the friendship was over, if ever it had really existed. Starrett was later to write that "although Machen and I made up our differences when I visited him in London, it was long before I was able to think of him as anything but cynically ungrateful."[61] (He was to write to Machen in June 1924 that "had I been able to see this final chapter when I penned my first letter to you, back in 1914, I assure you that my admiration would have remained forever a secret."[62]) For his part, Machen appears to have used every opportunity to say unpleasant things about Starrett.

During the 1930s, Starrett's recognition of Machen's genius was echoed by H. P. Lovecraft in his *Supernatural Horror in Literature*. Lovecraft, whose library contained some ten volumes by Machen,[63] was to write that,

> Of living creators of cosmic fear raised to its most artistic pitch, few if any can hope to equal the versatile Arthur Machen, author of some dozen tales long and short, in which the elements of hidden horror and brooding fright attain an almost incomparable substance and realistic acuteness. Mr. Machen, a general man of letters and master of an exquisitely lyrical and expressive prose style, has perhaps put more conscious effort into his picaresque *Chronicle of Clemendy*, his refreshing essays, his vivid autobiographical volumes, his fresh and spirited translations, and above all his memorable epic of the sensitive aesthetic mind, *The Hill of Dreams*....[64]

Lovecraft concludes his assessment by recognizing Machen's role in the creation of "The Bowmen": "Too well known to need description here is the tale of *The Bowmen;* which, taken for authentic narration, gave rise to the widespread legend of the 'Angels of Mons'—ghosts of the old English archers of Crecy and Agincourt who fought in 1914 beside the hard-pressed tanks of England's glorious 'Old Contemptibles.'"[65] Lovecraft's colleagues were to write verse and tributes to Machen, but they do not appear to have corresponded with him, and their praise does not seem to have stimulated his sales.

Machen's final years were alcoholic and impoverished, though he was in his 80th year granted a much-needed pension by the Crown.[66] He died on 15 December 1947, preceded by Purefoy, survived by their two children. The *Chicago Daily Tribune* published two accounts of Machen's death. The first, an anonymous notice in the daily paper, consists of one sentence stating that he "originated the World War I legend of the Angels of Mons."[67] Though the obituaries in *The New York Times*[68] and *The Times*[69] are longer, mentioning Machen's novels and collections, they too discuss "The Bowmen" as his best known work. Starrett's memorial was published nearly two weeks later: it is a touching tribute, describing Machen as an old friend, providing a charming account of the Machens at home, and revealing that despite their earlier differences, he and Arthur Machen had continued to correspond. He does not mention "The Bowmen."[70]

IV

The publication history of "The Bowmen" is not complex. As stated above, *The Evening News* published a story in each issue. Starting with the issue of 7 May 1887, and continuing for nearly all of its nearly 100 years of existence, *The Evening News* published literally thousands of short stories, with one Paul Feakes—"a foreign banker who wrote in his spare time"—contributing the most original stories, 397 signed pieces of fiction.[71] Furthermore, at the time "The Bowmen" was published, readers of *The Evening News* could immediately identify the short story, for it was headed "Our Short Story." Most of these stories remain unreprinted.

Although Arthur Machen wrote prodigiously for *The Evening News*,[72] he had but seven pieces of fiction in the newspaper. Furthermore, when he wrote "The Bowmen" for the issue of 29 September 1914, there was already a story scheduled to appear under the "Our Short Story" heading, Alexander Crawford's "A Scrap of Paper."[73] Machen's story was thus headed "The Bowmen: The Angels of Mons" and, although by-lined, it was not identified as fiction.

In addition, and perhaps more importantly, the story is in quite a number of respects a strikingly *unoriginal* work of fiction. The opening sentences are a mass of journalistic cliché piled upon journalistic cliché: "the most awful day of that awful time, on the day when ruin and disaster came so near that their shadow fell over London far away; and without any certain news, the hearts of men failed within them and grew faint; as if the agony of their brothers on the battlefield had entered into their souls." There is also melodrama, ladled on: "there comes a moment in a storm at sea when people say to one another: 'it is at its worst; it can blow no harder,' and then there is a blast ten times more fierce than any before it. So it was in these British trenches." Finally, there is, a fair amount of facile patriotic jingoism: "There were no stouter hearts in the whole world than the hearts of those men [in the trenches] ... they shook hands, some of them. One man improvised a new version of the battle song: 'Goodbye, goodbye to Tipperary,' ending with 'And we shan't get there!' And they all went on firing steadily." One could thus, if so inclined see "The Bowmen" as a fervid retelling of the events of recent past. Machen even quotes the Amiens Dispatch in explaining the survival of the "retreating and broken army" that was nevertheless "not an army of hunted men."

Paradoxically, the narrative of "The Bowmen" is effective precisely because it does not make many intellectual or stylistic demands upon its readers. Machen's cleverness lay in emphasizing the ordinary, largely eschewing dialogue until the conclusion, and in presenting small details—the "queer vegetarian restaurant in London where he had once or twice eaten queer dishes of cutlets made of lentils and nuts that pretended to be steaks" that had on its plates "a figure of St. George in blue, with the motto, *Adsit Anglis Sanctus Georgius*"—that assume importance after they are linked to the larger narrative, and even having them figure again at the conclusion. Had Machen's soldier not known "Latin and other useless things," had this soldier not eaten at this "queer vegetarian restaurant," and had this soldier not at a moment of crisis "uttered the pious vegetarian motto," then there would be no story.

Next, as the story develops, the fantastic elements are themselves reassuring and familiar. While some have attempted to establish Machen's literary models for "The Bowmen," this is essentially a pointless endeavor, for virtually all of its contents were drawn from general knowledge and would have been instantly recognizable to any even moderately aware Englishman or woman.[74] The readers of *The Evening News* would not be surprised at learning of Saint George, the English patron saint. Similarly, angelic visitations were common and familiar devices in English literature and histories; the histories of England and Agincourt stressed the powerful English longbowmen and the steadfast soldiers; and, of course, the disastrous affair at Mons of the previous month and the Amiens Dispatch would have been fresh in readers' minds. A specific "queer vegetarian restaurant" that used a Latin tag on its plates has not been located, but such may also have existed and been recognized by the readers of *The Evening News*.

Nevertheless, these attributes do not explain what sparked the interest and belief in "The Bowmen" that is mentioned at the beginning of this essay. As Machen recounts, he consented to requests to reprint the story, for somehow it was reaching an audience larger than the readership of *The Evening News*, and this audience was responding to its message, accepting fiction as fact. Doubtless the majority of the readers wanted to believe in the rightness and justness of the English cause and the story gave them something familiar and reassuring in which they already believed, but this facile response does not explain how this particular story traveled so rapidly and achieved such widespread recognition, and an alternative theory is thus somewhat diffidently suggested in the next section.

By the middle of 1915 Machen attempted to reclaim his property. He explained and detailed its composition in "The Mons Angels: The Growth of a Miracle Fiction," which was published in *The Daily Mail* rather than *The Evening News*.[75] He likewise pulled together half a dozen similar stories, found a publisher, and rewrote and expanded "The Mons Angels" as its introduction. In both instances he chose to emphasize that his account was fiction, nothing more, and while he did not in as many words state that the claimants who said they had seen angels were liars, he strongly implied it. Furthermore, he quietly revised his story. The most significant revision occurs in the conclusion. In the text given in *The Evening News*, the German leadership originally speculated that the "the contemptible English must have employed turpenite shells," a reference that would have meant much to a contemporary readership, as turpenite was rumored to be a terrible explosive in the possession of the French that emitted gasses that killed all within 400 yards of the explosion. On 1 October 1914 the *New York Times* published an article stating that its existence has "not been authenticated," and soon after turpenite faded from the news. Doubtless aware of this change in technology, Machen's rewritten version had the German leadership speculating that "the contemptible English must have employed shells containing an unknown gas of a poisonous nature."[76] On 10 August 1915 *The [London] Times* noted the appearance of this little book:

> Messrs. Simpkins, Marshall, Hamilton, Kent and Co. (Limited) have issued, at the price of 1s [1 shilling], "The Bowmen and Other Legends of the War," by Mr. Arthur Machen. Mr. Machen's story of "The Bowmen" originally appeared in the *Evening News* in September, and since then has attracted a considerable amount of attention, for, while the author in the introduction to the present volume, declares that the story is fiction and has no basis whatever in fact, many other people have insisted of late that the Bowmen of Mons were actually seen by many of the British soldiers who took part in that retreat. Mr. Machen attributes this to the fact that angels, with certain reservations, have retained their popularity, and so, when it was settled that the English Army in its dire peril was delivered by angelic aid, the way was clear for the general belief and for the enthusiasms of the religion of the man in the street. And so soon as the legend got the title "The Angels of Mons," it became impossible to avoid it.

The English edition of *The Bowmen* is known to have gone through two printings, the second having textual changes and a portrait included. Furthermore, there was an American edition, a reprint by a major publisher.[77] Machen had obviously hoped that his account would make money, and so it did, but as he noted glumly, the money was not for him: "the sale, I believe, was a very large one, but for reasons into which I need not enter, the book was not highly remunerative to me. However, it is always a satisfaction to find that one has put a little money into the pockets of good men."[78] It is not unreasonable to ask why, if the sales were good, Machen did not profit from *The Bowmen* or its American edition, but no answer is available. It must nevertheless have galled him that his works of art barely sold enough copies to keep him alive, whereas a work of journalism that he (literally) dashed off in one sitting was enormously popular and made everybody else money. Only rarely does he seem to have committed any of these feelings to paper.[79]

V

A few words must be said about the claimants, which is to say, the many who attested to the veracity of angelic visions. These come in two kinds: those who exploited the vision for their ends, which were generally testimonies of faith; and those who claimed to have seen the angels themselves. Of the former, relatively little needs to be said: one would like to believe in their piousness, in their sincerity and honour, but to the modern reader, many of their accounts seem little more than opportunistic and grasping, revealing aspects of their personalities and a side to their culture that has barely been explored.

Researchers have taken the latter claimants seriously, and when possible, when names have been provided, their claims have been investigated. They have uniformly been shown to be fraudulent. In some cases, the person who attested to the angels has been shown never to have existed; in others, the person has been shown not to have been present at the Battle of Mons. Speculations as to why people would fabricate these witnesses and their angelic experiences are generally beyond the scope of this introduction, though they too not only come across as opportunistic and grasping but also as pathologically mendacious and psychologically warped.

There is, however, one account that remains genuinely intriguing, that of Brigadier-General John Charteris, C.M.G., D.S.O. Born 8 January 1877, Charteris was of a distinguished academic family, and entered the Royal Military Academy in Woolwich in 1893. "He was commissioned in the Royal Engineers in March 1896 and posted to India," states his entry in the *Dictionary of National Biography*, adding most importantly that "his career did not take its characteristic shape until 1907, when he entered the staff college at Quetta, from which he emerged in 1909 with a reputation as the outstanding graduate of his year. His elevation to staff officer also brought him into contact with the man who was to dominate his professional life, Douglas Haig, then chief of staff to the commander-in-chief, India. Haig had a liking for young officers with quick wit and lively conversation, provided that they were dedicated, competent, and loyal. Charteris scored on all points."[80] Under Haig, Charteris continued his rise, and during the First World War, Charteris distinguished himself: he was a Captain in 1914 and a Brigadier General when the War concluded in 1918. He retired from the army in 1922 and led what from all accounts appears to have been an exemplary life as a civilian, serving as conservative MP for Dumfrieshire, writing accounts of his life and Haig, and dying on 9 March 1946.

The account under consideration is *At G. H. Q.*[81] It purports to reprint Charteris's letters and extracts from his letters, and two of these mention the Angels of Mons. The first, dated 1914, states:

> Then there is the story of the "Angel of Mons" going strong through the 2nd Corps of how the angel of the Lord on the traditional white horse, and clad all in white with flaming sword, faced the advancing Germans at Mons and forbade their further progress. Men's nerves and imagination play weird pranks in these strenuous times. All the same the angel at Mons interests me. I cannot find out how the legend arose.[82]

What is extraordinary about this account is that the letter purports to date to the 5th of September, thus predating Machen's claim to originality by more than three weeks. Charteris later provides an answer as to how the legend arose:

The impossibility of answering those *whys* as regards the Germans are explained in the easy philosophy of the men by the "Angel of Mons" theory, of which I told you when I was at home. I have been at some trouble to trace the rumour to its source. The best I can make of it is that some religiously minded man wrote home that the Germans halted at Mons, AS IF an Angel of the Lord had appeared in front of them. In due course the letter appeared in a Parish Magazine, which in time was sent out to some other men at the front. From them the story went back home with the "as if" omitted, and at home it went the rounds in its expurgated form.[83]

If these accounts were genuine, Machen's claims would be demolished, and "The Bowmen" would simply be his adaptation of a legend he had somewhere encountered. Nevertheless, Charteris is not to be trusted. The scholar David Clarke investigated Charteris's claim extensively, to the point of examining Charteris's original manuscripts in the War Office. His conclusion—"the absence of an original letter referring to the Angel of Mons among the Charteris collection leads me to conclude that the testimony provided by him dates not from 1914, but from 1931"[84]—is magisterial and damning.

It has not hitherto been noted that Charteris provides an identically structured story to another legend of the First World War, including a similar and equally spurious genealogy about the Russians, who were *not* passing through England at the time of the war:

> One other yarn has been traced to its source. The Russians in England (whom poor M's sister saw!) were undoubtedly the Territorial units moving through Great Britain on their way to ports of embarkation that at a wayside station one bearded warrior, asked where he came from, said truthfully enough, Ross-shire, which sounded like Russia. Even without this embellishment, the explanation is adequate. We shall have many more such rumours before the war ends.[85]

Like turpenite, the story of the Russians was also around at the beginning of the First World War and was sufficiently widely known that Sir Almeric Fitzroy would mention and debunk it in his 1925 *Memoirs*:

> There is nothing more remarkable than the persistence and universality of the legend that large bodies of Russian troops, brought from Archangel to Aberdeen, have been passing through England *en route* for the seat of war. Originally started, perhaps, by some inventive humorist, or more probably owing to someone having seen the weird figures of Lovat's Scouts and heard them talking Gaelic, it is now an article of faith with residents in the country throughout Great Britain. Though no one can be produced who has actually seen a Russian, an incredible number of persons have seen someone who has heard from others that Russians have most certainly appeared at places so far apart as Bath, Reading, and Northampton. In all parts the railway service has been held up for trains, with blinds drawn, loaded with Russians: drawn blinds are, it appears, the most infallible evidence, and you cannot question

the accuracy of the rumor, or dispute the data upon which it is alleged to rest, without incurring a scarcely veiled incredulity or even a suggestion of mendacity. I very nearly forfeited Lord Haversham's good opinion by venturing to doubt the grounds of his confidence, and two days afterwards received a letter which is a most signal example of the use of hearsay to prove a point. Meanwhile, neither the Foreign Office nor the War Office have the slightest information on the subject, and A. Nicholson tells me that he has ceased to contradict the report. The paucity of authentic news is perhaps responsible for the avidity with which fiction is devoured.[86]

Why then would John Charteris, a man of apparently the utmost probity, fraudulently claim prior knowledge of two pieces of folklore and create for each a spurious genealogy? Clarke's answer to this is, essentially, that Charteris was a propagandist for the English Army. He cites Charteris's role in "the embryonic field of black propaganda,"[87] specifically his spreading of the Corpse Factory story, in which it was claimed that the Germans were recycling their dead "for use in shells and animal feed in a secret factory hidden behind the front line."[88] The spreading of this story involved forged and fraudulent documents, and although Charteris was to deny a newspaper report that he had once claimed credit for the story, his denials in the end were not seen as carrying much weight: there was little doubt that he had invented or played a key role in at that particular piece of invention.

If this is so, why did Charteris write what he did in 1931? He almost certainly was sworn to secrecy, but why did he proffer several lies, readily recognizable as lies, rather than simply avoid all mention of the issues? A possible answer contains a statement he makes near the beginning of G. H. Q., that "we were trained for war. It was the task for which we had been preparing ourselves for years. We could not but appreciate that it was only in war that we could fulfil our life's work."[89] In this theory, Charteris was proud of his accomplishments and wanted recognition for his life's work but felt that he could not overtly reveal his role in its creation without having his volume suppressed. He thus provided wartime accounts that would easily satisfy any potential censors but that those who were in the know would recognize as false, hoaxes whose origins could only lie with the man reporting them, John Charteris himself. It is Charteris's backhanded way of claiming the credit.

Nevertheless, here too Charteris cannot be trusted, for his claim is certainly disingenuous. He may have conceived the idea, but the credit for its initial dissemination more than likely goes to Machen's colleague Harold Begbie. Little has been written on the man, and he has not before been connected to Charteris; indeed, like Charteris he seems at first a figure of the utmost probity and sincere patriotism. Almost certainly the two met because Begbie was active in the recruitment effort; his 1914 poem "Fall In!" was enormously popular.[90] Although it cannot be proved, it seems likely that Charteris convinced

Begbie to lend his pen to the dissemination of the story of the Angels of Mons, and Begbie stirred up interest among the faithful and wrote *On the Side of the Angels*, an odd combination of personal attack on Machen, "scientific explanation," religious fervor, and psychical mish-mash that proved sufficiently popular that it received three additional editions. As shown in the section devoted to *On the Side of the Angels*, Begbie's testimonials are as false as Charteris's memoirs.

At the end, the story of the Angels endures, as do Machen's writings, and regardless of who may or may not have played a role in the dissemination, there is no denying that "The Bowmen" went viral and a century ago became widely understood and accessible as a cultural referent. As with *The Battle of Dorking*, one is left with the wonder that it was as popular as it was and that, whatever their motivation, so many people once cared and felt compelled to write so many responses.

• Two •

Arthur Machen and *The Bowmen: The Angels of Mons*

First publication: *The [London] Evening News*, 29 September 1914.
First book appearance: *The Bowmen and Other Legends of the War*. London: Simpkin, Marshall, Hamilton, Kent, 1915.

This section reprints Arthur Machen's "The Bowmen" plus the *introduction* and *postscript* first published in *The Bowmen and Other Legends of the War* by Simpkin, Marshall, Hamilton, Kent, in late 1915. What has not hitherto been noted is that this text of "The Bowmen" differs slightly from that published in *The Evening News* on 29 September 1914. These differences are so noted. In general, they are stylistic, but in several cases Machen appears to have made changes to add greater dramatic emphasis to his text; e.g., "the singing arrows darkened the air; the heathen horde melted from before them," given in *The Evening News*, becomes "the singing arrows fled so swift and thick that they darkened the air; the heathen horde melted from before them."

Perhaps the most significant textual change occurs in the story's conclusion. The German leadership originally speculated that the "the contemptible English must have employed turpenite shells," a reference that would have meant much to a contemporary readership, as turpenite was rumored to be a terrible explosive in the possession of the French that emitted gasses that killed all within 400 yards of the explosion. On 1 October 1914 the *New York Times* published an article stating that turpenite's existence has "not been authenticated,"[1] and although stories of its lethality briefly continued to circulate, turpenite rapidly faded from the news.[2] Doubtless aware of this, Machen's altered version concludes with the German leadership speculating that "the contemptible English must have employed shells containing an unknown gas of a poisonous nature."

Introduction

I have been asked to write an introduction to the story of "The Bowmen," on its publication in book form together with three other tales of similar fashion. And I hesitate. This affair of "The Bowmen" has been such an odd one from first to last, so many queer complications have entered into it, there have been so many and so divers currents and cross-currents of rumour and speculation concerning it, that I honestly do not know where to begin. I propose, then, to solve the difficulty by apologising for beginning at all.

For, usually and fitly, the presence of an introduction is held to imply that there is something of consequence and importance to be introduced. If, for example, a man has made an anthology of great poetry, he may well write an introduction justifying his principle of selection, pointing out here and there, as the spirit moves him, high beauties and supreme excellencies, discoursing of the magnates and lords and princes of literature, whom he is merely serving as groom of the chamber. Introductions, that is, belong to the masterpieces and classics of the world, to the great and ancient and accepted things; and I am here introducing a short, small story of my own which appeared in The Evening News about ten months ago.

I appreciate the absurdity, nay, the enormity of the position in all its grossness. And my excuse for these pages must be this: that though the story itself is nothing, it has yet had such odd and unforeseen consequences and adventures that the tale of them may possess some interest. And then, again, there are certain psychological morals to be drawn from the whole matter of the tale and its sequel of rumours and discussions that are not, I think, devoid of consequence; and so to begin at the beginning.

This was in late August; to be more precise, on the last Sunday of last August. There were terrible things to be read on that hot Sunday morning between meat and mass. It was in The Weekly Dispatch that I saw the awful account of the retreat from Mons. I no longer recollect the details; but I have not forgotten the impression that was then on my mind. I seemed to see a furnace of torment and death and agony and terror seven times heated, and in the midst of the burning was the British Army. In the midst of the flame, consumed by it and yet aureoled in it, scattered like ashes and yet triumphant, martyred and for ever glorious. So I saw our men with a shining about them, so I took these thoughts with me to church, and, I am sorry to say, was making up a story in my head while the deacon was singing the Gospel.

This was not the tale of "The Bowmen." It was the first sketch, as it were, of "The Soldier's Rest," which is reprinted in this volume. I only wish I had been able to write it as I conceived it. The tale as it stands is, I think, a far better piece of craft than "The Bowmen," but the tale that came to me as the blue incense floated above the Gospel Book on the desk between the tapers: that indeed was a noble story—like all the stories that never get written. I conceived the dead men coming up through the flames and in the flames, and being welcomed in the Eternal Tavern with songs and flowing cups and everlasting mirth. But every man is the child of his age, however much he may hate it; and our popular religion has long determined that jollity is wicked. As far as I can make and modern Protestantism believes that Heaven is something like Evensong in an English cathedral, the service by Stainer[3] and the Dean preaching. For those opposed to dogma of any kind—even the mildest—I suppose it is held that a Course of Ethical Lectures will be arranged.

Well, I have long maintained that on the whole the average church, considered as a house of preaching, is a much more poisonous place than the average tavern; still, as I say, one's age masters one, and clouds and bewilders the intelligence, and the real story of "The Soldier's Rest," with its "sonus epulantium in aeterno convivio,"[4] was ruined at the moment of its birth, and it was some time later that the actual story, as here printed, got written. And in the meantime the plot of "The Bowmen" occurred to me. Now it has been murmured and hinted and suggested and whispered in all sorts of quarters that before I wrote the tale I had heard something. The most decorative of these legends is also the most precise: "I know for a fact that the whole thing was given him in typescript by a lady-in-waiting." This was not the case; and all vaguer reports to the effect that I heard some rumours or hints of rumours are equally void of any trace of truth.

Again I apologise for entering so pompously into the minutiae of my bit of a story, as if it were the lost poems of Sappho[5]; but it appears that the subject interests the public, and I comply with my instructions. I take it, then, that the origins of "The Bowmen" were composite. First of all, all ages and nations have cherished the thought that spiritual hosts may come to the help of early arms, that gods and heroes and saints have descended from their high immortal places to fight for their worshippers and clients. Then Kipling's story of the ghostly Indian regiment got in my head and got mixed with the medievalism that is always there; and so "The Bowmen" was written.[6] I was heartily disappointed with it, I remember, and thought it—as I still think it—and indifferent piece of work. However, I have tried to write for these thirty-five long years, and if I have not become practised in letters, I am at least a past master in the Lodge of Disappointment. Such as it was, "The Bowmen" appeared in The Evening News of September 29th, 1914.

Now the journalist does not, as a rule, dwell much on the prospect of fame; and if he be an evening journalist, his anticipations of immortality are bounded by twelve o'clock at night at the latest; and it may well be that those insects which begin to live in the morning and are dead by sunset deem themselves immortal. Having written my story, having groaned and growled over it and printed it, I certainly never thought to hear another word of it. My colleague

"The Londoner"[7] praised it warmly to my face, as his kindly fashion is, entering, very properly, a technical caveat as to the language of the battle-cries of the bowmen. "Why should English archers use French terms?" he said. I replied that the only reason was this—that a "Monseigneur" here and there struck me as picturesque; and I reminded him that, as a matter of cold historical fact, most of the archers of Agincourt were mercenaries from Gwent, my native country, who would appeal to Mihangel[8] and to saints not known to the Saxons—Teilo,[9] Iltyd,[10] Dewi,[11] Cadwaladyr Vendigeid.[12] And I thought that that was the first and last discussion of "The Bowmen." But in a few days from its publication the editor of The Occult Review wrote to me.[13] He wanted to know whether the story had any foundation in fact. I told him that it had no foundation in fact of any kind or sort; I forget whether I added that it had no foundation in rumour, but I should think not, since to the best of my belief there were no rumours of heavenly interposition in existence at that time. Certainly I had heard of none. Soon afterwards the editor of Light wrote asking a like question, and I made him a like reply. It seemed to me that I had stifled any "Bowmen" mythos in the hour of its birth.

A month or two later, I received several requests from editors of parish magazines to reprint the story. I—or, rather, my editor[14]—readily gave permission; and then, after another month or two, the conductor of one of these magazines wrote to me, saying that the February issue containing the story had been sold out, while there was still a great demand for it. Would I allow them to reprint "The Bowmen" as a pamphlet, and would I write a short preface giving the exact authorities for the story? I replied that they might reprint in pamphlet form with all my heart, but that I could not give my authorities, since I had none, the tale being pure invention. The priest wrote again, suggesting—to my amazement—that I must be mistaken, that the main "facts" of "The Bowmen" must be true, that my share in the matter must surely have been confined to the elaboration and decoration of a veridical history. It seemed that my light fiction had been accepted by the congregation of this particular church as the solidest of facts; and it was then that it began to dawn on me that if I had failed in the art of letters, I had succeeded, unwittingly, in the art of deceit. This happened, I should think, some time in April, and the snowball of rumour that was then set rolling has been rolling ever since, growing bigger and bigger, till it is now swollen to a monstrous size.

It was at about this period that variants of my tale began to be told as authentic histories.[15] At first, these tales betrayed their relation to the original. In several of them the vegetarian restaurant appeared, and St. George was the chief character. In one case an officer—name and address missing—said that there was a portrait of St. George in a certain London restaurant, and that a figure, just like the portrait, appeared to him on the battlefield, and was invoked by him, with the happiest of results. Another variant—this, I think, never got into print—told how dead Prussians had been found on the battlefield with arrow wounds in their bodies. This notion amused me, as I had imagined a scene, when I was thinking out the story, in which a German general was to appear before the Kaiser to explain his failure to annihilate the English.

"All-Highest," the general was to say, "it is true, it is impossible to deny it. The men were killed by arrows; the shafts were found in their bodies by the burying parties."

I rejected the idea as over-precipitous even for a mere fantasy. I was therefore entertained when I found that what I had refused as too fantastical for fantasy was accepted in certain occult circles as hard fact.

Other versions of the story appeared in which a cloud interposed between the attacking Germans and the defending British. In some examples the cloud served to conceal our men from the advancing enemy; in others, it disclosed shining shapes which frightened the horses of the pursuing German cavalry. St. George, it will be noted, has disappeared—he persisted some time longer in certain Roman Catholic variants—and there are no more bowmen, no more arrows. But so far angels are not mentioned; yet they are ready to appear, and I think that I have detected the machine which brought them into the story.

In "The Bowmen" my imagined soldier saw "a long line of shapes, with a shining about them." And Mr. A. P. Sinnett,[16] writing in the May issue of The Occult Review, reporting what he had heard, states that "those who could see said they saw 'a row of shining beings' between the two armies." Now I conjecture that the word "shining" is the link between my tale and the derivative from it. In the popular view shining and benevolent supernatural beings are angels and nothing else, and must be angels, and so, I believe, the Bowmen of my story have become "the Angels of Mons." In this shape they have been received with respect and credence everywhere, or almost everywhere.

And here, I conjecture, we have the key to the large popularity of the delusion—as I think it. We have long ceased in England to take much interest in saints, and in the recent revival of the cultus of St. George, the saint is little more than a patriotic figurehead. And the appeal to the saints to succor us is certainly not a common English practice; it is held Popish by most of our countrymen. But angels, with certain reservation, have retained their popularity, and so, when it was settled that the English army in its dire peril was delivered by angelic aid, the way was clear for general belief, and for the enthusiasms of the religion of the man in the street. And so soon as the legend got the title "The Angels of Mons" it became impossible to avoid it. It permeated the Press: it would not be neglected; it appeared in the most unlikely quarters—in Truth and Town Topics, The New Church Weekly (Swedenborgian) and John Bull. The editor of The Church Times has exercised a wise reserve: he awaits that evidence which so far is lacking; but in one issue of the paper I noted that the story furnished a text for a sermon, the subject of a letter, and the matter for an article. People send me cuttings from provincial papers containing hot controversy as to the exact nature of the appearances; the "Office Window" of The Daily Chronicle suggests scientific explanation of the hallucination; the Pall Mall in a note about St. James says he is of the brotherhood of the Bowmen of Mons—this reversion to the bowmen from the angels being possibly due to the strong statements that I have made on the matter. The pulpits both of the Church and of Nonconformity have been busy: Bishop Welldon,[17] Dean Hensley Henson (a disbeliever),[18] Bishop Taylor Smith (the Chaplain-General),[19] and many other clergy have occupied themselves with the matter. Dr. Horton preached about the "angels" at Manchester[20]; Sir Joseph Compton Rickett (President of the National Federation of Free Church Councils)[21] stated that the soldiers at the front had given testimony of powers and principalities fighting for them or against them. Letters come from all the ends of the earth to the Editor of The Evening News with theories, beliefs, explanations, suggestions. It is all somewhat wonderful; one can say that the whole affair is a psychological phenomenon of considerable interest, fairly comparable with the great Russian delusion of last August and September.

Now it is possible that some persons, judging by the tone of these remarks of mine, may gather the impression that I am a profound disbeliever in the possibility of any intervention of the super-physical order in the affairs of the physical order. They will be mistaken if they make this inference; they will be mistaken if they suppose that I think miracles in Judoea [sic]credible but miracles in France or Flanders incredible. I hold no such absurdities. But I confess, very frankly, that I credit none of the "Angels of Mons" legends, partly because I see, or think I see, their derivation from my own idle fiction, but chiefly because I have, so far, not received one jot or tittle of evidence that should dispose me to belief. It is idle, indeed, and foolish enough for a man to say: "I am sure that story is a lie, because the supernatural element enters into it"; here, indeed, we have the maggot writhing in the midst of corrupted offal denying the existence of the sun. But if this fellow be a fool—as he is—equally foolish is he who says, "If the tale has anything of the supernatural it is true, and the less evidence the better"; and I am afraid this tends to be the attitude of many who call themselves occultists. I hope that I shall never get to that frame of mind. So I say, not that super-normal interventions are impossible, not that they have not happened during this war—I know nothing as to that point, one way or the other—but that there is not one atom of evidence (so far) to support the current stories of the angels of Mons. For, be it remarked, these stories are specific stories. They rest on the second, third, fourth, fifth hand stories told by "a soldier," by "an officer," by "a Catholic correspondent," by "a nurse," by any number of anonymous people. Indeed, names have been mentioned. A lady's name has been drawn, most unwarrantably as it appears to me, into the discussion, and I have no doubt that this lady has been the subject to a good deal of pestering and annoyance. She has written to the Editor of *The Evening News* denying all knowledge of the supposed miracle. The Psychical Research Society's expert confesses that no real evidence has been proffered to her Society on the matter. And then, to my amazement, she accepts as fact the proposition that some men on the battlefield have been "hallucinated," and proceeds to give the theory of sensory hallucination. She forgets that, by her own showing, there is no reason to suppose that anybody has been hallucinated at all. Someone (unknown) has met a nurse (unnamed) who has talked to a soldier (anonymous) who has seen angels. But that is not evidence; and not even Sam Weller[22] at his gayest would have dared to offer it as such in the Court of Common Pleas. So far, then, nothing remotely approaching proof has been offered as to any supernatural intervention during the Retreat from Mons. Proof may come; if so, it will be interesting and more than interesting.

But, taking the affair as it stands at present, how is it that a nation plunged in materialism of the grossest kind has accepted idle rumours and gossip of the supernatural as certain truth? The answer is contained in the question; it is precisely because our whole atmosphere is materialist that we are ready to credit anything—save the truth. Separate a man from good drink, and he will swallow methylated spirit with joy. Man is created to be inebriated; to be "nobly wild, not mad." Suffer the Cocoa Prophets and their company to seduce him in body and spirit, and he will get himself stuff that will make him ignobly wild and mad indeed. It took hard, practical men of affairs, business men, advanced thinkers, Freethinkers, to believe in Madame Blavatsky[23] and Mahatmas and the famous message from the Golden Shore: "Judge's plan is right; follow him and stick."[24]

And the main responsibility for this dismal state of affairs undoubtedly lies on the shoulders of the majority of the clergy of the Church of England. Christianity, as Mr. W. L. Courtney[25] has so admirably pointed out, is a great Mystery Religion; it is the Mystery Religion. Its priests are called to an awful and tremendous hierurgy; its pontiffs are to be the pathfinders, the bridge-makers between the world of sense and the world of spirit. And, in fact, they pass their time in preaching, not the eternal mysteries, but a twopenny morality, in changing the Wine of Angels and the Bread of Heaven into gingerbeer and mixed biscuits: a sorry transubstantiation, a sad alchemy, as it seems to me.

The Bowmen

It was during the Retreat of the Eighty Thousand, and the authority of the Censorship[26] is sufficient excuse for not being more explicit. But it was on the most awful day of that awful time, on the day when ruin and disaster came so near that their shadow fell over London far away; and, without any certain news, the hearts of men failed within them and grew faint; as if the agony of the army in the battlefield[27] had entered into their souls.

On this dreadful day, then, when three hundred thousand men in arms with all their artillery swelled like a flood against the little English company, there was one point above all other points in our battle line that was for a time in awful danger, not merely of defeat, but of utter annihilation. With the permission of the Censorship[28] and of the military expert, this corner may, perhaps, be described as a salient, and if this angle were crushed and broken, then the English force as a whole would be shattered, the Allied left would be turned, and Sedan would inevitably follow.

All the morning the German guns had thundered and shrieked against this corner, and against the thousand or so of men who held it. The men joked at the shells, and found funny names for them, and had bets about them, and greeted them with scraps of music-hall songs. But the shells came on and burst, and tore good Englishmen limb from limb, and tore brother from brother, and as the heat of the day increased so did the fury of that terrific cannonade.[29] There was no help, it seemed. The English artillery was good, but there was not nearly enough of it; it was being steadily battered into scrap iron.

There comes a moment in a storm at sea when people say to one another, "It is at its worst; it can blow no harder," and then there is a blast ten times more fierce than any before it. So it was in these British trenches.

There were no stouter hearts in the whole world than the hearts of these men; but even they were appalled as this seven-time-heated hell of the German cannonade fell upon them and overwhelmed them and destroyed them.[30] And at this very moment they saw from their trenches that a tremendous host was moving against their lines. Five hundred of the thousand remained, and as far as they could see the German infantry was pressing on against them, column upon column, a grey world of men, ten thousand of them, as it appeared afterwards.

There was no hope at all. They shook hands, some of them. One man improvised a new version of the battlesong, "Good-bye, good-bye to Tipperary,"[31] ending with "And we shan't get there." And they all went on firing steadily. The officers pointed out that such an opportunity for high-class, fancy shooting[32] might never occur again; the Germans dropped line after line; the Tipperary humorist asked, "What price Sidney Street?" And the few machine guns did their best.[33] But everybody knew it was of no use. The dead grey bodies lay in companies and battalions, as others came on and on and on,[34] and they swarmed and stirred and advanced from beyond and beyond.

"World without end. Amen,"[35] said one of the British soldiers[36] with some irrelevance as he took aim and fired. And then he remembered—he says he cannot think why or wherefore[37]—a queer vegetarian restaurant in London where he had once or twice eaten eccentric dishes[38] of cutlets made of lentils and nuts that pretended to be steak. On all the plates in this restaurant there was printed a figure of St. George in blue, with the motto, *Adsit Anglis Sanctus Georgius*—May St. George be a present help to the English.[39] This soldier happened to know Latin and other useless things, and now, as he fired at his man in the grey advancing mass—300 yards away—he uttered the pious vegetarian motto. He went on firing to the end, and at last Bill on his right had to clout him cheerfully over the head to make him stop, pointing out as he did so that the King's ammunition cost money[40] and was not lightly to be wasted in drilling funny patterns into dead Germans.

For[41] as the Latin scholar uttered his invocation he felt something between a shudder and an electric shock pass through his body. The roar of the battle died down in his ears to a gentle murmur; instead of it, he says, he heard a great voice and a shout louder than a thunder-peal crying, "Array, array, array!"

His heart grew hot as a burning coal, it grew cold as ice within him, as it seemed to him that a tumult of voices answered his summons.[42] He heard, or seemed to hear,[43] thousands shouting: "St. George! St. George!"

"Ha! messire; ha! sweet Saint, grant us good deliverance!"

"St. George for merry England!"

"Harow! Harow! Monseigneur St. George, succor us."

"Ha! St. George! Ha! St. George! a long bow and a strong bow."

"Heaven's Knight, aid us!"[44]

And as the soldier heard these voices he saw before him, beyond the trench, a long line of shapes, with a shining about them. They were like men who drew the bow, and with another shout, their cloud of arrows flew singing and tingling through the air towards the German hosts.[45]

#

The other men in the trench were firing all the while. They had no hope; but they aimed just as if they had been shooting at Bisley.

Suddenly one of them lifted up his voice in the plainest English.[46]

"Gawd help us!" he bellowed to the man next to him, "but we're blooming marvels! Look at those grey ... gentlemen, look at them! D'ye see them? They're not going down in dozens, nor in 'undreds; it's thousands, it is. Look! look! there's a regiment gone while I'm talking to ye."

"Shut it!" the other soldier bellowed, taking aim, "what are ye gassing about?"[47]

But he gulped with astonishment even as he spoke, for, indeed, the grey men were falling by the thousands. The English could hear the guttural scream[48] of the German officers, the crackle of their revolvers as they shot the reluctant; and still line after line crashed to the earth.

#

All the while the Latin-bred soldier heard the cry:

"Harow! Harow! Monseigneur,[49] dear saint, quick to our aid! St. George help us!"

"High Chevalier, defend us!"[50]

The singing arrows fled so swift and thick that they darkened the air; the heathen horde melted from before them.[51]

\#

"More machine guns!" Bill yelled to Tom.

"Don't hear them," Tom yelled back. "But, thank God,[52] anyway; they've got it in the neck."

In fact, there were ten thousand dead German soldiers left before that salient of the English army, and consequently there was no Sedan. In Germany, a country ruled by scientific principles, the Great General Staff decided that the contemptible English must have employed shells containing an unknown gas of a poisonous nature, as no wounds were discernible on the bodies of the dead German soldiers.[53] But the man who knew what nuts tasted like when they called themselves steak[54] knew also that St. George had brought his Agincourt Bowmen to help the English.

Postscript

While this volume was passing through the press, Mr. Ralph Shirley,[55] the Editor of "The Occult Review," called my attention to an article that is appearing in the August issue of his magazine, and was kind enough to let me see the advance proof sheets.

The article is called "The Angelic Leaders." It is written by Miss Phyllis Campbell.[56] I have read it with great care.

"Miss Campbell says that she was in France when the war broke out. She became a nurse, and while she was nursing the wounded she was informed that an English soldier wanted a 'holy picture.'" She went to the man and found him to be a Lancashire Fusilier. He said that he was a Wesleyan Methodist, and asked "for a picture or medal (he didn't care which) of St. George ... because he had seen him on a white horse, leading the British at Vitry-le-François, when the Allies turned."

This statement was corroborated by a wounded R. F. A. man who was present. He saw a tall man with yellow hair, in golden armour, on a white horse, holding his sword up, and his mouth open as if he was saying, "Come on, boys! I'll put the kybosh on the devils." This figure was bareheaded—as appeared later from the testimony of other soldiers—and the R. F. A. man and the Fusilier knew that he was St. George, because he was exactly like the figure of St. George on the sovereigns. "Hadn't they seen him with his sword on every 'quid' they'd ever had?"

From further evidence it seemed that while the English had seen the apparition of St. George coming out of a "yellow mist" or "cloud of light," to the French had been vouchsafed visions of St. Michael the Archangel and Joan of Arc. Miss Campbell says:—

"Everybody has seen them who has fought through from Mons to Ypres; they all agree on them individually, and have no doubt at all as to the final issue of their interference."

Such are the main points of the article as it concerns the great legend of "The Angels of Mons." I cannot say that the author has shaken my incredulity—firstly, because the evidence is second-hand. Miss Campbell is perhaps acquainted with "Pickwick," and I would remind her of that famous (and golden) ruling of Stareleigh, J.[57]: to the effect that you mustn't tell us what the soldier said; it's not evidence. Miss Campbell has offended against this rule, and she has not only told us what the soldier said, but she has omitted to give us the soldier's name and address.

If Miss Campbell proffered herself as a witness at the Old Bailey and said, "John Doe is undoubtedly guilty. A soldier I met told me that he had seen the prisoner put his hand into an old gentleman's pocket and take out a purse"—well, she would find that the stout spirit of Mr. Justice Stareleigh still survives in our judges.

The soldier must be produced. Before that is done we are not technically aware that he exists at all.

Then there are one or two points in the article itself which puzzle me. The Fusilier and the R. F. A. man had seen St. George "leading the British at Vitry-le-François, when the Allies turned." Thus the time of the apparition and the place of the apparition were firmly fixed in the two soldiers' minds.

Yet the very next paragraph in the article begins:—

"'Where was this?' I asked. But neither of them could tell."

This is an odd circumstance. They knew, and yet they did not know; or, rather, they had forgotten a piece of information that they had themselves imparted a few seconds before.

Another point. The soldiers knew that the figure on the horse was St. George by his exact likeness to the figure of the saint on the English sovereign.

This, again, is odd. The apparition was of a bareheaded figure in golden armour. The St. George of the coinage is naked, except for a short cape flying from the shoulders, and a helmet. He is not bareheaded, and has no armour—save the piece on his head. I do not quite see how the soldiers were so certain as to the identity of the apparition.

Lastly, Miss Campbell declares that "everybody" who fought from Mons to Ypres saw the apparitions. If that be so, it is again odd that Nobody has come forward to testify at first hand to the most amazing event of his life. Many men have been back on leave from the front, we have many wounded in the hospital, *many soldiers have written letters home. And they have all combined, this great host, to keep silence as to the most wonderful of occurrences, the most inspiring assurance, the surest omen of victory.*

It may be so, but—
Arthur Machen

• THREE •

Harold Begbie and *On the Side of the Angels: A Reply to Arthur Machen*

Publisher: London: Hodder and Stoughton, 1915

Harold Begbie was one of the more beloved Edwardian literary figures, a versatile writer adept at practically everything to which he was to turn his pen. He seems to have had few enemies and many friends, and even those with whom he disagreed seem to have liked him. In life he was to count as friends such luminaries as Sir Oliver Lodge, Sir William Crookes, Lord Morley, Albert, the Fourth Earl Grey, William Booth, and Arthur Machen, to say nothing of many additional politicians and novelists. Perhaps because he was such an amiable personality, controversy did not accompany him, and he seems generally to have been taken for granted. Indeed, although he contributed several substantial biographical entries to the *Dictionary of National Biography*, he was not profiled by that set following his death; for all that he was significant as an early twentieth-century figure, he does not appear to have been the subject of any academic study, though he does figure in the memoirs of others and in an occasional encyclopedia entry.

Edward Harold Begbie was born on Midsummer Day (21 June) 1871, in Suffolk. Like Arthur Machen, Begbie was the son of a clergyman, his father being the Reverend Mars Hamilton Begbie. Also like Machen, he was a voracious reader of his father's religious library, and much of his childhood was spent out of doors, enjoying nature. Where the two men differed, however, was that Begbie came from a large family, being the fifth of six sons. He was educated at the Merchant Taylor's School, after which he held briefly a variety of jobs, then married Gertrude Seale; the couple moved to Devon, where they farmed.

Needing to support his growing family—the Begbies had three daughters, two of whom lived into adulthood—Harold Begbie went to London, where he made the acquaintance of the politician and writer G. W. E. (George William Erskine) Russell, who introduced him to H. W. (Henry William) Massingham, who was then editor of *The Daily Chronicle*, a newspaper to which Begbie began submitting prose and verse. In 1898 he became associated with the *Globe* newspaper as a columnist, and he began publishing, his first book being *The Political Struwwelpeter* (London: G. Richards, 1899). During the First World War, he became active in the recruiting effort, his best-known effort, the 1914 poem "Fall In!" published immediately following the Battle of Mons and the Amiens Dispatch, becoming enormously popular.[1] Following the First World War, Begbie's inside knowledge of politics and politicians led him to write *The Mirrors of Downing Street* as by "A Gentleman with a Duster" (London: Mills & Boon, 1920). It received high praise but his authorship was not confirmed until following his death on 8 October 1929. His wife and two daughters survived him.

At the time of Begbie's death, he had published more than 50 books: novels, verse, children's stories, travel books, and biographies, in addition to much journalism. He was a devout Christian and wrote a two volume biography of General William Booth of the Salvation Army (London: Macmillan, 1920), and his reaction to Arthur Machen's "The Bowmen" is aptly illustrated by its title: *On the Side of the Angels: The Story of the Angels at Mons. An Answer to The Bowmen*. It went through four printings.

On the Side of the Angels would appear a sincere expression and a testimonial of his genuine religious faith, but there were doubters, and one of the earliest was Arthur Machen. In a 1918 letter to Vincent Starrett, he wrote, "I don't think anything about Harold Begbie or his books. 'On the Side of the Angels' was a publisher's commission; I don't think that Harold believes in a word of it. I don't think he's fool enough to do so."[2] Was Machen in error, cynically imputing base motives to somebody whose sincerely held beliefs and genuine religious faith could not be reconciled with what Machen knew to be the origins of "The Bowmen"? Or is it reasonable to see *On the Side of the Angels* as Machen did, a cold and calculated attempt to exploit the contemporary interest in Machen's "The Bowmen"?

Answers emerge from examining the volume itself. Even allowing for credulity on Begbie's part, it is impossible to believe that a seasoned and responsible reporter—such as Begbie unquestionably was—could seriously accept the mass of unsupported and contradictory anecdote as genuine as well as claim unequivocally that telepathy existed. *Religious* does not mean *unquestioning*, nor should it be taken to mean *naïve* or *stupid*. Begbie was none of these, and his other writings show a sharp and inquisitive intelligence, perhaps equal to Machen's. There seems little doubt that Begbie had been given an assignment and told to fill a certain number of pages; indeed, in the last chapters of the first and most interesting edition *On the Side of the Angels*, it is clear that his invention has flagged, for he is reduced to copying articles from the *Proceedings* of the Society for Psychical Research and translating addresses from Henri Bergson in order to meet his word requirements.

Next, comparing the texts of the different editions of *On the Side of the Angels* yields some intriguing results. The text of the first edition is reproduced here. In the second edition, however, Begbie began defending himself against the charges of including erroneous information, particularly when his hastily inserted anecdote involving Private Cleaver was revealed to be false: Begbie stated that "at this, the first opportunity, I have, of course, taken out the letter which I quoted without comment from *The Daily Mail*").[3] He likewise occasionally responded to reviews, stating that "a critic in the *Church Times* pompously cites this sentence as a proof of his statement that my style is 'atrocious.' It is amusing to find a judge of literature mistaking for American slang an old-fashioned word employed, exactly as I employ it, by Milton and Swift."[4] Furthermore, he greatly reduced his mentions of Phyllis Campbell, preferring to provide more unverifiable anecdotes rather than continue his lengthy support for her testimonials. This was more than likely due to either the "scandal" that she had experienced[5] or to the Society for Psychical Research's investigation into Ms. Campbell's claims, with by its damning conclusion that "allowance must be made for inaccuracy of memory, the force of suggestion, and other common sources of error."[6]

More intriguingly and most damningly, Begbie seems to have manufactured the letters of his ostensible supporters and their supposed evidence. The correspondents he names and quotes at times have the names of actual people, but these people did not occupy the positions Begbie ascribes to them: the Reverend G. G. Monck, for example, does not appear to have been the Prebendary of Wells and the Rural Dean of Martock although somebody by this name was in 1901 appointed Rector of Closworth, Sherborne, Dorset. Other examples abound. There are, additionally, occasional changes in the names of his supporters: Miss M. Courtney Wilson of the first printing of *On the Side of the Angels* becomes Miss M. Courtenay Wilson and also Miss Courtenay Wilson in the later printings.

Harold Begbie's seeming probity and rectitude are thus, at least in this instance, polite fictions. He should rather be recognized not only as one of the people responsible for the spread of the story of the Angels of Mons but also as a person willing to fabricate data and alter his stories to suit somebody. One is left wondering who was paying him and his publisher.

Preface

Curiosity, interest, and something which transcends both curiosity and interest, have been created in this country by various rumours concerning the appearance of angels at the Battle of Mons. Nor is it to be wondered at, in an hour of such universal bereavement, that curiosity and interest in a story of this kind should intensify into hunger and thirds of the soul—a hunger and thirst after assurance that life upon this earth is bound up with universal existence.

My main quarrel with Mr. Arthur Machen, whose explanation of this mystery is the only excuse I can urge for my own interference in the matter, is concerned with what seems to me a most lamentable failure upon his part to realize the acuteness of human suffering and the intense eagerness for consolation which are now lying at the heart of English existence.

Mr. Machen, for whose imagination and rather sinister genius in the region of short stories many good judges of literature entertain a sincere admiration, tells us that all these various rumours of angels at the Battle of Mons may be traced back to a story which he wrote in August, 1914, entitled "The Bowmen"—a story originally published in the *Evening News* on September 29th, 1914.

He now publishes this story in book form, and sets before it an Introduction of agreeable charm and grace, in which he offers us his quite simple and pardonably egoistic explanation of the mystery. He would have us believe that his story, which had no basis in fact, is the root of all these rumours. To his surprise and entertainment he who has been for so long "a past master in the Lodge of Disappointment" finds himself the indirect creator of a snowball of rumour "now swollen to monstrous size." Ideas which he rejected as "over-precipitous even for a mere fantasy" accumulated with rumour: "I was therefore entertained when I found that what I had refused as too fantastic for fantasy was accepted in certain occult circles as hard fact." He speaks of the "evidence" for these rumours with amused scorn—"not even Sam Weller[7] at his gayest would have dared to offer it as such in the Court of Common Pleas." In short, he credits none of these legends, "partly because I see, or think I see, their derivation from my own idle fiction...."

Now it will probably occur to many people to ask themselves whether an apology for having written it would not make a more seemly introduction for such a story than an explanation of the rumours which Mr. Machen thinks have come from the tale. But it will certainly strike the vast majority of people as unfitting and indecorous that this Introduction, though very engagingly and modestly written, should wear so smiling a face. For men fell at the Battle of Mons who will never rise again. Because of those graves in France, thousands of people here in England feel that the goodness is wrung out of life, and that darkness must henceforth encompass all their ways. Men who were the joy and beauty of existence to many men, and women, and children, are now numbered among the unspeaking dead; and for these many men, women, and children, the silence of those dead is an almost intolerable agony.

To have entered upon a scene of such awful havoc and desolation for a story of mystery is, in itself, I think, an act very near to sacrilege, but having got the story from that dreadful scene, and by that story having created a thousand hopes and a thousand consolations, quietly to turn a smiling face to the world, and airily dismiss the legends with a playful reference to Sam Weller—this, I am sure, is behaviour for which Mr. Machen in his quieter and less popular moments will feel a very sincere regret and perhaps a sharp contrition.

Mr. Machen, it must be understood, is not a satisfied materialist who thinks that mechanism can account for mind, nor does he disbelieve in miracles. "It is idle, indeed," he says, "and foolish enough for a man to say: 'I am sure that story is a lie, because the supernatural element enters into it'; here indeed, we have the maggot writing in the midst of corrupted offal denying the existence of the sun." People, he tells us, will be mistaken if they suppose that he thinks "miracles in Judea credible, but miracles in France or Flanders incredible." He is on the side of the angels, but not the angels of Mons.

This makes it, obviously, more difficult to understand the lack of tenderness in his explanation. One can imagine how a hothead of infidelity would seize upon such an opportunity to lay about him, how he would laugh at the fools of the earth for their credulity, and how he would rub his hands over so sublime a hoax; but how is it possible that a man who is so passionate a Christian that he lectures the Clergy of the Church of England for preaching "a twopenny morality" instead of realizing that they are priests "called to an awful and tremendous hierurgy," how is it possible, we ask, that such a man, having created hopes in the hearts of suffering men and women, can assume the posture of jauntiness and in the tones of amusement proceed to tell them that those hopes are but the baseless fabric of a dream?

Perhaps it may be permitted to us to suggest that had Mr. Machen paid more serious attention to such simple morality of what is called the Sermon on the Mount, and had kept a firmer hold upon his reason when "the blue incense floated above the Gospel Book on the desk between the tapers," he might have thought more of the sorrowful mourner here upon earth than of "the dead men coming up through the flames ... and being welcomed in the Eternal Tavern with songs and flowing cups of everlasting mirth." It is so easy to sneer at morality—as the superficial philosophers of Germany have taught the whole world[8]—and it is natural, I suppose, for certain sensuous temperaments to mistake the dramatic and picturesque ceremonies of symbolism for actual mystery; but Mr. Machen would surely have been saved from committing what I feel to be a grievous sin in the region of taste if he had reflected long enough upon the moral teachings of Christ to create within himself something of the sublime character of that gentle Teacher; and perhaps—who can tell?—in such reflections he might have come to see that this gracious and attractive Christ Who is, after all, the very centre of Mr. Machen's "awful and tremendous hierurgy," chose rather the intellectual and spiritual labour of teaching than the posturing and abasements of the Jewish temple—hierurgical enough, we should have thought, to satisfy the most cabalist hierophant.

But, however this may be, it is decisively clear that Mr. Machen's book as it stands must add to the bitterness of this present grief and lamentation. Hunger and thirst for consolation is treated to an Introduction which will possibly please lovers of a pretty style, but which will certainly not medicine the agony of the human heart. Nor, we think, will Mr. Machen's affirmation of his own faith in the possibility of miracles seem to such as be sorrowful anything more than a wounding anti-climax to a story of shining hope fabricated at the very grave of their youthful dead.

That the sprightly *allegro* of Mr. Machen's Introduction may communicate its unseemliness to others, spreading pain and sorrow in ever widening circles, we have evidence in the *folâtre*[9] criticism of his book which appeared recently in a Literary Supplement of the *Times*. I quote this criticism as an example—a strange and almost incredible example—of that flippant, frolicsome, and perky attitude towards the sorrows of others which justifies those foreign critics of England who accuse us, not only of lightness and frivolity concerning serious things, but of a very deep and incurable vulgarity of the soul. It is almost impossible to believe that the writer of this criticism, like Mr. Machen himself, can have realized that the death of young men in France is a grievous bereavement to living men and women here in England, or that War has changed the whole "psychological atmosphere." But here is the thing to speak and swagger for itself:—

Long after the war is over, and the facts of it have been recorded in histories, one of the most widely known events will be the appearance of St. George and his angel-warriors fighting in defence of the British during the retreat from Mons. We say "known"; because posterity will "know'" that the guardian Saint came down. People "know" it already. The papers are full of the occurrences, and testimony pours in from all sides. And here is Mr. Arthur Machen roundly declaring that none of the testimony yet given is worth a rap; that the whole thing arose out of a story which he himself made up, out of his own head, in church, and sent to the *Evening News*. Mr. Machen, as those acquainted with his writings well know, is the last man to be skeptical about miracles. He has a positive faith in the existence of the Christian saints, and would regard the appearance of St. George in Flanders to-day as no more surprising than the appearance of an omnibus in Regent Street. If Mr. Machen believes that the only foundation for the story of the "Angels of Mons" is his own yarn (which does not mention angels, but only "shapes with a shining about them," that "were like men who drew the bow"), that is merely because, though a believer in miracles, he has some idea of the nature of evidence, and has seen no evidence yet that satisfies him. This case makes a very pretty study in the origin and growth of legend.

> The pity of it is that the discussions may rob Mr. Machen's tale of due credit as a work of imaginative art. It is very well told. Mr. Machen knows the value of homely detail; and when he makes the occasion of the miracle to be a half-jesting prayer uttered by a soldier who remembered the St. George on the plates at a certain vegetarian restaurant, he does what a writer of fiction ought to do, and convinces the reader that the story, whether the incident happened or no, is true. There are three other stories in the book on much the same lines. In one of them he shows us a very cheerful and Chestertonian heaven; in another "frightfulness" comes home to one of its perpetrators in a manner more frightful than any bodily torture could be; in the last the return to old devices and implements of warfare is cleverly used for an effect that will perhaps give rise to another legend when people are tired of discussing the Bowmen. And, to close the book, that entertaining writer, "The Londoner,"[10] supports Mr. Machen's contention and talks of Greece and Rome.

I would remind this critic, and Mr. Machen as well, of a saying of Sainte-Beuve[11] in his essay on Joubert[12]: "Taste, for him, is the literary conscience of the soul."

It is, then, rather to undo, so far as my powers will permit, the mischief wrought by this elegant but inappropriate Introduction, than to cross swords either with Mr. Machen on the one hand, or with rejoicing materialists on the other, that I set about the composition of this book.

I would beg all those who have rested the burden of their heavy grief on what they are now told is the shifting sand of legend to pause before, despairing of light or hope, they put a greater faith in this theory of delusion than perhaps they gave in their most expansive moments of belief to the stories of the angels. It may be that he who points most suavely to delusion is himself deluded; and of a veritable certainty it is as sure as the motion of the earth and the existence of boundless space that the spirit of man is for ever moving into fields of fuller and more abundant life. Death is a change, not an end.

"Not to believe is to believe." Not to believe in the angels is to believe in a mindless, meaningless, and soulless universe—it is to believe in the achievement by blind and irrational forces of order, beauty, and goodness; is to believe in a miracle infinitely more miraculous than the existence of God. And to believe in the angels is not to believe in all this, but to believe that spiritual life has created the material mechanism of life, that evolution came from mind and did not precede mind, and that the thrust, drive, propulsion, and passion of evolving and self-conscious life is upward and onward through eternal ages to the Maker of heaven and earth, the Giver of Life, and the

Fount of Love, Who is both the High and Lofty One Who inhabiteth eternity and the Father of all who call upon Him.

I

I remember reading at the time of the Crippen[13] murder trial that some years before a sensational novelist had published a book which resembled very closely and in many astounding details, even to that of some of the names in the case, the actual and sordid crime which brought Crippen to the dock. But I did not read that this novelist ever wrote a subsequent Introduction to his story claiming for himself the authorship of the murder or accusing Crippen of plagiarism. There is such a thing as coincidence.

Mr. Machen wrote his story *after the retreat from Mons and under the influence of that retreat which he read in the newspaper*; it was published for the first time in the last days of September. It was imagination in part, but not prophetic. The thing had occurred. He had read "an awful account of the retreat from Mons," and even to-day, although he can no longer recollect the details he has not forgotten, he tells us, the impression that was then made upon his mind:

> I seemed to see a furnace of torment and death and agony and terror seven times heated, and in the midst of the burning was the British Army. In the midst of the flames, consumed by it, scattered like ashes and yet triumphant, martyred and for ever glorious. So I saw our men with a shining about them, so I took these thoughts with me to church, and I am sorry to say was making up a story in my head while the deacon was singing the Gospel.

Now, there is not only such a thing as coincidence, but there is such a thing as telepathy. No man of science who has examined the phenomena of telepathy would dispute for a minute the thesis that Mr. Machen, on that Sunday morning, when he read with supreme sympathy that "awful account" in his newspaper, or stood stunned and bemused in church, while "the blue incense floated above the Gospel Book on the desk between the tapers," may have received from the brain of a wounded or a dying British soldier in France some powerful impression of the battlefield at Mons. The thing is possible. I could fill a book with instances of a like kind. One of the most remarkable and convincing ghost stories of the South African War, investigated by a man of science, was explained to me by the acutest sceptic of spiritual phenomena as a simple and common case of telepathy, and so dismissed. Telepathy is not a theory; it is not even a dogma of spiritualism; it is a fact of the physical world. Far from being impossible, it is quite possible that a man at home reading with so profound a sympathy an account of this battle that he became lost in it, might unconsciously produce within himself a condition of mind which would draw to itself and receive the agonized impressions of some

Three • Harold Begbie and *On the Side of the Angels*

stricken soldier in France. And, therefore, if we admit that Mr. Machen's story was first in the field, and even if we go so exceeding far as to say that every testimony to the appearance of spirits during the battle is derived from that story, still we are not committing ourselves to the dogmatic statement that no angels thrust themselves between the British Army and destruction at the Battle of Mons.

But when we have made it quite clear to ourselves that it is possible for this piece of fiction to have had a telepathic origin, and reminded ourselves that Mr. Machen's phrase of "the tale being pure invention" is a loose expression, both hazardous and unscientific, we must not fear to go forward and ascertain so far as we can do it whether there is any evidence for our belief in this telepathic origin, or whether we must conclude with Mr. Machen that "the whole affair is a psychological phenomenon of considerable interest, fairly comparable with the great Russian delusion of last August and September."

The best evidence for a telepathic origin of the story would be the statement by a living man of good character and sound reason present at the Battle of Mons that he had seen a vision with his own eyes.

Is it possible to produce such a man?

Such a man exists.

Before I proceed to speak about this man I should like to remind the reader that of all those gallant men who fought at the Battle of Mons only a remnant is left. In his *Postscript* Mr. Machen pounces upon a loose phrase used by a lady whose testimony I shall examine presently, and with an avidity which is hardly worthy of his reputation, cries out that if "everybody" who fought from Mons to Ypres saw the apparition, it is "odd that Nobody has come forward to testify at first hand to the most amazing event of his life."

> Many men have been back on leave from the front, we have many wounded in hospital, many soldiers have written letters home. And they have all combined, this great hose, to keep silence as to the most wonderful of occurrences, the most inspiring assurance, the surest omen of victory. It may be so, but—

The wounded soldier now lying in an English hospital who says that he saw angels at Mons is one of only five men left out of his whole battalion. That Battle of Mons, which saved the British Army from annihilation, was for most of those who fought with the angels a sepulchre. They saved the British Army, but they saved it with their lives. No "great host" withdrew from that field of destruction; the great host strewed the ground with their bodies; only a remnant of those who stood in the actual furnace of Mons escaped with their lives.

Then let us remind ourselves that a vision is no palpable and tangible thing. It comes into sight and disappears. Its duration is seldom so protracted as to outlast incredulity or so vivid as to outlive astonishment. And in the madness steaming up from the brains of furious, hard-pressed, and despairing men, and in the tumultuous hurly of a most bloody and ferocious battle, it is surely not to be looked for that veridical appearance or puzzling hallucination should wear the definitive outline of a calmly contemplated and steadfast object. Rather should we conclude that any graphic, coherent, and entirely convincing description of such vision or hallucination was the almost certain fructification of what is called after-belief.

Mr. Machen will perhaps remember his own words: "I seemed to see a furnace of torment and death." "So I saw our men with a shining about them."

He saw or seemed to see these things. Did he cry out with amazement at the sight of them? Did he feel that he must straightway publish to all the world the story of this "most amazing event"? Did he feel that he was combining with his own soul "to keep silence" as to this "most inspiring assurance, the surest omen of victory"? He saw "our men with a shining about them"— and he was at home in a chair with a newspaper in his hand, far beyond the range of the Prussians' heavy guns. Did he see them clearly and decidedly, or in a flash of thought? Did the vision last? Did he feel quite certain that he had seen them? Can he produce evidence that his imagination really and truly did present to him the vision of our men with a shining about them?

No clearer, no more definite, and no more convincing, as a rule, is the actual vision of a spirit.

It is true that a man may justly say even of such a protracted and well-attested vision, "How can we be certain that the thing is not hallucination?" We cannot be certain. But a wise man in this case, who desires rather to discover truth than to confirm his own prepossessions, will ask himself if the story of the Angels fits into the history of its occasion. And if it be found in the authentic history of this battle that the victorious Prussian host, at the very moment which delivered up the British Army to their sword, suddenly swerved away and let their most hated enemy escape, then the wise man will at least listen attentively and respectfully to the testimony of one who fought upon that day, and perhaps will come to Hamlet's famous conclusion that there are more things in heaven and earth than are dreamed of in our philosophy.[14]

Mr. Machen may have explained some of the rumours on this subject; but he does not explain that miraculous "side-slip" of the German onslaught, nor can he explain, I think, the testimonies which follow.

II

There is a wounded soldier lying in an English hospital who has made a definite statement concerning a vision in France. This statement was first made by him in conversation with a nurse, who repeated it to the Lady Superintendent of the Red Cross. The Lady Superintendent subsequently wrote it down, submitted her written record to the soldier for his approval, and later on, when Mr. Machen raised his controversy, this statement was published in a London newspaper.

Miss M. Courtney Wilson, of Moorlands, Bitterne, the Lady Superintendent,[15] is one of those good and devoted women who are to be found in most English counties –sensible, cheerful, keen, and self-sacrificing, who do all the drudgery of Church work and keep the life of a village from stagnation. She is practical, reliable, and conscientious. She is also charming, benevolent, and gracious. It is impossible to doubt her word or to suspect her of hysterical imaginings.

She describes the soldier as a man "not at all imaginative or highly strung. He is a decent, plain-speaking fellow, a married man with a family." She declared to the interviewer who saw her: "I am certain that he never thought of making a statement to the newspaper, and I am personally convinced that the vision was actually seen by this man."

A friend of mine who saw the soldier just before he underwent an operation in this hospital, spoke to me of the man as follows:

"Lance-Corporal _____ is of the artisan type, a slow-speaking and deliberate-mannered man, the last person you would suspect of hysteria or nervous ideas. He is a soldier of many years' service with a clean military record. I should take him to be a man of two or three and thirty. He spoke to me of his vision in a cool, calm, matter-of-fact way, as of something he had certainly seen. He made no attempt either to theorise or to dogmatise about it. His whole narrative was marked by sincerity. He spoke quietly and soberly of this strange thing, as of something that had happened and that he knows to have happened."

I asked my friend if he felt perfectly satisfied of the soldier's sincerity. He replied, with some emphasis, "Look here, I'll tell you what I am perfectly certain about. You might go down to see that man in an utterly skeptical frame of mind, but you would simply have to believe that he is relating something which to him is an actual experience and an absolute fact. You could come to no other conclusion. You might say that the man was speaking of an hallucination, but you could not possibly say that he was telling a lie."

"What did you gather concerning his religious ideas?" I asked.

"I should say," replied my friend, "that he is a man with no pre-conceived religious belief. In fact, he told me that while he doesn't now disbelieve in God, he couldn't say what he thought about God. He assented when I asked him if he were a bit of a fatalist, and smiled when I said to him that he was like so many soldiers and sailors who say, 'When Jimmy the One[16] has got my number up I've got to go, and it doesn't matter whether I'm ashore or afloat.'

I should say quite certainly, though he never used the word himself, that he is a fatalist. Almost every soldier is. At any rate, I am sure that he has never been curious or imaginative about religious matters."

This soldier will not allow his name and regiment to be mentioned because there is a definite military order that soldiers are not to speak of their experiences at the front for purposes of publication until after the War. And, further, Miss Courtney Wilson does not want the man to be made the centre of any public curiosity. Quite rightly she regards his experience as too sacred, too holy a thing for such clamour. But she is so anxious the truth should be established in this matter that she is kind enough to let me give here her name and address as a definite witness to the accuracy of my record.

It may be as well to remember that the soldier dictated his statement before undergoing an operation, a time when few men are given either to boastfulness or deceit.

Here follows the verbatim statement of this dependable lance-corporal:—

I was with my battalion in the retreat from Mons on or about August 28th. The German cavalry were expected to make a charge, and we were waiting to fire and scatter them so as to enable the French cavalry who were on our right to make a dash forward. However, the German aeroplanes discovered our position and we remained where we were.

The weather was very hot and clear, and between eight and nine o'clock in the evening I was standing with a party of nine other men on duty, and some distance on either side there were parties of ten on guard. Immediately behind us half of my battalion was on the edge of a wood resting. An officer suddenly came up to us in a state of great anxiety and asked us if we had seen anything startling [the word he used was "astonishing"]. He hurried away from my ten to the next party of ten. When he had got out of sight I, who was the non-commissioned officer in charge, ordered two men to go forward out of the way of the trees in order to find out what the officer meant. The two men returned reporting that they could see no sign of any Germans; at that time we thought that the officer must be expecting a surprise attack.

Immediately afterwards the officer came back, and taking me and some others a few yards away showed us the sky. I could see quite plainly in mid-air a strange light which seemed to be quite distinctly outlined and was not a reflection of the moon, nor were there any clouds in the neighbourhood. The light became brighter and I could see quite distinctly three shapes, one in the centre having what looked like outspread wings, the other two were not so large, but were quite plainly distinct from the centre one. They appeared to have a long loose-hanging garment of a golden tint, and they were above the German line facing us.

We stood watching them for about three-quarters of a [sic] hour. All the men with me saw them, and other men came up from other groups who also told us that they had seen the same thing. I am not a believer in such things, but I have not the slightest doubt that we really did see what I now tell you.

I remember the day because it was a day of terribly anxiety for us. That morning the Munsters[17] had a bad time on our right, and so had the Scots Guards.[18] We managed to get to the wood and there we barricaded the roads and remained in the formation I have told you. Later on the Uhlans[19] attacked us and we drove them back with heavy loss. It was after this engagement when we were dog-tired that the vision appeared to us.

I shall never forget it as long as I live. I lie awake in bed and picture it all as I saw it that night. Of my battalion there are now only five men alive besides myself, and I have no hope of ever getting back to the front. I have a record of fifteen years' good service, and I should be very sorry to make a fool of myself by telling a story merely to please anyone.

Now, here we have a simple, plain, but quite emphatic statement of a supernatural experience. It is a statement originally made in conversation. It did not arise from the controversy on the Angels of Mons. It did not develop from a discussion on supernatural matters. A wounded soldier lying in an English hospital, "going over again in his mind what happened during the great retreat," mentioned this incident to a nurse who repeated it to a Red Cross Lady Superintendent. It surprised him when she expressed such interest in his story that she proposed writing it down. He says that he had no idea the occurrence would interest Miss Courtney Wilson as it will always interest him. Nothing was further from his mind than the notion that his story should be made public.

I do not know that a more convincing and satisfactory statement on a subject of this nature has ever been made. It is quite impossible, I think, for any fair-minded man to doubt it. Every element in the story contributes to its cogency. The man is a soldier of unblemished record: his temperament is neither religious nor imaginative: he says of visions "I am not a believer in such things": he claims that others beside himself saw this shining in the night-sky, that they saw also three figures in the midst of the light, and he declares, "We stood watching them for about three-quarters of an hour." He made this statement in England when he was recovering from a serious wound. The lady to whom he made it, experienced in sick nursing and a practical organiser, is unshakably convinced that it is a true statement. A friend of mine, in whose judgment I have confidence, tells me that after talking to the soldier he is certain the thing occurred.

Everything I heard about this man so impressed me that I determined to try to see him for myself. I not only wanted to present the doubting reader with one definite case of first-hand evidence, but I wanted to see the soldier for my own personal satisfaction. I am extremely glad that I put myself to this trouble.

He is a man well above the middle height, of a powerful build, and without quickness of movement. His face, which is very dark and rather pitted, suggests a stubborn and almost a sullen disposition. He is a man, I should say, who would resent injustice, would find it difficult not to bear a grudge, and who would answer back if falsely upbraided. And yet when he smiles the heaviness and sulkiness of his face disappear, and a look of great gentleness comes into his eyes. You can see that he might be terrible with a bayonet at one moment and quite tender with a child at the next. His eyes, which are round and rather prominent, are blue-grey in colour and heavily lashed. Very friendly and rather pathetic eyes, but eyes which have seen a vision. The man, I found, is deeply affected by this experience in France.

A less hysterical, a less imaginative man I doubt if one could meet; and he is slow, awkward, and clumsy in speech—almost an inarticulate man. It is not until sympathy is well established that he begins to speak without self-consciousness, but when sympathy is established and he is speaking freely, he looks you full in the face, and there is a steady light in his eyes at such moments which is very impressive.

I asked him several questions, and he told me many things which do not appear in the statement. I asked about the officer, Captain R____: Was he a nervous or excitable man? "Far from it," replied the corporal; "he did not know what fear was, a proper officer he was; as good and brave as you'll find; and we were all sorry to lose him." I asked him how he knew that the vision lasted forty-five minutes. "That's wrong; that is," he said, "I told Miss Wilson it was somewhere about that, but I know exactly how long it lasted: it was thirty-five minutes." "How do you know that?" I inquired. "Because we were marching that very night, and I had my eye on the clock, as you might say. It was just before nine o'clock when the officer came up, and thirty-five minutes afterwards we started. We marched thirty-two miles that night."

"Now, tell me," I asked him, "what was the effect of the vision on your feelings, and the feelings of the other men?"

"Well, it was very funny. We came over quiet and still. It took us that way. We didn't know what to make of it. And there we all were, looking up at those three figures, saying nothing, just wondering, when one of the chaps called out, 'God's with us!'—and that kind of loosened us. Then when we were falling in for the march, the captain said to us, 'Well, men, we can cheer up now; we've got Someone with us.' And that's just how we felt. As I tell you, we marched thirty-two miles that night, and the Germans didn't fire either rifle or cannon the whole way."

"Did the effect last?—the moral effect?"

"There was a certain non-commissioned officer with us," he replied, slowly, "who was a fair coward, not fit to be a soldier, much less a non-commissioned officer. And that man—well, he was a fair honest coward and make no mistake about it!—became quite different from that night. He didn't mind what happened to him. He set a good example. That's a fact. He got killed at Wipers."[20]

I asked about other changes in the men.

"We were a decent lot of men on the whole," he replied, "and of course fighting keeps a man quiet; but there was one very rough fellow along with us who was always cursing and swearing, and going for all the drink he could get—not exactly a bad fellow he wasn't, but he was rough, very rough, and not particularly about himself. Well, that man was changed right through by the vision. I think it had more effect on him than on any of us. He didn't speak about it, but we could see for ourselves he was different. It made a man of him."

"Have you met, since you got back here, any of the men who saw the vision?"

"Only one. He's lying in Netley Hospital at this moment. He's in the Scots Guards. I saw him the other day and asked him about it. He remembers it just the same as I do. Of course, these chaps in here won't believe it. They think I must have dreamed it. But the sergeant in the Scots Guards could tell them. It was no dreaming! I've never seen anything like it before or since. I know very well what I saw."

Miss Courtney Wilson told me that he described the three figures to her as being midway between the earth and the sky—in mid-air: over the German lines and facing towards the British. They kept growing brighter and brighter, he said. The centre figure was much taller than the other two and had shining wings which seemed to protect the lesser figures on either side of him. Miss Wilson asked him if the figures resembled anybody, and he replied –these are his exact words:—"You could discern there were faces, but you couldn't see what they were like." He told her that under the feet of the three figures was a bright star, and that when the figures disappeared the star remained. "We found out afterwards," he told her, "that it was the Morning Star."

Such is the vision seen by a living man here in England, who has another witness to the truth of his narrative also in England.

It is not my business to discuss the explanations which can so easily be fabricated for experiences of this kind. My purpose is secured if I can dispel from the mind of those who accept Mr. Machen's theory the idea that all such stories have their origin in rumour, and that no first-hand evidence exists for any of them. But I should like to impress upon the reader, before passing on to a narrative of further evidence, the great need for exercising caution in the acceptance of explanations. Nothing is more easy than to dismiss such a story as this, nothing more difficult than to explain the explanation.

Quite by accident I encountered in Hoxton on the 26th August, 1915, a young dispatch rider home on leave from the front for the first time since the outbreak of hostilities, who could also confirm this account of a vision. He added something which I had not heard before. After speaking of the bright light between earth and sky, which he saw quite steadily, he said: "And then there's the shells. A shell bursts pretty close in front of you; the smoke and dust go up in the air; and presently you see in the middle of the smoke—well, it's like a woman, and she's looking at you, with her arms spread out. I've seen that many times. And it's not imagination. It gives you a strange feeling to see it. It's not real looking, but it's there—quite plainly."

A wounded Grenadier Guardsman tells me that the vision at Mons was common talk on the great retreat. "I've heard young fellows just enlisted at Chelsea Barracks talking about religion and denying a Supreme Being. They say, 'If there's a Supreme Being, why don't He stop the War?' And I say to them, 'Chums, you wait till you get out there. You'll be praying to a Supreme Being,' I says, 'before very long.' I know I prayed out there often enough, standing, sitting, and marching; yes, and I don't disown that I did it neither." He himself saw nothing supernatural; but he heard men out there speaking of the visions, and he was definitely conscious, he tells me emphatically, of a supernatural presence. This splendid type of Guardsman is a very convincing witness to a change in the "psychological atmosphere." He wishes to warn young man in England that if the Germans ever land in this country they'll make a cemetery of it." He has seen dreadful things.

Just as this book goes to press, the following statement by a justice of the peace in Flintshire makes its appearance in the *Daily Mail*:—

> Sir,—Private Cleaver, of the 1st Cheshire Regiment, was frequently in Birkenhead some months ago, but I did not hear of him until near the end of his stay, and failed to meet him. I thought he had left England. He frequently spoke to his friends in the canteen of what he had seen at Mons.
> To my great joy I learnt last week that he was only forty miles away, and the next day went to see him. He gave me the following words in writing: "I myself was at Mons, and saw the Vision of the Angels." He also expressed his willingness to sign an affidavit to that effect. Well content, I returned home, and the following day procured an affidavit and again travelled forty miles to see him sign it. A copy is enclosed.
> Geo. S. Hazlehurst
> Beaconsfield, Devonshire Place,
> Birkenhead, Aug. 22[21]

III

I propose to examine now an article written by Miss Phyllis Campbell which appeared in the August number of the *Occult Review*, and which Mr. Machen criticises in the Postscript to his book.

Miss Campbell, I am told, is the daughter of Mrs. Francis [sic] Campbell, the novelist, and a cousin of Lady Archibald Campbell.[22] She is a student of singing, and was in Germany studying music just before war broke out. The war caught her in France, where she was educated as a girl, and with great enthusiasm she threw herself into the work of nursing the stream of wounded which soon began to pour through the land. So great has been her service, and so conspicuous her devotion that I understand she is to be decorated by the French Government.

Although quite young she seems to possess extraordinary powers of self-control and endurance. She is extremely pretty, childlike, and sensitive; but she has been through scenes that would drive many people mad, and has actually helped in surgical operations that would try the nerves of a trained nurse. I shall not easily forget this child's account of how she held a man's leg for amputation, and how the leg came away in her hands.

In this article she tells of "the torrent of blistered, bleeding, stony-eyed Belgian refugees which had poured through our hands unceasingly, night and day, for the first hot breathless weeks of last August." She tells us that "the miseries of those first wounded cannot ever be written." These early days were followed by the unforgettable weeks of the great retreat. Miss Campbell says that there was a perceptible change in the wounded during these weeks which she found "utterly unaccountable."

> The French, who had tolerantly accepted badges and medals of the saints from the Catholics of our [medical] post, now eagerly asked for them, and were profusely grateful for "holy pictures"—those little prints of saints and angels so common in all Catholic communities. But what puzzled the post was that these men, without a solitary exception, demanded invariably "St. Michael" or "Joan of Arc."

Further, she tells us that these men in spite of their wounds and exhaustion from loss of blood were in a state of "singular exaltation."

> We thought at first some of them had been supplied with wine, but that was clearly impossible, as our post was the first stop and the trains came right through from the clearing station, without attention of any sort, as the fighting was then at its fiercest.
>
> This curious mental condition in the wounded continued during the long retreat on Paris. Many of the wounded died in our hands, but the living no longer urged us to fly; they "died in hope," as if they were mentally visioning victory, where their immediate forerunners had only seen defeat.

Miss Campbell does not give in this article the full story of her dreadful experiences; but I may tell the reader that she and those devoted women who worked with her, very often had to lift dead men from off the bodies of wounded men in unloading the railway trucks which came down from the battle line. But she does tell us that she did not take her clothes off for the whole of that week, first because she was too weary to undress or to eat and simply fell fast asleep on her bed; and secondly, because the summons was always coming, by night as well as by day, to arise and help fresh arrivals of wounded men.

Such was the state of things in those early days of the war when the following incident occurred. She was one day bandaging the broken arm of a French soldier while a surgeon was stitching up a horrible gap in his head, when the French lady in charge of the post, coming to replace her, said, "There is an Englishman in the wagon. He demands a something—I think a holy picture." Miss Campbell went to find the soldier, wondering that an Englishman in such a scene of blood and misery should ask for a holy picture. She found him to be a Lancashire Fusilier.

> He was propped in a corner, his left arm tied up in a peasant woman's head kerchief, and his head newly bandaged. He should have been in a state of collapse from loss of blood, for his tattered uniform was soaked and caked in blood, and his face paper-white under the dirt of conflict. He looked at me with bright courageous eyes and asked for a picture or a medal (he didn't care which) of St. George. I asked if he was a Catholic. "No," he was a Wesleyan Methodist (I hope I have it right), and he wanted a picture, or a medal, of St. George, because he had seen him on a white horse, leading the British at Vitry-le François, when the Allies turned.

I will interrupt her narrative at this point, because of a rather fiddling criticism by Mr. Machen, to point out that the mention of Vitry-le François was not intended by Miss Campbell to be taken as an utterance of the soldier. The sentence is carelessly written, but not more carelessly than we should expect from one who is not yet a practised writer; it will be clear from what follows that Miss Campbell merely mentioned here the name of the place for the reader's benefit because she herself afterwards ascertained it. She does not mean to put it into the soldier's mouth.

She says that as she was talking to this Lancashire Fusilier, another wounded man who was sitting beside him on the floor, and who noticed her look of amazement, said to her, "It's true, Sister. We all saw it. First there was a sort of yellow mist like, sort of risin' before the Germans as they come to the top of the hill, come on like a solid wall they did—springing out of the earth just solid, no end to 'em. I just give up. No use fighting the whole German race, thinks I; it's all up with us. The next minute comes this funny cloud of light, and when it clears off there's a tall man with yellow hair in golden armour, on a white horse, holding his sword up, and his mouth open as if he was saying, 'Come on boys! I'll put the kybosh on the devils.' Sort of 'This is my picnic' expression. Then, before you could say knife, the Germans had turned and we were after them, fighting like ninety. We had a few scores to settle, Sister, and we fair settled them."

Miss Campbell asked them where exactly this took place. Neither of the men could say.

"They had marched, fighting a rearguard action, from Mons, till St. George had appeared through the haze of light, and turned the Germans.

They both knew it was St. George. Hadn't they seen him with his sword on every 'quid' they'd ever had? The Frenchies had seen him too, ask them; but they said it was St. Michael."

Now this reference to the French is a matter on which I would like to lay some emphasis. Mr. Machen, I take it, will not claim that such a conviction among the French soldiers arose from the publications of his story in the London Evening News [sic]. His answer would be, of course, that the French soldiers have not seen any visions. But this puts him into the somewhat unpleasant quandary of charging Miss Campbell, for one, with telling a deliberate untruth. Until he makes such a charge—and Miss Campbell will surely give him the opportunity in a book which she is now preparing for the press—I shall not attempt to argue against so unwarrantable suggestion. But I would ask the reader carefully to observe that there are as many stories in France of the French soldiers having seen Joan of Arc, as there are stories in England of our troops having seen Angels or St. George. The Revd. Oswald Watkins,[23] a chaplain at the front, tells how the French speak of a mysterious nurse at the Battle of Ypres, who tended the wounded, comforted the dying, and who appeared to them as the Virgin Mary. Here, too, is another statement made by Miss Campbell:—

> "As for *petite* Jeanne d'Arc," said one soldier, "I know her well, for I am of Domrémy. I saw her brandishing her sword and crying 'Turn! Turn! Advance!'" Yes, he knew others had seen the Archangel, but little Joan of Arc was good enough for him. He had fought with the English from Mons—and little Joan of Arc had defeated the English—*par exemple*! Now she was leading them. There was a combination for you. No wonder the *Boches* fled down the hill.

Miss Campbell is also able to state that a Russian princess wrote to some of her friends by the last mail that got through, stating that St. Michael had been seen during the battles in Russia. This letter arrived in France before the 14th of September, 1914. The princess is a voluntary nurse, and in her letter says that the numbers of Russian wounded testified to seeing the visions. "Strange things," she wrote, "are happening in the trenches."

Miss Campbell says that in discussing this matter with the nurses and the wounded, they came to the conclusion that the French soldiers of all ranks had seen two well-known saints—Joan of Arc, to whom many of those delirious with the torrid heat and loss of blood were praying, St. Michael the Archangel, clad in golden armour, bare-headed, riding a white horse, and flourishing his sword as he shouted "Victory!" while for the English the saint was St. George, also in golden armour, also bare-headed, also riding a white horse, and crying while he held up his sword "Come on!"

> There were individual discrepancies, naturally, but in the main the story was the same, seen in cold blood at a moment of despair, and continued in the

realisation of victory. It was always related quietly and sanely, in a matter-of-fact fashion, as if it were a usual and quite expected occurrence for the lords of heaven to lead the hosts of earth. Of one thing all were assured—that the Germans represented the powers of evil, and that so doubtfully did victory hang in the balance, that the powers of good found it necessary to fight hand to hand and foot to foot with the Allies, lest the whole world be lost.

She then goes on to remark, which I think is very important, that she and her fellow nurses heard the same tale again "from the lips of a priest." She also heard the same story that same night from two officers, and three men of the Irish Guards. "These three men were mortally wounded, they asked for the Sacrament before death, and before dying told the same story to the old abbé who confessed them."

Now this statement is one upon which a true critic of Miss Campbell's article will surely fasten. He will ask for that priest to be produced. He will ask, at any rate, for a sworn statement by that priest; and he will say that no one has any right to ask a rational man to accept such a story on the mere word of a single young lady about whose antecedents and character he knows nothing at all. This is a perfectly justifiable attitude. It is one, I think, from which Miss Campbell herself would not dissent—if she chooses to consider that her place is the witness-box. But all I ask the reader to do is to keep his mind open on the whole question, and not by any means to conclude that Mr. Machen has solved the entire question by his assertion that he published a story of a somewhat similar character in an English newspaper towards the end of September 1914. I have no doubt that when all the hurly of the war is overpassed, it will be quite possible for Miss Campbell or others to produce written statements by reliable witnesses concerning all these things. The great point I have in my own mind is the prevention of incredulity likely to result, I am afraid, from the very singular coincidence which forms the only arguments of Mr. Machen's position.

For myself I may say that I am entirely satisfied of these two main matters. First, that Miss Campbell is neither neurotic nor untruthful. Second, that there are many others besides Miss Campbell, both in France and England, who could make a like testimony if they were so minded. Moreover, the reader of this book comes upon the remarkable narrative of Miss Campbell after reading the statement made by the lance-corporal in an English hospital which forms the matter of the last chapter. It is not as if Miss Campbell was the sole witness to these visions. There are many others. Harm has been done, I freely admit, by these mere gossips who have heard some story of mystery, have straightaway embroidered it, added I know not what fantasy to its simplicity, and passed it on as veritable gospel. But the sane and just-minded reader will not be dissuaded from a search after truth because he meets on his road those who either offend or disgust him. As well might a man going up to the Temple to pray turn back and cease to believe in a God, because of the beggars he encounters on his road, offering him grubby and ridiculous relics of the saints.

We must also constantly keep in our mind the fact that the British Army was saved in those days in a manner which puzzles the intellectuals of all soldiers. Miss Campbell speaks of that matter in the following way:

> For forty-eight hours no food, no drink, under a tropical sun, choked with dust, harried by shell, and marching, marching, marching, till even the pursuing Germans gave it up, and at Vitry-le François the Allies fell in their tracks and slept for three hours—horse, foot and guns—while the exhausted pursuers slept behind them.
> Then came the trumpet call, and each man sprang to his arms to find himself made anew. One man said, "I felt as if I had just come out of the sea after a swim. Fit! just grand. I never felt so fit in my life, and every man of us the same. The Germans were coming on just the same as ever, when suddenly the 'Advance' sounded, and I saw the luminous mist and the great man on the white horse, and I knew the *Boches* would never get Paris, for God was fighting on our side."

We shall no doubt hear much more of all of this when the war is over, but certainly there is even now the historic fact that when all seemed utterly hopeless for the Allies, and when destruction of the British Army looked utterly inescapable, suddenly the whole German army swerved on its road, disappeared from sight, and the situation and the cause of the Allies were saved.

Miss Campbell tells us of another man who spoke to her of these things:— "Poor Dix, when he came into hospital with a bleeding gap where his mouth had been, and a splintered hand and arm, he ought to have been prostrate and unconscious, but he made no moan, his pain had vanished in contemplation of the wonderful thing he had seen—saints and angels fighting on this common earth, with common mortal men, against one devilish foe to all humanity. A strange and dreadful thing, that the veil which hangs between us and the world of Immortality should be so rent and shrivelled by suffering and agony that human eyes can look on the angels and not be blinded. The cries of mothers and little children, the suffering of crucified fathers and carbonised sons and brothers, the tortures of nuns and virgins, and violated wives and daughters, have all gone up in torment and dragged at the Ruler of the Universe for aid, and aid has come."

If Miss Campbell is at all credible, and if the editor of the *Occult Review* is a man of honour,[24] this article contains a statement which should finally dispose of Mr. Machen's contention:—

> Much of what I have written here is not new to the Editor of this Review, because when I had a moment to spare I wrote to him after August 4th last

year, and much also I wrote to friends whose names I enclose with this, mentioning these things as they came, with the time. Naturally, these friends may not like their names mentioned, so I do not publish them; but the Editor may, I am sure, if he so desires, communicate with them for his own satisfaction.

I have asked the Editor of the *Occult Review*, Mr. Ralph Shirley, whether he feels perfectly satisfied in his own mind that Miss Campbell is a credible witness, and he has assured me that he is entirely satisfied in this respect. Therefore, I think Mr. Machen's theory is very badly damaged by the fact stated in this last quotation from Miss Campbell's article, that she wrote about these things to Mr. Ralph Shirley as early as August, 1914. There is either a conspiracy between Miss Campbell and Mr. Shirley to deceive the British public (object not stated!) or Mr. Machen's theory does not hold water.

In conclusion, I would ask the reader once more carefully to keep in his mind that there are witnesses in France to the fact of the French soldiers seeing visions as well as witnesses in England to the fact of British soldiers seeing visions of a similar nature. And according to Miss Campbell, there are those in Russia who can testify to the same thing.

If Mr. Machen has so travelled the earth and bewitched humanity, he has proof at least of his own immortality.

IV

Let us see what Mr. Machen has to say of Miss Campbell's narrative. His objections are four in number.

1. Miss Campbell does not produce the soldier.
2. The Fusilier and R. F. A. man contradict themselves about the locality of the vision.
3. The soldiers' apparition does not correspond with St. George on the English sovereign.
4. Miss Campbell says that "everybody" who fought from Mons to Ypres saw the apparition, and yet "Nobody has come forward to testify...."

We will examine these very trivial criticisms, which smack of the police-court, one by one.

Miss Campbell does not produce the soldier. I would remind Mr. Machen that only a very limited body of people have the power to move soldiers from place to place. Moreover, when Miss Campbell wrote her articles no one had challenged her either to produce the soldier or to give his name and address. She wrote an account of what she had seen and heard for the sympathetic audience she would expect to find among readers of the *Occult Review*. No one had risen at that time to dispute the truth of her statements. She was relating an experience, not conducting a controversy. I have no doubt that if she feels disposed to answer those who accuse her of a very willful and wicked attempt to deceive men and women, Miss Campbell will be able to give a number of names and addresses.

The contradiction as to locality. As I remarked in the last chapter, Mr. Machen has merely seized upon a girl's looseness in composition to trumpet what he mistakes to be a masterly stricture. Miss Campbell does not say that the soldiers told her the vision appeared at Vitry-le François. But does Mr. Machen truly think that a person so monstrously wicked as to spin a succession of lies on a most solemn subject would be also so inexcusably stupid, so incredibly foolish, as to say "Yes" in one place, and "No" to the same question a dozen or so lines lower down?

St. George and the Sovereign. We are very glad to think that Mr. Machen's contribution to literature is in the region of imaginative fiction and not in the sphere of criticism. Criticism of all kinds, since the days of Matthew Arnold,[25] has fallen low indeed, but not yet, let us thank the complacent stars, has it descended to such pitiable depths as Mr. Machen reaches in this paltry objection. Really it is disturbing to find that one who has done such admirable work as an imaginative artist (and I commend to lovers of sombre mystery and insidious horror not yet aware of them Mr. Machen's absorbing books), it is disturbing, I say, to find that a man who is really an artist and who has undoubted genius in his own genre, should bring forward with a ludicrous effect of pomposity a criticism so manifestly without life or force. Is not the very inaccuracy rather a proof of the story's genuineness? Will Mr. Machen assure us with his hand on his heart that before he proceeded to tell us exactly how St. George appears on the English sovereign (in order to contradict Miss Campbell) he did not put his hand into his pocket for the auriferous image? Are we to expect, too, that men in battle should be observers of minutest detail, and, coming out of battle, should be mathematically exact in their conversational reports of the things they have seen? Moreover, is the method of the police-court either the fairest or the best to arrive at the truth of such occurrence? Would Mr. Machen be content to leave the truth of the religion to which he is devoted with so mediaeval a surrender of his reason, to the decision of lawyers? How would the documents of that religion fare in such a wrangle? But one need not continue. The objection is mean.

The word Everybody. Miss Campbell is guilty in this writing as most of us speak. We say "everybody saw it," when we mean two or three, perhaps four or five, out of some twenty or thirty people. Miss Campbell should not have written in this fashion, and if she had been addressing a skeptical or a critical audience I think she would not have written in this fashion. But to object to her total narrative on this ground is as if a man threw over the Gospel of St. Mark, because discrepancies exist in the two versions of Creation related in the Book of Genesis. At the same time, I am quite of Mr. Machen's opinion that more men should testify to the visions. My own book does afford such testimony, and I hope that after the War is over a volume of equally reliable evidence may be collected and published.

These are the full sum of Mr. Machen's objections, and having dealt with them we are bound to consider their implications.

According to these objections Miss Campbell has told a tissue of lies. No man in the Lancashire Fusiliers, and no man in the Royal Field Artillery spoke to her of visions. There was no "poor Dix." There was no abbé who spoke to Miss Campbell about soldiers' visions. The nurses associated with Miss Campbell never discussed the visions. She has made it all up in her own head—and she made it up in her own head, not in August, 1914, when she first wrote as the editor of the *Occult Review*, but after September 29, when Mr. Machen's story of "The Bowmen" appeared in the London *Evening News*.

To quote Mr. Machen, "It may be so, but—."

I am on the side of the angels and on the side of Miss Campbell. Nothing that Mr. Machen has said shatters my faith in the least degree. And I shall be surprised if the accumulation of evidence on this matter does not presently bring Mr. Machen, hat in hand, before Miss Campbell with the confession that he is converted, perhaps with the apology he could so graciously frame for his vanity in preferring his fiction to her word.

To believe in Miss Campbell does not rob Mr. Machen of any credit he deserves for writing "The Bowmen."

V

Lest the reader should think that only the few cases mentioned in the foregoing pages have come to light, I will here make a chapter of various instances which have come my way in the course of a week or two:

The Rev. G. G. Monck, M. A., Prebendary of Wells and Rural Dean of Martock,[26] has received a letter from a personal friend concerning the Angels at Mons in which the following passage occurs:—

> The account I sent you was taken down from the lips of a wounded man in hospital in London by one of Sir H.'s sisters who was working there. She knew the man well, and had reasons for believing him to be depended on. Curiously enough, about two months ago in Oxford I met a young second lieutenant of the _____ who had been all through the retreat from Mons and had been wounded at Neuve Chapelle. I asked him if he knew the story. To this he replied, "Yes, I read it in hospital. It is simply miraculous, but it is perfectly true." He then added, "Do you know that almost the same thing happened at Neuve Chapelle?"

If this statement is not a pure invention by Prebendary Monck, his personal friend is either telling the truth or willfully deceiving his correspondent.

In the *Observer* of August 22nd, 1915, appeared the following paragraph:—

Three • Harold Begbie and *On the Side of the Angels*

The Rev. A. A. Boddy,[27] Vicar of All Saints, Sunderland, who has just returned home after two months ministerial work at the front, says he had several opportunities of investigating the story of the "vision" at Mons.

The evidence, he says, though not always direct, was remarkably cumulative, and came through channels which were entitled to respect. Supernatural angel forms had, he believed, been seen. He was reminded of one of the Biblical prophecies that at the time of a great crisis on the earth "great signs shall there be from Heaven."

A lady, whose name and address he holds, while nursing in a convalescent hospital, was told by a patient that at a critical people in the retreat from Mons they saw an angel with outstretched wings, like a luminous cloud, between the advancing Germans and themselves. And at that moment the onslaught of the Germans slackened. Unable to credit the story, she was discussing later with a group of officers, when a colonel looked up and said: "Young lady, the thing happened. You need not be incredulous. I saw it myself."

"A.M.B.," writing in the *Church Times* from Paris on July 28th, 1915, gave the following testimony from a German source:—

A lady in Germany at that time, who is well known for her work among English girls there, tells me that there was much discussion in Berlin because a certain regiment who had been told off to do a certain duty at a certain battle, failed to carry out their orders, and when censured they declared that they did go forward but found themselves absolutely powerless to proceed with their orders, and their horses turned sharply round and fled like the wind and nothing could stop them. The explanation given by the German soldiers was in these words: "We simply could not go on, those devils of Englishmen were up to some devilry or other, and we could do nothing—we were powerless."

This same lady had the opportunity of a conversation with one of the lieutenants of the regiment in question, and as the affair had made some stir in Berlin owing to the severe reprimand given to the men, she asked him what really happened. He said, "I cannot tell you. I only know that we were charging full on the British at a certain place, and in a moment we were stopped. It was most like going full speed and being pulled up suddenly on a precipice, but there was no precipice there, nothing at all, only our horses swerved round and fled and we could do nothing!" My friend adds that the Germans are most superstitious and dread anything touching on the supernatural, and would not go to a séance for anything, which accounts for the explanation given.

This was the story told in Berlin after the battle of Mons. It seems to show that something out of the common happened—the Germans ascribed it to the work of the devil, the English are said to have seen "angels," but the Germans only saw the English, whom they stigmatized as "devils," while the English saw themselves delivered as by a miracle from the Germans. That is how the facts stand, but a hiatus is left; and one dare not say that in that moment of stress and danger to the English, there was not a glimpse given to some of a supernatural aid. Of this one may be absolutely sure; that if anyone is still living who saw the glimpse, he is the last person who would wish to hold it up to scientific research.

The following extract is taken from *Light* (July 10th, 1915):—

"Pax," a correspondent of *Light*, who has been active in pursuing inquiry into the stories of visions at the battle-front, sends the following extract from a letter received from an artilleryman on the 26th ult:—

With regard to the stories which you have heard about "angels and spirits" appearing to our chaps in the trenches, I can only say that I have not seen them myself, but then, of course, we do not stop in the trenches long and have not the experience of them as have the infantry. I have heard several fellows discussing this subject and they absolutely vouch for the truth of it. They may be right, but of course, you must remember that trench work is mind-straining as well as nerve-wracking, and that may account somewhat for a lot of these stories.

The "Notes of the Month" in the current issue of the *Occult Review* deal at considerable length with the matter, citing several of the accounts which have appeared in *Light*. The editor, Mr. Ralph Shirley, remarks on the considerable discussion which has taken place in the Press regarding the alleged psychical phenomena at the Battle of Mons, and referring to the attack made by the *Evening News* on the statements of Mr. Sinnett in the *Occult Review*, and to the (unfounded) claim of the evening paper that the record was derived from Mr. Machen's now well-known story, he says:—

"Seeing this attack I at once wrote a rejoinder giving the true state of the case. I regret to have to state that, deviating from every tradition of self-respecting journalism, the *Evening News* failed to insert my reply."

Mr. Shirley relates that he has interviewed two English ladies who have been nursing at a hospital at St. Germain-en-Laye, in the neighbourhood of Paris. These ladies stated that the accounts in question were in France "not merely implicitly believed, but were absolutely known to be true," and they added "that no French paper would have made itself ridiculous by disputing the authenticity of what was vouched for by so many thousands of independent eye-witnesses."

It is only fair to the Editor of the *Evening News* that I should mention his newspaper's honourable part in the later stages of this controversy. Whether he should have published Mr. Shirley's letter I cannot say, but I can testify that he has since published evidence in favour of the theory of Angels, and evidence entirely destructive of the Machen theory. For example:—

If the "Angels of Mons" were really seen by numbers of soldiers, why is it so difficult to obtain first-hand and authenticated evidence? That is the question thousands of people are discussing to-day owing to the enormous popularity of Mr. Machen's story.

The author himself asks the question in a postscript to "The Bowmen":—

Many men have been back on leave from the front, we have many wounded in hospital, many soldiers have written letters home. And they have all combined, this great host, to keep silence as to the most wonderful of occurrences, the most inspiring assurance, the surest omen of victory. It may be so, but—

> "Mr. Machen is frankly incredulous," said a sergeant who was at Mons to an *Evening News* representative. "But Mr. Machen overlooks the real reasons. There are not hosts of soldiers about to-day who were in the crucial fights of the Mons Retreat. There are precious few of us alive to tell any tale, let alone of visions. One of the Hampshire battalions is an instance. To-day there are only six survivors who were at Mons. Much of the evidence that came in at the time was from mortally wounded soldiers."
>
> This particular sergeant was most reticent about his own experiences, but upon pressure admitted that he himself saw the phantom warriors.
>
> "I'm not talking about it," he insisted. "I'm not a spiritualist. But I know what I saw."

We may surely take it that the Editor of the *Evening News* (in whose columns Mr. Machen's story appeared) satisfied himself that this emphatic testimony by a sergeant from Mons came from the lips of a real sergeant, and did not reach the representative of the paper at second or third hand.

Here is a further emphatic testimony, for which the Editor of a respectable Roman Catholic organ is responsible:—

> An extraordinary story, which recalls an incident in the Crusades, reaches the "Universe" from an accredited correspondent, who is, however, precluded from imparting the names of those concerned.
>
> The story is told by a Catholic officer in a letter from the front, and is told with a simplicity which shows the narrator's own conviction of its genuineness.
>
> "A party of about thirty men and an officer was cut off in a trench, when the officer said to his men, 'Look here; we must either stay here and be caught like rats in a trap, or make a sortie against the enemy. We haven't much of a chance, but personally I don't want to be caught here.' The men all agreed with him, and with a yell of 'St. George for England!' they dashed out into the open. The officer tells how, as they ran on, he became aware of a large company of men with bows and arrows going along with them, and even leading them on against the enemy's trenches, and afterwards when was talking to a German prisoner, the man asked him who was the officer on a great white horse who led them? for although he was such a conspicuous figure, they had none of them been able to hit him. I must also add that the German dead appeared to have no wounds on them. The officer who told the story (adds the writer of the letter) was a friend of ours. He did not see St. George on the white horse, but he saw the archers with his own eyes."
>
> The former appearance of St. George on the battlefield was at a time when the infidel forces were pressing the Christians very closely, and even the reckless valour of Richard Coeur de Lion[28] seemed powerless to restore the fortune of the fight. It is said that at this critical moment St. George appeared mounted

on a white horse and led the Christians on to victory. Previously, it is recorded, St. George appeared to Geoffroi de Bouillon[29] at the Siege of Antioch.

Then we have a lady, Miss March, of 90, St. Andrew's Road, Southsea, writing to the Editor of *Light*, with the following strange story of a vision:—

I should like to mention that my young nephew, who enlisted for the period of the war at Portsmouth, told us on Sunday evening that the Garrison Church in the morning, during the service, the chaplain told them of a sergeant who was sitting where they sat only a short time ago. He was gazing at the altar, and suddenly the altar disappeared and he saw distinctly the form of the Lord Jesus Christ standing with outstretched arms towards him. "That sergeant is now dead, killed at the war," added the chaplain sadly. "I shall never see him again on earth, but I hope to do so in heaven."

Mrs. F. H. Fitzgerald Beale,[30] writing to the same journal from Ireland, says:—

We have among other wounded soldiers home from the war a soldier of the Dublin Fusiliers who was injured at Mons. I told him of the story and asked him whether it was true. He said, "Yes, I saw it myself—a thick black cloud; it quite hid us from the enemy."

The following testimonies reach me from one in whose judgment I have confidence, and for the character I have a sincere admiration:—

Lady ____ was lunching with me, having been the previous day at Stepney. In the course of the afternoon she told me that a poor woman in the Soldiers' and Sailors' Meeting said she had just received a letter from her husband who was at the battle of Neuve Chapelle. "In the course of the battle," he wrote to his wife, "I saw the angels all round us."

A Mrs. ____, a neighbour of a friend of mine, went to see a wounded cousin in Bucks. He is a silent, rather taciturn man. On hearing of his escape from death, she said, "It is nothing short of a miracle." "You may well say that," he replied, and proceeded to give her the following account:

He was told to take a certain wood, and started with his troop. On reaching a road at right angles which he was to follow, to his surprise his horse stopped dead, and nothing would induce the animal to move. Turning to his A.D.C., he found the same thing had happened, and not only so, but to the whole troop—the horses refused to move; finding it useless to waste time, he followed a parallel road further on. Afterwards they found that a strong German ambush awaited them along the road from which they had been so strangely turned by the conduct of their horses.

When asked why the Germans had turned back from Paris, the answer was given by more than one prisoner, "How could we advance when we heard of the immense army ready to take us in the flank?"

In a sermon preached by the Rev. R. F. Horton,[31] and published in the *Manchester Guardian*, the following incidents are narrated, one of them, at

Three • Harold Begbie and *On the Side of the Angels*

least, reaching this well-known and greatly respected minister direct from the actual witness:—

> There are (he said) wonderful stories coming to us in this time of war—some of them verified and some of them floating about and difficult to verify and to fix—but they are stories which show quite distinctly how men to-day are kept in the secret places of the most High, under the shadow of the Almighty, in the midst of unexampled peril. There is a story—repeated by so many witnesses that if anything can be established by contemporary evidence it is established—of the retreat from Mons. A section of the line was in imminent peril and it seemed as if it must inevitably be borne down and cut off. Our men saw a company of angels interposed between them and the German cavalry and the horses of the Germans stampeding. Evidently the animals beheld what our men beheld. The German soldiers endeavoured to bring the horses back to the line, but they fled. It was the salvation of our men.
>
> I had news from the Dardanelles last week but one. A sailor on one of our transport ships told me in the simplest language—just narrating the fact of the moment—how airships of the enemy came over the troopship dropping bombs. The captain, who is a man of God, gave the order to the men to pray, and they did pray. They knelt on the deck and prayed and the Lord delivered them. The eighteen bombs, which seemed to be falling from overhead, fell harmlessly in the sea.
>
> Respecting another story which he told, Dr. Horton said he did not know how far they must take it literally. "Now and again," he continued, "a wounded man on the field is conscious of a comrade in white coming with help and even delivering him. One of our men who had heard of this story again and again and had put it down to hysterical excitement had an experience. His division had advanced and was not adequately protected by the artillery. It was cut to pieces and he himself fell. He tried to hide in a hollow of the ground, and as he lay helpless, not daring to lift his head under the hail of fire, he saw one in white coming to him. For a moment he thought it must be a hospital attendant or a stretcher-bearer, but no, it could not be; the bullets were flying all round. The white-robed came near and bent over him. The man lost consciousness for a moment, and when he came round he seemed to be out of danger. The white-robed still stood by him, and the man, looking at his hand, said 'You are wounded in your hand.' There was a wound in the palm. He answered, 'Yes, that is an old wound that has opened again lately.' The soldier says that in spite of the peril and his wounds he felt a joy he had never experienced in his life before."[32]

Testimony of a similar kind appears in the following letter addressed to the *Church Family Newspaper*:—

> Sir,—I do not quite understand why suddenly in many papers and parish magazines the story of the appearance of angels at the battle of Mons has been suddenly revived, but discussing it with the daughter of the late Rector here, she told me that she had received a letter from a friend, Miss Stoughton, whose sister was nursing soldiers in the hospital at Tekleton, near Saffron

Walden, which carried the matter a step further, and with her permission, I read it in the pulpit at Evensong on Sunday. Miss Stoughton wrote: "There is a wonderful story of a man called by the soldiers 'A Comrade in White,' who is going about at the front, helping the wounded.[33] A man told my sister that, though he had not seen Him himself, he knew many soldiers who had. He was supposed to be 'The Angel of the Covenant,' our Lord Himself. He has been seen at different places." Yours truly, Ernest J. A. Fitzroy[34]

Weeken

Mrs. Hubert Barclay,[35] devoutly religious, clear-headed, and not in the least mentally careless, vouches for the truth of the following statement. She says:—

In February, 1915, I was speaking to a friend who told me that a commanding officer on leave from the Front had told him that this War had convinced him that the days of miracles were not over—that at one time our men were so few that the line had to be held by them at a distance of fifteen yards apart, and that nothing would persuade him that the trench had not been held by superhuman agency. It was humanly impossible, for there was a whole German Army Corps against us in that place.

"In March a friend of mine was addressing a soldiers' meeting at Witley. In the course of her talk she told them the foregoing story as I had told it to her. After the meeting a man pressed forward through the crowd and said, '"Eh! ma'am, it's a funny thing your telling that story. It was way back in October on the Aisne, and I was there and I saw them! but people won't believe me."

This lady who addressed the meeting at Witley is Mrs. Burnett Smith, very well known to a considerable public as Annie S. Swan.[36] She has written to me, and in her letter she says: "I believe all these stories. *I have heard so many at first hand*, and further, I have seen into the hearts of our Fighting Men when I was in France, and they know they are fighting on the side of the angels; therefore 'these ministers of His that do His pleasure' are on their side at the supreme moment." The statement which I have ventured to italicize, coming from such a source, is of the very highest importance. Mrs. Burnett Smith is a witness for whom it is impossible not to feel the sincerest respect. I am glad of this opportunity to pay my tribute of admiration to her quite noble and most inspiring work among our soldiers both in France and at home.

From the columns of the *Evening News* I take the two following paragraphs:—

"The Angels at Mons" was the subject of a sermon by Dr. Richardson last evening at St. Mary-at-Hill, E.C. In the course of his remarks Dr. Richardson told the well-known stories in regard to the soldiers' visions of angels referred to in the *Evening News*.

The skeptics, he said, did not disprove the existence of eyewitnesses or make any slur upon the veracity of their evidence. The question now was—

Could soldiers who had seen the angels at the front be got to give public evidence; or was it possible to get testimony from folk who had seen soldiers' letters vouching for such visions?

"I should like to ask," said Dr. Richardson, "whether there is anyone in the congregation who has letters in his possession or has seen such letters from any soldiers who can tell of seeing angels on the battlefield? If there is such a person here to-night will he stand up?"

Thereupon a lady in the back of the church stood up and declared that she had seen letters from three different soldiers.

"In each one," said this lady, "was clear and convincing testimony that these soldiers had themselves seen the angels."

The letters were not hysterical outbursts, but were written in a calm and sober fashion. These soldiers stated that the Germans had been kept back by a troop of angels, and averred that the French soldiers too declared that they had seen the vision.

Continuing, Dr. Richardson said Christian folk need not be incredulous. If Christians wanted to cut out all references to angels in the Bible, then a great deal would be destroyed.

Mrs. Quest, of St. Leonards-on-Sea, is the lady who testified on Sunday at St. Mary-at-Hill Church to having seen soldiers' letters relating their visions of the Angels of Mons.

She called at the *Evening News* office yesterday and said about a month ago she was travelling from St. Leonards to London when a hospital nurse just back from France got into a conversation with her. "She spoke to me," said Mrs. Quest, "because I was wearing my son's regimental badge. He is an Australian officer recently wounded in the Dardanelles.

"The nurse showed me three letters from different soldiers. All testified to having personally seen the angels, and mentioned that the French soldiers claimed to have seen St. Michael leading a troop of horsemen.

"This intervention, the soldiers said, came at the most critical stage, and certainly made the German horses stampede. Some German prisoners vowed the English had contrived to tamper with their horses beforehand. Other Germans said they fled because of 'large reinforcements,' which the English soldiers declare was the phantom army."

Here, then, are a number of instances, gathered in a brief period into a small space, which must surely impress the impartial reader as strangely corroborative evidence of the spiritual thesis. And now, in conclusion, I will give a case where faith in the vision goes side by side with an explanation which seeks to get rid of the Angels.

An English lady of great energy and the most practical common sense, who has established a rest-house and club for our soldiers in France, and who has seen and heard many of the worst horrors of war, tells me the following incident:—

"A dying soldier said to me one day, 'It's a funny thing, sister, isn't it, how the Germans say we had a lot of troops behind us?' It never struck me that he was speaking of phantasms, and I simply replied by the question, quite lightly uttered, 'Do they say that?' He went on to assure me that German prisoners had said, 'How could we break through your line when you had all those thousands of troops behind you?' And he added, 'Thousands of troops! Why, we were just a thin line of two regiments with nothing behind us.' Now, I believe in a life after death, but I don't believe in angels on earth, and so I said to the soldier, 'Well, it seems to me fairly easy to understand. When a man is killed, in the very thick of a fight, and with all his angry passions at white heat, I suppose his soul remains for some time on earth, and is unable to tear itself away from the battle.' At this another man on the opposite side of the ward joined in, and said to me, 'You're quite right, sister. I've many times heard a shot man in the trenches say to those who were looking after him, just before he died, "Never mind, mates, I'll be there to help you!" I've heard that said many times.' This man, who was a sergeant-major, afterwards told me that he had heard a British officer talking to a German prisoner, and that the prisoner talked of the crowd of troops behind the British line, saying that all the Germans had seen them."

After having narrated this incident, the lady said to me, "I am quite convinced from what I heard in France that many of our soldiers are conscious of some mystery in these battles. They do not easily talk about this. And those of us who are there to do everything we can to alleviate their sufferings are too occupied with our work to dream of collecting information. Besides, who would think of cross-examining a sorely wounded or a dying man! Pray do not think that I am arguing on the side of the angels; I know people who are absolutely convinced that angels have appeared, but that is not my own opinion. I don't say that angels or spirits could not appear, but I am not sufficiently orthodox or interested in orthodox religions to believe in such stories. At any rate, I have never taken the smallest trouble to find out what the soldiers are thinking in that direction. All I can tell you is this, that many of our splendid men who fought at Mons and who fought in the terrible battles of Ypres, are persuaded that very extraordinary things have occurred. If I had known the great interest which was being taken in this country about such matters, I might have written down what I heard and taken the names of the soldiers who spoke about such things. But it is only now, when I am home for a few days' rest, that I learn of this public interest. Out there one works from morning to night, doing every mortal thing in one's power to cheer and comfort our dear Tommies, hearing scraps of conversation, listening sometimes to very solemn request from dying men, and striving to help the wounded man with every ounce of one's strength. But while I think the explanation of all these many and various stories is a more or less physical explanation, I can certainly assure you that a great number of our soldiers, both officers and men, are conscious of some mystery on the battlefields. It is certainly quite preposterous to suppose that something written and published at home can account for this feeling. Soldiers were speaking of mysterious things in August 1914. I don't believe in the angels, as I told you, but I do believe, I can't help believing, that our soldiers, many of them, are aware of something supernatural in this War. They talk about it among themselves, some of them; and I suppose that they would talk as freely as they are able to others if those others showed them sympathy. But I am positive they even deny having seen anything at all, if they were questioned by one who appeared to them skeptical and superior. Tommy is much more sensitive than people suppose."

The main value of this testimony is the destruction it brings to the Machen theory of an *Evening News* origin for all the legends and rumours concerning the Angels at Mons. Here is a lady who does not believe in the legends and rumours, but who nevertheless, from a long and remarkable experience in France, can assure us with absolute conviction that the soldiers themselves are aware of strange things in battle. I have met many people in France, and, since my visit to France, here in England, who have told me of the vital change in the British soldier after he comes back from the trenches. Some of them are entirely and profoundly changed, some of them are only slightly changed, but all of them are marked by a new gravity. It is not to be supposed that every man would see visions, or that every man would feel himself touched by supernatural forces. Nor is it to be supposed that the new gravity in many of the men will survive convalescence and a return to the materialism of civilisation. But it is certainly clear that for many soldiers, in a certain condition of soul and body, experience of war has brought home the conviction that the visible phenomena of this earth are not the only bounds of reality.[37]

This is not the place to examine the theory of this particular lady, but I should like to say it is a theory consonant with the ideas of many people who have examined occultism. It is held by a number of investigators that the soul remains in the neighbourhood of its body and follows the line of its chief tendency for some time after death, and particularly in a case where the most powerful passions are in full play. Reflection will assure us (if we believe in a spirit at all) that men who die with the fierceness of battle burning like a conflagration in their souls, whose last passion and impulse is to kill, might be still in the thick of the conflict after their bodies had collapsed. I do not say for a moment that this is an explanation of the visions which have been seen on the battlefield, but I am confident in my own mind that those who are fighting in the body are compassed about by a very ocean of spiritual vibrations, whose consequences, be they what they may, are at least an influence in the strife.

VI

I have tried in the foregoing pages to prove, so far as proof is possible in this high matter, that there is a life after death—or at least to suggest that from the evidence now in our possession there is reason to suppose that death does not end everything.

My idea now is to leave this evidence with all its difficulties behind me, and for a moment to look steadily at the question from quite another standpoint. I want those who have lost in this War men inexpressibly dear to them to consider whether they have not sure and unshakeable ground for faith in the persistence of life after death quite apart from any of the evidence adduced in the foregoing pages. With as great simplicity as possible I will try to suggest the theory of life which the best science and philosophy of our period is beginning to formulate.

It is of the first importance to consider what we mean by the supreme word of all our discussions, the word Life. What is *Life*? We know that there are certain things visible and tangible which are without life, and we know that there are things also visible and tangible which have life. But what is the thing called *Life* animating those visible and tangible object which we say have life, and differentiating them so mysteriously from the other things? It is invisible and intangible. No man has ever seen it; no man has ever touched it. We look into the eyes of a fellow creature and think that we see there something that answers to us and is in sympathy with us. But no life and no soul are visible in eyes. The eye has been described to me by an oculist as nothing more than a bag of water; the pupil is only a hole in that bag of water; and through that hole it is possible to look by the aid of an instrument straight through to the optic nerve. When one has looked right through an eye, straight on to this little white nerve, one realises that the expression of a human eye, however sympathetic and responsive, is no more a central manifestation of life than the hand or the foot. Behind the physical mechanism of the body there is a spirit which is absolutely invisible and intangible. This spirit uses the machinery of the body to express itself, but is no more the machinery of the body than a chauffeur is the engine of a motor-car. Whatever life may be, it is something which has energy, and nothing physical has any energy without life. We therefore come to the conclusion that life is a spirit which is using matter for some purpose of its own. It becomes incarnate in matter and pushes matter forward to some goal of which it is in search. In the body of a mastodon it reaches an enormous strength and power, and ceases to exist. In the body of a tiger it reaches extraordinary cunning and muscular agility and ends in the cages of a menagerie. Alone in the body of man it reaches self-conscious existence, and in self-conscious existence this thing we call life becomes aware of the almost infinite difference between order and chaos, beauty and ugliness, right and wrong.

Now, is it rational to suppose that having worked its way up from the amoeba to man this invisible and intangible thing which we call life—this veritable ghost of the physical world—should cry a halt to its evolution? Is

Three • Harold Begbie and *On the Side of the Angels*

it not much more reasonable to suppose that man represents but a stage on its journey, and that having become in man self-conscious it should thrust forward to fuller and more perfect realization of itself?

We should constantly remind ourselves that this little planet is not isolated from the rest of the universe, but is itself an absolute part of a universe which is demonstrably infinite. The universe has been likened by a man of science to one of those jellies which contain cherries separated from each other by certain distances. It is an enormous universe of ether, with planets and stars swimming in the midst of it. Our little planet, however insignificant some people like to think it, is as much a part of this immense universe as the greatest of the stars or the mightiest of constellations. We belong to the universe, and the universe belongs to us. *Life* is at work here just as much as it is at work elsewhere. To suppose that we have nothing to do with the rest of the universe is as ridiculous as to suppose that an electric light in an attic or a scullery has nothing to do with the dynamo which produces its electricity. If, then, our planet belongs to the universe, can we believe that accident to the machinery of the body, the final accident of death, puts a definite full stop to the period of our personality? Is it not philosophically more rational to believe that the collapse of the body merely sets free the invisible and intangible life which animated it to search in some other way for opportunities and self-realisation?

It is slowly coming home to those people who fell under the unfortunate influence of Huxley[38] that nothing in Darwin's[39] great theory can account for the very alphabet of Beauty and Goodness. Every thinker is now convinced that the theory of natural selection has no explanation whatever to offer us for the existence of Beauty and Goodness in this struggling world. They perceive that life has been *moving* from its first appearance on this earth to reach forward to Beauty and to Goodness. Stay your mind on the thought of *motion*—the movement of invisible life. Struggle for existence took the mastodon straight to annihilation, and took man towards Beauty and Goodness. It is perfectly clear that nothing in the muddy origins of life can account for this desire to reach Beauty and Goodness unless from its very inception life itself was conscious of Beauty and Goodness.

All our thoughts have been darkened and obscured by the old-fashioned deism of our fathers, which pictured an Almighty Being seated upon a throne in a heaven of singular dullness, regarding His creature man at one moment with a frown of disapproval, and at the next with a smile of love. We no longer think of the Infinite Life in this manner. We no longer attempt to define the Almighty or to dogmatise about His properties. When we dare to think about the Infinite One, we fail, as Pasteur[40] said, prostrate upon the pavements of our temples, annihilated by the thought of infinity. But we find it natural to seek for manifestations of this infinite God here upon earth, and His supreme manifestation for us is the soul of Man. In Man we see the Life which comes from God thrusting forward on a wide circle of return to God, with discontent for what has gone before and longing for something quite indefinite which is to come. In the spirits of the most perfect men and women who have inhabited this earth we see the intention of life, the purpose of creation, and the direction of evolution. And we must never forget that when we ask the most perfect men and women who dwell upon this earth what they think to be the meaning of existence, without one single exception they tell us that life is good and that after death there is a fuller and more abundant life. IT does not matter whether they are Christians or not Christians, whether they are European or Asiatic; in all countries of the world the very best men and women who have influenced human history have been teachers of a life after death.

The late Professor Alfred Russel Wallace[41] told me that Huxley had put his finger upon the surest reason for belief in spiritual existence when he pointed to the definite dogma of another man of science that *life must have preceded evolution.* So many loose thinkers are apt to believe that mud and water became, in some fashion which they never attempt to explain, the parents of evolution. But one has only to reflect for a moment to see that life must have preceded the organization of life, and that there could not have been any organisation at all without life. When we look up to the sky and see the stars flowing in a definite rhythm through infinite space, obeying laws which the soul of Man finds it possible to understand, and shining with a beauty to which his spirit eagerly responds, do we not feel entirely convinced that some mind akin to our own brought all this material universe into existence, and that no material universe could possibly have brought into existence this invisible and intangible thing which we call mind?

Let us constantly remind ourselves of the great danger of mistaking words to which we have become so used that we hardly think about their meaning, for the things of which they are but the very feeblest symbols. The word which we should more especially hold now in our consciousness, with a supreme concentration of thought, is the word Life. To reflect upon that word is to convince ourselves that no definition of the term Life can satisfy our desire to know what life really means. Life is definitely invisible, intangible, inexplicable. It is as great a mystery as God. The man who looks into our eyes and whose body we can touch, is as definitely a spirit as the invisible hosts of heaven. No surgeon can put his hand upon the life in that man; no concentration of light upon his body can reveal to us the life within it. We see only the structure and its clothing of flesh. There is something in each one of us greater than we ourselves know, far greater be it remembered than our normal consciousness, which reigns over that body like an autocrat, and which only uses the body for purposes of its own which are entirely spiritual. The soul of a man is not satisfied as the soul of an animal is satisfied with eating, drinking, and shelter. Even in those animal passions which we share with all other living creatures there is something beyond them and transcending them all which man seeks even when he surrenders himself to them. And beyond those appetites of the body there is an almost infinite sphere of feeling wherein the soul of man spreads its wings and never encounters the soul of bird or beast. In that sphere he hungers and thirsts after beauty. He feels wonder and reverence. He longs for knowledge, he perceives the loveliness of self-sacrifice, and he loves. Nothing in his body can account for this vast range of feeling. Nothing in history can explain the origin of these desires. And it is only on the theory that in man life has found a door through which it is possible to pass forward on a road of eternal progress that we can arrive at any rational definition of life.

In these few words I have endeavoured to make a summary of modern thought, and brief as they are and simple as they are, I hope that they may at least suggest to those who are now comfortless and sorrowful, that whether angels have been seen on the battlefields of France or not, whether if seen they were purely delusions of the senses, still there is solid ground under our feet and an immovable heaven over our heads, for the faith that after death the life of those we love follows some road of self-consciousness, seeks some goal of further self-realisation, and is still as much in the universe, and of the universe, as it was here upon earth. Let me assure any who may be inclined to doubt, that men who have most thoroughly investigated the phenomena of the material universe are most convinced that noting in materialism can explain the mystery of Life.

VII

Now, since I know the almost insuperable difficulties which present themselves to the vast majority of people in confronting any spiritual theory, and since among these unconvinced and unconverted minds, imprisoned by materialism, must be many at this time longing for consolation and hope, I will conclude my answer to Mr. Machen's claims with a few quotations developing the ideas expressed in the last chapter.

And before I do so, let me relate an experience of the last few minutes. A friend of mine home from India has just been to see me in my London rooms. He saw my table in disarray with papers and books, and asked me what I was about. I told him that I was writing on the question of visions in France. He instantly exclaimed, "Don't touch that. Leave it alone. There's nothing in it. The whole thing is bunkum. Take my advice and have nothing to do with it." I replied by stating what I believe to be the attitude of the highest science and philosophy to this whole question of the spiritual universe, and my friend gradually diminished his indifference and finally withdrew his negation. "I'll tell you," he said, "rather a strange thing in my own experience. When I was a boy, I was one day shooting with two young cousins of mine in Ireland. We were making our way along a narrow path through a wood, walking in single file, the branches of the trees brushing against our heads. All of a sudden I heard a voice shout to me, 'look out, Jack!'—and as I ducked, a gun went off just behind me, bringing down a branch just over my head. Well, we held a council of war and decided not to say anything about this matter in case my uncle took away our guns. That was our chief concern! We didn't discuss anything else. But as we walked on, it suddenly occurred to me as a funny thing that my cousin should have warned me that the gun was going off if the shot were an accident! I turned round and asked him why he had shouted to me. He said he hadn't shouted at all. But someone had shouted, and shouted too, just in time for me to duck before the splutter of shots, which must have killed me, went over my head. But neither of my young cousins had shouted. Neither the one nor the other had heard a sound."

I tell this story because it helps one to see that even those who most contemptuously brush away all stories of ghosts or visions, rationally argued with, and quietly pressed, may perhaps come not only to admit the possibility of a spirit world, but even to relate some experience in their own lives which is wholly inexplicable on material hypotheses.

But I am well aware that there are those who would not be persuaded though one rose from the dead. I am neither angry nor impatient with such people. For all those unhappy ones whose minds are made up, whose eyes are closed, and whose ears are stopped, I am profoundly sorry. They seem to be in like case with the man who is dead to loveliness, who is moved neither by the beauty of a building nor the majestical procession of the stars; what can one say to such a man? They seem to me, too, to miss that sweet music of life, that marching accompaniment of all existence, the humming of the wheels of creative evolution. They appear to be, nay, but they veritably are, living with no real idea of what is happening on every side of them, blind to the beauty, deaf to the music, and dead to the energy, of that which penetrates and transfuses all physical appearance,—the spirit Life.

To those who would believe if they could, I hope this book may be of some modest and initial service, particularly to those who are comfortless and sorrowful. Let me remind all such as are willing to seek truth that just as there are conditions in the physical, so there are conditions in the spiritual world. Close your eyes, and you will see neither the heavens nor the earth. Stop your ears, and you will hear neither the song of the lark nor the whisper of the wind. To take a photograph you must observe certain conditions: you must not expose the plate to the sun. To do your best in anything you must be in a certain condition of health. No man's will, however arbitrary, can do away with the conditions of achievement.

Now, in the spiritual world these are the conditions, *Faith in the Goodness of God: serenity of mind: the desire for perfection.* Let those who mourn, taking encouragement from these stories of visions on the battlefield, quietly and with a child's exquisite confidence, cultivate within themselves a waiting, receptive, and desiring spirit. Let them empty their minds of prejudice and self. Let them rest in the thought of their own inward unity with the love and goodness of the universe. Let them detach themselves more and more from the material obsessions of worldly life. Serenity is the path by which the Thoughts of God travel to us; and faith is the invitation which brings them to the table of our souls.

Whether a vision comes to us or not, of a certainty that which is greater than any vision will come tenderly yet powerfully to our soul, namely, the assurance of God's existence. And to believe in God, as Christ saw and as He taught, is to solve every riddle of life, to feel at home in this vast universe, to be neither shaken nor cast down by calamity, and to *know* that life is eternal.

Ask yourself very quietly but very honestly, before you throw away the hope of a revelation and return to the dullness and cares of a worldly existence, Have you really, truly, and earnestly observed the essential conditions in seeking the consolations and the transfiguring joys of faith in God? And the question you must most honestly confront, even if there be tears on your face, sobs on your lips, and a veritable agony in your soul, is this—*Do you really want to believe?* I would reverently call you not to mistake either violence of grief or exceeding bitterness of soul for the steadfast desire of a heart quietly set upon communion with God and patiently waiting, in the conviction of His love, for the moment of illumination and the long after-hours of increasing assurance.

And now let me conclude with a few quotations which may help you to believe that there are at least reasons which should persuade you to ignore the darkness of disbelief and to turn your face towards the light of faith.

Here is an extract from a letter which has just come into my hand from a friend already mentioned in the pages of this book, a very noble and most gracious woman. She answers to me for its truth:—

> M—my dearest, thank you for your letter. It is hard but it is wonderful. Oh, my Dear, he is not gone from me. He came to me at once, and so I knew before ever the news came, and he died so perfectly if one may call it death. I know now the great strength of love, and I know how death cannot touch it, and that I have a great help to me in all my loneliness. There is no touch of despair in it all—not one. He died most gallantly, and he went without pain at the very perfect moment of his dear life. And I shall not know separation in any awful sense, because it does not exist, and I m so *proud* of him, my Beloved, and I just do my best until I too can say "Finitum est."

The following cases of appearance after death may help the skeptical reader to understand that there is at least some reason for serious inquiry into the phenomena of such mysteries:—

In the *Proceedings* of the Psychical Research Society, Vol. V., pp. 412–415, will be found the remarkable experience of a Colonel H. who was known to Edmund Gurney, and who did not believe in the supernatural. He awoke one morning to find an old brother officer, who was fighting in the Transvaal War, at his bedside, and so real was the appearance that for a moment he imagined himself back in the barrack room, and sprang up asking if he were late for parade. The figure, however, was dressed in an unwonted uniform, and wore a black beard—Colonel H. had never seen him with one. The figure then told him that he was shot, and when Colonel H. asked where, it said in the right lung. He asked what his friend was doing at the time, and the apparition replied that the General had sent him forward. Then it vanished. Colonel H. told a friend the same day, but it was not or two days after that the death of his friend (Major Poole, of the Royal Artillery) was announced, and by calculating the hour of the battle (of Lang's Nek) and of the appearance of the ghost, he arrived at the conclusion that his friend must have come to him about the time of his death. Not till six months later did he succeed in discovering that he died in the dress and wearing the beard of the ghost, and only after a year did he learn that he was shot in the right lung.

In Vol. VI., and on page 27 of the *Proceedings*, will be found a most interesting story of an apparition seen by two people, one of whom had never seen the person in life. Only initials are given, but there appears to be good reasons for this, and the story is confirmed by both witnesses, and by a Doctor C. and his wife, to whom it was told at the time.

Briefly, a wife was feeding her child at night by lamp-light when she saw a naval officer leaning on the bed-rail, his face concealed by the shadow of his peaked cap. Her husband turning at her touch, and seeing the figure, cried out, "Good God, sir, what are you doing here?" Drawing itself up, the form said in a commanding yet reproachful voice, "Willie! Willie!" It stalked across the room and vanished into the wall. The husband instantly made a search, and then returning trembling to his wife asked if she knew who they had seen: she had not recognised anyone, but wondered if it had something to do with her brother who was lost at sea. The husband told her that it was his father, and then confessed that he had been in considerable financial difficulties, and had been about to take the advice of a man who would have brought them to ruin, if not worse.

The most interesting facts of the story are these:—The man's father had been dead fourteen years, the son had only once or twice seen him in uniform, as he had left the Service before the son's birth, and the daughter-in-law had never seen him at all.

In "Miracles and Modern Spiritualism," by the late Professor Alfred Russel Wallace,[42] the two following stories occur:—

Three • Harold Begbie and *On the Side of the Angels*

Sir John Sherbroke and General George Wynyard were Captain and Lieutenant in the 33rd Regiment, stationed in the year 1785 at Sydney, in the island of Cape Breton, Nova Scotia. On the 15th of October of that year, about nine in the morning, as they were sitting together at coffee in Wynyard's parlour, Sherbroke, happening to look up, saw the figure of a pale youth standing at a door leading into a passage. He called the attention of his companion to the stranger, who passed slowly through the room into the adjoining bedchamber. Wynyard, on seeing the figure, turned as pale as death, grasped his friend's arm, and, as soon as it had disappeared, exclaimed, "Great God! my brother." Sherbroke thinking there was some trick, had a search immediately made, but could find no one either in the bedroom or about the premises. A brother officer, Lieutenant Gore, coming in at the time, assisted in the search, and at his suggestion Sherbroke made a memorandum of the date, and all waited with anxiety for letters from England, where Wynyard's brother was. The expected letter came to Captain Sherbroke, asking him to break to his friend the news of his brother John's death, which had occurred on the day and at the hour when he had been seen by the two officers. In 1823 Lieutenant-Colonel Gore gave his account in writing to Sir John Harvey, Adjutant-General of the Forces in Canada. He also stated that some years afterwards Sir John Sherbroke, who had never seen John Wynyard alive, recognised in England a brother of the deceased, who was remarkably like him, by the resemblance to the figure he had last seen in Canada. Mr. Owen has obtained additional proof of the correctness of these details from Captain Henry Scott, R. N., who was told by General Paul Anderson, C. B., that Sir John Sherbroke had, shortly before his death, related the story to him in almost exactly the same words as Mr. Owen had given it, and which was communicated in manuscript to Captain Scott.

The evidence in this case of the fact of the appearance of the same apparition to two people (one of whom did not know the individual) is very complete; and I cannot rest satisfied with any theory which requires me to reject such evidence without any intelligible explanation of what occurred.

Philip Weld, a student at a Catholic College, was drowned in the river at Ware, Hertfordshire, in the year 1846. About the same hour as the accident, the young man's father and sister, while walking on the turnpike road near Southampton, saw him standing on the causeway with another young man in a black robe. The sister said, "Look, papa, there is Philip." Mr. Weld replied, "It is Philip indeed, but he has the look of an angel." They went on to embrace him, but before reaching him a labouring man seemed to walk right through the figures, and then with a smile both figures vanished. The President of the College, Dr. Cox, went immediately to Southampton to break the sad news to the father, but before he could speak, Mr. Weld told him what he had seen, and said he knew his son was dead. A few weeks afterwards Mr. Weld visited the Jesuit College of Stonyhurst in Lancashire, and in the guest-room saw a picture of the very same young man he had seen with his son, similarly dressed, and in the same attitude, and beneath the picture was inscribed "St. Stanislaus Kotska," saint of the Jesuit Order, who had been chosen by Philip for his patron saint at his confirmation.

The following account comes from a lady known to me, who prefers that her name should not be given.

March, 1889.

My mother died on June 24, 1874, at a house called The Hunter's Palace, Silima, Malta, where we were then residing for her health. She had always a great fear of being buried alive, and extracted a promise from my father that wherever she died he would not allow her to be buried for a week, and I remember he had to get special permission, as it is it the custom to bury within three days in a hot climate. The third day after the death was the last time I saw her, and I went into the room with my father, and we cut off all her hair, which was very long and curly. I have no remembrance of being at all nervous or in the least frightened. On the seventh day after death she was buried, and it was on that night she appeared to me. I slept in a little dressing-room opening out of the larger nursery, which, like many old houses, had two steps leading into it. The smoking room, where my father usually spent his evenings, was across the hall, and my little room also had a door opening on to the hall, so that it was not necessary for me to go through the nursery, where my two little brothers slept, to get out. On this particular evening the weather was stiflingly hot and intensely still. I had been put to bed earlier than usual, and had no light in the room; the Venetian shutters were open as far as they would go, and the night was so beautiful that the room was quite light. The door into the nursery was only partially closed, and I could see the nurse's shadow as she leaned over her work, and I gazed at the shadow of her hand moving up and down with an irritating regularity until I fell asleep. I seemed to have been sleeping some time when I woke, and turning on the side towards the window saw my mother standing by her bedside crying and wringing her hands. I had not been awake long enough to remember that she was dead, and exclaimed quite naturally (for she often came in when I was asleep) "Why, dear, what's the matter?" and then suddenly remembering I screamed. The nurse sprang up from the next room, but on the top step flung herself on her knees, and began to tell her beads and cry. My father at the same moment arrived at the opposite door, and I heard his sudden exclamation of "Julia, darling." My mother turned towards him, and they to me, and wringing her hands again retreated towards the nursery and was lost. The nurse afterwards declared that she distinctly felt something pass her, but she was in such a state of abject terror that her testimony is quite worthless. My father then ordered her out of the room, and telling me that I had only been dreaming, stayed until I fell asleep. The next day, however, he told me that he, too, had seen the vision, and that he hoped to do so again, and if she ever came to see me again I was not to be frightened but, tell her that "papa wanted to speak to her," which I promised faithfully to do, but I need scarcely say that she never appeared again.

What has struck me as curious since then is that I saw her as she usually came to see me the last thing at night, dressed in a white flannel dressing-gown trimmed with a band of scarlet braid and her long hair loose and flowing. She was not buried in that dressing-gown, and we had cut off all her hair.

Years afterwards, when we were speaking of it, my father told me that she had always promised to come back after death if such a thing were possible. That being the case it is curious that she should have appeared to me. The nurse from that time forward refused to sit alone in the nursery, and predicted no end of dreadful things as likely to happen, but when a few weeks afterwards I sickened for a long and serious illness she was quite satisfied. She was a Maltese, and when we left the island we quite lost sight of her. My father died just three years ago, so that I am now the only eye-witness left. My father's second wife has, however, heard the story from him, and will sign this paper.

The lady was eight years old at the time, had never heard of ghosts, and neither before nor since then has she seen an hallucination. She is not the very least nervous.

From the *Proceedings* of the S. P. R., Vol. X., pp. 385–386:—

The account of the percipient, Baron B. von Driesden, was written in November, 1890, and has been translated from the Russian by Mr. M. Petrovo-Solovoro, who sent us the case.

(Baron von Driesden begins by saying that he has never believed and does not believe in the supernatural, and that he is more inclined to attribute the apparition he saw to his "excited fancy" than to anything else. After these preliminary remarks he proceeds as follows:—)

I must tell you that my father-in-law M. N. J. Ponomareff, died in the country. This did not happen at once, but after a long and painful illness, whose sharp phases had obliged my wife and myself to join him long before his death. I had not been on good terms with M. Ponomareff. Difficult circumstances, which are out of place in this narrative, had estranged us from each other, and these relations did not change until his death. He died very quietly, after having given his blessing to all his family, including myself. A liturgy for the rest of his soul was to be celebrated on the ninth day. I remember very well how I went to bed between one and two o'clock on the eve of the day, and how I read the Gospel before falling asleep. My wife was sleeping in the same room. It was perfectly quiet. I had just put out the candle when footsteps were heard in the adjacent room—a sound of slippers shuffling, I might say—which ceased before the door of our bedroom. I called out, "Who is there?" No answer. I struck one match, then another, and when after the stifling smell of the sulphur the fire had lighted up the room, I saw M. Ponomareff standing before the closed door. Yes, it was he, in his blue dressing-gown, lined with squirrel furs and only half buttoned, so that I could see his white waistcoat and his black trousers. It was he undoubtedly. I was not frightened. They say that, as a rule, one is not frightened when seeing a ghost, as ghosts possess the quality of paralysing fear.

"What do you want?" I asked my father-in-law. M. Ponomareff made two steps forward, stopped before my bed, and said, "Basil Feodorovitch, I have acted wrongly towards you. Forgive me. Without this I do not feel at rest there." He was pointing to the ceiling with his left hand whilst holding out his right to me, I seized this hand which was long and cold, shook it, and answered, "Nicolas Ivanovitch, God is my witness that I have never had anything against you."

(The ghost of) my father-in-law bowed (or bent down), moved away, and went through the opposite door into the billiard room, where he disappeared. I looked after him for a moment, crossed myself, put out the candle, and fell asleep with the sense of joy which a man who has done his duty must feel. The morning came. My wife's brothers, as well as our neighbours and the peasants, assembled, and the liturgy was celebrated by our confessor, the Rev. Father Basil. But when all was over, the same Father Basil led me aside, and said to me mysteriously, "Basil Feodorovitch, I have got something to say to you in private." My wife having come near us at this moment, the clergyman repeated his wish. I answered,—"Father Basil, I have no secrets from my wife; please tell us what you wish to tell me alone."

Then Father Basil, who is now living in the Koi parish of the district of Kashin (Gov. of Tver), said to me in a rather solemn voice, "This night at three o'clock Nicolas Ivanovitch (Ponomareff) appeared to me and begged me to reconcile him to you."

(Signed) Baron Basil Driesden.

The priest's confirmation of the Baron's story is given in a letter which he wrote in answer to inquiries.

And now, in conclusion, I would make a few quotations from the Presidential Address delivered by Henri Bergson[43] to the Psychical Research Society in 1913—an address which, so far as I am aware, has not yet been translated:—

The more we accustom ourselves to this idea of a consciousness which overflows the organism, the more natural and apparent shall we find the hypothesis of the soul's survival of the body. Indeed, if the mental is firmly moulded on the cerebral, if there is nothing more in human consciousness than can be read in the brain, we might admit that consciousness follows the destiny of the body and dies with it. But if facts, impartially studied, lead us on the contrary to consider the mental life as much vaster than the cerebral, the survival becomes so probable that the obligation of proof devolves on him who denies it, rather than on him who affirms it; for as I said elsewhere, "the one reason we can have for believing in the extinction of consciousness after death is that we see the body become disorganized, and this reason has no longer any value if the, at least, partial independence of consciousness with regard to the body, is, too, a fact of experience."

Some time ago, at a fashionable gathering at which I was present, the conversation turned on the phenomena which occupy your Society, and more particularly on the facts of telepathy. One of our greatest doctors, who is also one of our greatest men of Science, was there. After having listened attentively for some minutes, he addressed us, and expressed himself almost in these words: "All that you have said interests me very much, but I ask you to reflect before coming to a conclusion. I know, too, an extraordinary occurrence. And I can guarantee its authenticity, for it was told me by a very intelligent lady, whose word inspires me with absolute confidence. The husband of this lady was an officer. He was killed during an engagement. Now at the very moment when the husband fell, the wife had a vision of the scene, an exact vision, which confirmed to the reality at every point. Perhaps you will conclude from that, like the lady, that it was clairvoyance or telepathy? ... You forget only one thing; it is that it often happens that a wife dreams that her husband is dead or dying, while he is quite well. We notice the case when the vision happens to be right, we don't count the others. If they were all known, we should see that the coincidence is simply the work of chance."

The conversation turned on some other subject; besides, it was out of the question to enter upon a serious discussion—it was not the right place or the right time. But, as we left the table, a very young girl, who had paid great attention, came to me and said, "I think that Dr. X argued badly just now. I don't know what was the flaw in his reasoning, but there surely must be a flaw." Well, yes, there was a flaw. It was the young girl who was right, and the great savant who was wrong. He shut his eyes to the concrete in this phenomenon. He reasoned thus: "When we dream that a relation is dead or dying, it is either true or untrue, the person either does die or does not. And consequently, if the dream happens to be right, we must, before we can be sure that it is the work of chance, compare the number of cases which were right with the number of cases which were wrong." He did not see that the apparent force of his argument lay in that he had replaced the living and concrete description of the scene—of the officer falling at a given moment, in a given place, with such and such soldiers round him—by this dead an abstract formula: "The lady was right in her dream, not wrong." Ah, if we accept this transposition into the abstract, we certainly ought to compare *in abstracto* the number of true cases with the number of false ones; and perhaps we shall find that there are more false than true, and our doctor will be right. But this abstraction consists in ignoring what was most essential—the picture seen by the lady, which turned out to be identical with a scene very far away. Can you conceive the idea of a painter, drawing on his canvas an incident in a battle, trusting to his imagination in doing it, and being so well served by chance that he discovers he has painted the portraits of real soldiers, really present at that day in a battle where they took the very attitudes lent them by the painter? Evidently not. The computation of probabilities, which are invoked here, will show us that it is impossible, because a scene in which given persons take given attitudes is a thing unique in its kind, because a human face, even isolated, is already unique in its kind, and consequently each personage—especially when found together in one scene—is decomposable into an infinity of separate details so that an indefinite number of coincidences would be needed for chance to make the picture of imagination identical with a real scene. In other words, it is mathematically impossible that a picture brought forth by the painter's imagination should represent exactly as it is a scene in a battle. Now the lady who had a vision of an incident in a battle was in the place of the painter. Her imagination executed a picture. If the picture was the representation of a real scene, it is surely necessary that she was in communication with this scene or with a consciousness which had perceived it. I need not make the comparison of the number of "false cases" with the number of "true ones"; statistics have no place here: the one case suffices for me directly I retain what is concrete in it. That is why, if it had been the time to discuss with the doctor, I should have said to him: "I don't know if the story told you was true; I don't know if the lady of whom you speak had the exact vision of the scene which took place far away; but if this point was confirmed, if I could only be sure that the physiognomy of one soldier whom she didn't know, who was present in the scene, appeared to her as it was in reality—well, then, even if it had been proved that there had been thousands of false cases and that there was no other veridical hallucination than this, I should hold the existence of telepathy, or of some cause, whatever it may be, which makes us perceive objects and events situated out of reach of our normal senses, definitely and rigorously established."

For my part, when I remember the results of the admirable inquiry continually carried on by you during more than thirty years, when I think of all the precautions you have taken to avoid mistakes, when I see how, in most cases you have approved, the story of the hallucination had been told to several people, often written down, before the hallucination was found to be veridical, when I take note of the enormous number of facts and, above all, of their resemblance, of their family likeness, of the agreement of so many independent witnesses, all examined, controlled, criticized—I am led to believe in telepathy as I believe, for example, in the defeat of the invincible Armada. It is not the mathematical certitude which the demonstration of the theorems of Pythagoras gives me; it is not the physical certitude that I have concerning the law of the fall of bodies; it is, at least, all the certitude you get in historical or judiciary matter.

Here, then, let us leave the matter, at least for the present. Be sure of this, the War has powerfully changed the "psychological atmosphere," and the thoughts of a great multitude are turned towards the spiritual aspect of existence.

In this vast but connected universe we are not the only self-conscious beings. Life is working, here as elsewhere, for some sublime purpose. The day is at hand when we shall turn from the childlike amusements and excitements of physical science to the unimaginable adventures of super-physical discovery; and in that day we shall not only flash our messages to the stars but hold communion with our Dead.

• FOUR •

Phyllis Campbell and *Back of the Front*

First Publication: *The Occult Review* July–September 1915
First Book Publication: London: George Newnes, 1915

Despite her centrality to the narratives surrounding the Angels at Mons, surprisingly little is known about Phyllis Campbell, and that little is often contradictory.[1] Nevertheless, she does not appear to have been a "Scotch girl," although W. L. Courtney's[2] introduction to Campbell's *Back of the Front* so describes her, presumably with her approval. This description is repeated verbatim in E. W. Walter's 1916 *Heroines of the World-War*.[3]

Phyllis Campbell's middle name was Frances. Her mother was Phyllis Vivian Campbell of Toothill, Ongar, Essex; her father, Howard Douglas Campbell, may have been a brother or a cousin of the Duke of Argyll.[4] In addition to being related to nobility, his was a family of some military repute. Phyllis's paternal grandfather, also named Howard Douglas Campbell, was Captain in the 78th Highlanders and died of cholera on 16 August 1857; he is buried in All Souls Church, Cawnpore.[5]

One of the few newspaper articles about Phyllis Frances Campbell states that she was born in Australia in 1894, was removed to England at the age of seven, and "a few years later ... went with an elder sister to France, and since then she has lived in Paris."[6] This appears accurate, but it is also deliberately incomplete. The family's removal to England may have been for medical reasons, for shortly after the family's return, young Howard Douglas Campbell was to die a suicide, shooting himself in a hansom cab in March of 1901. His death made international news: the *New York Times* reported it, the headline stating "Duke's Relative a Suicide," although the body of the article questioned the relationship.[7] The contents of his suicide note, a pathetic document at best, were also internationally distributed:

> Pathetic indeed was the last letter of Mr. Howard Douglas Campbell, who blew his brains out in a hansom cab one day last month in Marylebone, Lon-

don. Before committing suicide the poor fellow wrote to the Coroner: "Dear Sir, There need be no mystery about my death. My father was Captain Campbell, of the 78th Highlanders. Ten years ago I was in the Government service in Queensland, and one night whilst on duty I had a very heavy fall. I ruptured an artery in the cavity of my chest, and the doctor then almost gave me up for dying. But, unfortunately, I had a stroke of paralysis three years ago, and I went home. I find I am not gaining strength, and rather than be a burden to my people I am going to slip my moorings. I believe this sort of thing is called cowardly. I do not think so myself. I was brought up by a good lady—my mother—who was a member of the free Church of Scotland, and very religious. So I know, after death comes the judgment.—Howard Douglas Campbell." At the inquest it transpired that the dead man, who had taken to roaming about the country, had shown symptoms of mental disorganization, and that his wife had been taking medical opinion on his condition, physical and mental. The doctor's opinion was opposed to the idea that any improvement would take place, and poor Campbell appears to have been well aware that in both respects he could only expect to go from bad to worse. The jury, of course, returned the merciful verdict of suicide whilst of unsound mind, but it is open to question whether a man hopelessly bankrupt, physically and mentally, and recognising his state, can be deemed mad if he seeks relief in death.[8]

Following her father's death, Phyllis Frances Campbell was raised by her mother, who turned to journalism to make a living. In June 1912, Phyllis Vivian Campbell—now a novelist of some repute, as well as a journalist/correspondent of some note[9] and, perhaps, also a spy—was in the news following a disastrous Mediterranean voyage aboard the *Carib Prince* during which she claimed to have been given a filthy and pestiferous cabin and to have contracted ptomaine poisoning from badly prepared quail, after which she lost the use of her left eye. Phyllis Vivian Campbell thus sued the Prince Line of Newcastle-on-Tyne for breach of contract and negligence, and young Phyllis Frances Campbell testified in her support, stating that the food was "very tough and uneatable. The cabin was swarming with cockroaches."[10] The case of *Campbell v. The Prince Line (Limited)* was reported in the London *Times* as well as various colonial newspapers. During the testimony, Phyllis Vivian Campbell claimed that she had made the trip at the behest of the late W. T. Stead,[11] who had paid her £300.00 for her services:

> Mr. Stead asked me to go out and bring back a certain package. He pointed out to me that it might be at great risk to myself, and that I was to keep it secret. I was to go in such a manner that I would not be noticed, and I was to come back, if possible, in the same ship that I went out in.[12]

The contents of this package were not revealed, it having vanished mysteriously, and the defendant's cross-examining lawyer, Mr. F. E. Smith, K. C., cast significant doubts upon all of Phyllis Vivian Campbell's claims, the reporter for *The Standard* reporting him stating that "the whole story was so ridiculous that no one outside of Bedlam would have accepted it, and very few people, he hoped, would have invented it."[13] Nevertheless, the issue was not whether W. T. Stead had given Phyllis Vivian Campbell a package but the condition of the ship, and on 26 June 1912 the jury presented its verdict:

> Mr. Justice Avory, having summed up the case, left the following questions to the jury, the answers of which are appended. On the question of the conditions contained in the ticket: (1) Did the plaintiff [i.e., Phyllis Vivian Campbell] know that there was writing or printing on the ticket?—Yes. (2) Did she know that the writing or printing contained conditions relating to the terms of the contract of carriage?—Yes. (3) Did the defendants [i.e., the Prince Line] do what was reasonably sufficient to give the plaintiff notice of the conditions?—Yes.
> As to the other parts of the case: (1) Were the accommodation, food, and attendance reasonably good and sufficient for first class lady passengers, having regard to the kind of vessel and to the fare paid?—Yes. (2) Were defects due to or did they arise from the act, neglect, or default of the master or other servants of the company?—No.
> Judgment was entered for the defendants.[14]

Following this disastrous episode, young Phyllis Frances Campbell was sent to France to finish her education and thereafter lived in Paris and Brittany. In 1913 she began publishing in the *Occult Review*, signing herself "Phil Campbell."[15] So far as can be determined, she never gave any interviews about her family, and it is not yet known whether she ever again met her mother or even when her mother died. Nor is it known whether the general hatred of Germans revealed in *Back of the Front* has an autobiographical component or if her descriptions of the Highlanders are somehow autobiographical: it is quite conceivable that, as a little girl, she was shielded from the news of her father's suicide and knew nothing of his regimental history. And of course it is unknown how she—a legitimate care-giver and a very good writer—learned of the stories of the angels and chose to embellish her first-rate narrative with them. Harold Begbie's *On the Side of the Angels* states that Phyllis Campbell "is extremely pretty, childlike, and sensitive," but whether this statement is based on personal acquaintance is, again, not known.

For all that Begbie endorsed Campbell's narrative, its contemporary reception was at best mixed and reviews tended towards the negative. Indeed, the Society for Psychical Research dismissed it with the statement that "allowance must be made for inaccuracy of memory, the force of suggestion, and other common sources of error."[16] Unlike Machen and Begbie, Campbell does not seem to have defended her narrative, and it is probably significant that although a contemporary market for it existed, *Back of the Front* was not reprinted. She thus vanishes from view in 1915. It is possible that she turned to fiction and authored two novels published in 1920 by Mills and Boon, *Lined with Rags* and *The White Hen*; the latter was filmed in 1921. She may likewise have been the writer of "The Hand of Thais," a ghost story that was read over the English radio on 23 December 1937[17]; if so, this appears to be her last identifiable publication.

An intriguing comment comes from Arthur Machen, who in 1918 wrote to an American correspondent that "Phyllis Campbell ... became involved a little later in a scandal in which an officer was also concerned; I believe her to have become a conscious liar in the matter."[18] The nature of this scandal has not yet been discovered, nor has the date of her death.

Below are W. L. Courtney's introduction and the two chapters of *Back of the Front* that mention the angels.

Introduction

Every reader gives to a book as much as he takes away; he decides on its merits in accordance with his own special predilections. I cannot therefore tell what impression this little volume may make on the general public; I can only say that coming to it, so far as is possible without any bias or prejudice, I have found it a very pathetic and interesting record. But there is something more in it than its interest or its appeal to human sympathy. It is quite unpretentious and therefore convincing; it is written wholly without arrière pensée[19] and therefore bears its credentials on its very surface. I do not think that anyone who peruses these pages will fail to believe, that a narrative so simple and sincere is precisely what it intends to be—a straightforward account of certain poignant experiences undergone by a Scotch girl when she was nursing French and British wounded during the opening months of the Great War. But I may be permitted to say a few additional words. I have had the welcome opportunity of seeing the author and hearing from her own lips an account of similar incidents and experiences. I have been shown the various documents which prove that she was an accredited nurse with the French Red Cross. I have seen her photographs, her medals, her diploma and the insignia of her office. Above all I have read some of the numerous letters which she has received (and still receives) from her grateful patients in which the tale is told of a nurse's devotion and of her exceeding great reward. It is the more necessary for me to give this testimony, because I understand that some doubts have been expressed as to the credibility of a narrative which to my mind carries conviction from its first page to its last, and in reality requires no external proof. Of course it may be difficult in some cases to distinguish between memoranda taken at the time and the results of mere memory. But in the book before us the authoress very evidently gives a picture of the impressions she gathered at the time—very vivid and unforgettable impressions, printed on a retentive brain during months of poignant suffering and strenuous and self-sacrificing service.

Four • Phyllis Campbell and *Back of the Front*

Frankly I do not know what to say about the "visions" which wounded soldiers narrated to Miss Campbell, as they have done also to other witnesses. She only tells the tales as they were told to her, and carefully avoids expressing any judgment on their merits or their veracity. Notice that she draws a distinction between the attitude of the early sufferers in the war, as they were brought back from the battle-field to her nursing-station, and that of the later arrivals. The former were dumb, stricken, paralysed; the latter seemed to have a rapt expression on their faces as though uplifted by some inner experience. It was the second of these two classes who for the most part referred, apparently with some shyness and reserve, to their belief in celestial aid. The French saw Joan of Arc—especially any who might come from the vicinity of Domrémy—and St. Michael; the English saw a warrior on a white horse whom they identified with St. George. Mr. Arthur Machen in his imaginative story makes his soldier suddenly think of a figure of St. George seen on the plates of a restaurant,[20] and so become aware of stout English bowmen fighting on his side. It is as easy to suppose that the image of the patron saint might have been remembered from the obverse of a sovereign. Anyhow some of these men saw, or thought they saw, a great light or a golden cloud, with a divine champion riding at their side and driving back the enemy. Let us leave it at that. It is a beautiful legend, far too beautiful to be vulgarised by rationalistic comment or a too inquisitive press. In moments of extreme nervous stress many men in history have seen visions or dreamed dreams and found a real inspiration therein. Shall we dare to tell them that they are the victims of a purely subjective delusion, when in the strength of their faith they have won the victory?

There is a curious comment which Miss Campbell records among these impressions of hers. "The English," she heard some critic remark, "have mercy without judgment; the French have judgment without mercy." Expressed in this epigrammatic form, the statement contains obvious untruth. Both English and French are civilized fighters who do not war with the wounded or the dead. One cannot imagine their indulging in such frantic orgies of lust and cruelty as have for ever tarnished the good fame of German soldiers. But the sentence aptly illustrates a certain difference in the temper in which French and English commenced this war. To our Allies the present war is the logical sequel of the campaigns of 1870. They remember or have been told of what their countrymen suffered more than forty years ago; they discovered then the essential qualities of the Teutonic temperament: they knew how implacable and remorseless and brutal was the enemy with whom they had to deal. In a real sense therefore this great struggle is to them a war of righteous vengeance in which the strong arm and the pitiless heart must nerve themselves to deal summary execution on foes of the whole human race. We could not have the same feelings when the campaign began; we had not the same experience. It was difficult in those early days for Englishmen to conceive what a German army was capable of.

Besides, our country had not been invaded: even now we do not know what it means to see English land trampled under the arrogant foot of an invader. The French know only too well and perhaps we too are gaining lessons which make mercy difficult. It is part of the dreadful business of the war that as the months go by, each with its catalogue of horrors, the temper of the combatants grows sterner. There seems no place for pity when men are fighting for their liberty and their lives.

It is the merit of Miss Campbell's book that it is full of pictures. She makes us see the little town and the forest through which the soldiers pass and the trains which come back with their loads of wounded. We get to know the men and the women by whose side she worked and whose gratitude she earned by her devotion. And the horizon is always lighted by ruddy fires and the ear is perpetually stunned by the ominous sound of approaching battle. The very atmosphere is tense with apprehension and suspense. Only five miles separated the nurses from the oncoming Germans in their desperate rush on Paris. Only by this slight interval was their safety won.

VI

"Mesdames," said François, as we reached the station, "the train is not yet arrived. I would like to show you a very curious thing, just one instant."

He propped his bicycle against the wall, and beckoned us across the road where a sentry-box guarded the forest avenues.

"There! What do you think of that curious thing?"

The curious thing was an outline drawing in black crayon of a cow, with her head up, looking at the sky. It was a biggish drawing, crude and awkward—evidently the artist had never studied anatomy. It might have been the work of a child, but there was something in it which did not suggest childhood.

"I ask you," resumed François, "because yesterday I bicycled to Pontoise with Madame la Brazilienne, and while I sought information, she made a drawing similar to that, but much larger. I caught her at it—there is no harm in drawing cows, mesdames—yet—I am full of unease. For instance, does one keep sheep in Brazil?"

"I don't think so."

"Nor do I—thanks, mesdames. I will talk to the Commandant—or the captain."

We entered the Post and found the Brazilian lady washing up cups with a great clatter. She had beside her a large piece of the ham and garlic sausage so beloved of the soldiers, and a piece of fresh loaf. At intervals she would take a huge bite of sausage and a mouthful of bread. Latty came sailing along to meet us, and glanced at her.

"Stop, madame," she cried. "Where did you get that sausage?"

The Brazilian lady pointed a thumb over her shoulder at the canteen. Her mouth was too full to answer.

"H—y—m," snorted Latty. "I thought so. Now mark me well, young lady, the food in this canteen is for the soldiers, and not for the workers at the Post. *Buy* your food in the town."

I thought the Brazilian was about to throw the cup she was drying at Latty's head, but suddenly she averted her blazing eyes and, mumbling something, went on with her work. As soon as Latty's back was turned, she rushed down the platform, and I saw her ride across the place on her bicycle, followed quickly by François, and almost immediately afterwards by the Commandant's car full of soldiers.

I was not surprised when François told me the Brazilian was a German boy—one of their cleverest spies. A good deal of information was found on him, and the reason why he drew cows.

Captain P_____ went across to the sentry-box with a bucket of whitewash and obliterated the drawing; according to a code of signals it showed the size of the garrison at C_____, and that there were aeroplanes scouting.

While we were sitting making bandages, and rolling cigarettes, old Pierre came in, dressed in ragged old regimentals. He carried a beautifully arranged bouquet for Nancy and me, and a little basket of peaches for Aunt Margaret. He had come to say *au revoir*, he was going to look for his second son—news had reached him that André was wounded.

"*Au revoir*," he said, smiling cheerfully. "The good God will no doubt permit that I kill a Boche[21] or so—a man whose wife prays all day is entitled to some compensation."

He turned at the gate. "The news is bad," he said. "But all is not lost while we have the English—the English *never* give up."

He went just as the train came in—and we began our work—there were very few of us now, and the work was heavy. It was the twenty-fourth of August, and the wounded came from the retreating army; they flowed out over the platform and waiting-room into the green spaces under the trees, and with them began the Week of Terror and Faith. The wounded were in a curious state of exaltation—they talked not of defeat, but victory, and spoke of Joan of Arc and St. Michael riding white horses and turning back the foe. Some of the men spoke also of the Germans falling dead in their ranks where Joan of Arc and her Companion, Michael the Archangel, had intervened between the contending hosts. The Allies were fighting a rearguard action all the way. It had begun on Sunday, they had been falling back from Mons, fighting, fighting all the way.

The men's wounds were horrible—they were in a state of absolute physical exhaustion, yet not one of them was depressed or despondent. There was a boy of about twenty-two, two of whose fingers on the right hand were hanging by a thread—the forefinger was pulp, yet he refused to have it amputated.

"I don't mind the others," he said, looking at us with fever-bright eyes, "but if you take off that one, Doctor, I cannot go back to the firing-line."

"You may die of blood-poisoning."

"Better that than be useless to France," declared the boy. "I would be in the march to Berlin."

"Looks like it —" groaned the doctor, "with the Boches in Paris."

"They will never be in Paris," declared the boy. "I have seen St. Michael fighting by my side. We shall have the victory. The Boches are doomed."

The *majeur* patted him affectionately on the back, and ordered me to fetch the brandy. He gave the boy, now almost swooning from loss of blood, a huge nip—and we carried him back to the train. He had a great wound in his leg, a wound in his shoulder, and two of the fingers off his right hand, but he was going back to the firing line—and I know he did.

A man whose right leg had been blown away showed me a piece of shell. It was smeared inside with a curious greenish-bluish substance.

"What do you think that is, my sister" he asked.

It smelt curiously—but I could not place it. The captain did, however. "It is phosphorus," he said. "Where did you get this, *mon enfant*?"

"It is part of the shell that took my leg," responded the soldier.

The captain's face darkened, and the teeth met on his lower lip.

"The hogs!" he groaned, "the dirty hogs—murderers—"

He walked away, and the soldier, returning the piece of shell to his pocket, let me pad the hard wood with cushions under him, and light his cigarette. They were also washed, bandaged and fed—comforted as far as we could comfort them—given a cigarette, and sent on.

The English boys were more reticent than the French; they did not confide in us so easily, nor were they so easily comforted.

Their faces were hard and set, and they held themselves with a pride that brought tears to my eyes. Mostly their boots were falling off their feet—some had none at all; their wounds were nearly all shrapnel, or bullets, in the head or shoulders. They all had the same strange, "exalted" look—and also they, after their wounds were dressed, spoke of St. George on a white horse.

A boy whose right arm had been amputated, told me the Field Hospital where he was had been shelled by the Germans, and most of the men in it killed. "They're not men, sister," he flamed, "they're devils—that's why St. George is fighting for us."

There was a big Highland boy propped in a corner, bleeding from a shoulder wound. Latty insisted on his being taken out and sent to the hospital in the town. He, however, wanted to go on. "My poor boy!" wept Latty, "you will die."

The Highlander looked up at her with deep mystical eyes, flaming with fever.

"Na! Na!" he said. "I'm no goin' west yit—I've a bit German killin' tae do first. In Belgium yonder I saw twelve wee lassies—just wee bit slips of lassies—mebbe the eldest would be nine or ten—an' for ivery one of them I'll hae twa German fathers—jist that—I'll no die—no fear."

All the soldiers implored us to run away—they all told us that the Germans were brute beasts and devils. At length Nancy and I replied in the same words. We would work so long as we were necessary, but we would never fall into the Germans' hands alive, they might be sure of that.

The brave, kind boys! In all their agonies they thought of the safety of the two English girls, who could do so little for them. But that little, how gladly we did it!

In one waggon I found Aunt Margaret washing the blistered feet of an English boy who had marched the soles off his boots. She had given him a basin of hot milk, but he could not hold it, and I fed him with it in spoonfuls, as if he were a baby. Not easy, because all the time he was saying to himself in a dull quiet voice, "I was at Mons—I was at Mons—I was at Mons."

"Weren't you all at Mons?" asked Aunt Margaret, as she sponged and dried the weary feet.

"Yes, Ma—we were so," replied a big gunner. "His head's a bit dazed, that's all. We've been retiring since Sunday, you see, no time for food or drink, or a sleep—that's done it. He's only a kid."

In the next truck we found a Tommy trying to feed a little boy-baby of two or so, with pieces bitten out of a peach Nancy had given him. Nancy had gone for Latty about the baby, the boy had picked it up in the road and carried it in the retreat till he was wounded—and so tightly did the child cling to its preserver that it was flung with him into the train.

"He's such a nice little chap, sister," said the Tommy, "an' a rare good plucked one—not a cry out of him since I picked him up."

At what a cost to himself this brave boy had carried the baby! His right arm was just pulp, and his left wounded above the elbow.

He did not want to be parted from the baby, but Latty pointed out the advantages of leaving it with her—and he agreed—whereon Latty kissed him soundly, and called him a "brave gosse," greatly to his embarrassment.

"How did you manage to pick up the child under the German guns?" I asked. He shifted a little uncomfortably, then looked bravely into my eyes.

"It's a bit of a queer thing I'm going to say—but it's *true*" he said. "It was a kind of golden cloud between us and the Germans, and a man in it on a big horse—and then I saw the child in the dust on the roadside, and I picked it up."

"Yes, sister," he added. "Lots of other chaps saw it too."

There was a murmur of confirmation. "The minute I saw it," he continued, "I knew we were going to win. It fair bucked me up—yes, sister, thank you. I'm as comfortable as I could be."

So another train steamed out, carrying its load of shattered humanity to haven—and we made ready for the next.

One after the other the trains came in with their terrible loads. We sifted the dead from the dying, and did what we could, and made ready for the next. Just before sunset a Taube came over us, circling round and round above the treetops—and we waited apprehensively a bomb. Suddenly out of the blue came a French aero-plane, and the German turned to fly. But it was cut off. For nearly half an hour they circled and plunged, and rose in the air, each trying to get above the other. A train came in, and we worked with feverish haste to get it off before the German could fulfil his mission.

Then in an instant it was over, and the black bird of Death came plunging sideways down into the forest—with the Frenchman planing down easily after him. Both pilot and observer were dead, and the captured Taube was taken to the aerodrome.

We could not return home—there was no time, so we spent the night at the Post, where we slumbered between whiles on chairs and benches. My dress had a wet border of scarlet round it, and so had Nancy's. We were all in the same plight—stained and weary, and sick with horror. Aunt Margaret got a tub and washed everything she could lay hands on, and we put them out to dry on the shrubs and benches. We went out on the line and collected the dirty dressings and burnt them. The Commandant shrouded his cigar in the waiting-room, and we sat together listening to the dull sound ever-nearing that had begun like a throbbing in the ears the day we were in Paris. It was now like the rolling of distant thunder, and there was a smokiness in the air and an acrid smell.

All night there was a fluttering and piping in the forest, and sometimes a flight of confused and skirling birds would sweep past and settle in the trees. It was very strange to feel the birds flying in the moonlight, they roosted everywhere, on the edge of the platform, and on the roof, and on every twig and branch of the undergrowth along the line—as if the little woodland folk were seeking to shelter beside the Croix Rouge also.

The soldiers had collected the cattle strayed into the forest from the great mobs driven up to Paris, and put them in an enclosure opposite the Post. They moaned and cried all through the dark, and the horses stamped and jingled their harness. The soldiers made coffee at their fire and brought it over to us, and we all drank together, listening to the distant growling in the murky air.

I wondered what we would do when the first Uhlans[22] came out of the forest and rushed at the Post. What Latty and Aunt Margaret and Madame L_____ would do—and Madame P_____ and Raoul, the brave and tender, with his beautiful boyish face and gay smile. How good he had been that day—how thoughtful and kind as a woman!

Well, anyhow, one thing we had silently agreed on—none of us women would fall into the German hands alive: we remembered the Belgian girls.

At dawn, with Raoul and Nancy, we walked to the little station in the town for a paper. There was no one in the street, but as we passed the church the old Abbé came down the steps, with two peasant women, both weeping bitterly.

"No! no!" protested the Abbé cheerfully, "there is no need to weep like this. My children, you can come to me and I will protect you."

"Alas! alas!" wept the elder woman, "that would be to add your death to our own, Father. They always kill priests, old women and children."

"Ah, perhaps!" said the Abbé. "We are the most ready to face God. The children are sinless, and we have had time to repent. Therefore have courage, my children. Come!"

He gave them a cheerful benediction and hurried over to us, greatly rejoiced, apparently, that we too had not fled.

"I am alone in my street," he said cheerfully, "and I have not given up my revolver. I may have at least one Boche to my credit."

The morning sun was just beginning to light the place, and as it brightened his white hair and his saintly old face, I did homage to a brave man.

VII

The booming came nearer and nearer with each hour of that dreadful time till the morning of 1st of September dawned smoky red, with the roar of the guns filling the air. We saw the French artillery falling back on Paris—a long procession of dusty, worn-out horses, barely staggering along in the breathless heat, with the men nodding in their seats, and on their beasts—bloody heads and wounded arms and legs a-plenty—and all day long the trains poured in choc-a-bloc with broken men. The tales they told of the Germans were beyond belief. One man rescued by his comrades had the soles of his feet burnt off. He had been tortured for information—which they did not get. Other things we heard were too horrible to repeat. They were such things as only fiends from the Bottomless Pit could have imagined or carried out.

The old Abbé came down to the Post with a little basket of peaches, and we discussed the story of the Archangel and Joan of Arc. With the boom of the German guns in our ears and the sight of the devilish work they had executed on our brave boys, I was conscious of a bitter resentment against St. Michael and his companion. Why, if they had power to lead the Allies had they not led them to victory? Why—if God was God, had He not driven the Huns back to their own place? Why had He not blasted them out of existence in one great flame of fire?

The old Abbé looked at me sorrowfully. "It is for the purification of the whole world," he said. "The Germans are the Power of Evil. I have seen it since *soixante-dix*. They represent all that makes for wickedness—and they have poisoned the body of the world—and you English, *chère mademoiselle*, are to blame most of all, for you have given them great places—and much honour—yes, they have poisoned the body of the world—but most of all England, and she will suffer most in expiation. As for France"

"Is it that God has forsaken us?" asked Captain P____.

"M. le Capitaine," said the Abbé," I never saw you at Communion before Sunday—why did you come then?"

The Captain coloured slightly. "*They*," he waved his hand to the forest, "are coming up—I made my peace with Him."

"Exactly," said the Abbé. "So with all. When France calls upon God He will hear her. No—the Germans will not conquer." He gave us his blessing and departed, and a rushing of wild birds fled after him on the hot wind.

"*They* come nearer!" remarked the Captain.

He went down the platform, and presently all the soldiers crossed the line and disappeared in the forest. Early in the afternoon the crackling of rifle-fire—shouts and cries and rushings of horses' feet in the forest aisles reached us at our work. The Commandant seemed rigid at the entrance to the station, his eyes fixed on the forest. We worked with feverish haste, never speaking. The afternoon wore on, and night came. In one of the carriages we found a Prussian officer in a British uniform. He insolently demanded champagne and fresh bread. We pulled him out and the Commandant disarmed him and tied him up. A man asked Nancy to lift him up to drink, and clasping his hands round her arm, died holding her—and in that dead grasp she was held for nearly fifteen minutes. We had gangrene, too, and tried to isolate them—by setting aside one of our number to guard them.

"Where are *They* now?" I asked Raoul.

"Coming up to Meaux," he whispered. "The news are bad."

Aunt Margaret and Latty were never off their feet that long night. "Come back, Ma," the English soldiers would call.

"Ma" took messages, washed grimy faces, and feet that had marched for seventy hours. "Seventy hours, Ma," said one boy stolidly. "Ain't it a miracle I've got a foot at all?"

Oh, the tales of simple heroism we heard in that dreadful night. Whether we lived to remember them, or died with our wounded—we were filled with the glory of their deeds and the splendour of their devotion—French and English alike. The stars in the dark sky were not more glorious than their souls.

And in the night a train came suddenly through, carrying the telegraphic apparatus, and wireless, from the station beyond, and warning us to be ready to evacuate at any moment. The thunder of the guns went on till just before dawn, when it suddenly ceased—but the trains came steadily in, it was as if all the Allies had been broken in this awful fray.

Morning came, and *They* had not arrived. Captain P____ came out of the forest—grimy and grim. A patrol of Uhlans had got through at Compeine—but "it was disposed of." So there had been fighting in the forest!

Aunt Margaret came down to speak to us. Her hair was a kind of dusty white, and her face so changed I scarcely recognised her. As I stood, basin in hand, staring at her, François came up on his bicycle, with Raoul racing beside him.

"The news are good!" he cried joyously. "We have them surrounded. Mesdames, we have turned!"

The Allies had turned at Vitry-le-François and were attacking.

In the afternoon the Abbé came to tell us Monsieur P____ had found Jean—unwounded, and given him a change of clothing and some food. We rejoiced with Raoul and Madame P____, and turned to our work again. Our hands were full.

"Now," said Latty, "you will see the others returning, and we shall be inundated. But my little English, I shall not forget how *we* faced the Boches together." She kissed us all affectionately, and we set about our various tasks. The heat was tropical, there was a plague of wasps and flies—and the stench of the station was terrible. If I had owned the world, I would have offered it in exchange for half an hour's sleep—but there was no time for sleep.

The wounded came through from Vitry-le-François, and we heard again strange tales from the wounded. The Allies had fallen back for seventy-eight hours—marching, marching, fighting a rearguard action all the way. No food, no drink, harried by German shell, and German horse—marching night and day, day and night—the men falling dead asleep in the ranks, to be kicked to their feet by the officers—of the officers falling off their feet drunk with sleep, and being pushed and kicked to their feet again by the men—of horses that fell dead in the traces and being replaced by men, who could barely pat one blistered foot before the other—yet dragged on their guns; of motor transport that drove itself, with the drivers hanging dead asleep over the wheels, or sitting with wide-open eyes and dead hands, steering food and munitions to safety, till at last the Germans fell in their tracks and both armies slept.

Then came the trumpet call, and the Allies sprang to their feet new men—one man said he felt as if he had just come out of the sea after a swim—"fit for anything!" Then as the immense wall of the German army came up, a kind of luminous mist settled down between it and the Allied forces—and out of the mist came two mounted figures—Joan of Arc and St. Michael, on white horses.

The men who related these stories varied them in this wise—that the British saw St. George and the French St. Joan and St. Michael. There did not seem to be any *religious* sentiment in the stories, but those who told them had left the fight in the certainty that victory was with the Allies.

One man, a Breton, practically echoed what the Abbé had said one night before. "It must be a pretty hard case for us, when God has to send His best fighting man to our aid. You see, Mademoiselle Mees, it is an ancient feud between Satan and St. Michael. He got him out of heaven—now he will get him off the earth, but it will take time."

One soldier told me he had seen Joan of Arc brandishing a sword, and crying to them to "Advance!"

This man was from Domrémy, and was familiar with the tradition of the shepherd girl. He had fought with the English all the way from Mons— and little Joan of Arc had defeated the English—*par example!* Now she was leading them—there was a combination for you! No wonder the Boches fled.

We had three tall men of the Irish Guard who died that night—and another who survived. These men told the Abbé a tale of St. George riding on a white horse between them and the Germans. A Lancashire Fusilier and a man of the R.F.A. also told me a similar story. All the French asked eagerly for medals of Joan of Arc and St. Michael, and these two men demanded a medal, or a picture, of St. George—because they had seen him—these men all came from in or about Vitry-le-François—where the Allies turned. These men were sure they had seen St. George, because they were familiar with his figure on the English sovereign, and had recognised it.

When this train had gone out we had another discussion. The Commandant wavered between belief and doubt. "Seventy-eight hours afoot," he summed up. "I wonder they didn't see the Devil!"

Raoul, however, advanced no opinion, and the Captain was silent. We also—like many—pondered it in our hearts and said nothing. If God was— why should this thing not be?

"Why should He not, seeing the Powers of Hell about to prevail, send His best fighting men?" said Madame P_____. "It is like this—the Pope makes saints—but does God accept the Pope's ultimatum? that's the stumbling-block."

Madame P_____ is a Huguenot—and mourns always deeply that this war is caused by a Protestant nation—though the Captain assures her the Germans do not worship her Protestant God, but a good old god of their own—Odin to wit.

With that dreadful night ended our work at the Post. In the morning we were informed that we must present ourselves at the Hospital, and be entered for service. We were mobilised with the French Army, and had our numbers, and were liable to be called upon for service anywhere.

About noon then, we crawled homewards, and on the way met Jean, Latty's younger son, running down to the Post. The automobile had been smashed by a shell, and he had walked all the way back from Chantilly. He had seen the Germans, millions of men in grey with faces of the devil. Robert was driving an ammunition waggon, and would not return. He could drive quite well with the left hand. The Germans were in retreat—all was well—but all the pretty little towns and villages were in ruins—and the Boches killed babies—yes, truly—tore them out of their mothers' arms and thrust a bayonet through them.

We went on, while Jean ran to the Post, where Latty sat nodding on her hard bench beside the wounded. We had forgotten what it was like to sleep in a bed. We had slept in odd snatches—but never enough to give one the feeling of rest. We began to think that at any moment we, too, might see visions.

In the kitchen sat Peter—thin as a rake. His shrivelled old hands about a little damp ball of blackness.

"See, Mademoiselle," he cried, holding it out to me. "Behold this little '*Blessé*'—I have brought it to you."

A little black Persian kitten—one of its eyes gouged out, one tiny fluffy paw broken, and hanging helplessly.

"I killed him," said Peter, with a satisfied indrawing of his breath. "I killed the dirty pig who did it to the little animal. André, my big son, had a German rifle—good! I killed the Boche—he had tied the little animal to a tree, would you believe it—and he was torturing it. Oh, I assure you, he died thoroughly, that one! Yes, I thought always the good God would compensate me for having a wife who prayed all day. And the little cat will be a beauty, *pansez* its little hand, MdlleMees [sic]—the eye I have attended to myself—so—courage now, my *dear* friends! I will make you coffee and all will be well. Thank God the Germans are now in retreat. Oh, I can tell you a thing or two about what we have done. *Allons!* sit in the salon and I will bring coffee."

I sat down and bandaged the little black hand—of all the devilish cruelties I had seen none brought home to me the utter depravity of the German soul as this innocent little victim of their lust of hate.

"Dogs!" I heard a Canadian call them, his eyes like hot steel at the remembrance of what he had seen. But that was too high praise—to rank them with the faithful friend of man. They are nothing but themselves. All the wickedness, the lust, the hate and cruelty and greed—the filthiness unimaginable that exists can be summed up in one word: *German!*

When I saw the German prisoners the next day, and went about like all the others holding my nose—I thought they were distinctly a race that is something apart from Humanity, as we understand the word.

When they stood blinking in the sun with their square heads and putty-coloured faces, colourless eyes and lashes—furtive yet unspeakably sinister in their grey uniforms—they suggested to me a creation of some monstrous spirit of evil. We call them Huns—and do so without understanding that in reality they are a something more than Huns, and less—for the Huns were at least individuals. But these are merely so much of the mechanism that goes to make the gigantic whole of Germania—and each unit has no more individuality, no more soul, than any other steel cog, or wheel, or spring, or catch in the machine that is moved by the mind of the Kaiser and his crowd.

Is it strange, then, that saints and angels should fight against this dreadful foe—or that the veil which hangs between us and Immortality should be rent and shrivelled by such suffering and agony of the innocent as this world has never seen. Is it strange that the cries of virgins violated, of crucified sons and fathers—of brothers and sons carbonised, of nuns tortured and burnt—of priests tortured and impaled, of little children done to death in such ways that they cannot be spoken of, is it strange that the torment of these has dragged at the feet of the Ruler of the Universe till He sent aid.

I have seen no vision. But in my heart I believe that the Captains of God are leading the Allies to victory, through untold suffering, through loss, and privation and sacrifice this nation is being brought to re-birth. Already have I seen France rise from her own corruption, a splendour of white youth—filled with Holy Vengeance, silent, alert, implacable. And they say in France this thing:

"The English are mercy without judgment. But we—'*are judgment without mercy.*'"

• FIVE •

A Churchwoman and *The Chariots of God*

Published: London: Arthur H. Stockwell, n.d.

Though appearing without a date, *The Chariots of God* has been dated to 1915 or 1916. The former date would appear to derive from the introduction; the latter, from its receipt by the British Library. The preface of *The Chariots of God* is signed with the initials M. C. H., which the British Library has identified as Mary Coultman Horne, though its evidence for doing so is unclear.

If the Churchwoman who wrote *The Chariots of God* is indeed Ms. Mary Coultman Horne, then she may also be the holder of at least five patents designed to improve the lives of invalids. Four of these are English patents[1]; the fifth, French.[2] That all five patents were issued well before the start of the First World War would strongly imply that Ms. Horne was a highly practical woman, had some personal acquaintance with the issues faced by the invalids of the time, and may have been a nurse who spoke French and was resident at least for a time in France. That her names does not appear in the English censuses from 1901 and 1911 may also be significant.

Reprinted from *The Chariots of God* are Ms. Horne's introduction and her account of the Battle of Mons. They are the accounts of a devout and unquestioning believer whose faith was strengthened by the story. What her accounts lack in literary polish they make up for in fervor.

Introduction

To-day is the Feast of St. Michael and All Angels.[3] It seems fitting in this time of unparalleled crises that we should commemorate it by paying more special attention to the teaching of the Church on the subject of the Holy Angels.

That I may be able to offer some new thought, or some old thought newly-presented, to the comfort and enlightenment of some heart, anxious or bereaved, is my great desire.

That I may be able to strengthen the belief that the Holy Angels, as Messengers of Mercy, are Great Realities; that they are about our path, and are specially appointed to succour and defend us and ours in times of danger,—this is my home and aim.

The Powers of Darkness, against which we contend, must eventually be dispersed before the Light of the New Day which is coming.

September 29, 1915

Following the introduction, Churchwoman opens her account of the Battle of Mons by stating that:

"The War may be divided into three phases—the first, in which the Allies retreated without being beaten; the second, advanced without beating; and the third, in which they will both advance and beat."

These words are taken from a leader in one of the daily papers. The second phase partakes still of the nature of the first, and we are far from realizing the third.

The War has dragged its weary length all through the Summer and Autumn hearts have been sick with longing for the third development. May we hope now that it is beginning?

We look back to those terrible days when the first phase was the only one of which we had any experience—those days which preceded the Victory of the Marne. We feel that we can hardly credit the evidence of the dates, which testify to the terrible rapidity of the onrush of the German hordes, which in less than three weeks had overrun the greater part of Belgium, and laid it in ruins. It was when our gallant little Army was confronted with what promised to be irretrievable disaster that those events occurred that have been the subject of more discussion than perhaps any subsequent events in the course of the war.

This is followed by accounts of the battle and the English retreat, after which she introduces the Bowmen. The punctuation and phrasing are hers:

On September 29, 1914, appeared in the "Evening News" a piece of fiction which was to have an unique history. It was re-printed in the same paper on July 20 last year, and later in book form, with other legends of the War.

In it is graphically depicted the Battle of Mons, with the marvelous Retreat. The author had read the account in the "Weekly Dispatch," and this inspired him to write more than one piece of fine imaginative fiction. It is, however, only "The Bowmen" round which a controversy has raged. Although this controversy has subsided, it seems worth while recalling the circumstances, partly because it gave rise to what may be called the "Angel Books."

"A thousand British soldiers are occupying a salient against a furious cannonade from ten thousand Germans. To hold this salient is vital. Its capture means the turning of the Allied left flank, and *that* means ruin for France and England.

"The British see that the position is hopeless. Their guns are overwhelmed and shot to bits by the enemy's artillery; their numbers are reduced from a

Five • A Churchwoman and *The Chariots of God*

thousand to five hundred. They know that they are doomed to death beyond all hope or help; and they shoot on as calmly as if they were at Bisley.[4]

"Then a soldier remembers the motto that appears on all the plates in the vegetarian restaurant in St. Martin's Lane[5]: 'Adsit Anglis Sanctus Georgius'—'May St. George be a present help to the English.'[6] He utters this prayer mechanically; and falls instantly into a waking vision. He hears a voice, mighty as a thunder-peal, crying: 'Array, array, array!' and the spirits of the old English bowmen obey the command of their patron and ours. The soldier hears their war-cries: 'Harow, Harow, St. George, be quick to help us.' 'Dear Saint, succor us!' He sees the flight of their arrows darkening the air.

"And the other men, to their amazement, see the Germans melting from before them. In a moment a whole regiment crashes to the ground. The men cannot make out what is happening: they suppose a reserve of machine guns may have been brought up. At all events, as one says to another, 'the Germans have got it in the neck.' And the soldier who is in the world of vision goes on shooting till the man next to him clouts him on the head, and tells him not to waste the King's ammunition on dead Germans."

Such is a brief outline of the story.

There is something quite pathetic in the sequel to this romantic story. People persisted in believing it was true! Might not the author have foreseen this, and guarded his readers and himself from the results?

One man writes about the "gross materialism of the age." Another, of the general spiritual revival during the last fifteen or twenty years, and speaks of the "boom" in supernatural fiction as evidence of this!

The feature of this modern type of story is its realism of detail, which, dealing with the commonplace, gives the illusion of truth.

Such devices for deceiving the imagination are perfectly justifiable, one would agree, when it is of *no consequence* to the reader whether he is deceived or not!

But the case is far different when such a subject as the awful struggle between the forces of Right and truth and Honour and the barbarous cruelty of Might and False-dealing (in which the latter for the moment triumphs) is the subject! Add to this that there is scarcely a heart in England which is not wrung with agony for some one or more dear ones who are spilling their life's blood in that contest. In such a light how can one regard that very charmingly-written fantasy? So realistic is "The Bowmen," and, if it were true, so comforting, so helpful!

"All a myth! Pure fiction; all made up out of his own head!" This is the assertion thrown, as it were, at a suffering nation. But more than that—or by now it might have been forgotten—the Author insists that all other stories of Divine Intervention have their source and origin in this attractive bit of fic-

tion! It was to combat this that Mr. Harold Begbie wrote his "On the side of the Angels [sic]."[7]

He shows conclusively that numbers of such stories were being circulated in France, Russia and England before Mr. Machen wrote "The Bowmen." Whether these stories are all true or not is beside the mark. Sufficient that they do not owe their origin to Mr. Machen's imagination. To deny this is now impossible with all the evidence forthcoming. Therefore we are driven back on the theory of thought transference—or mere coincidence, neither of them being at all unlikely.

The Editor of the "Church Times" says that Mr. Machen's little tale "could easily be recognised as fiction by anyone of intelligence who read it." And yet, how many thousands of readers have been deceived! Are we to consider them lacking in intelligence? I think not. The style, the subject, the use of realistic detail, and the intense desire of the readers, all tended to delude them. It was more easy to deceive the public because people were asking themselves how it was that the triumphant onward march of the irresistible German Army had suddenly been thrown back at the battle of the Marne, in disastrous and ignominious retreat.

If "On the side of the Angels [sic]" had concluded with the early part of Section VIII, it would have conveyed to many minds more strength and consolation in this agonizing struggle which we are enduring, than can be the result of proceeding to the arguments of the last part of the section. This brings the whole argument from a spiritual to a spiritualistic plane. Ghost stories, pure and simple (one of them being mischievous, if not meaningless and only two being of the nature of warnings to avert a catastrophe), go far to remove the high state of confidence and hope in the ever present guardianship of Angels which should be the final and abiding conviction of the sorrow-stricken and anxious.

After reading the concluding lines one closes the book with the question: "But are these things desirable?"

Another of the "Angel-Books" is quite a small pamphlet by Mr. Ralph Shirley.[8] He makes much of the strange appearances in the sky, which appeared some months *after* the battle of Edgehill. He regards this manifestation as a true case of psychic exaltation, but, in any case, the sign being long after the event cannot be regarded as on parallel lines to the otherwise similar manifestations in our own days. It was not a warning—in that therefore unlike the very remarkable account of an aerial display of warfare in the heavens, which preceded the overthrow of Louis of Nassau.[9]

One paragraph I will quote, as it contains a theory likely to be the true solution of some of these "evidences" which have not the quality of Divine Intervention.

"It appears, indeed, that in some peculiar way great wars open up fresh channels for the psychic senses, and the physical struggle of great armies appears ever to have its counterpart on the spiritual plane by the bringing into action of psychic forces, working for good or evil, on the side of Light or of Darkness—principalities and powers mustering their unseen array upon whose efforts, no less than upon the efforts of those now living on the physical plane, the great and final issues of this vast world-conflict ultimately depend."

This is quite in line with Mr. Sinnett's theory in the article on "Our Unseen Enemies and Allies" in the *Nineteenth-Century* for October.

This unforeseen contest in which we may take part by our prayers and aspirations, and by our habitual frame of mind, is it not that to which St. Paul refers in his Epistle to the Ephesians (Chap. vi. v. 12), "For we wrestle not against flesh and blood, but against principalities, against powers, against the rulers of the darkness of this world, against spiritual wickedness in high places." In the margin "heavenly" is given instead of "high." This is worth noting, for its bearing on the above theory.

Stories from the Front
A Lance-Corporal's Evidence

A "Daily Mail" representative gives the following account taken from the lips of a Lance-Corporal, in hospital, waiting to undergo an operation.

> I was with my battalion in the retreat from Mons, on or about August 28. The German cavalry were expected to make a charge, and we were waiting to fire and scatter them, so as to enable the French cavalry, who were on our right, to make a dash forward. However, the German aeroplanes discovered our position, and we remained where we were.
>
> The weather was very hot and clear, and between eight and nine o'clock in the evening I was standing with a party of nine other men on duty, and some distance on either side were parties of ten on guard. Immediately behind us half of my battalion was on the edge of a wood resting. An officer suddenly came up to us in a state of great anxiety and asked us if we had seen anything startling.
>
> He hurried away from my ten to the next party of ten. When he had got out of sight I, who was the non-commissioned officer in charge, ordered two men to go forward, out of the way of the trees in order to find out what the officer meant. The two men returned reporting that they could see no sign of any Germans; at that time we thought that the officer must be expecting a surprise attack.
>
> Immediately afterwards the officer came back, and taking me and some others a few yards away showed us the sky. I could see quite plainly in mid-air a strange light, which seemed to be quite distinctly outlined and was not a reflection of the moon, nor were there any clouds in the neighbourhood. The light became brighter, and I could see quite distinctly three shapes, one of the centre having what looked like outspread wings, the other two were not so large, but were quite plainly distinct from the centre one. They appeared to

have a long loose-hanging garment of a golden tint, and they were above the German line, facing us.

We stood watching them for about three-quarters of an hour. All the men with me saw them, and other men came up from other groups who also told us that they had seen the same thing. I am not a believer in such things, but I have not the slightest doubt but that we really did see what I now tell you.

I remember the day because it was a day of terrible anxiety for us. That morning the Munsters had a bad time on our right, and so had the Scots Guards. We managed to get to the wood and there we barricaded the roads and remained in the formation I have told you. Later on the Uhlans attacked us and we drove them back with heavy loss. It was after this engagement, when we were dog-tired, that the vision appeared to us.

I shall never forget it as long as I live. I lie awake in bed and picture it all as I saw it that night. Of my battalion there are now only five men alive besides myself, and I have no hope of getting back to the front. I have a record of fifteen years' good service, and I should be very sorry to make a fool of myself by telling a story merely to please anyone.

A Lieutenant-Colonel's Testimony

The following story is that of a Lieutenant-Colonel, "Somewhere in France," whose identification and undoubted standing and repute are vouched for by "The Evening News."

On August 26, 1914, was fought the battle of Le Cateau. We came into action at dawn and fought till dusk. We were heavily shelled by the German artillery during the day, and in common with the rest of our division had a bad time of it.

Our division, however, retired in good order. We were on the march all the night of the 26th and on the 27th with only about two hours' rest.

The brigade to which I belonged was a rearguard to the division, and during the 27th we took up a great many different positions to cover the retirement of the rest of the division, so that we had very hard work, and by the night of the 27th we were all absolutely worn out with fatigue—both bodily and mental fatigue. No doubt we also suffered to a certain extent from shock; but the retirement still continued in excellent order, and I feel sure that our mental faculties were still quite sound and in good working condition.

On the night of the 27th, I was riding along in the column with two other officers. We had been talking and doing our best to keep from falling asleep on our horses.

As we rode along I became conscious of the fact that, in the fields on both sides of the road along which we were marching, I could see a very large body of horsemen.

These horsemen had the appearance of squadrons of cavalry, and they seemed to be riding across the fields and going in the same direction as we were going, and keeping level with us.

The night was not very dark, and I fancied that I could see squadron upon squadron of these cavalrymen quite distinctly.

I did not say a word about it at first, but I watched them for about twenty minutes. The other two officers had stopped talking.

At last one of them asked me if I saw anything in the fields. I then told him what I had seen. The third officer then confessed that he, too, had been watching these horsemen for the past twenty minutes.

So convinced were we that they were really cavalry that, at the next halt, one of the officers took a party of men out to reconnoiter, and found no one there. The night then grew darker, and we saw no more.

The same phenomenon was seen by many men in our column. Of course we were all dog-tired and over-taxed, but it is an extraordinary thing that the same phenomenon should be witnessed by so many different people.

I myself am absolutely convinced that I saw these horsemen; and I feel sure that they did not exist only in my imagination. I do not attempt to explain the mystery—I only state facts.

A Private's Story

I scarcely think Private J. Easy, of the 9th Lincolns, would have laid himself open to be got at by the public and by his comrades if he had not been "fully persuaded" that he was only telling the simple truth about what he had seen, and that he could bring many others to support his testimony.

In a letter published in the "Evening News" on October 14th, he says:—

The third division marched into Mons through a street of flags and excited Belgians. I can picture it all over again as I write. But little did they think what had to happen in a short time.

We were given two hours' leave with certain boundaries. We had not been out long when a Sergeant came round to tell us to return at once.

When we were all to arms we were told there would be a lot of street fighting, but we thought it was all bosh. We had no more idea of seeing a German in Mons than we had of seeing the Angels of Mons.

We were set to work cutting trees down, pulling up the road, and making a strong barricade. This finished, No. 16 Platoon was posted in a house facing up the street. Still we thought it was all bosh, and we laughed at the very idea of Germans. I was leaning out of the window when I heard the order given, "Rapid fire."

"What are they firing at?" said one man. Then a man who was looking out of another window shouted, "Look." And we all flocked to the window.

Yes, sure enough, there they were. A huge mass of grey forms staggering on under our heavy fire. Our men fought bravely. The Germans were dropping like sheep, but they were too many for us. We were forced to retire.

We turned back when it got dark and found ourselves nearly in the place we had left. When morning broke the firing began. If you have ever been in an earthquake you will have a good idea of what it was like. We had about four hours of this. We did our best, but it became too hot for us, and we would not retire unless a covering party was left behind. So they prepared to fight a rear guard action. I was one of the men left, and I was one of those who saw the most marvellous things which have happened in history.

I saw "The Angels of Mons."

Yes, when the main body had retired, the Huns seemed to have spotted the move, and they came on thicker and stronger than before. But every one of us behind that barricade seemed to be gifted with an iron nerve. Every man took a steady aim, just the same as I have seen them do on Browndown Range, when they have been firing for their pay. Bang, bang, rap, ping, just like thunder. They were coming nearer, nearer. We looked at each other, I don't know how I looked, but the others looked as white as a sheet, but not afraid.

Nearer, still nearer they came. "God help us," murmured one, as he took steady aim and fired.

"We're done," gasped another, and as I looked at him I saw him staring in front with wild eyes. And, as if by magic, the whizzing, buzzing, and whirling stopped. I followed the man's gaze, and, sure enough, there, not two hundred yards in front of us, was a long line of white forms, stretching from house to house. They were making mysterious motions with their arms.

"Good lor!" said one man, "What is it?"

But no man answered. Yet every man felt in his heart that the white barricade had been sent by some Unseen Power to protect that small body of English.

"We retired. No one spoke until we were well clear of Mons. I said they were Angels, and not a man contradicted me."

Of some hundreds of letters which Private J. Easy has written to enquirers the following, which reached me on New Year's Eve, contains some interesting additional details.

After some preliminaries of a personal nature, he goes on:—

It was the second day the British were in action. We had retired once, but wishing to check the enemy's advance, and at the same time surprise them, we went back in the night, and took up a position on the opposite end to where the Huns were. But they got to know, and got their guns trained on to our trenches, which we had dug with our small entrenching tools, and when daylight broke it was like Hell upon earth.

They dug us out of our small trenches with those fearful shells. They ploughed the ground at every foot. Houses, hospitals, buildings as big as St. Paul's, were cast like dust before the wind!

We retired from barricade to barricade, until the officers found out we couldn't stick it any longer, so they prepared us to fight a rearguard action. Now, I suppose you know what a rearguard action is? A certain portion of the men are left behind, as covering party, while the majority get clear. It's just like sacrificing the minority to save the majority.

I was amongst the men left behind. The main body got clear, and we few men had a kind of "creepy" feeling, when we discovered there was only about 300 to face about a hundred times that many.

To cut a long story short. We could see those "grey devils" swooping down upon us—down this narrow street—and when we thought we should all be cut up—

A wonderful thing happened!

Five • A Churchwoman and *The Chariots of God*

A white line of Angelic forms appeared between us and the advancing German, and held them back. Every gun was still!

We couldn't believe it, until after the second look—and there they stood! Beautiful, majestical—defying those "cut-throats" to advance another step!

By this Act of Providence we few men were able to retire, and the next day gained the remainder of the Army.

And they were very much surprised to see us!

The three foregoing stories are at first hand—the accounts given by eye-witnesses—whose identity can be verified. There are many others, of hearsay evidence, which, nevertheless, bear the stamp of truth.

Such for instance is that of Mr. Lancaster, a Weymouth clergyman, who told his congregation that he had had a letter from a soldier who said that his regiment was pursued by a large number of German cavalry, from which they took refuge in a quarry, where the Germans found them and were on the point of shooting them. "At that moment," said the writer, "the whole top edge of the quarry was lined by Angels, who were seen by all the soldiers and the Germans as well. The Germans suddenly stopped, turned round, and galloped at top speed."

Among other stories given by the Vicar of All Saints, Monkwearmouth, who was with the troops for two months in France, is the following:—

> A soldier of the third Canadians stated that after the second battle of Ypres, when their battalion was retiring through their communication trenches towards their rest camp, they were obliged to halt where a West Riding regiment was stationed. During the halt one of the men of this regiment was narrating to those around him a strange experience of his own. He had seen, he said, what appeared at first to be a ball of fire. Afterwards it took the form of an Angel with outstretched wings standing between the British front line and that of the enemy.

• SIX •

T. W. H. Crosland and
Find the Angels: The Showmen: A Legend of the War

Published: London: T. Werner Laurie, Ltd., 1915

If T. W. H. Crosland is remembered at all, it is because he was the ghostwriter for Lord Alfred Douglas's *Oscar Wilde and Myself*,[1] writing a volume that is known to be "full of inaccuracies, untruths and attempts at self-justification, even going to the extent of denying that he knew Wilde was homosexual until the trials...."[2] Lord Alfred Douglas was to repudiate *Oscar Wilde and Myself* while simultaneously emphasizing that Crosland was its co-author,[3] thus ensuring that the deceased Crosland was blamed as the source for the mistruths. The truth, of course, is that both dealt harshly with Wilde. Crosland did indeed possess what critics have termed a "pathological hatred of Wilde"[4] and, before attacking him in *Oscar Wilde and Myself*, self-published *The First Stone: On Reading the Unpublished Portions of "De Profundis"* that begins:

> Thou,
> The complete mountebank,
> The scented posturer,
> The flabby Pharisee,
> The King of Life,
> The Lord of Language
> With the bad teeth;
> The whining convict
> And Prince of Hypocrites,
> That slouchest
> Out of the shameless slime[5]

Douglas considered this vitriol an "astonishingly brilliant indictment of Wilde."[6]

Crosland nevertheless was more than Douglas's hired pen, and if he was at times no better than an attack dog, there were many times when he showed himself to be, though certainly not the leading literary light of his time, a strong secondary illuminator. His biographer, W. Sorley Brown, was to describe him as "a man of genius—great poet, sane and acute critic, scathing satirist, great Bohemian and patriot, fearless pugilist, the last brilliant journalist of the Victorian era, and one of the most original and remarkable men that ever wielded a pen in Fleet Street,"[7] and an examination of Crosland's sad life tends to agree with this assessment. He was unquestionably all that Sorley Brown claims for him, but he was also a severe alcoholic, terribly self-destructive, bigoted, homophobic, and possessed too what today would perhaps euphemistically be referred to as "anger management issues." Even the staid *The Times* noted these traits in its obituary of Crosland, stating that "a sense of humour would have saved him from his worst extravagances," as his bluster usually left his opponents "unmoved and unharmed."[8]

Thomas William Hodgson Crosland was born in Leeds, England, on 21 July 1868. He was educated privately and began to drink early: an anecdote recounted by Sorley Brown has him, at age 12, going to Leeds, getting drunk, and remembering nothing until he "found himself in Manchester practically penniless."[9] He likewise began to write early—Sorley Brown notes a poem published in *The Leeds Mercury Weekly Supplement* in 1885[10]—and 1890 he removed to London and went to work as a miscellaneous journalist, then editor. States his obituary in *The Times*, "from 1899 to 1902 he was assistant editor of the *Outlook*. Afterwards for six months he became assistant editor of *Vanity Fair*, and then, in 1905, editor of the *English Review*. In 1908 he joined the *Academy* as assistant editor, but he resigned when the paper was sold in 1911. He then became editor of a paper called *P.I.P.*, but resigned a year later."[11] He was to rejoin the *Academy* in 1915 as editor and owner, but it soon ceased publication. After lengthening periods of ill health, many of which can be directly traced to his alcoholism, he died on 23 December 1924. His family and friends—and friends he had, though few—genuinely mourned him.

As a fellow journalist, Crosland knew Machen well enough to joke with him, even about his name,[12] and it seems to be in this spirit that *Find the Angels: The Showmen* was written. At the same time, the resulting book is remarkable for several reasons. It is certainly the most topical of the responses to Machen, riddled with references and allusions that only contemporary readers would recognize. In addition, it overtly recognizes the flimsiness of the testimonials disagreeing with Machen and is almost as quick to mock and ridicule them, while at the same time pointing out that it was religion that kept men fighting:

> There is not a soldier's wife ... or a soldier's mother in England who doesn't overtly or covertly believe in the existence of angels. It is an angel who brings the boy back, perhaps hurt and maimed—but back. It is an angel that goes

with him from Waterloo platform to his death, and makes that death an honour to himself and a glory to his country, and tolerable and even beautiful to those who loved him. If it were not for angels no woman would ever say 'Go.' And if it were not for angels no man who has seen another man blown into a crimson mist with bits of rag in it would ever fight again.[13]

Finally, in its series of increasingly (and deliberately) desperate appendixes, Crosland demonstrates the capacity for a very appealing self-mockery and genuine patriotism.

Nevertheless, for all that *Find the Angels: The Showmen* is a singular and informed reaction, its brash mockery and cultural criticism appear to have had no noticeable effect on the Angels of Mons controversy, and the work was never reprinted. Had it been more readily available, Crosland might be remembered for more than his pathologies.

Introduction

I have been asked to write an introduction to the famous story of "The Showmen." Frankly, I hesitate. Introductions are nothing in my line. They belong to the same category as a dish of spiced meat before mass. That is to say, they take the edge off the spiritual appetite. But whether one likes it or not, books have to be filled out both in front and behind (see Appendices), and one needs must when the publisher drives.

How did I come to write "The Showmen"? What moved me to put down on paper a fiction which turns out to be so true that people go about asserting that I was intended by Heaven for a war correspondent rather than a writer of poignant short stories. From first to last it has been the oddest of odd affairs. As you will see for yourselves, the story itself is nothing; yet the hubbub and pother it has raised impinge on the phenomenal. Everybody is talking about it: everybody swears that Private Sweets and Private Cheese are real persons; that they were really visited and succoured in their extremity by a real angel; that the angels have been seen by all manner of sober folk in all manner of places, including Boulogne, Furnes, Auteil, Bexhill, Sandown Park, Chaudfontein, Shipley Glen and Islington; and that when I say, as I do say, that to the best of my knowledge and belief there is no angel (save a certain charming young lady to whom I send violets fresh from Piccadilly Circus every morning) I am an unmitigated promulgator of falsehood, or, in plain terms, a liar. What is one to do? Psychological considerations might tempt me to bow before the storm of popular belief and desire, and admit for the edification of mankind at large that Private Cheese and his angel really exist, but psychology is poor stuff compared with hard fact. And the harder the fact the closer we ought to cling to it, as the nightingale clings to the thorn. So let me begin at the beginning.

It was last week; to be more precise, on the only Sunday of last week. There were terrible things to read in the Sunday paper—there always are. Between breakfast and evensong I read terrible thing after terrible thing, and if the Sunday papers brought out night editions I should probably have read more. After evensong—the dean preached a rather vapid sermon about second-century heresies—I went to a recruiting meeting. The principal speaker was a fine Yorkshire tommy who had been gassed and scorched with liquid fire and jabbed with German bayonets and bashed over the head with the butt ends of German rifles till he thought he was dead. But the stretcher-bearers and the doctors had saved him, and he was here, leaning on a stick and telling all the old men and women and children round him of his wonderful escape and the equally wonderful escape of a friend of his, who had been blown twelve feet in to the air by high explosives and was now in Charing Cross Hospital, sitting up and taking nourishment. I felt proud of this Yorkshireman and his friend. I loved them for the dangers they had passed, like Desdemona loved Othello, and I particularly loved the orator, because he said in his splendid Yorkshire way, "All that me and my pal ask is that we may be spared to go back and, with the help of Divine Providence, 'warm the Germans' jackets.'" When I was a small boy my Yorkshire nurse—a kindly comfortable saint of sixty—used to threaten to warm my jacket for me. Once she did it (without the help of Divine Providence), and I knew what it meant. One way and another, therefore, I was filled with a sort of enthusiasm at this meeting. I would have recruited myself on the spot and gone cheerfully off with my orator in khaki were it not for the fact that while anybody lies who says that Lord Kitchener[14] bars bantams, his lordship certainly has no use for asthmatical bumpers and borders afflicted with arterio-sclerosis and chronic vertigo and burdened with two sticks; so I determined to go round and get some shellwork next morning; but when I applied at the Labour Exchange they smiled broadly upon me and took my name and address—that was all. For thirty-one long years—that is to say, since I was eighteen—I have trailed a pen and been vexed in consequence by a sempiternal want of pence, and the thought came to me, "If I cannot fight with my doughty Yorkshireman and his friend, I can at least invent a story about them—and maybe sell it to profit." And I did. "The Showmen" is the story.

When I took the manuscript to an editor and asked him to read it then and there, he did not fall out of his chair. He said; "We are eaten up with footle of this sort, but, as I daresay you are feeling the general pinch, I don't mind giving you a guinea for it on the nail." He said "on the nail" with a stress and empressement *which convinced me. I remarked that it was a "go" or "deal," and he summoned by telephone a hard-hearted owl from below stairs, who gave me a single pound treasury note and one shilling and requested me to write a receipt. After which elaborate ritual the editor turned to me affably and observed, "You know, So-and-so (meaning me), human, palpitating stuff like this, with a touch of the supernatural in it, is exactly what everybody is wanting just now. I am astonished you have not buckled to before and made a fortune* out of it. For your encouragement I prophesy that 'The Showmen' will sell my paper like old Harry. Within a month you will be translated in to Danish, Bulgarian, Italian, French, Welsh, Choctaw, Hindustani, Chinese, Basque, and various other languages; I shall then invite you to write further little things in the same manner, and you will be rich and famous at last." I looked wistfully at my guinea and, stretching forth my hand, took back my receipt and scrawled upon it "For serial rights only." I am Yorkshire too.

The reader will naturally inquire why in the name of wonder he should be worried with these squalid financial details. But the reader has probably never written an introduction to a work of high literary intention—otherwise he would know better.

After the appearance of my beautiful story "The Showmen" in print I began to be pestered by editors of parish magazines requesting permission to reprint it. These requests I immediately granted with the proviso that the name of the paper in which the story had first appeared should be prominently displayed and my own name as author printed in big type top and bottom. The editors very properly agreed. Then bishops and prebendaries and vicars and even curates began to bombard me with awkward communications. "You are perfectly well aware," wrote one eminent ecclesiastic, "the 'The Showmen' is the truest story ever written. I suspect that you took it down from the lips of the uncle of an officer, and if you do not write to the Times at once and avow the proper facts it may become my painful duty to unmask you." I liked the "may become" in this hoity-toity note, and told the writer by return of post that he might burn me at the stake if he liked, but I should not recant. Another gentleman of the cloth advised me that he had the honour to include among his parishioners a highly respectable laundress of the name of Rynde who happened to be a cousin by marriage to Private Thomas Henry Cheese, and that she had lately visited Cheese's parents in Yorkshire, who informed her that every word in "The Showmen" had been written by Cheese in a letter which he had dispatched to them from the front, but which had, unfortunately, miscarried and fallen into my hands. Cheese, they said, was indignant about the matter and threatened proceedings. In order to avoid an exposure, and in some material, if inadequate, way to recompense Cheese for the wrong I had done him, the reverent gentleman suggested that I should forward notes ("not a cheque") for ten pounds to Cheese's mother, who would expend the money in comforts for her boy, now laid up at a base hospital with fresh wounds of which the angel in the story had as yet, apparently, neglected to take notice. I was somewhat perturbed by these tidings, as a literary reputation, like the cathedral at Rheims or the bloom on a peach, when once destroyed can never be supplied. Accordingly I parlayed with my correspondent, assuring him of my absolute professional integrity and pointing out that there were doubtless many Cheeses in the world, and that, while I would not venture to doubt that his particular Cheese had in fact written a story similar to mine in a letter which had miscarried, I flattered myself that there was a literary touch and finish about the story of "The Showmen" which plainly proclaimed it to be the work of an accomplished author rather than a common soldier. I received a quick and distinctly jolting reply, to the effect that I now stood condemned out of my own mouth, and that it was common soldiers who were bearing the brunt of the present fearful struggle while accomplished authors skulked at home in their easy-chairs, embellishing with literary touch and finish the work of honester hands.

At this I gave it up. In the Society jottings of that evening's papers I caused it be announced that I had left the country for Paris in charge of a body of voluntary workers, who would, it was hoped, be allowed to proceed to the front for the purpose of reading the works of Mr. Charles Garvice[15] to overwrought hospital nurses at the various bases, and that letters would not be forwarded. But if I imagined thus to escape from the consequences of my careless yarn-spinning, I was doomed to bitter disappointment, for the first thing I read in the French newspapers was a paragraph in which it was stated that the celebrated author of "The Showmen" would arrive at the Gare du Nord that night, "his mission being," continued the paragraphist, "to discover and, if possible, have speech with the angel of his famous story." "We have no doubt whatever," ran a gallant comment, "that in a city like Paris, M. So-and-so (meaning me) is sure to succeed in his quest, but if, perchance, he should fail, it seems to us that he may return confidently to Londres, which, as we have always understood, is a city of angels."

Later that self-same evening the representative of a famous cinematograph firm called upon me at my hotel to tell me that his principals were prepared to pay me £10,000 in advance of royalties on the film rights of my story, provided that I would deliver the angel (strongly bound) at their studios in Provence. I said that if they cared to cough up a couple of thou. as a guarantee of good faith, I would see what could be done.

As the present introduction will soon be as long as Mr. Arthur Machen's, I may deal summarily with a few further important points. It should be observed that both the private soldiers in my story are Yorkshiremen. The casual reviewer may conceivably jump to the conclusion that in this regard I derive myself in some degree from Mr. Kipling,[16] who has a Yorkshire soldier in certain of his stories. But I would respectfully urge that while Mr. Kipling give us only one Yorkshire soldier, I, being perhaps of a less parsimonious disposition, have treated my county and the British public to two. I would also mention that Yorkshire enjoys a world-wide reputation as the county of broad acres and pretty women. There are certainly more acres in Yorkshire than there are words in the Bible and more pretty women than there are letters. But I never saw a winged angel there in my life—excepting once at a pantomime, and she was the daughter of a pork butcher who sold excellent sausages and noble raised pies at his handsome shop or emporium in Meadow Lane, Leeds.

With all of which facts at your disposal, you will conclude, if you are a reasonable being, that my story "The Showmen," is, as I have said, a pure exercise in invention—a figment or fantasy of a playful, if considerably disordered, imagination, and not for one moment to be reckoned among those great, and it may be small, things which we call truth.

And lastly, for the benefit of the scoffers and to eke out another introductory page or two, I should like to say that for a single glimpse of a real angel with wings and a long trumpet—such an angel, possibly, as rolled the stone away, or even such an angel as drove foolish Adam and weeping Eve out of Paradise—I would give the eyes out of my head, or, for that matter, as Mr. Stacpoole[17] has it, "all the wives I have not married." William Blake[18] publicly confessed that he had seen a tree full of angels at Hampstead, and I once thought I saw a churchful of them in the by no means over-holy city of Nice. But I didn't know William Blake to speak to, and I am very uncertain about angels at Nice. I expect plenty of people feel as I feel in respect of angels generally. Every one of us wants just a single glimpse of them. Then we would cease from publishing shilling books, and go to mass with Mr. Machen like good little children. And in the night I think we would all of us, rich and poor, old and young, strong and feeble, put on a sort of spiritual khaki and stream forth somehow to Flanders and the Argonne and there so shine upon and frighten the Germans that they would run shrieking to their black fastnesses across the Rhine, and never come out again till the Day of Judgment.

And it may be—and this is the best wish I can wish them—that perhaps all soldiers (on our side) do see a real angel before they die.

The Showmen: A Legend of the War

Private William Sweets and Private John Henry Cheese, familiarly known and relished as "Sweets and Cheese"; both homely soldiers; both, prior to the war, concerned together in the useful if humble avocation of "professional busking"; both from Yorkshire, and both passionately devoted to harmony and beer.

Fate has delivered one of her nastiest slaps at Privates Sweets and Cheese, for they are lying in a Flanders ditch, where they have been left for dead after an affair of bayonets v. liquid fire, chlorine gas, portable machine guns and so forth. Private Sweets has a hole in his chest through which you could put your fist. Cheese is beautifully shattered about the thigh, and not quite sure whether he has lost one eye or two. They are soaked to the skin with drizzle and ditch-water. Their hands and faces are sticky with blood. Over them is nothing but the Flanders dark (and in spite of reports to the contrary it can be fairly dark in Flanders), and round them nothing but stillness and blackness; though, very far away they can hear the desultory booming of guns.

This is the thirty-sixth hour of their sojourn in the ditch. Thirty-six hours ago they were fit as fiddles, and, according to Cheese, "didn't care a damn for the cat."[19] Now—well, Private Sweets has, delicately and with much beating about the bush, just confided to Private Cheese his belief and conviction that their "numbers are up" and that neither of them "will ever see Low Moor any more."

Such an announcement coming from one military gentleman to another naturally provokes ribaldry in the other. And when a Yorkshireman wants to be ribald with a person who talks about dying, he invariably says, "Well, I hope you'll die a blanky good colour," a remark which by common Yorkshire consent represents the height of punning waggery, not to say humorous disdain. This is what Private Cheese said to Private Sweets. He also told Private Sweets with some emphasis (*a*) that he was worse than Lloyd George[20]; (*b*) that cocking one's clogs (Anglice "departing this life") miserably in ditches was no job for Yorkshire lads; (*c*) that if Private Sweets did so far forget himself as to die, he, Private Cheese, was damned if he would ever speak to him again.

But in his heart of hearts Private Cheese knew that both of them were hard set. Having pushed them thus roughly into the tight place, it was even betting that the order of things might finish them clean off, merely for fun as it were.

B-rr! Private Cheese did not like it.

By a sort of blind instinct, however, he kept talking to, and at, Private Sweets. "What about Jane Lizzie? A grand lass Jane Lizzie, and tha wert a blanky fool not to marry her before tha started. But she'll be waitin' for thee a t'station, when we get home, I'll be bound! And there's thi mother. I had to promise her I'd bring thee back safe and sound before she'd let tha 'list. Poor owd girl! A promise is a promise, isn't it Bill? and I shouldn't look to a lad like thee to let a'body down. Then there's t'business. Damn it man, there's t'business. By gum, what a time we shall be having next season at Blackpool, or if tha likes, Moorcum, or t' Isle o'Man!—'Return visit of Sweets and Cheese,' 'Direct from the Trenches,' 'Sweets' Soldier Songs,' 'Witty Wheezes from the War,' 'Cheerful Cheese Chirrups Coolness under Fire,' ''Ero Sweets on the old original Mouth Organ!' I wish we was at it *now*, Bill—dang me if I don't!

'Whiter than the whitewash on the wall,
'Whiter than the whitewash on the wall,
'Wash me in the water where you wash your dirty daughter
'I'll be whiter than the whitewash on the wall!'"[21]

Private Cheese positively sang aloud in his enthusiasm.

Private Sweets was stirred, after a fashion. Jane Lizzie, and his mother and the business! He did his best to join with Private Cheese in his fantastic and unholy vocalism; but there was something in his voice which frightened Private Cheese, who stopped singing and reaching out his hand, put it on Private Sweets' soggy tunic.

"Bill," he said, "I know, lad—I'll tell 'em at home, Bill. I'll give 'em thy love.... Say tha' prayers, Bill. Say 'Our Father which art in....' Bill! ... Bill!!"

Then something really happened.

There were the sea, the sands, and the summer sunshine, and crowds of little children with spades and buckets, and some old ladies in deck chairs, and a stout gentleman with a panama hat over his eyes lying full length by the old ladies. And Private Cheese became suddenly conscious that his face was blackened and that he wore a silly little straw hat, and that Private Sweets, whose face was also blackened and who wore a brim with no hat, was struggling valiantly with a fierce and wheezy harmonium, and that he, Cheese, was roaring at the top of his voice a beautiful new song which appeared to tickle everybody to death, and which he sang and sang over and over again and did not get tired of.

And all the time the crowd was growing bigger and bigger and he could see moving among the people a wonderful young woman whom he had never seen before. Tall and white was this stranger, with a white gown which fluttered in the breeze, and glistened to the sun as though it were made of silk shot with silver, and she was collecting money from the crowd in a big shell. And everybody seemed to give, and presently she came to Private Cheese, with a shining smile, and emptied the shell into his hands. And he took off his foolish little hat and said "Thank you very kindly, Miss." And the lady in white smiled again and turned to go, and as she turned, Private Cheese noticed that her feet were bare and very white and shining, and that beneath her robe were the points of golden wings. And he called to Private Sweets, "Bill, look, look!" And Bill said, "Yes, I see. *It's only a angel!*"

In a cowshed at the back of a ruined farm, which according to Eye-Witness had been taken by the Germans and retaken by the English a dozen times, sits Lieutenant Swift of the R.A.M.C.,[22] smoking an inferior brand of cigarettes, lately looted from an enemy trench.

Before him stand Private Sweets and Cheese, very ragged, very grimy and wet, and, if the truth must be told, a trifle nervy and shame-faced.

"What's all this damned nonsense?" rasps the Lieutenant. "You fellows ought to be bally well ashamed of yourselves, skulking in filthy ditches till the trouble's over and then coming here with your cock-and-bull taradiddles. You're a disgrace to the British Army. I'm not so sure you didn't ought to be shot out of hand. Now, you first, Cheese; own up, and get done with it."

Private Cheese clears his throat after the manner of a man who must lie or die, and replies:

"All I have to say, sir, is that it's true, so 'elp the British Army!"

And for his part Private Sweets, without invitation, remarks, "I didn't see her myself, sir, but John Henry has the money, and my wound's healed and so is John Henry's."

"Rats!" snaps the Lieutenant. "You are a pair of bally funkers!"

"But here's the money, sir," argues Private Cheese, producing from his pockets handfuls of coppers intermixed with threepenny bits and sixpences.

"And here's the blood all over us, sir, and here's the healed place on my chest, sir," adds Private Sweets, ripping open his tunic.

Lieutenant Swift knows a newly-healed wound when he sees one, and he perceives that Private Sweets has had it pretty stiff somehow. But his experience of soldiermen's excuses has induced in him an abounding caution. On the other hand there is no getting over Private Sweets' wound. For once in his life the Lieutenant is puzzled. But a bright idea strikes him. In a voice of thunder he says: "*You will be kept in custody till the state of your minds can be inquired into.* Right about turn. Quick march!"

And Privates Sweets and Cheese go stolidly off with a Corporal, who, twenty yards from the "office," throws himself down and rolls on the ground in an uncontrollable fit of laughter.

The Showmen and Other Wonders: By "The West-Ender"

There was a journalist—readers of the higher critical weeklies may remember the initials of his name; I never can—who lately sat down to write a story.

I say "sat down to write a story," though I believe the journalist I have in mind never sits down to anything, unless it be trouble. Anyway he started in, or began, or commenced, to write a story. Of course it had to be about the war. Stories about anything else are not wanted at the moment, and what is not wanted at the moment is obviously no good. So the story had to be about the war. And the journalist made a story with two soldiers and an angel in it. The soldiers were put in because it is difficult to write stories about the war without mentioning soldiers, and the angel was put in for luck, pretty much on the principle which induces kindly housewives to put half a sovereign in a Christmas pudding.

The journalist said he made up the story by himself, and that he sat down or stood up manfully, and wrote it out of his head; which I can well believe, because he says himself that his story is "nothing." However, he wrote the story out of his head—didn't borrow it from Maupassant,[23] or Kipling,[24] or Lewis Sydney,[25] or anybody, and didn't have it told him by a postman who has an uncle at the War Office, or a parlourmaid who has a young man who is sure to get the V.C. one of these days.

Well, the journalist wrote his story out of his own head, as I keep on saying, and, strange as it may seem (or let us say, *mirabile dictu*), "others" will have it that he did nothing of the kind. "Others," whoever they may be, aver that the things in the story must really have happened. For example, I remember a clergyman, whose credit was so good that the tradespeople never sent him any bills, who told the journalist to his face that he was a wicked man to pretend he had written the story out of his head, when it was common knowledge and all up and down the front that Private Sweets and Private Cheese had really and truly been assisted by an angel as they lay in a ditch grievously hut, and trying to cheer each other up with snatches of popular melody.

For my part I know he wrote "The Showmen" out of his head, because I actually saw him at the detestable and pernicious job of doing it. You may take it from me that writing stories, especially about the war, is a detestable and pernicious job. It looks easy, but it makes even strong men sweat. I hope you have all heard about the famous actor who, after playing the part of Hamlet for the first time, came off the stage in a high state of perspiration and said to Charles Brookfield,[26] "What do you think of my Hamlet, Charles?" To which Brookfield replied, "Very fine, dear boy, and" (looking him up and down) "your skin appears to act splendidly too."

Well, the journalist's skin acted quite splendidly during the six hours he expended over that story; and when you mention it to him now his skin acts with greater splendor still. For, as bad luck will have it, the tale has proved nothing more nor less than the bane of the poor fellow's life. True, it is selling at the rate of 3000 copies per diem, and if it isn't, it isn't his fault; true, he draws wonderful royalties from it,[27] and gets his name printed in all the parish magazines. But what are royalties and parish magazines to a soul in pain, or a spirit wracked with fearful and gnawing doubts, not to mention bitter regrets?

Good people, do you know, that this excellent man, who sat down to write a story out of his own head and for the perfectly legitimate purpose of earning an honest shilling (an exceedingly rare thing among journalists, by the way), do you know that this good, great and innocent man has been so pestered and harassed by the persistent attacks of people who know of their own knowledge that the story of "The Showmen" is true, that he is actually beginning to believe they may be right when they call him a liar?

Isn't it terrible? This sensitive person of genius, a poet easily the equal of the author of the "Fireman's Wedding,"[28] and whose work has been proclaimed by no less an authority than C.K.S. of the *Sphere*[29] to be worthy of a place in any anthology, a prose man, too, of distinction, as witness his recent brilliant articles on "Conscription and Sleeping Out" in the *Embankment Times*,[30] a kindly, inoffensive, slow-lunching wight, once as cheerful as the morning and gay as a linnet, till quarter day came round, now goes about under a sinister cloud, suffering from the benumbing consciousness that while he knows and I know that he wrote "The Showmen" clean slap-bang out of his head and out of nothing else, there are hundreds, nay thousands of his fellow creatures who think they know better than both of us, and don't scruple to tell us so.

Again I ask, isn't it terrible? Psychologically of course, the affair is most interesting—though that doesn't appreciably assist my poor friend. But for the comfort of himself and the enlightenment of the town, I will reveal here and now the true psychological inwardness of the situation. When I was at Oxford they made me read some fellow called Butler, not the "Erewhon" man,[31] but another—a bishop, if I remember rightly.[32] This fellow appeared to me to be a fearfully involved rhetorician, but there was a considerable substratum of shrewd sense in him. One of the things he said was this: "Men readily believe what they wish to believe."[33]

I am not sure I have got the words right, and perhaps it wasn't Butler who wrote them. It may have been Paley[34] or Plato[35]; one dabbles in any old author when one is young. But the sense is there, I trust. And really this phrase of Butler, or Paley, or Plato, or somebody else, applied as I now apply it to this matter of "The Showmen," is not only most apposite but extremely flattering to our British manhood. People believe in the real existence of the angel in "The Showmen" because they desire strongly to believe in it. We are commonly supposed to be a nation of so materialistic a turn of mind that the dirtiest little fact is worth rubies to us, while we dismiss the most glorious imaginative or spiritual truth as being of less value than a tinker's damn [sic].

You go to a man of business—there are always plenty at hand in war time—and tell him you want to borrow a five-pound note on the strength of your possessions in the stars, which, let me tell you, are the only things you really do possess, though you may not know it. What will the businessman do? As likely as not he will say you are trying to blackmail him, and threaten to ring up the police. But ask him to lend you a trifle on your gold watch or the diamond ring your wife gave you on your birthday and he will produce a fifth of the probable value without a murmur.

And yet it is this same business man, this Englishman if you like, who is determined to believe in my poor friend's unfortunate angel, and insists on believing in her, no matter if the heavens fall and it thunder to the tune of "Keep the Home Fires Burning."[36] And between ourselves, I like him for it. To say the least it shows he has a good spirit, and shows also that the teaching which those of us who were fortunate got at our mother's knees has not been wasted. More than that, it shows that, deep down, we are actually not business men at all, but keen on angels and the bright and kind and happy and innocent things which angels mean for us when we think about them properly.

So that my journalist friend must do his best to bear up. Despite his fame and his royalties he is a martyr if ever there was one. Of its essence martyrdom is nothing but sheer triumph, and my friend has triumphed indeed. Let him carry himself erect amongst us as of yore. Let him take our doubts about "his own head" in good part. Let him reflect that unless his angel did indeed and in fact appear to Private Cheese and help him and his friend Sweets out of their sore plight, we are most of us undone, and worse than undone.

There is not a soldier's wife, or a soldier's mother in England who doesn't overtly or covertly believe in the existence of angels. It is an angel who brings the boy back perhaps hurt and maimed—but back. It is an angel that goes with him from Waterloo platform to his death, and makes that death an honour to himself and a glory to his country, and tolerable and even beautiful to those who loved him. If it were not for angels no woman would ever say "Go." And if it were not for angels, no man who has seen another man blown into a crimson mist with bits of rag in it would ever fight again.

Let us keep our weather eye open for angels. Perhaps one day we might see them. Up to now only the men at the front, and possibly a few unhonoured saints at home have seen one. I am told they are very good to look on, and I should judge by all accounts that it is worth waiting and suffering and being patient a long time ultimately to compass such a sight.

Appendix I: P. C. Grubb and the Old Lady

Not the least entertaining of an astonishing series of events in regard to "The Showmen" has been the extraordinary episode of Police-Constable Grubb of the XYZ Division and the elderly lady. Grubb is, or was, a police officer of seventeen years' standing in the Potromelitan force. A man of fine presence and dignified manner, his superiors have taken something of a pride in keeping him on what is known as point duty. Day by day, summer and winter, year in and year out, he has commanded the traffic at one of the most dangerous "crossings" or "circuses" in our mighty cosmopolis.

In the whole period of his service there had never been a complaint or a black mark against him. Like many another competent man, he has repeatedly refused promotion, because he believed that his usefulness lay in one direction and one direction only. At "the point" he felt himself to be in his element, and "at the point" he steadfastly remained till the other day. A tolerant and complacent observer of human nature, and not averse from a quiet joke, Grubb enjoyed the respect and confidence of all sorts and conditions of people. He had faith in two things—duty and civility. "Duty," he once finely said, "must be done, and civility costs nothing." Beneath this simple and perhaps commonplace philosophy, however, he concealed a kindness of heart and an inclination to unostentatious philanthropy, which are not commonly associated with policemen.

As a matter of fact police constables and retired colonels are really the most sentimental people in the world. The general public is unaware of this importance circumstance, but it is nevertheless true. If ever you lose your purse in a part of London where you have no acquaintance, and you desire the immediate use of small money, go straight to the nearest policeman. No matter how ridiculous your situation, you will find in him a respectful listener and an unassuming Samaritan. In certain accidental difficulties which may overtake you once in a lifetime, you will be better treated by a policeman than you would be by a millionaire. I speak from knowledge, having tried both.

And if ever you happen to be editing a newspaper and you want some passable "lovey-dovey" verses wherewith to please your lady readers, write at once to any colonel on the retired list. By first post next morning, if not by special messenger same day, you will receive a bushel of the real article rhymed and finished to a "t"—and not a penny to pay, unless you like to send a cheque for the easing of your conscience.

However, to return to P.C. Grubb. His kindness of heart, coupled perhaps with his innocent turn for a harmless jest, brought him to the one trouble of his life. On the Wednesday morning after the publication of my famous story, an old lady who happened to have read it, and indeed was carrying in her hand a copy of the book, approached Constable Grubb and asked him if he would be kind enough to tell her how to get to Highbury. It so happened that short of taxi-cabs, which are said to be expensive, the best way from Grubb's point to Highbury is to take a 'bus bound for the Elephant and Castle and change at Ludgate Circus into a 'bus which passes the Angel Hotel at Islington.

Constable Grubb had been asked the way to Highbury many a time and oft before my old lady swam into his ken so to speak, and more or less subconsciously, he had elaborated a kind of joke about it, the which joke he delighted to fire off on those comparatively infrequent pilgrims who desired to travel Highburywards. So that when my dear old dame put her perfectly prompt question, Grubb had his answer prompt and pat:

"Yes, madam," he remarked, with a bland smile, "the best way to get to Highbury is to get into an Elephant and change into an Angel at Ludgate Circus." And then he laughed, as who should say, "Now that's really funny, isn't it?"

But the old lady, whose mind was running somewhat on angels, and who didn't know that for the saving of his breath your proper Cockney calls an Elephant and Castle 'bus an "Elephant," and an Angel at Islington 'bus an "Angel"; yet did know that she carried in her hand a copy of "The Showmen," jumped to the, perhaps, not unnatural conclusion that in answering her as he had done, Police Constable Grubb was endeavouring to be waggish at her expense, or as the vulgar have it, "trying to take a rise out of her."

She turned "The Showmen" picture-side to her flurried bosom, and demanded to know the constable's number. "I shall report you for incivility," she told him; and hurrying to the pavement passed into the crowd of pedestrians.

Police Constable Grubb was cut to the quick, by what seemed to him her altogether inexplicable asperity. He would have explained if she had given him time to open his mouth; and he could not follow her on to the pavement, because the traffic was just then pretty heavy and "duty must be done." So he made a note of the occurrence in that wonderful pocketbook, and with that hunk of stubby pencil a policeman always carries, and reflected that "some females are rummy goes," and that it behoves even the most experienced officer to exercise unremitting caution in his dealings with the public; and so dismissed the matter from his mind. But my old lady, who by the way was an old lady of a certain consequence, did not dismiss it from her mind. On the contrary, she wrote at great and indignant length, on paper headed Belgrave Square, to P.C. Grubb's superiors; with the unfortunate result that, for the first time in his life, P.C. Grubb was hauled over the coals at headquarters.

Discipline is a thing which no unbiased layman can ever hope to understand. It is a thing of cut-and-dried rule and rote, tied up with plenty of red tape; no doubt useful and necessary in its place, but sometimes bearing more than heavily on entirely well-intentioned persons. And it fell out that P.C. Grubb was held by Discipline to have transgressed. He admitted the bald facts set forward in his accuser's letter. He admitted that she was a just old lady and had given a truthful account of her question and his answer. He denied that he had seen the book in the lady's hand—at any rate "to know that it was a book about angels," and he admitted that his answer was couched in terms which might be considered witty, though it was an answer he said which he had bestowed on inquirers for years without offence, and for that matter with occasional twinkles and winks of appreciation. And he pointed out that it was the standing and common joke of the "point" and so well known that it had been appropriated and printed by one of the comic journals.

To all of which, Discipline listened with stern brows and uncompromising tickings-off of passages in the accusation; ultimately informing P.C. Grubb (1) that he had exceeded his duty by being unduly familiar in his tone and manner of speech to a female member of the public; (2) that as an intelligent officer he ought to have had eyes enough to see what manner of book the lady was carrying; (3) that he must apologize to her; and (4) that he would be advised further as to his fate when the matter had been considered by a higher authority.

Now P.C. Grubb was in full possession of the free and proud spirit of the man who has always managed to preserve a clean slate; also he had money in the War Loan and a nice house with a bit of garden at Kensington. Wherefore, in a fit of desperation and outraged *amour propre*, he took the bull by the Horns, so to say, and resigned from the force, of which he had been an ornament and example for so many happy years. His comrades got up on his behalf the usual testimonial and illuminated address, to which the authorities and many admirers in the City liberally subscribed, and with the purse of sovereigns which was handed to him on the presentation, he was also made the recipient of a handsomely bound copy of "The Showmen"; wherein he subsequently begged of me to do him the favour to write my name "as a memento of the occasion." This I did, placing above my signature the following garblement by a famous feminine poet.

Laugh and the world laughs with you,
More often than not.[37]
Rather neat, eh?

Appendix II

My reason begins to rock upon its throne. As these bright sheets are passing to the press a provincial journal, which shall be nameless, rushes into print with the appended affidavit. The blanks are a tribute to the Censor.

I, Thomas Henry Cheese, a private in the King's Own Royal Bombardiers, commonly known as "The Devil's Own Boys," "The Pill Pushers" and "The German Perils," make oath and say as follows:

(1) I enlisted in the aforesaid regiment on the ... day of ... 1914.

(2) In pursuance of orders I subsequently proceeded to—in Flanders and was there wounded in the thigh and also over the left brow, probably by shrapnel.

(3) In consequence of these wounds I became unconscious.

(4) On regaining my senses I found myself lying in a wet ditch side by side with Private William Sweets of the gallant regiment above named, who informed me that he had received a bad wound in the chest, and was about to hand in his checks.

(5) The said Private William Sweets and I had been friends before the war, and were for some years associated together in business as professional buskers or seaside minstrels under the well-known style and title of "Sweets and Cheese."

(6) For the purpose of cheering Sweets in his last moments, and putting a little spirit into him, I reminded him *inter alia* of our business connexion, and sang to him various ditties, including "Whiter than the Whitewash on the Wall," which had been highly popular in the trenches during our service there.

(7) Sweets endeavoured to join with me in the chorus of the aforesaid vocal exercise, but collapsed from exhaustion.

(8) I declare that immediately thereupon, I had a vision of the English foreshore, and saw there a crowd of holiday makers, in the midst of whom I sang a

new song, the words of which I am unable to remember. My face was blacked and I wore the ordinary habiliments of my profession. Sweets, whose face was also blacked and who was arrayed in similar garb to my own, played an accompaniment for me on a portable harmonium.

(9) I declare that while I sang and Sweets played, a young lady dressed in white, who, to the best of my knowledge, recollection and belief I had never previously seen, went round among the crowd with a shell, in which she collected monetary offerings.

(10) This money she brought to me, and I thanked her for it. As she turned to go away, I noticed that she had very white and shining feet, and that the tips of two golden wings protruded from beneath her cloak or robe. I shouted to Sweets, "Look Bill, look!" or words to that effect. And Sweets replied, "I see her. It's only an angel," or words to that effect.

(11) When the vision disappeared Sweets and I both stood up in the ditch. Our wounds were healed, though our clothes were still covered with blood. In the pockets of my trousers I found a good deal of English money, which I declare had not been there before, namely and to wit, £1 19s. 1½d. in bronze, 13s in sixpences, and 6s 9d in threepenny bits. There were no buttons.

(12) I told Sweets what had happened, and while he said that he had not seen the lady, he had no doubt whatever about the money, which he helped me to count, biting the sixpences and threepenny bits with his teeth to make sure they were good.

(13) We afterwards made our way across country, and coming across a British outpost, were taken before Lieutenant Swift, an officer of the R. A. M. C., to whom we told our story.

(14) The said Lieutenant Swift ordered us to be kept in custody until the state of our minds could be inquired into.

(15) Some days later we were examined by the Army doctors and pronounced to be sane. We were also certified to have been seriously wounded, but now fit for service. We were sent again to the trenches, where, unfortunately, Sweets was killed, and I myself received further wounds from which I am at present recovering.

(16) I wrote an account of these circumstances in the form of a letter to my parents, but I am informed and verily believe that the said letter was not received by them, and was lost in the post.

John Henry Cheese

(17) Sworn before me ... a Commissioner for Oaths in the day ... of ... 1915.

On perusing this document I at once entrained for Yorkshire, and proceeding to the office of the solicitors, desired to be informed of the whereabouts of Private John Henry Cheese. The solicitor said that Cheese had left their establishment immediately after swearing the affidavit. On inquiry at the local newspaper office I was given Cheese's address and went to visit him in a hired motor-car. On the road the car broke down, and repairing to a local tavern, where I chanced to speak about Cheese with the landlord, I was informed that Mr. Cheese was at that moment in the bar taking half a pint with his friends. I went into the bar and spoke to him, telling him who I was, and that I should like a little private conversation with him. He thereupon became very abusive and said that he was "fed up" with newspaper men, and that if I didn't go away, he would give me the biggest hiding I ever had in my life. Perceiving that he was fully capable of carrying out his threat, I left, and was subsequently informed by the recruiting authority of the district, that though Cheese had indeed offered himself for service, he had been rejected on account of a physical defect, and that if I wanted to know more about him, I had better see the proprietor of the Angel Hotel where the man had formerly been employed in the humble capacity of "boots."

And there, dear reader, so far as Cheese is concerned, we may let this curious matter drop. I am inwardly satisfied; though, as one might say, a good deal shaken in my view of human nature, never at any time too rapturously rosy. My story, "The Showmen," stands for what it is worth, and will so stand till it is forgotten. I have just received from the publishers a translation of it in Yiddish with a foreword by an eminent Rabbi.

This gentleman, though obviously possessed of literary and perceptive powers beyond the ordinary, stumbles into the old, old pitfall.

"I cannot help thinking," says he, "that the author of 'The Showmen' has not been altogether frank with us. He tells us that he invented this beautiful story, and that the persons mentioned in it, and particularly the Angel, are simple figments or fictional figures created 'out of his head,' and real only so far as they appeal to the imagination. I wonder if by any chance the talented author happens at any time to have come into contact with a well-known and highly respectable tradesman of our community of the name of Angell. This worthy man, a glazier by profession, visits periodically all parts of London in pursuance of his calling, and may easily have mended windows either for the author of 'The Showmen' or his friends.

"It is no reflection on Angell to say that he is fond of talk and wonderfully proud of his boy Izzy, who, as we are all aware, enlisted in the 51st Highland (Kilted) Brigade with his friend Solly Suett (a cognomen, by the way, which might readily be corrupted into Sweets), and on returning covered with honourable scars, was found to possess a great deal more English money than he started with. Izzy asserts that both he and Solly were wounded in the same trench on the eve of the Shaboth, but that on the next morning they found themselves miraculously recovered from their hurts and their pockets heavily laden with copper and small silver coins. Certainly it is not within my knowledge that Izzy and Solly went 'busking' together, though they are both ambitious members of our dramatic Club. But Angell, Suett (or Sweets) and Izzy—the bare names are philologically suggestive! 'Tizzy,' I am informed, is a cant name for 'sixpence' in common use among pedlars and travelling *Showmen*. My only real trouble is the surname 'Cheese.' The nearest I can get to it, is the substantive 'shiksa,' which is our word for a young lady or 'flapper,' and brings us again close to Angels. And I once heard Izzy tell his father to 'cheese it' when he wished to hint that the old man should stop talking.

"However these things may be, we have to thank the Author of this story for so kindly bestowing upon us the rights of translation without charge or fee, and if out of a misguided modesty he has attributed to his own inventiveness something which is the rightful property of the Jewish race, we may content ourselves with the observation that Israel has forgiven the Gentile for so much that she can well afford to forgive him for just a little bit more."

Upon which I am constrained to remark, in the words of the poet, S-O double L-O-M-A-N spells Solomon.[38]

Appendix III

While the press was still waiting for the foregoing pages I received the following cable by wireless, via New York and Berlin:

> Have captured Angel. Can deliver her f.o.b.[39] and passage money paid, port you name, for ten thousand dollars. Wire anything doing.—Long Dick Kalamazoo, Buffalo County, U.S.A.

I have telegraphed to the cinema people in Paris, and we shall see what happens. Of course, Long Dick's angel cannot be mine, but she might do.

Certainly the Americans are an enterprising people, if a trifle "proud."

Appendix IV

The book is not yet full. People requires o much for their money nowadays! So we must e'en go on. My wife has just read the proofsheets of my introduction. I expected her to be pleased, but she isn't. In point of fact, the fat is in the fire. She is upstairs now, thrumming out on our old piano—a wedding present of, ah! so many years ago—"Every morn I bring thee violets."[40] Of course, of course, of course! The poor dear has rumbled that stupid passage of mine about the charming young lady to whom I send violets fresh from Piccadilly Circus every morning. Foolish child! When will our unfortunate better halves learn that we jackasses who write must keep on saying silly things about ourselves or perish? The charming young lady of the violets is pure fantasy. I put her in solely to liven up the introduction, just as I put the angel into "The Showmen" to liven up the reading world.

And now my angel in the house is playing "I'll never get married again."[41] By which, of course, she means that she has made a note of Stacpoole's useful line about "all the wives I have not married."[42] The trope, the metaphor, and the quotation are treacherous affairs, and Art—well, Art is the natural born enemy of domesticity. I shall have to "explain," and I hate explaining.

It is the fault of life that everything about it can be explained. And the happiest and most successful people are good explainers. Consider Mr. Belloc explaining the war,[43] and be wise. Consider Mr. Lovat Fraser[44] explaining Mr. Belloc and be wiser still. I remember seeing in one of the illustrated weeklies the portrait of a harmless-looking person in evening dress pointing with a long stick to a blackboard. And underneath, the editor—good, easy man—had printed these words: "Portrait of Professor So-and-so explaining the Riddle of the Universe." This was a serious caption to a serious picture in a serious paper, and I have worshipped that editor ever since. He will review "The Showmen," and do it handsomely while he is about it. And if he explains it, nobody will be better pleased or more greatly edified than myself.

Other things being equal in the way of reward, remuneration and emolument, I could explain it myself—in a work of thirteen octavo volumes. The more I think about it the surer I am that "The Showmen" is a story of profound significance and entirely deserving of thorough explanation. Any story or other literary product which has gripped the public by the heart-strings is worthy of explanation. There is the world-famous song "Tipperary,"[45] for example. For a whole year all England has lived and died to it. The way of a ship at sea, of an eagle in the air, and of a man with a maid,[46] puzzled one of the noblest minds, but what would that mind have thought about "Tipperary" in its relation to Armageddon? There are subtle undercurrents of relativity which pull one up aghast at times.

Just now the ha'penny press of this great country is hard at work explaining Charlie Chaplin.[47] I can explain him in a phrase. He is a showman. Most persons of consequence, from Mr. C. B. Cochran[48] to Mr. Lloyd George,[49] can be explained handily in this way. I once tried, and, as I think, nearly succeeded in explaining "In the Shadows" to Mr. Herman Finck.[50] When the tide of national affairs serves, I will explain Mr. E. V. Lucas[51] to Mr. Albert de Courville[52] and Mr. Frank Harris[53] to Lord Kitchener,[54] who, I am sure will do me the honour to like "The Showmen." Meanwhile I must explain to my only angel upstairs that "charming young lady" who doesn't get the violets, and Mr. Stacpoole's "wives I have not married."

Which, as everybody who is acquainted with the prevailing trend of feminine thought will agree, may or may not require a bit of doing.

Appendix V

The printers have sent along to say that still further manuscript is required. Desperate ills need desperate remedies. I have just dispatched a swift maid-of-all-work with a shilling to the Tube bookstall to purchase a copy of Mr. Harold Begbie's chaste volume "On the Side of the Angels."

Mr. Begbie is a poet. He wrote:

> Oh, no, I wasn't the first to go,
> But I went, thank God, I went.[55]

These immortal lines (I hope I have quoted them correctly) are said to have caught the eye of Lord Kitchener, who saw in them great possibilities for what may be termed recruiting by mural advertisement. The result, need one say?—is Kitchener's Army. Great oaks from little acorns grow. If anybody had told the late Field-Marshal the Duke of Wellington[56] or the equally late Admiral Lord Nelson[57] that a British Army, of the Kaiser[58] doesn't know how many million hefty fellows, would one day be recruited with the assistance of poetry stuck on the walls, they would have said, "Shipton, thou should'st be living at this hour"[59]—or, in a word, "Bosh!" Yet I happen to know that the Iron Duke[60] was himself a bit of a poet, and everybody knows that Horatio Nelson, whose very name sounds like an Iliad, wrote better prose prayers than the Archbishop of Canterbury. The Duke of Wellington might have cursed somewhat over "The Showmen," but I am morally convinced that Nelson would have taken to it as a duck takes to water. He had an eye for an angel, Nelson had. When I get a chance I am going to secrete a copy of "The Showmen" in the finest laurel-wreath I can afford to buy, and put it on his monument in Trafalgar Square for the sake of the *réclame*.

But to get back to Mr. Begbie. He has undoubtedly accomplished, or helped to accomplish, absolute marvels for this England of ours. Wellington (or was it Nelson?) used to shout for "the sweepings of the gaols" when he wanted fighting men. Not so Lord Kitchener. "Give me men," says he, "who are stirred by the divine cadences of 'I went, thank God, I went,' and who can appreciate the palpable dying fall in 'Good-bye, Piccadilly; *Good*-bye, Leicester Square.'"[61] And he gets them—without compulsion and by the tens of hundreds of thousands.

I am not quizzing or sneering or writing with my tongue in my cheek. I mean what I say. These are high and solemn matters, even though we take them cheerfully, and it may seem humorously; and I tell you that, in spite of all the slaughter and bloodshed and sacrifice, the dead young boys, the maimed hard men who have looked at death as eagles look at the sun, the anguished women, the sorrow and the mourning, we are living in the finest world that the best of us ever deserved to live in. We must never say a word in mitigation or condonation of the wickedness of the Germans, and we must never say a word that might be construed into the smallest hint of mercy for them; but if such a word could be said, we might say that we owe them a sort of gratitude, inasmuch as their evil has lifted up our good and their devilries have brought us nearer and closer to our angels. For if there be not angels at the back of all these great happenings I am a neutral, tea-smuggling, Zeppelin-spying Dutchman and not worthy to have my name written on the National Register.

And once more to get back to Mr. Begbie, whom I am trying my hardest to congratulate on, "I went, thank God, I went," though it is very difficult: his book has arrived, and we shall now proceed to compose a further excellent chapter called "The Other Side of the Angels," a parody of a poem of Mr. Rudyard Kipling[62] and a postscript to "The Showmen," which together, it is hoped, will about fill the bill.

The Other Side of the Angels

Mr. Harold Begbie has done for Mr. Machen and the British public exactly what was required to be done. He has taken the shine out of Mr. Machen, and left the British public in triumphant possession of the shine of the angels at Mons, and all the other angels. I for one thank him from the bottom of my heart.

But Mr. Begbie says nothing about my own particular angel—that is to say the Angel in "The Showmen." This is not exactly neglectful of him, as he may not yet have heard of her. But when he does read my beautiful story, as he doubtless will after concluding his voyages and travels on the Thames, I trust that he will oblige us with a small treatise about her. She is worth it. If ever an angel clamoured to be expounded and exegised and supported with evidence, mine is the Angel. Mr. Begbie is just the man for the work. His exegesis is powerful, and he is the finest hand at evidence I remember to have encountered.[63] He also knows about telepathy and visions, and people revisiting the glimpses of the moon after they have died. What could he not do with my beautiful story, "The Showmen," if he would only try?

But if he does try, I beg that he will remember that I am quite a different pair of horses from Mr. Machen. I am neither a High Churchman, nor an authority on the Fathers; but a plain blunt Methodist with a faith which, though a comparative failure as a remover of mountains, has at any rate prevented me from writing for the *Evening News*. Also I have never thought that "the average Church, considered as a house of preaching, is a much more poisonous place than the average tavern." I know all about preachers, having been nurtured in the business, and I will back myself to know as much about taverns as Mr. Machen does; but I also know something about "push and go" newspaper offices; and it is precisely this knowledge which has prompted me to write "The Showmen"—a really beautiful story, as everybody must admit.

Mr. Begbie calls his book "On the Side of the Angels," and I have called this Appendix "The Other Side of the Angels," because angels have another side. I met a man the other day who was selling roses out of a basket, and, among other things, he told me that on Chobham heights, beyond Woking, he had seen with his own eyes two angels. He declined to tell me what they looked like, or what they were doing, or what he did when he saw them, or the date on which he saw them, and he wouldn't give me his name and address. All I could get out of him was "I tell you I saw two angels on Chobham heights. There was nobody about at the time, and I don't want people to think I am 'balmy.'" That is just the trouble. People want to see angels, and whether they want to or not, do, as I believe, at times verily see them; but they are always afraid to speak definitely about it. And this is our fault, not theirs.

Let us suppose that next Saturday afternoon, a clergyman of similar "credit" to the one in Mr. Machen's book, were to see an angel in the back garden of his vicarage. And let us suppose, that being absolutely sure of himself and his vision, he went into the pulpit next morning and told his congregation of his experience. What would happen? The people in the church would immediately begin to doubt his sanity, and perhaps even his probity. When they went away, they would talk, and the local newspaper would get hold of the story. Then Mr. Machen might have wind of it and be instructed by his Editor to "go down and interview the old top." "There's probably nothing in it," the Editor would say, "but any way you can make a startler out of it." And Mr. Machen would approach our clergyman delicately; get from him the main lines of the episode, and write them up in the *Evening News* in his own accomplished and inimitable way. The *Evening News* would sell papers, there would be correspondence and counter correspondence, and a further article or so by Mr. Machen; the public would be mildly entertained, and the clergyman would hear from his bishop, and might even receive a friendly call from his doctor.

And for the rest of his life people would say of that clergyman behind his back, "Ah, Mr. So-and-So—the man who saw the angel!" and they would wink, or giggle, or wag their heads. The beautiful story of "The Showmen," let along Mr. Machen, proves beyond a doubt that angel-seeing, actual or fictional, is a risky business. I doubt whether if Mr. Machen himself, or for that matter Mr. Begbie, were to be fortunate enough to see an angel tomorrow, either of them would dare avow the fact in print. Like my Woking rose-seller, they don't hanker after the contempt of their fellows; and having seen and been blest, they would keep their own counsel.

Now it seems to me that what is wanted for the good and benefit of humanity is a Society of Persons who have Seen Angels and are Not Afraid to Say So. Mr. Begbie might be the President, Mr. Machen the Corresponding Secretary, and I would be the Treasurer. The need of such a Society is perfectly obvious. Quite a large proportion of the "evidence" in Mr. Begbie's book is spoilt, because it has had to be prefaced with "only the initials are given," "the following testimonies come to me from one in whose judgment I have confidence," "the following account comes from a lady known to me, who prefers that her name should not be given," and so on and so forth. On large matters human nature is a very doubting Thomas indeed, and it has more confidence in a name and address than in a wilderness of anonymity and initials, or even titles with dashes after them. The Society I have proposed would be a living and organized witness to the truth of something we all desire to believe, and if persons eligible for membership are afraid of the *Evening News*, they can easily secure themselves by making up their minds never to be interviewed and never to communicate anything to Mr. Machen without first putting him on his honour not to use it for professional purposes.

The other side of the angels is simply this. They know us. They know what children we are, and, excepting in extreme circumstances, how foolish and frightened and doubtful and faint-hearted we become when they let us see them, and so out of kindness, perhaps, they keep out of our way. None but the brave and the faithful and the hard-pressed ever see them. We are most of us hard-pressed enough. Let us be brave and faithful, also.

The White Feather Legion

The following verse are put into this volume partly by way of fill-up and partly to assist recruiting. A verse may find him who a sermon flies.[64] The author wishes it to be distinctly understood that he is no conscriptionist, and believes the stories about "slacking" and "shirking" on the part of our young English manhood to be gross exaggerations. But he has lately seen at various places of entertainment in London numbers of young men in apparently comfortable circumstances, who if they are half as fit as they look, ought certainly to be soldiering. Perhaps they are all munition workers. As the lines are obviously a close parody of a famous lyrical piece by Mr. Rudyard Kipling, the author desires to express his acknowledgement to that gentleman.

    1
There's a legion that's never been 'listed,
    That follows no colour or crest,
But split into silly detachments
    Loafs round in the bars of the West:
Our fathers have given us the blessings
    They taught us and groomed us and crammed,
We all part our hair in the middle
    But we mustn't go out and be damned,
        (Dear boys)
We mustn't get shot and be damned.
    2
So some of us cherish the flapper,
    And some of us run the cocotte,
And none of us wants to be "wounded,"
    Or "missing" or that sort of rot;
And some of us dawdle at Brighton
    And some of us shirk at Southend,
And some of us "rest" up the river
    In charge of a giddy young friend,
        (Of course)
Thank God for the giddy young friend.

3
We've painted the night clubs vermillion,
    We're hot at the "Palace" and "Pav,"
We're just a bit short of the ready,
    But by thunder we spend what we have:
We laugh at the world as we find it
    It's women and crooks and "bad men,"
And no one can make us downhearted
    For things'll soon straighten again
        (Dear boys)
They'll straighten and buck up again.

4
Big meals and fresh air are our portion
    The "niggers" and piers are our share,
When cruisers loom grim in the offing
    Both we and our glasses are there;
Yes, somehow and somewhere and always
    We're first when the shoutings begin,
We put up a howl for Old England
    The Kaiser can hear in Berlin
        (Dear boys)
He hears it and quakes in Berlin.

5
We prance at the head of the Army—
    That is when it walks through the street;
We wave little flags at the station
    And drink with whoever we meet;
We know that the row will soon finish
    And rifles be back on the shelves,
Then won't we be proud of our Country
    And shake the glad hand with ourselves
        (Good men)
Who is there so good as ourselves!

6
Then a health (we must drink it in whispers)
    To the flats on the field and the foam,
And also to us, the pacific
    Young Gentleman Slackers at home;
Yes, a health to ourselves ere we scatter
    In taxis to get the last train,
Cheer oh! For the White Feather Legion,
    Goes back to its females again.
        Regards!
Goes back to its slippers again
        Hurrah!
The Bass and the lager again,
        Here's how!

> The gin and dry ginger again,
>   Salue!
> The cigar and the night-cap again.

If Lord Kitchener should happen to consider this spirited outburst suitable for what is obviously one of the most excellent of his purposes, I beg respectfully to say that he is welcome to the poster rights, free gratis, and for nothing. I am as keen to do my bit—and have it well displayed—as any man.

Postscript

"The Showmen" will, I devoutly trust, trouble me no more. You pay your shillings, and you can't have them back even if you want them. That is the one glory of authorship—no money returned. But I hope you will be well content. If you have any doubts about angels I beg of you to get rid of them forthwith. The Bible is full of angels. Shakespeare knew about them, so does Mr. Begbie; and I cannot help thinking that, in spite of his haut en bas[65] attitude, Mr. Machen knows about them also. My last words to you are these: If ever you see an angel, and I hope you will, don't hesitate. Write at once to Mr. Begbie, c/o his publishers, and tell him he may print your letter and—your name and address.

T. W. H. C.

• SEVEN •

John Garnier and *The Visions of Mons and Ypres: Their Meaning and Purpose*

Publisher: London: Robert Banks and Son, 1915

Though it went through at least four printings, *The Visions of Mons and Ypres* was published anonymously. The identity of its author was not hard to deduce, however, for the pamphlet indicated that it was "by the author of 'The Great Pyramid,'" and the advertisements for this book, conveniently given in the back of the pamphlet, would rapidly lead one to discover that it had been written by Colonel John Garnier, Late of the Royal Engineers. The profile given in A. E. Garnier's *The Chronicles of the Garniers of Hampshire During Four Centuries (1530–1900)*, is of sufficient length to indicate his life, interests, and ultimate obsessions:

> JOHN GARNIER, the eldest son of the Very Rev. Thomas Garnier, Dean of Lincoln, and Lady Caroline Garnier, was born August 24th, 1838, at Lewknor Rectory, Oxfordshire. He was baptized by his father in Lewknor Church, and his sponsors were Lady Parry, the Dean of Winchester, his grandfather, and the Rev. W. K. Hamilton. He eventually entered the Royal Engineers, retiring with the rank of Colonel in 1887.
>
> He has served with credit at Plymouth, Canada, the Cape, Chatham, Malta, Isle of Wight, and Guernsey, in the strengthening and construction of Fortifications. He married 26th June, 1869, at Trinity Church, St. Marylebone, Mary Caroline, second daughter of Christopher William Giles-Puller, Esq., M.P. of Youngsbury, Ware, Herts. He was a breeder of the British mastiff for many years, commencing when quite a boy, and his knowledge of the subject has caused him to become one, if not the greatest, of living authorities and judges of this noble breed of dogs. His famous dog, "Lion," which he himself bred, was the sire of that great dog, "Governor," reckoned to be the finest and most perfect specimen of the old British mastiff of the present century. *Vide* "The Dogs of the British Islands," edited by "Stonehenge." He is now a diligent

writer on theological subjects, and is the author of more than one excellent work: his chief effort being "Sin and Redemption" (published by Elliot Stock in 1893); but several other exhaustive theological treatises are at the time of writing in the press, the principal of which are "The Nephilim," "The True Christ and the False Christ," and in 1900 he was the author of "England's Enemies, a Warning" [published by W. H. Russell & Co.].[1]

The Colonel became a thoroughgoing eccentric during his retirement. In addition to being obsessed with what he believed was the falseness of Catholicism—which obsession can be seen emerging in *The Visions of Mons and Ypres*—he also became convinced that it was possible to identify what he described as "the British Race" with the Ten Tribes of Israel, publishing his findings in *Israel in Britain*.[2] He likewise became obsessed with the Great Pyramid of Giza (known also as the Pyramid of Cheops and the Pyramid of Khufu), but from a religious standpoint, and devoted the majority of *The Great Pyramid* to providing its measurements, establishing their correspondence to the Bible, and explicating their meaning as prophecy.[3]

John Garnier died on 29 April 1929[4] and is today remembered only as a crank, scholarly websites such as Bad Archaeology describing him as having "played a significant role in the creation and promulgation of the pseudo-science of pyramidology."[5] This availability *The Visions of Mons and Ypres* will probably do little to retrieve his reputation, but it should be mentioned that in his attempts at classifying and categorizing the nature of the visions, in his analyses of the inconsistencies of the account of Phyllis Campbell, and in his awareness of military processes, he shows a clear and analytic intelligence that is lacking from the majority of the other accounts.

The Visions of Mons and Ypres

Many people have read accounts of the visions said to have been seen by our soldiers in the early days of the war, and which have been called *The Angels of Mons*. The object of this pamphlet is to show their reality and to suggest the way in which they should be regarded.

In order to do this it is first necessary to give an account of the principal testimonies concerning them, as collected by Mr. Ralph Shirley and Mr. Harold Begbie.[6]

The first account is by *Miss Phyllis Campbell*, a cousin of Lady Archibald Campbell, and who has been a nurse at the front throughout the war. Speaking of "the awful days" of the retreat from Mons she said:—

> I paid little attention to the stories at the time. The Commandant had warned us to be ready for evacuating the base at a moment's notice. But we hung on.
> Train after train crept into the forest without lights, almost without sound. We went around with small lanterns, had to climb from the ground into cattle

trucks, and then sort the living from the dead. This post was the first stopping-place.

It was pitch dark, and I was attending a poor French fellow when the Lady President of the post called me. "Miss Campbell," she said, "there is an English soldier in the fifth wagon—he wants *a holy picture*."

It seemed an extraordinary thing to ask for in that awful scene, but I went to him. "*Miss*," he asked, "*please give me a picture of St. George. I want a picture or a medal, because I have seen St. George on a white horse!*"

An R.F.A.[7] man lying nearby corroborated this seeming madness. "*It's true, Sister*," he interjected, "*we all saw it.*"

While helping to make these men as comfortable as possible, I questioned them. Yes, they had seen it; others had seen it from different points of the battle. There was no doubt about it; St. George had saved them from utter annihilation.

They had seen him come out of a funny-looking cloud of light. He was a tall man with yellow hair, in golden armour, and was riding a white horse. He was holding a sword above his head. Then came the order to advance, and the German hordes were in full flight.

But why had they fled? None could say, for the British were hopelessly outnumbered.

Later, during that awful night, I tended French soldiers who all brought, in effect, the same testimony. But some of these poor fellows said it was Joan of Arc, while others said it was St. Michael.

"*When God sends St. Michael to fight for us,*" they said, "*then the case is hard indeed.*"

One French soldier—he was a sergeant-major, and has since been given an adjutancy—was particularly explicit and lucid in his account of the vision. He had seen Joan of Arc leading them on to victory. She was brandishing a sword and rode a white charger.

On this night there were six of us women at the post, including Madame de A_____, the President. Similar stories were told to all of us, except one, who was mounting guard over some wounded Germans.

When there came a lull in the work we compared notes. The accumulated evidence was from the lips of scores of wounded. Amongst these eye-witnesses were officers of high rank, a Roman Catholic priest, and English and French soldiers.

I had the testimony, amongst others, of three poor fellows of the Irish Guard. One of them was an enormous man who stood over 6 ft. 5 ins.

St. George was in Golden armour, bare-headed, and riding a white horse. He cried, "Come on!" as he brandished his sword. This had occurred at the most critical point of the retreat.

They had given themselves up for lost; nothing known to them could save them. Then suddenly there had been this interposition from heaven, and to their amazement the Germans were in full retreat.

The French testimony differed. Some said it was Joan of Arc, that she was bare-headed, riding a white horse and flourishing a sword as she called "Advance!" Others had seen St. Michael the Archangel, clad in golden armour, bare-headed, riding a white horse, and crying "Victory!" as he brandished his sword.

These eye-witnesses came from widely-separated points of the field of battle. I cannot give names of places; not even could the officers do this. They had been retreating and fighting for days and nights. None knew where they were.

Miss Campbell said that her French colleagues at "The Place in the Forest" could supply corroborative testimony. She would see, she said, if she could get written statements to that effect.

In another account of the same facts, Miss Campbell says that "while bandaging a shattered arm the President of the post, Madame de A____ (presumably a Catholic), came and took her place, asking her to attend to an Englishman who was begging for *a holy picture*. The idea of an English soldier making such a request at such a time seemed curious enough, but she hurried off to attend to his needs. He proved to be a Lancashire Fusilier."

"He was propped up in a corner" (says Miss Campbell), "his left arm tied up in a peasant woman's headkerchief, and his head newly bandaged. He should have been in a state of collapse from loss of blood, for his tattered uniform was soaked and caked in blood, and his face paper-white under the dirt of conflict. He looked at me with bright, courageous eyes and asked for a picture or a medal (he did not care which) of St. George. I asked if he was a Catholic. 'No,' he was a Wesleyan Methodist, and he wanted a picture or a medal of St. George, because he had seen him on a white horse, leading the British at *Vitry-le-Francois, when the Allies turned*. There was an R.F.A. man, wounded in the leg, sitting beside him on the floor; he saw my amazement, and hastened in, 'It's true, Sister, we all saw it. First there was a sort of yellow mist, sort of risin' before the Germans as they come on to the top of the hill, come on like a solid wall they did—springing out of the earth just solid—no end of 'em. I just give up. No use fighting the whole German race, thinks I; it's all up with us. The next minute comes this funny cloud of light, and when it clears off there's a tall man with yellow hair, in golden armour, on a white horse, holding his sword up, and his mouth open as if he was saying, "Come on, boys! I'll put the kybosh on the devils." (This is my picnic expression.) Then, before you could say "knife," the Germans had turned, and we were after them, fighting like ninety. We had a few scores to settle, Sister, and we fair settled them.'"

In another account Miss Campbell writes:—

For forty-eight hours no food, no drink under a tropical sun, choked with dust, harried by shell and marching, marching, marching, till even the pursuing Germans gave it up, and at *Vitry-le Francois* the Allies fell in their tracks and slept for three hours—horse, foot, and guns—while the exhausted slept behind them.

Then came the trumpet-call and each man sprang to his arms to find himself made anew. One man said, "I felt as if I had just come out of the sea after a swim. Fit, just grand. I never felt so fit in my life, and every man of us the same. The Germans were coming on just the same as ever, when suddenly the 'Advance' sounded and I saw the luminous mist and the great man on the white horse, and I knew the Boches would never get to Paris, for God was fighting on our side."

Miss Campbell further states that the French wounded were in "a *curiously exalted condition, a sort of rapture of happiness.* It was quite true, they maintained, the Germans were in full retreat and the Allies were being led to victory by St. Michael and Joan of Arc. One of the wounded French soldiers happened to have come from Domremy, Joan of Arc's native home, and declared he saw her brandishing her sword and crying, 'Turn, turn, advance.' No wonder, he said, the Boches fled down the hill."

Miss Campbell also refers to the case of the three soldiers of the Irish Guards, who were mortally wounded and asked for the Sacrament before death, and before dying told the same story to the old Abbe who confessed them.

She also says that "immediately before the apparition were seen all our wounded soldiers who were brought in expressed the conviction of swiftly approaching disaster, but that immediately afterwards there was a complete transformation of their attitude, the sense of despair giving place to *a state of strange exaltation and confidence of victory*."

Another nurse, *Miss Courtney Wilson*, gives the following statement by a lance-corporal:—

I was with my battalion in the retreat from Mons on or about August 28th. The German cavalry were expected to make a charge and we were waiting to fire and scatter them so as to enable the French cavalry who were on our right to make a dash forward. However, the German aeroplanes discovered our position and we remained where we were.

The weather was very hot and clear, and between eight or nine o'clock in the evening I was standing with a party of nine other men on duty and some distance on either side were parties of ten on guard. Immediately behind us, half of my battalion was on the edge of a wood resting. An officer suddenly came to us in a state of great anxiety and asked us if we had seen anything astonishing. He hurried away from my ten to the next party of ten. When he had got out of sight I, who was the non-commissioned officer in charge, ordered two men to go forward out of the way of the trees, in order to find out what the officer meant. The two men returned, reporting that they could see no sign of the Germans. At that time we thought that the officer must be expecting a surprise attack.

Immediately afterwards the officer came back, and, taking me and some others a few yards away, showed us the sky. I could see quite plainly in mid-air a strange light, which seemed to be quite distinctly outlined, and was not a reflection of the moon, nor were there any clouds in the neighbourhood. The light became brighter, and I could see quite distinctly three shapes, one in the centre having what looked like outspread wings; the other two were not so large, but were quite plainly distinct from the centre one. They appeared to have a long, loose-hanging garment of a golden tint, and they were above the German line facing us.

We stood watching them for about three-quarters of an hour. All the men with me saw them, and other man came up from other groups who told us they had seen the same thing. I am not a believer in such things, but I have not the slightest doubt that we really did see what I now tell you.

I remember the day because it was a day of terrible anxiety for us. That morning the Munsters had a bad time on our right, and so had the Scots Guards. We managed to get to the wood, and there we barricaded the roads, and remained in the formation I have told you. Later on the Uhlans[8] attacked us, and we drove them back with heavy loss. It was after this engagement, when we were dog-tired, that the vision appeared to us.

I shall never forget it as long as I live. I lie awake in bed and picture it all as I saw it on that night. Of my battalion there are now only five men alive besides myself, and I have no hopes of ever getting back to the front. I have a record of fifteen years' good service, and I should be very sorry to make a fool of myself by telling a story merely to please anyone.

Miss Wilson asked him if the figures resembled anybody, and he replied: "You could discern there were faces, but you couldn't see what they were like."

Miss Wilson also asked him, "What was the effect of the vision on your feelings, and the feelings of the other men?"

"Well, it was very funny. We came over quiet and still. It took us that way. We didn't know what to make of it. And there we all were looking up at those three figures, saying nothing, just wondering, when one of the chaps called 'God is with us'—and that kind of loosened us. Then when we were falling-in for the march the Captain said to us, 'Well, men, we can cheer up now, we've got Someone with us.' And that's just how we felt. As I tell you, we marched thirty-two miles that night, and the Germans didn't fire rifle or cannon the whole way."

Asked, "Did the effect—the moral effect—last?"

He replied slowly: "There was a certain non-commissioned officer with us who was a fair coward, not fit to be a soldier, much less a non-commissioned officer, and that man—well, he was a fair honest coward, and no mistake about it—he became quite different from that night. He didn't mind what happened to him. He set a good example. That's a fact. He got killed at Wipers" (Ypres).

Asked about other changes in the men. "We were a decent lot of men on the whole, and of course fighting keeps a man quiet, but there was one very rough fellow along with us, always cursing and swearing and going for all the drink he could get—not exactly a bad fellow he wasn't, but he was rough, very rough, and not particular about himself. Well, that man was changed right through by the vision. I think it had more effect on him than any of us. He didn't speak about it, but we could see for ourselves. It made a man of him."

On being asked whether he had met, since he got back, any of the men who saw the vision, he replied: "Only one. He's lying in Netley Hospital at this moment. He's in the Scots Guards. I saw him the other day, and asked him about it. He remembers it just as well as I do. Of course, these chaps in here won't believe it. They think I must have dreamed it. But the sergeant in the Scots Guards could tell them. It was no dreaming. I've never seen anything like it before or since. I know very well what I saw."

Miss Callow, Secretary to the Higher Thought Centre at South Kensington, also writes:—

> An officer has sent to one of the members of the Centre a detailed account of a vision that appeared to himself and others when fighting against fearful odds at Mons. He plainly saw an apparition representing St. George, the patron saint of England, the exact counterpart of a picture that hangs to-day in a London restaurant. So terrible was their plight at the time that the officer could not refrain from appealing to the vision to help them. Then, as if the enemy had also seen the apparition, the Germans abandoned their positions in precipitate terror. In other instances men had written about seeing *clouds of celestial horsemen* hovering over the British lines.

Miss Callow also adds that a nurse at the front on one occasion asked her patients why they were *so silent*, to which the men replied, "We have had strange experiences, which we do not care to talk about. We have seen many of our mates killed, but *they are fighting for us still.*"

Mr. Hazlehurst, a Justice of the Peace in Flintshire, wrote to the *Daily Mail*, on August 22nd, 1915, concerning Private Cleaver, of the 1st Cheshire Regiment. He said: "Cleaver frequently spoke to his friends in the canteen of what he had seen at Mons, and finding he was only forty miles off I went to see him. He gave me the following words in writing: 'I myself was at Mons, and saw the vision of angels.' He also expressed his willingness to sign an affidavit to that effect. Well content, I returned home, and the following day procured an affidavit and again travelled forty miles to see him sign it. A copy is enclosed."[9]

The Rev. G. G. Monck, M.A., Prebendary of Wells and Rural Dean of Martock,[10] quotes a letter he received from a friend concerning the angels at Mons, in which the following passage occurs:—

> The account I sent you was taken down from the lips of a wounded man in hospital in London by one of Sir H.'s sisters, who was working there. Curiously enough, about two months ago in Oxford I met a young lieutenant of the _____ who had been all through the retreat from Mons, and had been wounded at Neuve Chapelle. I asked him if he knew the story. He replied: "I read it in hos-

pital. It is simply miraculous, but it is perfectly true." He added: "Do you know that almost the same thing happened at Neuve Chapelle?"

The Rev. Alexander Boddy, Vicar of All Saints, Monkwearmouth,[11] who was for two months at the front with the troops, also gives an account of similar visions having been seen at *the second battle of Ypres*, when the British were attacked by overwhelming numbers of Germans. He says: "A soldier of the 3rd Canadians stated that after the second battle of Ypres, when the battalion was retiring through their communication trenches towards their rest camp, they were obliged to halt where a West Riding regiment was stationed. During the halt one of the men of this regiment was narrating to those around him a strange experience of his own. He had seen, he said, what at first appeared to be a ball of fire. Afterwards it took the form of an angel with outstretched wings, standing between the British front line and that of the enemy." Mr. Boddy also mentions a story told to the sister of a gentleman who had given up his house as a convalescent home for wounded soldiers. One of the wounded soldiers told the lady that "at a critical moment an angel with outspread wings, like a luminous cloud, stood between the advancing Germans and themselves. This figure appeared to render it impossible for the Germans to advance and annihilate them." The lady in question was subsequently speaking of this incident in the presence of some officers, and expressed her own incredulity. One of the officers, a colonel, looked up at this, and said, "Young lady, the thing happened. You need not be incredulous. I saw it myself."

Similar phenomena to those which have occurred in the present war were narrated of the siege of the British Legation by the Boxers at Pekin.[12] The occupants of the Legation found the house they occupied untenable, and were obliged to move to another position, and while the removal took place the British were in full view of the Chinese insurgents, who, they took for granted, would fire upon them. To their great surprise they failed to do so. An Englishman who was present on the occasion, and who knew Chinese as well as his own native language, took the opportunity afterwards of asking one of the Chinese soldiers why they missed such a fine chance. The Chinaman gave as a reason the fact that "there were so many people *in white* between them and the British that they did not like to fire."

In most of the records of the appearance the apparition of a luminous cloud is alluded to. One of these records narrates how "in this cloud there seemed to be bright objects moving. The moment it appeared the German onslaught received a check. The horses could be seen rearing and plunging, and ceased to advance." A soldier of the Dublin Fusiliers is cited as confirming this phenomenon, adding, with regard to the cloud, that it quite hid them from the enemy. Numerous references have been made in the pulpits to these phenomena, some of the clergy going so far as to read letters from soldiers at the front to their congregations. Mr. Lancaster, for instance, a Weymouth clergyman, read one of these letters from a soldier who said that his regiment was pursued by a large number of German cavalry, from which they took refuge in a quarry, where the Germans found them and were on the point of shooting them. "At that moment," said the writer, "the whole top edge of the quarry was lined by angels, who were seen by all the soldiers, and the Germans as well. The Germans suddenly stopped, turned round, and galloped away at top speed."

Dr. Richardson, in a sermon on the Angels of Mons, asked whether there was anyone in the congregation who had seen letters from any soldiers who could tell of seeing angels on the battlefield. A lady, Mrs. Guest, of St. Leonard's on-Sea, immediately got up and said that she had seen letters from three different soldiers. In each one she said there was clear and convincing testimony that these soldiers had themselves seen the angels. The letters were not hysterical outbursts, but were written in a calm and sober fashion. These soldiers stated that the Germans had been kept back by a troop of angels, and that the French soldiers also declared that they had seen the vision.

Mrs. Guest was travelling from St. Leonard's to London when a hospital nurse just back from France got into conversation with her. "She spoke to me," said Mrs. Guest, "because I was wearing my son's regimental badge. He is an Australian officer, recently wounded in the Dardanelles. The nurse showed me three letters from different soldiers. All testified to having personally seen the angels, and that the French soldiers claimed to have seen St. Michael leading a troop of horsemen."

"This intervention," the soldiers said, "came at a most critical stage and certainly made the German horses stampede."

Some German prisoners vowed that the English had contrived to tamper with their horses beforehand. Other Germans said they fled because of large reinforcements which the English soldiers said was the phantom army.

Another lady who has established a rest-house and club for our soldiers in France, relates the following incident—

> A dying soldier said to me, "It's a funny thing, Sister, isn't it, how the Germans say we had a lot of troops behind us?" He went on to assure me that the German prisoners had said, "How could we break through your line when you had all those thousands of troops behind you?" The soldier added, "Thousands of troops! Why, we were just a thin line of two regiments with nothing behind us."
>
> A Sergeant-Major afterwards told me that he had heard a British officer talking to a German prisoner, and that the prisoner talked of the crowd of troops behind the British line, saying that all the Germans had seen them.

The lady added, "I don't believe in the angels, but I do believe—I can't help believing—that our soldiers, many of them, are aware of something supernatural in this war. They talk about it among themselves, some of them; and I suppose that they would talk as freely as they are able to others if those others showed sympathy. But I am positive they would even deny having seen anything at all if they were questioned by one who appeared to them skeptical and superior. Tommy is much more sensitive than people suppose."

The following from A. M. B. in a letter to the *Church Times*, July 28th, 1915, is worth recording:—

> A lady in Germany at that time, who is well known for her work among English girls there, tells me that there was much discussion in Berlin because a certain regiment which had been told off to do a certain thing at a certain battle failed to carry out their orders, and when censured declared that they did go forward, but found themselves absolutely powerless to proceed with their orders, and their horses turned sharply round and fled like the wind and nothing could stop them. The explanation given by the Germans was, "We simply could not go on; those devils of Englishmen were up to some devilry or other, and we could do nothing; we were powerless."

The same lady asked one, the lieutenant of the regiment, what happened. He said, "I cannot tell you. I only know that we were charging full on the British at a certain place and in a moment we were stopped. It was almost like going full speed and being suddenly pulled up on a precipice, but there was no precipice there, only our horses swerved round and we could do nothing."

Mr. Ralph Shirley, referring to the visions seen by our men and the French, relates that he has interviewed two English ladies who have been nursing at a hospital at St. Germain en Laye, in the neighbourhood of Paris. These ladies stated that the accounts in question were in France "not merely implicitly believed, but were absolutely known to be true," and they added "that no French paper would have made itself ridiculous by disputing the authenticity of what was vouched for by so many thousands of eye-witnesses."

Similar visions were reported from Russia.

Miss Campbell states that a Russian princess wrote to some of her friends in France stating that St. Michael had been seen during the battles in Russia. The letter arrived September 14th, 1914. The princess is a voluntary nurse, and her letter says that numbers of Russian wounded testified to seeing the visions.

In a recent telegram also from Petrograd to *La France de demain* it is stated that many Russian sentries declare that they have seen the ghost of *General Skobeloff* (who gained fame in the Russo-Turkish war of 1877) in a white uniform, riding a white horse.[13]

"Exchange," *Pall Mall Gazette*, August 4th, 1915.

Remarks On the Visions

The records of the phenomena witnessed by numerous British and French soldiers, including officers, do not admit of any doubt as to their reality. The visions are not always the same. In one case a central figure is seen with a figure on each side. In other cases, a number of angelic forms are seen standing between our soldiers and the enemy at a critical moment. But the vision seen apparently by the greater number of both British and French soldiers was that of a warrior on a white horse, encouraging them to advance, and sometimes accompanied by other warriors.

The various interpretations of the latter vision are just what we might expect from the different points of view of the beholders. The British soldier believes he saw St. George of England, with which he was more or less familiar from pictures or coins. The French soldier believes he saw Michael the Archangel, or more generally Joan of Arc. The Russian soldier also sees St. Michael or else General Skobeloff. Each one clothes the vision in accordance with his preconceived ideas. These different interpretations of the vision are the best proof of its reality and that the same vision was seen by all. They are also wholly opposed to the suggestion that the phenomena were due to psychic hallucination induced by great mental and nervous strain; for in that case the different beholders, widely separated from each others, would have had greatly different hallucinations in accordance with the different idiosyncracies of each.

The fact that the warrior on the white horse was sometimes accompanied by other warriors appearing in a luminous cloud may explain the remark of some of the British wounded who said, "We have seen many of our mates killed, but they are fighting for us still." They doubtless alluded to the warriors who accompanied the rider on the white horse, and very naturally supposed they were their dead "mates."

It will be noticed that in one of Miss Campbell's accounts she speaks of the vision as the angels of *Mons*, and as having taken place after certain days and nights of the continuous fighting and marching which followed the battle of Mons on August 23rd. But in other accounts Miss Campbell speaks of the vision as having been seen at *Vitry Le Francois "when the Allies turned."*

Now Vitry Le Francois is on the Marne, more than eighty miles to the south-east of the position held by the British at the end of the four days' battle which commenced at Mons on the 23rd. Vitry Le Francois was the point at which General Joffre[14] ordered the retreat to stop and was followed by the counter attack of the Allies, which resulted in the complete defeat of the Germans and their being driven across the Marne and back to the Aisne with heavy losses. Vitry Le France was not on the British front, but being the point where the retreat of the French was stopped and their attack commenced, is no doubt became among our soldiers, ignorant of localities, a general term for the point at which the Allies turned.

It seems clear that Miss Campbell's accounts refer to two distinct occasions, on each of which there appeared the vision of the rider on the white horse, and that she has mixed the two incidents together. This might naturally be expected in the case of a young lady writing from memory after months of the stress and turmoil of war, and intent only on recording the facts connected with the vision itself, compared with which details of time and place would seem of secondary importance. It is in itself an evidence of the reality of the facts she relates, for in an artificially invented story particulars of time and space would have been given a prominent place.

There is a distinction to be observed in the accounts of the various visions. Where the British soldiers were hard pressed and in danger of being overwhelmed by the superior numbers of the enemy, the vision was generally of three or more angelic forms standing between them and the enemy, which had the effect of paralysing the latter's advance. But when the British and the French were intended to attack, the vision was always that of a single warrior on a white horse, urging them to attack,. This figure appears to have been seen not only previous to the Allies' attack and defeat of the Germans behind the Marne, but also during the retreat from Mons.

The battles of Le Cateau and Landrecies, by which the British checked for the moment the German pursuit, were fought on August 25th and 26th, the retreat being continued through the night of the 26th. But on August 28th the Allies, having retreated behind the Oise, turned upon their German pursuers, and the British cavalry inflicted two severe defeats on the pursuing German cavalry south of the Somme at Cerizy and near St. Quentin, while at the same time the French turned and attacked the German guard corps and two other German corps, completely defeating them and driving them back on Guise. In fact, so completely were the Germans checked at this time that it is a question whether the Allies could not have held the line of the Oise and Aisne instead of retreating to the Marne. It may be that it was at this time when the Allies turned on their pursuers that the vision of the rider on the white horse was seen.

On the other hand, it seems more probable that the vision may have occurred before the battle of Le Cateau, when the British turned and held the greatly superior forces of the Germans at bay for the greater part of the day, August 26th. This is supported by the allusion of Miss Campbell to *the Forest*, for a large portion of the British had just retreated from the position near the fortress of Mauberge through the Forest of Mormal.

But after the battle of La Cateau the weak British army was in great danger of being overwhelmed by the enormous forces of the Germans, three or four times their number, which had accumulated on their front and flank and threatened to envelop them. Yet it was just at this period that the German pursuit slackened, thereby enabling the British to retreat from Le Cateau with little or no molestation and reform their forces behind the Oise. Sir John French[15] in his report attributed this slackness of the German pursuit to the severe losses they had suffered at Mons, Le Cateau, etc. But considering the German recklessness of loss, their great numerical superiority, and their vindictive determination to crush the British, this is wholly insufficient to explain their sudden cessation of pursuit. May not the visions of the guardian angels who stood between our troops and the pursuing Germans, as recorded by various witnesses, account for this?

In the account of the lance-corporal, recorded by Miss Courtney Wilson, of the three angel forms seen by him and the men of his regiment, he says that it occurred *about* August 28th. It might be expected that in the storm and stress of that period he would lose count of days, and that speaking of the event a year afterwards he could not be certain of the exact date. It is clear from his account that the vision occurred on the night of the 26th.

From Sir John French's report, the forced march of thirty-two miles of which the lance-corporal speaks, took place after the battles of Le Cateau and Landrecies, nor was there any other such march during the whole of the retreat to the Marne. Sir John, recognizing the overwhelming forces of the Germans, determined to make this great effort in order to place the river Oise covering his front and left flank between him and the enemy. The retreat commenced by Sir Horace Smith Dorien's[16][sic] masterly withdrawal of his army corps from the position of Le Cateau. It commenced in the afternoon of August 26th, and had to be done gradually in the face of a greatly superior enemy, a most hazardous operation. The retreat was continued during the greater part of the night of the 26th and the whole of August 27th, and it was not until the 28th that the whole of army was collected and reformed behind the Oise between Noyon on the left and the fortress of La Fere on the right, the whole distance by road from Le Cateau and Landrecies being fully forty-five miles.

It is also clear from the lance-corporal's account that there had been heavy fighting on the day on which he speaks, and that the Munsters and the Scots Guards had suffered severely. Now, beyond the cavalry actions at St. Quentin and Cerizy, and some rear-guard actions in the in the forest of Compeigne, south of the Aisne, there was no serious battle after the battles of Le Cateau and Landrecies. It was at the latter place that the Scots Guards suffered severely, the Guards divisions having to withstand the attack of a whole German corps nearly four times their number.

This shows that the time spoken of by the lance-corporal was the night of the 26th, after the battles of Le Cateau and Landrecies, when his battalion had retreat some miles and was halted under cover of a wood to keep the pursuing German cavalry at bay. The further retreat of thirty-two miles, commencing that night, with of course intervals of rest, was clearly that spoken of by Sir John French as continuing through the night of the 26th and the whole of August 27th.

The vision of the guardian angels, therefore, must have occurred at what was undoubtedly the most critical moment of the war. For had the Germans pursued with their usual vigour, the British columns, separated from each other on a long line of retreat, would almost certainly have been attacked and overwhelmed in detail. As it was, the pursuit was feeble, and when the German cavalry did pursue they were attacked and defeated with heavy loss by inferior numbers of British cavalry.

Equally well authenticated records of similar visions of guardian angels were said to have been seen at the second battle of Ypres, where the Germans made their great attempt with vastly superior forces to break through our thinly-held lines, and in this case also the visions appear to have been guardian angels holding back the German onslaught. In every case this vision seems to have taken place at the critical moment when the British were in danger of being overwhelmed by greatly superior numbers.

We may here refer to the story of "*The Bowmen*," written by Mr. Machen. He claims that his story, invented by himself, was the real origin of the various visions; that it suggested the idea to the British and French soldiers and caused them to imagine they saw these visions, or in other words, that they were hypnotised by his story.

But apart from the practical impossibility of Mr. Machen's story having been read by soldiers who for days and nights had been marching and fighting with little or no time even for sleep, and the still greater unlikelihood of its having affected French soldiers, ignorant of English, there is the fact that the story was not published until September 29th, over a month after the time of the vision in the retreat from Mons and three weeks after the time when the Allies turned and attacked at Vitry-le-Francois. Mr. Machen's story could not therefore have suggested the vision. Moreover, with one exception of doubtful authority, the accounts of the visions were not of bowmen but of angelic forms.

Mr. Machen, in short, admits that his invention was suggested by the stories which he had read in the papers describing the terrible days of the retreat from Mons. He says, in rather high-flown and exaggerated language:—

> I seemed to see a furnace of torment and death and agony and terror seven times heated, and in the midst of the burning was the British army. In the midst of the flames consumed by it and yet aureoled by it, scattered like ashes and yet triumphant, martyred and for ever glorious; so I saw these men with a shining about them, so I took these thoughts with me to church and I am sorry to say was making up a story while the deacon was singing the gospel.[17]

Considering that there were no correspondents at the front and that no details of the retreat from Mons were known for some days afterwards, it is quite possible that during that time some rumours of the vision had reached

England and that a vague but forgotten mention of it had reached Mr. Machen, and unconsciously to himself had suggested his story—that, in short, the visions had suggested the story and not the story the vision.

It has also been pointed out by Mr. Harold Begbie that there is such a thing as *telepathy* or the transference of thought from one person to another without words, a fact which has been proved beyond dispute by numberless well authenticated instances. The telepathy between animals is often most wonderful, and there are many people who have had experience of it, generally of trivial importance, in everyday life between themselves and others with whom they had strong sympathies. It is therefore not impossible that Mr. Machen's mind, being wrought up to a high pitch of sympathy with our men in their retreat from Mons, may have had, unconsciously to himself, some telepathic communication of the vision seen by them.

But Mr. Machen was probably fully aware of the numerous traditions of supernatural appearances on the eve of great conflicts or at critical moments and this, in itself, would be quite sufficient to suggest his story, which it must be remembered differed considerably from the actual visions.

At the most, Mr. Machen's story and the actual visions were merely a partial coincidence, and the story was certainly not the *cause* of the visions.

Mr. Machen, however, is anxious to be thought the sole originator of the visions and to prove that they were merely hallucinations, the product of his suggestion. He therefore endeavours to throw discredit on their reality, and among other objections to them, he says that if these visions were seen by so many men how is it that none of them have come forward to testify of them.

But of the men who fought in the first battles of the war a large proportion are killed or prisoners, and probably not more than one-third now remain. Of these the majority are still fighting at the front, and their testimony is not available in England. The only testimony available is that of those among them who have been wounded and are still in hospital or incapable of further service, and these are necessarily very few.

It is not true that none of these have not testified to the reality of the visions, for many on being questioned have done so. But, as we have seen, they are loth [sic] to speak about them. The effect of the visions on them was to make them silent. They did not like to talk about them. They did not understand them, and there is nothing the British soldier shrinks from more than to be thought weakly credulous and foolish. Rather than be thought this by anyone affecting a skeptical superiority, he would deny the vision altogether.

There is little or nothing of this reticence among the French soldiers, who are only too willing to relate their experiences, and as the testimony of most of them is available on the spot, the reality of the visions is not even questioned in France.

Mr. Machen also, in support of his contention that the visions were a psychological illusion, compares them to the fact that many people in England were led to believe that they had seen large numbers of Russian soldiers passing in trains from the North for the embarkation to France, although no such soldiers existed. But this was not an illusion of the senses. The people who testified to the fact really saw what they *believed* to be Russian soldiers, and it seems that they were intended to do so. The mystery attending the transit of these soldiers in railway carriages with the blinds drawn down helped to confirm this belief, and it is stated on good authority that it was a ruse of Lord Kitchener's to create the belief that a powerful Russian force was about to be landed on the West Coast of France, in order to attack in flank the line of the German advance on Paris. It seems that the Germans also feared this, and it therefore was very possible that the Russian story had no little effect in inducing them to turn aside from Paris.

It is difficult to quite understand Mr. Machen's anxiety to prove that the visions were merely hallucinations suggested by his story of "The Bowmen."

How, then, are we to regard the visions the reality of which cannot be denied, and what did they portend?

It is clear that we are living at the time foretold in Luke xxi. 10, when "nation is to rise against nation, and kingdom against kingdom." For unlike former wars, when the fighting was confined to the regular armies of the States at war, this is a war of nations against nations, waged by the whole peoples of the nations engaged. It is in connection with these wars of the last days that *"fearful sights and great signs shall there be from heaven."* It would therefore be a serious error to reject the possibility of their taking place at the present time, or to receive with incredulity the strong evidence of their occurrence, as in the case of the visions of Mons and Ypres, lest in so doing we should reject the testimony of God vouchsafed for our benefit and encouragement.

It must further be remembered that the forces arrayed against us in this war, viz., the Ultramontane Rome and Germany, are wholly evil and opposed to God, and that their purpose in making this war has been to crush Britain as the stronghold of Protestantism, and the chief witness of God in the world, and the chief propagator of the Bible throughout the world. Moreover, we are fighting against foes who are not only opposed to God and the truth of God but whose methods of warfare, treachery, falsehood and ruthless cruelty are wholly Satanic.

The war must therefore be regarded as the beginning or foreshadow of the final great conflict which is to take place at the close of this dispensation between Satan and Christ—the *"battle* (or *war,* polemon) *of that great day of God Almighty"* (Rev. xiv. 4). See also Rev. xvii. 14.

In all wars between the people of God and the enemies of God, the former, as shown by the history of Israel, whenever they are true to God, were miraculously helped by God. The battle was not merely on earth but in heaven—as in the case of the defeat of Sisera[18]—"they *fought from heaven.* The stars in their courses fought against Sisera" (Judges v. 20). So also in the overthrow of Paganism by Christianity in the reign of Constantine the Great,[19] the conflict, although decided on earth, is represented as taking place also in heaven between Michael and his angels and Satan and his angels (Rev. ix).

Again, in Dan. X. we see the veil lifted which conceals the heavenly combatants in earthly conflicts. The description of the man clothed in white who appeared to Daniel and in whose presence Daniel's strength was turned to corruption, shows Him to be Christ, who appeared to John in Patmos, and before whom the apostle fell as dead (Rev. i. 13–18). The description in both cases is practically identical.[20]

He tells Daniel: "The prince of the kingdom of Persia withstood me one and twenty days: but, lo, Michael, one of the chief princes, came to help me; and now I remained there with the kings of Persia ... and now will I return to fight with [*i.e.,* on the side of] the prince of Persia: and when I am gone forth, lo, the prince of Grecia shall come" (Dan. X. 13, 20).

The words appear to refer to the raising up the power of the Persians for the overthrow of the Babylonian empire and to the establishment of the Persian empire as long as Christ remained *with them*; but that when He had "gone forth," or left them, the Greeks would come, by whom, under Alexander the Great, the Persian empire was in its turn overthrown.

It shows that behind the conflicts of early kingdoms there are unseen heavenly powers by whom the issues of these conflicts are decided.

We may also refer to the story of Elisha (2 Kings vi. 13–17), when the king of Syria sent an army to capture the town in which he lived, where we are shown that he was really defended by the invisible hosts of heaven. For "the angel of the Lord encampeth round about them that fear Him and delivereth them" (Psa. xxxiv. 7).

If, then, the present war is the beginning of the final great conflict between Christ and Satan, we may believe that Christ and the armies of heaven are, unseen, fighting on our side. But in all such conflicts the people of God have to suffer failures, reverses, and defeats before they finally overcome. It is part of their discipline and teaching either as chastisement for national sin, or in order that they may recognise the power and malignity of the enemy and their own dependence on God. In the same way the individual Christian has to suffer chastisement, failure, defeat, and overthrow in order that he may recognise the power of the evil he has to overcome, and be made humble and poor in spirit, and recognise more fully his dependence on Christ, whose strength is made perfect in his weakness.

It is at such times, whether in the case of the individual or the nation,

Seven • John Garnier and *The Visions of Mons and Ypres*

that faith and hope are liable to waver and fail. If, then, in the time of His great temptation an angel was sent to strengthen Christ Himself, there is nothing improbable that in times of overwhelming danger and need the eyes of some, like those of the servant of Elisha, should be opened and enabled to perceive the heavenly forces arrayed on their side, thereby filling them, as in the case of the soldiers in the retreat from Mons, with a strange confidence and exaltation of spirit. Nor would such vision be intended for them alone, but for all believers in Christ who in the dark hours of the war, and the still darker hours which the nation may yet have to pass through, might be tempted to despair.

Now the final battle of the great war between Christ and Satan is described in Rev. xix., where it is shown that Christ, followed by the armies of heaven, will appear on earth for the salvation of His people and the destruction of His enemies. Christ is therefore revealed as *a rider on a white horse*, Who "in righteousness doth judge and make war." We may, therefore, conclude that any previous manifestation of Him as an earnest of His presence for the purpose of strengthening and encouraging those who are fighting on his side would take that form.

Finally, it may be shown that in the great conflicts of the last days between Christ and Satan the chief earthly protagonist on the side of God is to be the British nation, who are to be specially raised up by God for this purpose. This has already been partially fulfilled in the present war.

Therefore, as many great signs from heaven are to appear during the final conflicts, it seems highly probable that they will come as special revelations to the British for their encouragement in the hour of their need, and should be received as assurance of the help of God in the dark hours which may yet await the British race.

False Signs and Lying Wonders

We are told that in these last days false Christs and false prophets are to appear, who shall show great signs and wonders, and deceive if possible the very elect (Matt. xxiv. 24). But Scripture tells us how we are to regard such signs and wonders. If their effect is to support idolatry or false religion, we are to give no heed to them. They are permitted by God as tests to prove the reality or otherwise of people's faith (Deut. xiii. 1–3).

But the case of the rider on the white horse in the vision of Mons is not of this character. If, as pointed out, the vision can only be a manifestation of Christ as an earnest that He is fighting, unseen, on our side, it must lead to faith in Him and not to idolatry. It would not only induce numbers to seek His aid in the hour of earthly need and conflict, but beget in many, hitherto ignorant of Him, the desire to know more of Him, and thence to seek His aid in spiritual things as "the only name under heaven given among men by which we can be saved," and Who has said "Him that cometh unto Me I will by no means cast out ... and I will raise him up at the last day" (John v. 37, 40).

But whatever evidence of truth is given by God to man, Satan will do his best to pervert it, or else neutralise its effect by sowing tares among the wheat so as to make it difficult for the world generally to distinguish between truth and error. The teaching of Romanism is wholly opposed to any direct appeal to or trust in Christ Himself. The sinner is warned that if he goes to Christ direct he will be rejected, and that he must first seek the mediation of the Virgin as "the only hope of sinners." As the Jesuits told the Rev. Hobart Seymour,[21] the religion of Rome is practically the worship of Mary; that is, Mariolatry.[22] We may therefore expect that the advocates and supporters of Romanism would endeavour as far as possible to either pervert, or wholly deny, visions such as those of Mons and Ypres, which, if believed, might lead numbers to put their trust in Christ.

Such is probably the explanation of the supposed appearance of the Virgin Mary with Christ in her arms to the Russian soldiers before the battle of Angustovo [sic].[23] Nothing would be more likely than that the priests or devotees of superstition would make use of the actual vision in order to support their false religion by persuading the ignorant soldiers that what they saw, more or less indistinctly in a luminous cloud, was a vision of "the Virgin and Child," which is the usual way in which the false Christ of both Paganism and Romanism is represented.

The above is not the only case in which these visions have been perverted by fables and inventions to teach idolatry and false religion. Such accretions and fables must be expected, and will doubtless deceive those who are not guided by the "Spirit of Truth" (John ii. 20, 27).

• EIGHT •

W. H. Leathem and "In the Trenches"

First book appearance: p. 11–19 in *The Comrade in White*. New York, London, etc.: Fleming H. Revell Company, 1916.

The angelic Comrade in White was a Mons-inspired battlefield story that made the rounds during the early days of the Great War. Begbie quotes the Reverend T. F. Horton's account of a Comrade in White in *On the Side of the Angels*, but it fell to the Reverend W. H. Leathem to write the account. It was apparently first published in *Work and Life*, then largely reprinted by *The Living Church*, and finally achieved monographic permanency in the well-received *The Comrade in White*.[1]

William Harvey Leathem was born in Belfast in 1875. He received his undergraduate degree at Queen's College (now Queen's University) Belfast and his degree in Theology at New College, Edinburgh. During the First World War, he served as Chaplain to the 1st Gordon Highlanders, after which he was called to St. Andrew's Presbyterian Church, as Minister. He was serving as Minister at the time of his death from cancer in 1937.[2]

The Reverend Leathem wrote but three books in his life, and *The Comrade in White* is his only work of adult fiction.[3] It is also one of the earliest works of fiction to connect the Angels to the conflicts of the First World War, and that it was written by somebody who had experienced the War firsthand gives it a certain cachet that is often lacking in the works of more professional fiction writers. It appears heartfelt and sincere in its expression of faith, and one wishes that Leathem had left an autobiographical explanation recounting how he learned of the Angels.

Hugh Black was almost certainly the Scottish-American author and Presbyterian theologian (1868–1953).

Introduction by Hugh Black

The Great War has put a strain on the resources of human nature, as well as on material resources. Men who have come through the hell of the trenches have discovered some of the secrets of life and death. Many of them have known a reinforcement of spiritual power. It is quite natural that this fact should often be described in emotional form as direct interposition of angels and other supernatural agencies. Among these the most beautiful and tender stories are those of "The Comrade in White." In essence they are all testimony to the perennial fount of strength and comfort of religion—the human need which in all generations has looked up and found God a present help in times of trouble.

The origin of the many stories brought back to England from the battle fronts by her soldiers is that to the average Briton this a religious crusade, and men have gone with an exaltation of soul, willing to make the ultimate sacrifice, willing to die that the world might live. Men and women are face to face with eternal realities, and are driven by the needs of their hearts to the eternal refuge. Unless we see this we miss the most potent fact in the whole situation.

The tender stories in this little volume are a reflex of the great religious stirring of the nation. They describe in a gracious and pathetic way the various abysmal needs of this tragic time, and they indicate how many human souls are finding comfort and healing and strength. They are finding peace as of old, through the assurance that "earth has no sorrows, that heaven cannot heal."[4]

In the Trenches

Strange tales reached us in the trenches. Rumours raced up and down that three-hundred-mile line from Switzerland to the sea. We knew neither the source of them nor the truth of them. They came quickly, and they went quickly. Yet somehow I remember the very hour when George Casey turned to me with a queer look in his blue eyes, and asked if I had seen the Friend of the Wounded.

And then he told me all he knew. After many a hot engagement a man in white had been seen bending over the wounded. Snipers sniped at him. Shells fell all around. Nothing had power to touch him. He was either heroic beyond all heroes, or he was something greater still. This mysterious one, whom the French called *The Comrade in White*, seemed to be everywhere at once. At Nancy, in the Argonne, at Soissons and Ypres, everywhere men were talking of him with hushed voices.

But some laughed and said the trenches were telling on men's nerves. I, who was often reckless enough in my talk, exclaimed that for me seeing was believing, and that I didn't expect any help but an enemy's knife if I was found lying out there wounded.

It was the next day that things got lively on this bit of the front. Our big guns roared from sunrise to sunset, and began again in the morning. At noon we got word to take the trenches in front of us. They were two hundred yards away, and we weren't well started till we knew that the big guns had failed in their work of preparation. It needed a stout heart to go on, but not a man wavered. We had advanced one hundred and fifty yards when we found it was no good. Our Captain called to us to take cover, and just then I was shot through both legs. By God's mercy I fell into a hole of some sort. I suppose I fainted, for when I opened my eyes I was all alone. The pain was horrible, but I didn't dare to move lest the enemy should see me, for they were only fifty yards away, and I did not expect mercy. I was glad when the twilight came. There were men in my own company who would run any risk in the darkness if they thought a comrade was still alive.

The night fell, and soon I heard a step, not stealthy, as I expected, but quiet and firm, as if neither darkness nor death could check those untroubled feet. So little did I guess what was coming that, even when I saw the gleam of white in the darkness, I thought it was a peasant in a white smock, or perhaps a woman deranged. Suddenly, with a little shiver of joy or of fear, I don't know which, I guessed that it was *The Comrade in White*. And at that very moment the enemy's rifles began to shoot. The bullets could scarcely miss such a target, for he flung out his arms as though in entreaty, and then drew them back till he stood like one of those wayside crosses that we saw so often as we marched through France. And he spoke. The words sounded familiar, but all I remember was the beginning. "If thou hadst known," and the ending, "but now they are hid from thine eyes."[5] And then he stopped and gathered me into his arms—me, the biggest man in the regiment—and carried me as if I had been a child.

I must have fainted again, for I woke to consciousness in a little cave by a stream, and *The Comrade in White* was washing my wounds and binding them up. It seems foolish to say it, for I was in terrible pain, but I was happier at that moment than ever I remember to have been in all my life before. I can't explain it, but it seemed as if all my days I had been waiting for this without knowing it. As long as that hand touched me and those eyes pitied me, I did not seem to care any more about sickness or health, about life or death. And while he swiftly removed every trace of blood and mire I felt as if my whole nature were being washed, as if all the grime and soil of sin were going, and as if I were once more a little child.

I suppose I slept, for when I awoke this feeling was gone. I was a man, and I wanted to know what I could do for my friend to help him or to serve him. He was looking towards the stream, and his hands were clasped in prayer; and then I saw that he too had been wounded. I could see, as it were, a shot-wound in his hand, and as he prayed a drop of blood gathered and fell to the ground. I cried out. I could not help it, for that wound of his seemed to me a more awful thing than any that bitter war had shown me. "You are wounded too," I said faintly. Perhaps he heard me, perhaps it was the look on my face, but he answered gently, "This is an old wound, but it has troubled me of late." And then I noticed sorrowfully that the same cruel mark was on his feet. You will wonder that I did not know sooner. I wonder myself. But it was only when I saw His feet that I knew Him.

"The Living Christ"—I had heard the Chaplain speak of Him a few weeks before, but now I knew that He had come to me—to me who had put Him out of my life in the hot fever of my youth. I was longing to speak and to thank Him, but no words came. And then He rose swiftly and said, "Lie here to-day by the water. I will come for you tomorrow. I have work for you to do, and you will do it for me."

In a moment He was gone. And while I wait for him I write this down that I may not lose the memory of it. I feel weak and lonely and my pain increases, but I have His promise. I know that He will come for me to-morrow.

• NINE •

C. Conway Plumbe and "The Angels of Mons"

First appearance: *Punch, or the London Charivari.* 6 October 1915, p. 293.

Punch is usually considered the English humor magazine *par excellance*, but its humor was almost invariably topical, dependent on the socially attuned reader being able to recognize the people, events, and issues of the day, and there was nothing whatsoever irreverent or anarchic about its humor. *Punch* was infallibly and unquenchably patriotic, a proud voice for the English, the ways of England, and the defense of the English empire. Were *Punch's* humor ever to come into conflict with its patriotism, the latter's victory was guaranteed.

"The Angels of Mons" was published anonymously, but *Punch* published its own indexes, and these reveal that its author was C. Conway Plumbe, but thereafter, the trail becomes faint and confusing. The C. is probably Charles. He contributed verse to *Punch* indicating that he might have been Canadian,[1] but other verse indicates he may have been English.[2] He was probably the artist of this name whose paintings were displayed at the Royal Academy in 1927,[3] but might he also have been the civil engineer who in 1949 published *Factory Well-Being*[4] and in 1953 the *Factory Health Safety and Welfare Encyclopaedia*?[5] Was this also the person who in 1950 published the philosophical treatise *Release from Time*?[6] It is not inconceivable that a poet painted and earned a living as a civil engineer, but this can be neither proved nor disproved, and these may all be different men having the same name.

> It may be just that folks have flocked
> To glorify a pretty tale;
> It may be truth that Something blocked
> That desperate battle trail,
> And, anyhow, the story's growing stale.
> But, true or not, there's this is right,
> Sure as man lives and murder's done,

Fate never mixed another fight
Since wars were first begun
With so much Freedom to be lost or won.
And swearing Tommies, beaten back,
But rallying still their broken line
Against the howling Prussian pack,
May not have seemed divine,
But still did heroes' work and did it fine.
Whether they saw the shining crew,
St. George and all the rest of it,
Or only found a job to do
And meant to stand their bit,
Something or Someone gave them grip and grit.

• TEN •

Ralph Shirley and *The Angel Warriors at Mons: Including Numerous Confirmatory Testimonies, Evidence of the Wounded, and Certain Curious Historical Parallels. An Authentic Record*

Publisher: London: Newspaper Publicity Co., 1915

The Honorable Ralph Shirley was born in 30 December 1865, brother to the eleventh Earl Ferrers; he was thus a direct descendant of Robert Devereux (1566–1601), second Earl of Essex and a favorite of Queen Elizabeth prior to his execution. He matriculated Oxford, receiving his B.A. in 1890,[1] and soon thereafter he became director (and perhaps owner) of William Rider & Son, remaining so until 1925. William Rider & Son was England's leading publisher of occult material, and they published works by such notable figures as Elliott O'Donnell,[2] A. E. Waite,[3] H. Stanley Redgrove,[4] and Hereward Carrington.[5] Although occult material was the majority of William Rider & Son's stock, it must be observed that Shirley was, like any responsible publisher, attempting to discover and promote new talent, and William Rider & Son (later Rider & Company) was also among the first to publish works by such emerging figures as John Cowper Powys[6] and his brother Theodore.[7] In January of 1905 Shirley began his editorship of *The Occult Review*, also published by William Rider & Son; under various titles, it lasted until 1951 and was the leading publisher of news and scholarship concerning the occult. Shirley left his editorship in 1926 and, though largely retired, contributed occasional essays to *The Cornhill* and *The Contemporary Review*. He died on 29 December 1946, one day before his 81st birthday.[8]

Shirley was neither a simple nor a credulous man, and *The Occult Review* under his editorship published many articles that offered rational views and did much to debunk what charlatans claimed as supernatural events. Nevertheless, he was obviously a man of sincere faith in the supernatural, and *The Angel Warriors at Mons* is a sincere recapitulation of the events as he saw them, with a valiant attempt to link them to historical events that he saw as having similarities to the Angels of Mons. Like so many of the writers included in this volume, he initially trusted in the veracity of Phyllis Campbell's accounts as they first appeared in *The Occult Review*, but the Society for Psychical Research later dismissed them with the statement that "allowance must be made for inaccuracy of memory, the force of suggestion, and other common sources of error."[9] It is thus perhaps significant that *The Angel Warriors at Mons* was published not by the reputable firm of William Rider & Son but as a pamphlet for sale by the Newspaper Publicity Company, which also published inexpensive and noncritical works on graphology, astrology, dreams and omens, and strange prophecies.[10]

The Angel Warriors at Mons

The press in this country has recently given publicity to various stories claiming to be authentic of appearances of phantom warriors who are stated to have come to the rescue of the hardly-pressed armies of France and England at the time of the retreat from Mons. At this date it will be recollected that the German army was carrying everything before it in a triumphant advance towards Paris, and it seemed to the majority of people both in this country and across the Channel that nothing could prevent the capture of the French capital. Suddenly there came a change over the whole outlook—a change that was explained in all sorts of different ways according to the conceptions of the military situations as seen from the point of view of innumerable armchair strategists. An opinion which held favour with many, and which rumour loudly supported, was that a Russian army had come by sea to an English port, and passing through this country and across the Channel had landed on the French coast, and was threatening the German line of retreat. This bubble was soon burst, but people still continued to ask themselves how it was that the triumphant onward march of the irresistible German army had suddenly been thrown back at the battle of the Marne, in disastrous and ignominious retreat.

The Bowmen

It was about this time (September 29, 1914, to be precise) that a circumstantial narrative which might have been intended to be taken either as fact or fiction appeared in the columns of the *Evening News* under the title of *The Bowmen*. This story narrated how at a critical point in the retreat of the Allies an apparition of the army of English bowmen with St. George at their head had come to the rescue of the retreating forces of General Joffre[11] and Sir John French,[12] and had struck terror into the German armies. Many readers took this charmingly-written tale as a statement of fact, but a letter addressed to the author, Mr. Machen, by the present writer, elicited the response that the narrative had no foundation outside the writer's vivid fancy. Soon, however, correspondence began to reach the papers from various quarters giving records more or less circumstantial of appearances of phantom warriors who, it was confidently averred, had actually come to the rescue of the defeated armies at this critical moment. These correspondents would have none of Mr. Machen's statement that his story was pure romance. It might not be, they said in effect, that the phantom English bowmen had been seen on the battlefield (though one of the narratives actually maintained this), but they stoutly declared that of the apparitions of spirit warriors and especially of St. George on his white charger, there could be no possible doubt. These stories were in their turn borne out by the French wounded, many of whom maintained that while the English had seen the figure they took for St. George, they themselves had seen St. Michael, while many others had witnessed the apparition of Joan of Arc riding at their head in full armour.

Such stories had indeed been widely current in France at the time of the retreat from Mons—nearly a month before the appearance of Mr. Machen's story. Thus a lance-corporal, who was subsequently wounded, and is now in an English hospital, told his nurse (Miss C. M. Wilson) of his own experience on or about August 28. It is not so definite or circumstantial as some of the others, but it has the merit at least of being first-hand. "The weather," he states, "was at the time very hot and clear, and between eight and nine o'clock in the evening we were standing with a party of nine other men on duty. Immediately behind us half of our battalion was on the edge of a wood resting, when an officer suddenly came up in a state of great anxiety and asked if we had seen anything startling," the impression at the moment being that a German surprise attack was threatened. Immediately after this the lance-corporal's attention was drawn to a strange appearance in the sky.

A Lance-Corporal's Evidence

I could see quite plainly in mid-air (he said) a strange light which seemed to be quite distinctly outlined and was not a reflection of the moon, nor were there any clouds in the neighbourhood. The light became brighter and I could see quite distinctly three shapes, one in the centre having what looked like outspread wings, the other two were not so large, but were quite plainly distinct from the centre one. They appeared to have a long loose-hanging garment of a golden tint, and they were above the German line facing us.

We stood watching them for about three-quarters of an hour. All the men with me saw them, and other men came up from other groups who also told us that they had seen the same thing. I am not a believer in such things, but I have not the slightest doubt that we really did see what I now tell you.

In most of the records of the appearance the apparition of a luminous cloud is alluded to. One of these narrates how "in this cloud there seemed to be bright objects moving. The moment it appeared the German onslaught received a check. The horses could be seen rearing and plunging and ceased to advance." A soldier of the Dublin Fusiliers is cited as confirming this phenomenon, adding, with regard to the cloud, that it quite hid them from the enemy. Numerous references have been made in the pulpits to these phenomena, some of the clergy going so far as to read letters from soldiers at the front to their congregations. Mr. Lancaster, for instance, a Weymouth clergyman, read one of these letters from a soldier who said that his regiment was pursued by a large number of German cavalry, from which they took refuge in a quarry, where the Germans found them and were on the point of shooting them. "At that moment," said the writer, "the whole top edge of the quarry was lined by angels, who were seen by all the soldiers and the Germans as well. The Germans suddenly stopped, turned round, and galloped away at top speed." The *Universe*, a Roman Catholic paper, gives a story told by a Roman Catholic officer at the front, of an apparition of men with bows and arrows, and states that when he was talking to a German prisoner afterwards the man asked who was the officer on a great white horse who led them, for although he was such a conspicuous figure they had none of them been able to hit him. This is the single instance above alluded to where the story tallies with Mr. Machen's bowmen.

Such stories as that of the apparitions of Mons have been told in connexion with various great historical battles, but they have always been put down as legendary. The most famous instance of this that is so brilliantly utilized by Lord Macaulay[13] in his ballad entitled "The Battle of Lake Regillus,"[14] where two mysterious horsemen appear, who lead the Roman army to victory and are subsequently averred to have been the great Twin Brethren of Roman Mythology, Castor and Pollux. Among Bible records we have the story of the siege of Dothan by the King of Assyria, when Elisha is narrated as turning to his terrified servant and stating that, "They that be with us are more than they that be with them."[15] Elisha then prays that his servant's eyes may be opened, that he may see, and, continues the Bible narrative, "The Lord opened the eyes of the young man and he saw, and behold, the mountain was full of horses and chariots of fire round about Elisha."

A somewhat similar story is told with regard to the victory of Judas

Maccabeus[16] in the second century B.C. over Lysias, the General of Antiochus Epiphanes.[17] The army of Judas only consisted of 10,000 men whereas that of Lysias numbered 80,000. "When they were at Jerusalem," says the historian,[18] "there appeared before them on horseback one in white apparel shaking his armour of gold. Thus they marched forward in their armour, having an helper from heaven; for the Lord was merciful unto them."

Among the most important records of psychic phenomena occurring on the occasion of the Battle of Mons is that of Miss Phyllis Campbell, who has for many months of the war been a nurse at a hospital near the front. It fell to her lot to tend various wounded soldiers who had witnessed these strange phenomena and she gave a record of her experiences in the form of an article which appeared in the August issue of the *Occult Review*.[19] On one occasion while she was bandaging a shattered arm, the President of the post, Mme de A____, came up and took her place, asking her to attend to an Englishman who was begging for a holy picture. The idea of an English soldier making such a request at such a time seemed curious enough, but she hurried off to attend to his needs. He proved to be a Lancashire Fusilier.

St. George at Mons

He was propped in a corner [says Miss Campbell], his left arm tied up in a peasant woman's head kerchief, and his head newly bandaged. He should have been in a state of collapse from loss of blood, for his tattered uniform was soaked and caked in blood, and his face paper-white under the dirt of conflict. He looked at me with bright courageous eyes and asked for a picture or a medal (he did not care which) of St. George. I asked if he was a Catholic. "No," he was a Wesleyan Methodist, and he wanted a picture, or a medal of St. George, because he had seen him on a white horse, leading the British at Vitry-le François, when the Allies turned. There was an R. F. A. man, wounded in the leg, sitting beside him on the floor; he saw my look of amazement, and hastened in, "It's true, Sister," he said. "We all saw it. First there was a sort of yellow mist, sort of risin' before the Germans as they come on to the top of the hill, come on like a solid wall they did—springing out of the earth just solid—no end to 'em. I just give up. No use fighting the whole German race, thinks I; it's all up with us. The next minute comes this funny cloud of light, and when it clears off there's a tall man with yellow hair, in golden armour, on a white horse, holding his sword up, and his mouth open as if he was saying, 'Come on, boys! I'll put the kybosh on the devils.' Sort of 'This is my picnic' expression. Then, before you could say 'knife,' the Germans had turned, and we were after them, fighting like ninety. We had a few scores to settle, Sister, and we fair settled them."

Both these soldiers knew it was St. George, for "Had not they seen him with his sword on every quid they'd ever had?" The "Frenchies," however, they admitted, maintained that it was St. Michael. The French wounded Miss Campbell describes as being in a curiously exalted condition—a sort of rapture of happiness. It was quite true, they maintained. The Germans were in full retreat, and the Allies were being led to victory by St. Michael and Joan of Arc. One of the wounded French soldiers happened to have come from Domremy, Joan of Arc's native home, and declared that he saw her brandishing her sword and crying, "Turn! turn! advance!" "No wonder," he said, "the Boches fled down the hill."

A Dying Guardsman's Narrative

Miss Phyllis Campbell told Mme de A_____ her experience with the soldiers, and they agreed to compare notes with the rest of the staff. All but one had heard the tale of the angelic leaders, and this one had been detailed to guard three wounded Germans, and had therefore had no opportunity of conversation. Miss Campbell mentions the case of three men of the Irish Guard who were mortally wounded and asked for the Sacrament before death, and before dying told the same story to the old abbé who confessed them. The author of this remarkable article draws attention to the fact that whereas immediately before the apparitions were seen all the wounded soldiers who were brought in expressed the conviction of swiftly approaching disaster, immediately afterwards there was a complete transformation of their attitude, the sense of despair giving place to a state of strange exaltation and confidence of victory. It is only natural that long forced marches without adequate food, under a condition of intense strain and anxiety, should produce a condition of the nerves which is far from normal, and however ready we may be to grant the genuineness of the experiences above narrated, it must be borne in mind that men in such a state of tension will be far more susceptible to psychic influences than they would be under normal, everyday conditions. Granted, however, that such conditions were prevalent, it is noteworthy that very similar, though not identical, experiences were undergone, if the records are to be relied upon, by thousands of French and English soldiers.

The abnormal conditions induced by the intense strain of the long marches enforced by the rearguard fighting is made evidence by a curious passage which appears in a recently published work entitled *The Crucible*, by Mabel Collins.[20] She here cites a letter from a young officer who was killed immediately afterwards, who says, "I had the most amazing hallucinations marching at night, so I was fast asleep, I think. Every one was reeling about the road and seeing things." And again, of the following night, he adds, "I saw all sorts of things, enormous men walking towards me and lights and chairs and things on the road."[21]

Another contribution to the evidence on the subject of the apparitions at the front has been sent me by the Rev. Alexander A. Boddy,[22] Vicar of All Saints, Monkwearmouth.[23] Mr. Boddy was for two months at the front with the troops in France, and in the course of his work was the recipient of some

Ten • Ralph Shirley and *The Angel Warriors at Mons*   159

interesting communications. Among other stories he gives that of a soldier of the third Canadians who stated that after the second battle of Ypres, when their battalion was retiring through their communication trenches towards their rest camp, they were obliged to halt where a West Riding regiment was stationed. During the halt one of the men of this regiment was narrating to those around him a strange experience of his own. He had seen, he said, what appeared at first to be a ball of fire. Afterwards it took the form of an angel with outstretched wings standing between the British front line and that of the enemy. Mr. Boddy also mentions a story told to the sister of a gentleman who had given up his house as a convalescent home for wounded soldiers. One of the wounded soldiers told the lady that at a critical moment an angel with outspread wings like a luminous cloud stood between the advancing Germans and themselves. This figure appeared to render it impossible for the Germans to advance and annihilate them. The lady in question was subsequently speaking of this incident in the presence of some officers and expressed her own incredulity. One of the officers, a colonel, looked up at this, and observed—"Young lady, the thing happened. You need not be incredulous. I saw it myself." It is curious to note that similar phenomena to those which have occurred in the present war were narrated of the siege of the British Legation at Pekin. The occupants of the Legation found the house they occupied untenable, and were obliged to move to another position, and while the removal took place the British were in full view of the Chinese insurgents, who they took for granted would fire upon them. To their great surprise they failed to do so. An Englishman who was present on the occasion and who knew Chinese as well as his own native language, took the opportunity afterwards of asking one of the Chinese soldiers why they missed such a fine chance. The Chinaman gave as a reason the fact that "There were so many people in white between them and the British that they did not like to fire."

A valuable addition to the list of records in connexion with the phenomena at Mons was supplied by Miss Callow,[24] secretary of the Higher Thought Centre,[25] at South Kensington, to the *Weekly Dispatch*. She writes:

> An officer has sent to one of the members of the Centre a detailed account of a vision that appeared to himself and others when fighting against fearful odds at Mons. He plainly saw an apparition representing St. George the patron saint of England, the exact counterpart of a picture that hangs to-day in a London restaurant. So terrible was their plight at the time that the officer could not refrain from appealing to the vision to help them. Then, as if the enemy had also seen the apparition, the Germans abandoned their positions in precipitate terror. In other instances men had written about seeing *Clouds of Celestial Horsemen* hovering over the British lines.

Miss Callow also adds that a nurse at the front on one occasion asked her patients why they were so silent, to which the men replied, "We have had strange experiences, which we do not care to talk about. We have seen many of our mates killed, but they are fighting for us still."

Doubt has, not unnaturally, been cast upon the credibility of these records in England, owing to the publication of Mr. Machen's story and his persistent affirmation that this story was purely evolved from his own inner consciousness. There appears, however, to be no question that the time of his writing *The Bowmen* and for weeks before, these stories had been current, especially on the other side of the Channel, and if we are to accept the now generally admitted fact of telepathy, nothing is more likely than that a record passing from mouth to mouth might have reached Mr. Machen's subconscious intelligence and formed the basis of a story the main details of which, after all, only approximately corresponded to the experiences of the soldiers at the front.

Spiritual Exaltation

The spiritual exaltation above alluded to, which is always liable to accompany great battles, has indeed given rise in numerous authenticated instances of psychical phenomena of an entirely abnormal kind, and such phenomena on the present occasion have not been confined to only one theatre of the war. Stories have been widely current in the Russian army that many Russian sentinels have seen the famous ghost of General Skobeloff[26] in white uniform and riding his white charger. This apparition is supposed to appear when the armies of the Tsar are in imminent danger, and invariably to create a panic in the enemy's ranks. General Skobeloff, it will be remembered, played a conspicuous part in the Russo-Turkish War of 1877–1878, in particular the storming of the then Turkish fortress of Plevna.

A spiritual experience of another kind is also told in connexion with the battle of Augustovo in October 1914, in which the German army met with its first disastrous defeat at the hands of the Russians. The story, which was communicated by a Russian general who was with the army operating in East Prussia, runs as follows:

Vision of the Virgin Mary

While our troops were in the region of Suwalki, the captain of one of my regiments witnessed a marvellous revelation.

It was eleven o'clock at night, and the troops were in bivouac. Suddenly a soldier from one of our outposts, wearing a startled look, rushed in and called the captain. The latter went with the soldier to the outskirts of the camp and witnessed an amazing apparition in the sky. It was that of the Virgin Mary, with the Infant Christ on one hand, the other hand pointing to the west.

Our soldiers knelt on the ground and gazed fervently at the vision. After a time the apparition faded, and in its place came a great image of the Cross, shining against the dark night sky.

Slowly it faded away.
On the following day our army advanced westward to the victorious battle of Augustovo." [sic]

This strange state of psychic exaltation is also doubtless accountable for the remarkable and well-attested phenomena which took place nightly for some months after the Battle of Edge Hill, in the English Civil War, on the subject of which Lord Nugent[27] makes comment "that the world abounds with histories of preternatural appearances, the most utterly incredible, supported by testimonies the most undeniable."[28] Here is a ghost story of the most preposterous sort. "Yet is this story," he adds, "attested upon the oath of three officers, men of honour and distinction, and of three other gentlemen of credit, selected by the King as commissioners to report upon these prodigies, and to tranquillize and disabuse the alarms of a country town."[29] The record of these phenomena is given in a rare and curious tract entitled *A Great Wonder in Heaven, showing the late Apparitions and Prodigious Noyses of War and Battels, seen on Edge Hill, neere Keinton in Northamptonshire. Certified under the hands of William Wood, Esquire, and Justice for the Peace in the said Countie, Samuel Marshall, Preacher of Gods Word in Keinton, and other Persons of Qualitie.—London: Printed for Thomas Jackson, January 23, Anno Dom. 1642 (1643?).*[30] Its bearing on the question under discussion seems to me to warrant its republication here in the words of the narrator:

The Battle of Edge Hill

Between twelve and one o'clock in the morning (says our authority), was heard by some shepherds, and other country-men, and travellers, first the sound of drummes afar off, and the noyse of souldiers, as it were, giving out their last groanes; at which they were much amazed, and amazed stood still, till it seemed, by the neernesse of the noyse, to approach them; at which too much affrighted, they sought to withdraw as fast as possibly they could; but then, on the sudden, whilst they were in these cogitations, appeared in the ayre the same incorporeall souldiers that made these clamours, and immediately, with ensigns display'd, drummes beating, musquets going off, cannons discharged, horses neyghing, which also to these men were visible, the alarum or entrance to this game of death was strucke up, one Army, which gave the first charge having the King's colours, and the other the Parliaments in their head or front of the battells, and so pell mell to it they went; the battell that appeared to the Kings forces seeming at first to have the best, but afterwards to be put into equall scale continued this dreadful fight, the clattering of Armes, noyse of cannons, cries of souldiers, so amazing and terrifying the poore men, that they could not believe they were mortall, or give credit to their eares and eyes; runne away they durst not, for feare of being made a prey to these infernall souldiers, and so they, with much feare and affright, stayed to behold the successe of the businesse, which at last suited to this effect: after some three hours fight, that Army which carryed the Kings colours withdrew, or rather appeared to flie; the other remaining, as it were, masters of the field, stayed a good space triumphing, and expressing all the signes of joy and conquest, and then, with all their drummes, trumpets, ordinance, and souldiers vanished; the poore men were glad they were gone, that had so long staid them there against their wills, made with all haste to Keinton, and there knocking up Mr. Wood, a Justice of the Peace, who called up his neighbor, Mr. Marshall, the Minister, they gave them an account of the true passage, and averred it upon their oaths to be true. At which affirmation of theirs, being much amazed, they would hardly have given credit to it, but would have conjectured the men to have been either mad or drunk, had they not knowne some of them to have been of approved integritie; and so, suspending their judgements till the next night about the same houre, they, with the same men, and all substantiall inhabitants of that and the neighbouring parishes, drew thither; where, about half an houre after their arrivall, on Sunday, being Christmas night, appeared in the same tumultuous warlike manner, the same two adverse Armies, fighting with as much spite and spleen as formerly. The next night they appeared not, nor all the week, so that the dwellers thereabout were in good hope they had for ever departed; but on the ensuing Saturday night, in the same place, and at the same hour, they were again seene with far greater tumult, fighting in the manner afore-mentioned for four hours, and then vanished, appearing again on Sunday night, and performing the same actions of hostilities and bloodshed; so that both Mr. Wood and others, whose faith, it should seeme, was not strong enough to carry them out against these delusions, forsook their habitations thereabout, and retired themselves to other more secure dwellings; but Mr. Marshall stayed, and some others; and so successively the next Saturday and Sunday the same tumults and prodigious sights and actions were put in the state and condition they were formerly. The rumour whereof coming to his Majestie at Oxford, he immediately dispatched thither Colonell Lewis Kirke, Captaine Dudley, Captaine Wainman, and three other gentlemen of credit, to take the full view and notice of the said businesse, who, first hearing the true attestation and relation of Mr. Marshall and others staid there till Saturday night following, wherein they heard and saw the fore-mentioned prodigies, and so on Sunday, distinctly knowing divers of the apparitions or incorporeall substances by their faces, as that of Sir Edumund Varney,[31] and others that were there slaine; of which upon oath they made testimony to his Majestie. What this does portend God only knoweth, and time perhaps will discover; but doubtlessly it was a signe of his wrath against this Land, for these civil wars, which He in His good time finish, and send a sudden peace between his Majestie and Parliament.[32]

This strange psychic record is not indeed in any sense an exact parallel to the phenomena which have excited so great an interest at the present time, but it serves to show the effect that war is liable to produce upon the psychic atmosphere, and in this manner may render such incidents as those recently recorded credible to the minds of many who would at first sight be disposed to reject them as old wives' tales. If the phenomena following the Battle of Edge Hill so fully substantiated by contemporary evidence actually took place, why should it not be possible for psychic phenomena of a certainly no more remarkable kind, to be one of the concomitant circumstances of the greatest war in the world's history? Would it not rather be strange if it were otherwise?

These records do not in fact stand alone. The ghostly story of the Battle of Edge Hill which has been perpetuated in the *Memorials of John Hampden, His Party and Times*, by Lord Nugent, finds a close parallel in the record of the Battle of Mook-Heath of April 13, 1574, as narrated in *Motley's Rise of the Dutch Republic*.[33] In both cases were individual combatants identified. In both cases the phenomena were not confined to experiences of the sight alone. The shouts of the combatants and the discharge of cannon and the rattle of musketry were clearly audible in both instances. The main difference indeed lay in the curious fact that whereas the phenomena at Edge Hill followed the date of the battle, in the case of Mook-Heath they preceded it by some two months. It appears, indeed, that in some peculiar way great wars open up fresh channels for the psychic senses, and the physical struggle of great armies appears ever to have its counterpart on the spiritual plane, by the bringing into action of psychic forces working for good or evil, on the side of Light or of Darkness—"principalities and powers mustering their unseen array"[34]— upon whose efforts no less than upon the efforts of those now living on the physical plane the great and final issues of this vast world-conflict ultimately depend.

The Pros and Cons

One important point is inevitably raised with regard to these apparitions on the European battlefields. They have this in common, with many similar apparitions—that is they are not seen alike by all witnesses. Where one sees St. George another sees St. Michael, and a third Joan of Arc. Were all three of these heroes of the past actually present on the battlefield, or indeed were any of them? Even assuming that we accept the authenticity of the visions, we are not, I think, called upon to say that they were. Spirit is plastic. May we not rather say that it is Protean? It is clothed upon by the imagination of the beholder to an almost limitless extent. In a further account of Miss Phyllis Campbell's which she gave to the editor of the *Evening News*, she relates how a soldier of the Irish Guards, an enormous man who stood over six feet five inches, told her, narrating his own experiences, that "St. George was in golden armour, bareheaded, and riding a white horse." He cried "Come on!" as he brandished his sword. Why, we may ask, was St. George in golden armour? Doubtless because the Irish guardsman had seen him most recently on the back of a sovereign. Here also he is brandishing a sword. The apparitions which created such a sensation in the South of France a few months before the outbreak of war had the same tendency to vary according to the temperament of the beholder. Here, too, Joan of Arc was seen (among others) and foretold the fact that she was the harbinger of a great war, by making stars appear from out of a clouded sky at the request of the village curé. Who can doubt that if a Theosophist had been present at the retreat of Mons he would have witnessed an apparition of one of the Mahatmas, just as the Russian soldiers saw the phantom of General Skobeloff? The gods of ancient days, according to classical story, became visible to the heroes whose causes they espoused, in the guise of mortal men. The radiant forms of the spiritual hierarchies can only be made manifest to mortal eye in a form which the beholder can interpret. The spirit champion of British arms inevitably takes the form of St. George. He comes in the spirit and power of St. George to do St. George's work, and thus the British soldier interprets his spiritual leaders in terms of the ancient traditions of his race.

• ELEVEN •

Isabelle E. Taylor and *Angels, Saints & Bowmen of Mons: An Answer to Mr. Arthur Machen & Mr. Harold Begbie*

Published: London: Published for the Author by the Theosophical Publishing Society, 1916

According to the *Catalogue* of the British Library, I. E. Taylor's full last name is Stilwell-Taylor, and under Stilwell-Taylor responsibility are listed four Theosophically related titles published at about this time.[1] Unquestionably these works are by the same person, but that person was one Isabelle E. Taylor, and so she signed herself and was known to her publisher Swan Sonnenschein. It is not known why the British Library desexed her by referencing only her first initial, nor is it known why it assigned her the additional patronym. Nothing is known about Isabelle E. Taylor, however, although census records indicate somebody by this name born in Surrey circa 1862. She appears to have become completely inactive following the First World War and has vanished without a trace. The Theosophical Society in England today does "not know anything about this person."[2]

The central tenets of Theosophy are not easily or briefly stated. The name is "derived from the Greek *theos* (rod) and *Sophia* (wisdom), denoting a philosophical-religious system that claims absolute knowledge of the existence and nature of the deity."[3] The Theosophical Society was established in November 1875 by Helena Petrovna Blavatsky, Henry Steel Olcott, and William Quan Judge, the stated object being "to collect and diffuse a knowledge of the laws which govern the universe." They hoped "that by going deeper than modern science has hitherto done, into the esoteric philosophies of ancient times, they may be enabled to obtain, for themselves and other investigators, proof of the existence of an 'Unseen Universe.'"[4] They thus

165

believed that many of these proofs would and could be revealed by hidden Mahatmas of India and Tibet. Nevertheless, it cannot be determined if Taylor's assertions in *Angels, Saints & Bowmen* correctly reflect the teachings of Theosophy or if her statements would have been disputed and rejected by the Theosophists of her day.

Arthur Machen dismisses *Angels, Saints & Bowmen* in "The Angles of Mons: Absolutely My Last Word on the Subject" [q.v.], stating that "without any intention of disrespect, I must say that I can make nothing of Mr. [sic] Taylor," simultaneously giving the pamphlet more attention than it was to receive from the general press while not recognizing that Taylor was a woman. Machen is correct in his descriptions and assertions but misses the larger implications of his argument: the story of the Angels of Mons was so popular and so culturally pervasive that other faiths than Christianity were claiming it in their own support. Nevertheless, whether Ms. Taylor's Theosophically-inspired effort contributes anything substantive to the discussions is debatable.

Angels, Saints and Bowmen of Mons

Having read *The Bowmen*, by Mr. Arthur Machen, and also *On the Side of the Angels*, by Mr. Harold Begbie, I have taken up my pen for the purpose of dealing with the subject of the Angels of Mons from an aspect which would appear to have escaped the notice of these writers whose books mainly concern the physicist. From the point of view of the prophet, the theosophist and the occultist, the idea of the visions of our soldiers having resulted from the publication of Mr. Machen's story of *The Bowmen* is almost incomprehensibly ridiculous; and the reproduction, by Mr. Harold Begbie, of statement after statement in a necessarily fruitless endeavour to prove a spiritual reality to material understanding, is, from the above point of view, a lamentable waste of time and energy which might have been profitably employed in answering the only vital question which arises, namely: What is the meaning of the visions which the soldiers saw? The answer is long, but may be commenced on this wise: In the book of The Revelation of St. John the Divine we find a description of a certain war known as "the great day of the battle of God Almighty."

Into this war, which has also been mentioned by many prophets of the Old Testament (notably Isaiah, Jeremiah, Ezekiel and Daniel), every nation was destined ultimately to be drawn. ("I will call for a sword upon all the inhabitants of the earth, saith the Lord of hosts" *Jer.* xxv. 29.) And it will be remembered that the remaining remnant of the races surviving this appalling chastisement of the Almighty were to be gathered together "into a place called in the Hebrew tongue Armageddon"[5] (*Rev.* xvi. 16). For hundreds of years The Revelation of St. John the Divine and the books of the Prophets have been read and expounded by ecclesiasticism in our Churches without the aid of a single ray of light whereby to reveal their spiritual significance; and the consequence of this teaching is, that without warning, we have now arrived at that period of racial history recognised by the Prophets as "the latter days" of the Christian era and, equally without warning, have been thrust into the midst of this great "battle" of God Almighty which, while sounding the death knell of the sixth age of our world, is already introducing some of the spiritual conditions destined to obtain in the seventh. Judging this subject however from the aspect now in view, we cannot blame theology for its inability to cope with our present trouble; because theologians, during the time which was allotted to them, have more or less faithfully carried out the work with which they were entrusted; and the present conditions of our visible universe having resulted from divine prophecy which, irrespective of human creed or belief, has come right down through the ages to the present time, we are by these very conditions reminded, that the ecclesiastical term of office, which was never intended to be permanent, is due to terminate now; and, consequently, the hand of toddling material manhood is about to be withdrawn from the priest and placed in that of the prophet who is already beckoning across the awful chasm of world-wide material destruction, now separating this age from the next. "What then," the materialist may ask, "was the use of theology at all? Why were we kept in the dark about these things? What is the sixth age of the world? in short, where, in all this tangle of evolution, are we?" Let us first endeavour to disengage the thread of ecclesiasticism from the web of human evolution and examine its *raison d'être*.

Although, in so doing, the reader is warned that, as it is by no means easy to explain, in words which can be understood by persons trained in western thought, great Spiritual truths which, for millions of years, have lain under the cloak of an adequate symbology, it may be found necessary to set them forth in these pages in a manner which is neither purely theosophical nor purely scientific; and the tolerance of theosophists and scientists is therefore asked by the writer, whose present purpose is but to point out as simply and lucidly as possible, the relationship of the divine scheme of evolution to the signs of the present time. We all know that there was once a people called Israel which was Biblically recognised as "God's." Some of us know also, that the Israelites were forward in evolution albeit careless, slothful and intemperate.[6]

Moreover, ecclesiasticism has taught the masses that persistent indulgence in these and other vices, on the part of the Israelites finally incurred the "Wrath" of the Almighty who, about the year 606 BC laid upon his chosen people a curse of "blindness in part." Theology, however, has never given us any deeper reason for this seemingly severe punishment of the Israelites than "the wrath of God" and it is this omission which necessitates the loosening of the occult, theosophical, scientific and prophetic threads of the evolutionary web we are examining and binding them firmly round the defective, or "twopenny" parts of the morality which theology has taught.

By so doing the writer hopes to show that nothing—be it "twopenny" or otherwise—which appears in, or appertains to, the visible universe we inhabit, is without its peculiar significance and use. Theosophy teaches us that the visible universe is one of a chain of seven worlds resulting from divine ideation or Thought; and that its periods of activity are regularly succeeded by periods of rest; in other words, it appears and disappears periodically, returning after the performance of its cycle of evolution, into the Infinite essence from which it emanated and which Christians call "God." The Creation of Genesis therefore is recognised by the theosophist but as one of a series of similar creations, and theosophy considers humanity, also, as an emanation from Divinity on its return path thereto. There is naturally neither time nor space here and now to describe the doctrine of the Ancients concerning the life Cycles and root races of the human family after it has been launched by Divinity on its evolutionary course through-out a septenary chain of worlds; the reader who desires to pursue this subject will find it adequately dealt with in the various works of present day theosophists; nevertheless, in order to clear the way for a lucid explanation of the Israelitish curse, it is necessary to gather up a sufficiency of the theosophical thread, which we are now handling. Let us then understand that our earth is the visible representative of its six superior, though invisible fellow globes, and has to live, as have the others, though seven rounds, during the first three of which it forms and consolidates, during the fourth it settles and hardens, and during the last three it gradually returns to its ethereal form. Man—a facsimile of the universe—performs his evolutions (or works out his salvation) in the same way. Like the universe, he is septenary, like the universe he is an emanation from Atomic Deity, and commences his evolution ethereally; and similarly, as in mid ages, the universe forms, consolidates, settles and hardens, does man, in mid-evolution, materialize and develop physically and mentally.

Finally, in the same manner in which the Universe enters upon its predestined course of reversion towards the Spiritual, does man gradually redevelop the use of the corresponding senses within himself which attune him to spiritual sources of knowledge; and as divinity—otherwise nature—has ordained that all life should be vibratory, and that the rates of human thought and universal conditions should be determined by the degree of human or universal spiritual advancement, it follows that as soon as man realises that, in addition to his five physical senses, he possesses two others which connect him with knowledge and executive having their sources in the super-physical world, his thought vibrations become accelerated, and, lifting his vision and understanding to a higher plane of life, meet and mingle (at first but momentarily) with those of the Spiritual Beings functioning on one or other of the hitherto invisible prototypes of our globe which lying, as they have always lain, round about us in what materialists call "space" have suddenly become tangible and available through unity of vibratory thought-rate. In one of the most beautiful passages of the Gospel of St. John, our Lord refers, in the following words, to the graduated vibratory rate of progressive spiritual thought as it becomes available to man, in accordance with the measure of his fitness to receive it; that fitness being determined by the purity of his thought which, in its turn, determines the rate of his vibrations:

"In my Father's house are many mansions, if it were not so, I would have told you."—*St. John* xiv. 2.

In times of intense agony of mind, of great moral elevation, of bodily and mental exhaustion and of approaching death, we may see and speak to our fellow beings inhabiting one or other of these "many mansions" on the Spiritual, and—under ordinary circumstances—invisible planes of life. Indeed in cases of approaching death few of us fail to see either friends or relatives whom we have spoken of as "dead," or Beings from higher Spiritual mansions, whom we recognise as Angels; and the first (counting from our end of the chain) of the six invisible fellow globes of our own visible one being, so to speak, next of kin to the physical, closely surrounds and interpenetrates it; occupying what the physicist sees and describes as "space," and thus providing an immediately accessible "mansion" for the human soul, on its departure from physical existence, a rendez-vous for relatives and friends coming from various other Spiritual habitations to receive it, and a footing for the Angels, Saints and other great Beings from "mansions" of a far higher vibratory rate, who may appear upon it in order to watch the deeds of physical man; or to direct and take part in any great material struggle with which he would otherwise be unable to cope. The vibratory rate of this nearest invisible prototype of our world is attuned to the sixth (or first Spiritual) sense in man who, evolving sympathetically with the universe, is unfailingly supplied by it with whatsoever he is fitted to receive.

In the beginning, that is to say, when our present world, having newly emanated from deity, was performing its evolution on the ethereal line of life,[7] there were no mysteries; moreover, for millions of years after the Atomic soul of man had gone forth from Divinity on its evolutionary course in the visible world, it retained a clear recollection and appreciation of the nature of its divine source of being. As, however, material civilisation develops the physical and intellectual at the cost of the psychic and spiritual, the further man advances along the physical and (academically) intellectual line of life, the further he recedes from the spiritual until, in mid-mundane evolution, he entirely loses the use of his sixth and seventh senses, which become available again only when he begins cycling back towards his spiritual origin. Our present universe, since entering upon its material evolution, has passed through the five rounds or dispensations of graduated progression towards its predestined goal, which we recognise as the Edenic, Antediluvian, Noachian, Patriarchal and Mosaic, and has duly brought us to the end of the Sixth—Christian—Age, which marks that fateful period of our existence spoken of in the Book of Daniel as "the latter days," during which a stern Divine settling up of the moral accounts of all nations, kingdoms, governments, societies, and individuals, is required of us, before "back-sliding" Israel can be restored to his promised inheritance in the Holy Land. As far as the masses are concerned, the five material senses of man have sufficed for his evolution throughout these five material ages of the past; but the spiritual knowledge which was available for all in the beginning—has never departed from the universe wherein it still remains, attuned as heretofore, to the higher vibratory thought-rate of those whose capacity—momentarily or permanently—exceeds the limits of the physical senses.

Thus, though in all ages prophets, theosophists, occultists, scientists, poets, musicians, artists and dreamers of dreams, in accordance with the measure of responsive "light" within themselves, become vibratorily connected with the Divine invisible forces latent in the visible universe; no amount of material fact, however accurately set forth, in support of a Spiritual verity, can prove its reality to those who, still cycling exclusively upon the material line of life, are incapable of availing themselves of the faculty which enables "older souls" to receive such verities quite unsupported by proof. And this being the rock against which Mr. Harold Begbie has dashed his literary force, let us by means of further adequate and careful explanation endeavour to steer quite clear of its angularities.

If then we understand that the first invisible plane of life through which we pass on our way to one or other of those "many mansions" of our Father's house, closely surrounds and interpenetrates our present visible world, and that the only barrier which separates us from its inhabitants is dissimilarity of thought, we must also realise that, in order to connect ourselves with this progressive plane of life and to see Angels or speak to comrades functioning thereon, we need not necessarily (in theological parlance) "die," nor move an inch from where we physically stand, but that it is essential that by some means or other we should purify our thoughts; for thought, both Divine and human, being the creative power of all manifestation, is the strongest force which exists; and its action being reciprocal, a pure and earnest desire or prayer intelligently sent out to Divinity on the rapid vibrations of intuitive Spiritual faith in the unseen, as inevitably secures its exact measure of pure and powerful spiritual responsiveness, as the law of gravitation provides that, when we throw a ball into the air, it will come down again; for Divinity works through all the laws of reciprocity and periodicity which secure to man that wonderful exactitude of justice which enjoins that he shall reap precisely as he sows.[8] We cannot therefore reach and attune our vibrations to the higher rate of faith in the existence and conditions of the invisible world which is lying round about us, until we have altered the quality of our thought to the extent of bringing it into harmony with these more rapid spiritual vibrations which have hitherto—so to speak—passed over our heads, in the same manner as the significant value of the stories of the Angels of Mons has passed over the heads of the majority of readers of to-day. There are three methods by which man attunes his vibrations to the higher rates of spiritual sight, knowledge and executive; firstly, he arrives naturally at the point of ability to do so, after entering upon his spiritual line of evolution while in the material universe, and thus becoming what theosophists call an "older soul" and materialists either a "genius" or a "crank." Secondly, by "dying" and, as a natural consequence, waking up in the invisible universe in the possession of the faculties and knowledge in which, in material life, he systematically disbelieved; and thirdly, when, by heroic thoughts, noble deeds, fervent prayer (rightly offered) or menace of death, his spiritual senses are, by these sympathetic conditions, suddenly set free, when he may see "departed" comrades, or the Angels and Saints in whose existence he faithfully believes, and who are, in consequence of his belief, enabled visibly to approach him through sympathetic rates of thought vibration. To the physical eye the vibratory rates of thought appear to be coloured in accordance with their quality; the Spiritual being yellow, in shades varying from orange to light itself. The greater the purity of the thinker, the more rapid the vibratory-rate of his thought which, though invisible to the physical eye, surrounds him like a halo, and makes its soothing and strengthening influence felt by all who approach within the radius of its rays. The more rapid the vibrations the purer is the yellow shade of their colouring; and in cases of exalted Beings coming from those higher mansions of the soul, one of which St. Paul describes as "the third heaven" the thought-rate is so rapid that its action glows like golden dust forced into dazzling light, thus clothing the thinker in garments radiant as the sun. The low vibratory rate of materialism cannot, under ordinary circumstances, attune itself to the dazzling rapidity of that of the great Spiritual Beings who descend from these higher mansions; nor can their brilliant presence (consequently) be looked upon with the physical eye; therefore men's physical senses must first, through great bodily fatigue, illness, or other causes, have become dazed or suspended; or the whole body may be lying in what doctors describe as a "comatose condition" for—again to quote St. Paul—"Whilst we are at home in the body, we are absent from the Lord" (II. Cor. v. 6).

To many of our exhausted soldiers lying on the awful battlefields of this present war, great Spiritual Comforters have, in this way, come; and awakening the intuitions of these brave souls, shown them that there is a higher conception of Christianity and of God than ecclesiasticism preaches from the pulpit. In dealing, however, with that first invisible mansion which immediately encircles and interpenetrates our own world, we must remember that its vibrations are far lower and easier to reach from the physical plane than are those of the higher grades of spiritual progression, and that although Angels, Saints and prophets may repeatedly come down to it in order to watch the progress of great crises on the physical plane, this is not their natural habitat, inasmuch as their vibrations are attuned to the higher rates of higher conditions of life; for it is important that we should realise that the thought atmosphere of this first invisible plane is but one degree purer than our own. The man who dies a sinner in our own visible world does not wake up upon this plane a Saint, but a sinner still; he has changed nothing but his physical body; his tastes, habits and desires remain unaltered; and his predominating thought in physical life still (invisibly) draws him to the same haunts of vice which formerly he visibly frequented, and to which he is still vibratorily attuned; therefore through invisible influence over sinners such as he,[9] he may become a greater power for evil than he was in physical life. We see then that our strongest thoughts in the visible world influence our actions in the invisible one which interpenetrates it; and that the man suddenly cut off from physical life while in the endeavour to accomplish either a good or evil deed upon which his strongest thought was concentrated, remains for a time vibratorily attuned to the place in which his crowning efforts were made, to the conditions under which he strove or to the companions who shared his thoughts, so long as the vibratory-rates of place, conditions or human mind remain attuned, through the power of sympathy to his own. Hence we understand that the soldier killed in battle does not necessarily cease to fight. It is true that he has departed from the physical sight of his purely materialistic companions because the world of action which interpenetrates our own appears to the physical eye to be but empty space; nevertheless, at a given moment these same materialistic companions may, through exalted thought or anguished prayer, awaken within their physical eyes the spiritual sight which will reveal "departed" comrades fighting in this so-called "empty space" exactly as they fought before they fell.

It is noteworthy that both superphysical beings and superphysical conditions are readily sensed and seen by animals (especially the finer types, such as horses and dogs) where they may be quite unperceived by man; and if we examine still more closely, the theosophical thread of our evolutionary web, the reason for this phenomenon will naturally unfold. On page 10 of this work it has been stated that in the beginning there were no mysteries, and that for millions of years after the atomic soul of man has gone forth on its evolutionary career in the visible universe, it still retains a clear knowledge and appreciation of the nature of the Divine source from whence it came. Having passed through its ethereal course, the human soul enters the mineral kingdom wherein it gains its first experience of material life; thence it passes successively through the vegetable and animal kingdoms prior to its appearance in man as we recognise him to-day. The Spiritual capacity of man, as has already been pointed out, recedes in proportion as he advances along the material line of his evolution until, having arrived at perfection thereon, his reversion towards the Spiritual commences. During evolution in the animal kingdom, he lacked the power of speech, albeit on the other hand, he had not then outgrown the faculties of spiritual sight and intuition; for, not having reached material perfection, these faculties were available still, and a very striking illustration of their availability is afforded us in the twenty-second Chapter of the *Book of Numbers*, wherein we are told that it was not Balaam who first saw the Angel of the Lord standing in the way, but the ass; and it is easy to realise that had Balaam been a materialist pure and simple he never *would* have sensed the presence of God's messenger, but remained in a state of physical bewilderment very similar to that of the German soldiers whose experience is repeated by Mr. Harold Begbie, on page 67 of *On the Side of the Angels*, and which reads as follows: "A.M.B., writing to the *Church Times* from Paris, on July 28th, 1915, gave the following testimony from a German source:—A lady in Germany at that time ... tells me that there was much discussion in Berlin because a certain regiment who had been told off to do a certain duty at a certain battle, failed to carry out their orders, and when censured they declared that they did go forward but found themselves absolutely powerless to proceed with their orders, and their horses turned sharply round and fled like the wind and nothing could stop them. The explanation given by the German soldiers was in these words: 'We simply could not go on, those devils of Englishmen were up to some devilry or other, and we could do nothing—we were powerless.' This same lady had the opportunity of a conversation with one of the Lieutenants of the regiment in question, and as the affair had made some stir in Berlin owing to the severe reprimand given to the men, she asked him what really happened. He said 'I cannot tell you! I only know that we were charging full on the British at a certain place, and in a moment we were stopped. It was most like going full speed and being pulled up suddenly on a precipice, but there was no precipice there, nothing at all, only our horses swerved round and fled and we could do nothing!'"

Anent the above circumstance it has been explained that dissimilar rates of thought vibration will not blend; moreover that the most rapid and powerful vibrations proceed from the purest thought. Pure thought therefore is a positive force in nature which attracts towards it all that is good while repelling the evil; on the other hand, impure thought is negative, and attracts but the slow vibrations of evil. The vibrations of good and evil thought are therefore antagonistic, and the good being positive deflects the evil, which is negative, and returns it to its source. In charging full on the British, the Germans were unwittingly preparing ferociously to attack God's chosen people—the Israelites of the latter day house of Israel, with whom we are about to deal in the second part of this book, and even as Balaam was forbidden to curse the former Israelites when they came out of Egypt and pitched in the plains of Moab, so are their enemies forbidden to annihilate the latter day Israelites in the great "day of the battle of God Almighty" which precedes their restoration to the Holy Land. Between the lines of the opposing German and British forces an Angel or Angels stood, thus interposing an impassable barrier of pure thought between modern Israel and his foe.

The thought auras of Angels and men extend beyond them into space, and therefore when, preceded by massed unholy thought, the German hordes pressed on, the lower vibrations of this quality of thought had no sooner encountered the higher ones of the opposing Spiritual force than the shock of revulsion was felt, and the evil returned through the action of the Divine law of reciprocity, to its natural source. We are told that on this occasion the Germans saw nothing; but what did their horses see? Their action strangely resembled that of Balaam's Ass. Moreover on another occasion we find that in order to turn the battle in favour of the Allies it became necessary to awaken the Spiritual sight of the Germans, in the same manner as in days of yore, it was found necessary to "open the eyes" of Balaam; and that on this occasion the Germans saw in the superphysical "space" thousands of our fallen soldiers fighting in troops behind their physical comrades. This story told by an English lady, to whom a dying soldier was speaking, is also repeated by Mr. Begbie, and in the following words: "'It's a funny thing, sister, isn't it, how the Germans say we had a lot of troops behind us?' ... He went on to assure me that German prisoners had said, 'how could we break through your line when you had all those thousands of troops behind you?' And he added 'Thousands of troops! Why, we were just a thin line of two regiments with nothing behind us.' Now, I believe in a life after death" (continues this lady) "but I don't believe in Angels on earth, so I said to the soldier 'Well, it seems to me fairly easy to understand. When a man is killed, in the very thick of a fight, and with all his angry passions at white heat, I suppose his soul remains for some time on earth, and is unable to tear itself away from the battle.' At this another man on the opposite side of the ward joined in, and said to me, 'You're quite right, sister. I've many times heard a shot man in the trenches say to those who were looking after him, just before he died,' 'Never mind, mates, I'll be there to help you.' I've heard that said many times. Another German prisoner talked of the crowd of troops behind the British line, saying that all the Germans had seen them."

A vivid illustration of the effect which may be produced by sudden encounters of antagonistic thought Auras is afforded by the experience of a near relative of the present writer who in the year 1882 when a young lady of twenty-one years of age, told the following story:

> "In a certain village, a certain gentleman was conducting the education of a limited number of pupils in conjunction with that of his own sons, the eldest of the pupils being a youth of eighteen. In addition to these there resided at the house an eighteen year old nephew of a high dignitary of the church. It happened one day that some of the boys possessed themselves of an old Saloon pistol which had been carelessly left in a drawer by a visitor. The two eldest pupils secretly purchased some bullets and took the pistol into the garden to try its efficiency. An accident resulted; the nephew of the high dignitary of the Church was shot between the eye and the nose, the bullet penetrated the roof of the mouth and finally passed down the throat. No matter what followed. The accident is merely given as the cause to an effect. It suffices to say that being on intimate terms with the family, I, as a matter of course, walked over to the house one afternoon to enquire as to the state of the unfortunate sufferer. My friend, the gentleman's daughter, was nursing the patient who was then growing better, though of course his injuries must remain for life. As I rose to go, my friend said 'He would like to see you, will you come up?' I hesitated, thinking that to do so would be injudicious, considering the state of extreme prostration to which the patient had been reduced; but my friend urged that he had asked to see me, and, not wishing to disappoint him, I finally rose and followed her across the hall. The staircase was broad, with many landings. My friend had already tripped up to the first of these ere, placing my hand upon the stair-rail, I raised my foot towards the lowest stair in order to follow her, when, in an instant, I was struck by some invisible though overwhelming force, which held me rigidly fixed in that position, my body bent slightly forward—as one bends to an ascent—one hand resting upon the stair-rail, the other extended towards the opposite wall, my foot poised in mid-air between the floor and the first stair; and no more than I could have lifted the house upon my shoulders could I have moved one single nerve of my whole body. The nearest material similitude of the feeling which I can give was that of hopelessly trying to force my way against an impenetrable screen of solid iron which had suddenly slid down from above, and, pressing close against my chest, stood between me and the stair upon which I was about to place my foot. The sensation lasted but for a second, and I was then as suddenly liberated. My first feeling was one of complete bewilderment as to the nature and cause of this remarkable exhibition of invisible force which, without the least sign of approach, was capable, in an instant, of barring my progress far more effectually than could any tangible means of opposition. My next was a realisation of the warning it conveyed. I became conscious that there was some quality or some circumstance connected with the lad which was antagonistic to my own character, and ought to be avoided. Perhaps I was

being warned to turn back." Given in her own words, this is the young lady's story, to which should be added the following facts. Reared in seclusion, she was of a thoughtful, studious disposition; the predominating trait of her character being morality; on the other hand, the lad, though lovable, was of dissolute habits, and his career, as the result of the above-mentioned accident, having been completely ruined, he subsequently became an intemperate, immoral, reckless and dangerous man.

That in all ages our Guardian Angels have endeavoured to stand between us and threatened evil there is ample proof in the physical world to satisfy every living sceptic were it possible for the sceptic to receive it; but as it is Divine law that man shall receive only in accordance with the measure of his faith, it follows that whatsoever he firmly believes, for him shall be, or become real, and whatsoever he disbelieves, for him, shall be non-existent. Materialistic research is limited to the power of the five material senses of man because the materialist does not believe in the existence of the other two senses which connect him[10] with higher sources of knowledge. All along the lines of his physical research therefore he needs material proof until he has stumbled across the barrier between his fifth and sixth senses and discovered the Spiritual intuition which supplants material proof; then will he have quickened the vibratory rate of his thought and begun to connect himself with men and things which were hitherto invisible; then will he have made it easier for Spiritual Beings to aid him in distress; and then will he believe the stories of our soldiers when they speak of the Angels of Mons.

Part II.

The casual reader seldom discriminates between the supernatural and the superphysical, were it otherwise there would be less of the feeling of awe and creepiness which usually besets people when one speaks of having seen in the superphysical world, friends or relatives who have been understood to have been "dead" for years. It is hoped, however, that the explanations given in the first part of this book may help such readers to realise that it is not God who limits their vision to the physical plane of life, but their own disbelief in there being any other. To a large number of so-called "cranks" the superphysical world is as real as the physical; and these people see nothing extraordinary in the stories which have been told by our soldiers. But apart from Biblical sentiment, both logic and common sense must ultimately lead us all to the conclusion that the superphysical planes of life can only be available through the use of the superphysical senses in man which correspond with them; and that so long as material man looks upon these senses as "fancy," and the superphysical world as "supernatural," fancy and supernatural for him they must remain. Thus with the physicist pure and simple (otherwise the "younger soul") the sixth human sense is so clogged by material thought and custom that it is generally necessary for the material body to "die" before this sense can be liberated; in which case, though the dying man may describe to his bedside companions places and persons he sees in the superphysical as he approaches it, in passing into it, he carries his newly acquired knowledge away with him; and his material friends merely say: "Poor chap! he was rambling," or "quite light-headed," before he died. But there are occasions when in dangerous maladies men and women are carried to the threshold of death's door, see through it into the superphysical "Space" as do those who die, but instead of passing into it, recover, and return to physical life with their superphysical experiences indelibly stamped upon their souls; and this having been the case with the author, these explanations are not offered as hypotheses, but as experienced facts.

A soldier fighting in battle is in the same position as an invalid prepared to die in bed; in both cases it is realised that at a given moment physical life may cease; in both cases the thought of the individual is away from the body and concentrated on the beyond; in both cases the spiritual senses are thus awakened and the vibratory rate of thought quickened in proportion to its individual strength and purity; in both cases these quickened vibrations catch and attune themselves to whatever spiritual conditions are vibrating at a similar rate. We see, therefore, that when our soldiers, facing death in its most awful form, rise to the great moral heights of courage and self-sacrifice which carry them to the threshold of the superphysical world, their thought vibrations momentarily quicken to an equality with that of the inhabitants thereof; and they become vibratorily attuned to saints who have similarly sacrificed their lives in ages past, to comrades who have recently done so, to their own guardian Angels, to the Patron Saints of their people, or to still higher spiritual beings. It is but a question of vibratory rates of thought, which rates are determined by the purity and concentrative power of the thinker.

Having then explained the method by which our soldiers have, during this war, been put in touch with the inhabitants of superphysical spheres, it remains but to deal with the reason why, from the eyes of so many men of all nationalities, the scales of Spiritual blindness have so suddenly fallen. Let us therefore now proceed with the unwinding of the ecclesiastical thread of our web which during the reeling off of all this metaphysical matter, has lain inactive in our hands. It has already been stated that ecclesiasticism has never given us any deeper meaning for the curse of "blindness in part" which was laid upon the Israelites than the "wrath of God," and it must here be pointed out that it has not done so because that deeper meaning has not been understood by the Priesthood. Why so? Because orthodox Christianity has no esoteric foundation known to those who profess it; the successors of the Apostles never having recorded the secret doctrine of Jesus, and the "mysteries of the kingdom of heaven," which it was given to them (the apostles) alone to know, having been suppressed. Thus to succeeding generations there floated down upon the stream of time nothing but the maxims, the parables, the allegories, and the fables of Christianity, which of necessity, have been interpreted according to the fancies of the Fathers of the Secular Church; and, although it is not denied to them that there have been, and still are good men in the Church, as indeed there are in every other walk of life, who have always acted up to the highest light within them yet, having been specially deputed to teach a people, who, for a certain period, were destined to remain under a "curse" of Spiritual blindness, these Fathers of the Church were and are at best, but blind leaders of the blind.[11]

In examining the circumstances which have made them so, we must first grasp the fact that all esoteric Scriptures, including the Bible, are written emblems, or, in plainer language, a series of graphic pictures which allegorically explained, unfold an idea in a succession of panoramic views, recognisable only by the initiates but, in due season, to be taught by them to "those who are without"; next we must realise that the initiates of to-day are not the Clergy of the orthodox Christian Church of which the highest dignitary must, in these ominous times of our world's history be only too painfully aware that he knows absolutely no more of those "mysteries of the kingdom of heaven" which Jesus taught his disciples than does the most illiterate member of his Congregation; nay, bearing in mind that academical erudition cannot alone impart spiritual understanding we may go further and declare that he may know even less. From the earliest ages there has always been both a spiritual interpretation of divine truth for those who have ears to hear, and a dead letter rendering or external covering of the same for those who have not. Although this does not imply that those who have not ears to hear, never will have them; it simply means that they are "younger souls" who, not having evolved to the point of ability to receive Spiritual truths, must take their religion in the only form suited to their mental capacity.[12]

Theology then represents the dead-letter covering of the true Gospel of Christianity, and the keys to the "mysteries of the kingdom of heaven" which unlock the truth that ultimately sets our spiritual senses free, were never given into the hands of ecclesiasticism. What then was the *raison d'etre* of theology? We shall find it bound up with the evolution of God's chosen people, the Israelites, to whom we must now therefore turn our attention. At the termination of each successive age of our Universe a certain number of persons are "chosen of the Lord" to lead humanity through the changing conditions which mark the departure of the old age (or world) and the approach of the new. Noah and his family were the elect of the Antediluvian age and led humanity after the flood into the Noachian. In the Mosaic age the twelve tribes were chosen to lead, and in the Christian the twelve apostles constituted elect humanity. God's people are, theosophically speaking, "older souls"; that is to say, through repeated reincarnations they have gained experience and evolved to a point which connects them with the conditions of the incoming age before it comes, and thus enables them to pass from the worn out conditions of the old age, into the improved ones of the new, without experiencing the trials and troubles which fall to the lot of those who are evolving sympathetically with the age in which they live. It was part of the Divine scheme, if we may so speak—of Creation, that elect humanity, at the end of the Christian era, should be gathered from the house of Israel; that the remnant of purified mankind destined to pass from the sixth (Christian) dispensation of the visible world into the seventh (Millennial) and last visible age (during which elect humanity will be in direct communication with spiritual rulership and guidance) should be collected from the seed of the whole twelve tribes of Israel which, during the passing of the intermediate ages, was to remain scattered throughout the nations and kingdoms of the world.

It has been said that the Israelites were forward in evolution; that is to say, as "God's people" they possessed greater Spiritual knowledge than their contemporaries the Gentiles, having entered upon their material evolution in the physical world as "older souls"; had they, therefore, on taking possession of the land set apart for them by the Lord in Palestine, obeyed their spiritual intuitions and lived according to the rules prescribed by their spiritual senses, they would have so greatly out-distanced the Gentiles in their evolutionary race through the ages, as to have rendered associateship in the same physical world an impossibility, by reason of that dissimilarity of vibratory thought-rate which has already been explained. Obviously then, if the purpose of Divinity was to re-establish the Israelites in the Holy Land in the "latter days" of the Christian era while the Universe was still in its material form, their evolution must be retarded in order that they should, through numerous reincarnations, have evolved to the right point of Spiritual progression at the right time. Therefore, as Divinity and Nature are one and consequently Divinity always works in unison with the great fundamental laws of Nature[13]; as neither one jot nor one tittle shall pass from the Natural (otherwise Divine) law until all the evolution of the whole septenary chain of worlds be fulfilled,[14] and as the promise of the restoration of the remnant of the twelve tribes of Israel to their former possessions in the Holy Land was not intended to be operative until after the great "day" of the battle of God Almighty in the latter days of the Christian era, the Spiritual knowledge and recollection of divine truth which the Israelites had in the beginning, receded further and further from their use, as they accustomed themselves to the evolutionary conditions of the material line of life, upon which the masses of them were destined to remain until the present time. Always remembering then that the dead letter teaching of the Bible represents the allegorical cloak which hides its mysteries from the materialist, we trace the evolutionary course of the Israelites from the time of the "curse" to the present "day" of the battle of God Almighty, between the written lines of their material Biblical history.

While retaining our hold on the ecclesiastical thread of the web of evolution therefore, we have now to separate the two tribes called Judah as representing the Jews, from the other ten tribes Biblically recognised as the "lost sheep" of the house of Israel; for although the elect of the Christian era are chosen from the whole twelve tribes of "God's people" and although the whole twelve tribes alike came under the curse of "blindness in part," Judah's punishment, which commenced after that of the "lost sheep," was destined to terminate first. In other words, the Jews who, notwithstanding the curse, retained a clearer insight into the mysteries of the Kingdom of Heaven than the lost tribes,[15] were destined to return first to their former inheritance in the Holy Land,[16] whither, during the latter days of the Christian era, the remaining ten tribes were to follow them. By their waywardness, insobriety and foolishness, theologically speaking, the Israelites provoked the "wrath"[17] of God, and called down upon their heads the curse of a "seven times" punishment of" blindness in part." Theosophically speaking, however, the soul evolution of the Israelites was put back upon the material line whereon, as a natural and inevitable consequence, they lost the use of spiritual sight and understanding, and were placed on an evolutionary equality with the Gentiles under whose rule for a period of (circa) 2,520 years they were destined to remain. From the time of the commencement of the "curse," therefore, until that of its predestined removal, the Israelites have had neither ears to hear nor eyes to see the mysteries of the Kingdom of Heaven; those mysteries not having been destined to be revealed to them until the latter days of the Christian era in which we now are. Meanwhile the Gentiles, evolving also exclusively on the material line of life were destined to occupy the inheritance[18] of the Israelites in the Holy Land and to rule over them throughout the "seven times" (2,520 years) period of their punishment.

The casting back of the Israelites on to the material line of soul evolution whereon they were necessarily deprived of their Spiritual senses, is thus poetically referred to by St. Paul in the eleventh chapter and twenty-fifth verse of his *Epistle to the Romans*: "Blindness in part has happened to Israel until the fulness of the Gentiles be come in." Having been specially reserved, however, to represent elect humanity at the passing of the Christian era, it was necessary that the Israelites, more particularly than the Gentiles, should retain their hold on some outward semblance of the Spiritual Gospel of Christianity which was to be revealed to them at a later date; for although the Gentiles, also, were promised their "meat" in due season, being younger souls in the visible world, it would have antagonised the natural action of divine evolutionary law were they to have done so before the Israelites had received theirs; therefore, lest the prophecy of Esaias "which saith, By hearing ye shall hear, and shall not understand; and seeing ye shall see, and shall not perceive"[19]: should fail in its fulfilment, the Christian mysteries were clothed in materialism, the science of the Gospel shrouded in allegory, and into the spiritually darkened world came the personification of that "Light" which Israel had lost when his soul fell into matter under the curse of "blindness in part," but which he was destined to recover in "the latter days."

Israel then, being destined to pass from the Christian to the Millennial age of our chain of worlds, in order to people the highest, because the most spiritually perfect, world of the whole chain, we see that, as we can only qualify for high Spiritual positions by passing through much tribulation, it was of paramount importance that the Israelites should understand how, by material purity, love and self-sacrifice, they could win back their former Spiritual sight and knowledge. Whereas Judah, as aforesaid, having retained a clearer knowledge of the Spirit of Christianity than the ten tribes, and the Gentiles (with few exceptions) being cyclically unready to profit by it, these peoples could afford to stand more or less aside while Israel received the dead-letter rendering of the Gospel. "I am not sent," therefore, said Jesus of Nazareth in the fifteenth Chapter of the *Gospel of St Matthew*, "but unto the lost sheep of the house of Israel." And to these lost-sheep He taught the mysteries of the kingdom of heaven only in parables. At a later date St. Paul, the Apostle of ecclesiasticism whose mission was to gather the Gentiles (purely materialistic humanity) within the radius of his influence while preaching to the Jews the same veiled Gospel of Christianity which Jesus had taught the ten tribes, revealed the Christian mysteries only "through a glass darkly" whereas the ecclesiastical Priesthood which followed him and whose *raison d'etre* we now discover, had no knowledge of the mysteries and was consequently deputed to lead blind Israel, in company with the Gentiles, to the end of the Christian age. Thus in keeping the scales over the eyes of Spiritually [*sic*] blind Israel until the time appointed for their removal, theology has fulfilled its predestined purpose in the divine scheme of evolution.

Probably and very properly, the following questions may here arise, *viz*.: what is the meaning of a Biblical "time," and, by whose authority does the writer translate" seven times" into a period of 2,520 years. The answers to these questions, however, being with the questions[20] themselves side issues of the subject in hand, are necessarily crowded out of a work of this scope; and the reader is therefore referred to Mr. W. Redding's book entitled *Our Near Future*,[21] wherein he will find them admirably answered. Meanwhile we will proceed to consider the signs of the times in connection with the Biblical prophecies. Jesus of Nazareth did not tell his disciples when the Christian age would terminate and the yoke of material limitation of the senses, recognised as the "Curse," would be lifted from the necks of God's people; but all humanity was warned that certain signs were destined to precede it; and that therefore it would be highly necessary to watch for them in order intelligently to prepare for a time of Universal upheaval such as had not occurred at the termination of any other previous age, and should not again occur throughout the evolution of our whole Septenary Chain.

"Then," said Jesus, "*shall be great tribulation, such as was not since the beginning of the world, to this time, no, nor ever shall be.*"[22] It was said that false prophets would then arise, but inasmuch as we can never override the great fundamental law which obliges all men to reap as they sow, these prophets would necessarily be known by their fruits. There would be wars and rumours of wars[23]; signs and wonders in the sky; investigation, alteration, and in some cases complete overthrow of established religions, extermination of insincere social customs, false governments, Mosaic law; destruction of armies on the land and navies on the sea. There would be, in short, all the unspeakable suffering, the terror, brutality, starvation and universal chaos inseparable from the complete disruption of every worn out custom of the passing age prior to the establishment of the improved conditions of the new. During this terrible period of our history the spiritual senses of many persons would awaken and "they that understood among the people would instruct many,"[24] nevertheless all the representatives of the tribes of Israel would, in company with the Gentiles, continue "many days" to fall by the sword, and by flame, by captivity and by spoil. For we are Biblically told that the intention of the Lord was, during the latter days, "to gather the nations together to pour out His wrath upon them,"[25] by which passage, theosophically we understand that as no man can attain to spiritual perfection without passing through the fire of suffering; and as the greatest physical suffering results in the greatest Spiritual gain, God's people, as destined to pass on and reap the glorious benefits accruing from life in an age during which all rulers would be spiritually called to office instead of as now, being indiscriminately chosen by the people, it would be absolutely necessary that elect Israel should suffer equally with (and in some cases even more than) the Gentiles in the universal and painful breaking up of all those material methods by which man has, through the sixth age of our world, ruled over the spirit; and thus, though in falling the Israelites should be "holpen with a little help"[26] they were nevertheless destined to be plunged, with the Gentiles, into the chasm of unspeakable misery which, yawning between the Christian and the millennial ages of our world, represents the great "day" of the battle of God Almighty, which in purging from the minds of elect humanity all remaining traces of material Government, prepares the visible universe for the totally different methods of spiritual rulership destined to be operative through the thousand years' duration of the millennial age, which follows upon the heels of the Christian. Israel then, over whose spiritually blinded eyes ecclesiasticism was deputed to keep the scales, has been led blindfold by the Church to the brink of the chasm which separates the material from the Spiritual Gospel of the Christ; but though in his awakening Israel, for custom's sake, clutches at the gown of theology in its fall with him into that dark abyss, ecclesiasticism, in its present form, does not rise with him upon the other side, whereon the Spirit of the Christian Gospel kneels to help but Israel out.[27]

We are told that in the latter days signs and wonders shall appear in the sky, that St. Michael shall be seen in the physical universe,[28] that Angels shall take part in the battle of God Almighty[29] and that departed saints and others shall arise and appear to many. That though God's people, through their blind material judgment of all things, must be sorely tried, yet God will be with them and consequently victory will ultimately be theirs.[30] Both in the Old Testament and in the New we read of these things for ourselves, and Sunday after Sunday the clergy read of them in Church, yet when our soldiers, through sheer heroism, brought face to face with the living reality of the Gospel they have thus been taught, declare that they have seen the Angels, Saints and Spiritual Beings of whom the Bible and the clergy speak, ecclesiasticism refuses to believe them, thus denying that the Christianity it is teaching in our Churches to-day is as real and as practical as it was in the days when its great Master taught humanity the physical methods by which alone we can inherit its spiritual rewards. *O my people, they which lead thee cause thee to err, and destroy the way of thy paths.—Isa.* iii. 12.

Who then are God's people now? For it here becomes necessary to show that they also are as real to-day when the time is ripe for their return to their lost inheritance in Egypt as they were when, 2,520 years ago they were driven out of it under the "curse" of that spiritual blindness which still afflicts the Christian priesthood. It will be seen by those who are sufficiently interested in the Anglo-Israel subject to study it through the medium of the various able authors who have dealt with it, and which, be it said, the present reader is advised to do, inasmuch as in a work of this compass it is possible only to treat it cursorily, that the Israelites, who at the time of the "curse" were scattered among all the nations of the world, are now represented by the English, French, U.S. Americans and all Anglo-Saxon races, although in dealing with this subject in connection with the latter days it is important to remember that "they are not all Israel which are of Israel."[31] The Israelites were formerly, and will be again, the moral and religious branch of the seed of Abraham from which has been chosen the elect body of humanity destined to pass unharmed from the final chaotic material conditions of the sixth (Christian) age into the spiritually conducted ones which must obtain in the seventh (millennial), whereas the Edomites, so named from the word Edom meaning "red," were the ignorant, wild and vicious branch, formerly represented by Esau (whose birth allegorises the Christian age as that of Jacob allegorises the millennium which follows on its heels) and Ishmael; but which at the present time is represented by the Turks; as, however, all unprogressive peoples are Biblically styled "Gentile," it is as Gentiles in these latter days of the

Christian era that we now see the Turks, in accordance with the prophecy, "treading down" Israel's promised inheritance in the Holy Land. *"Jerusalem shall be trodden down by the Gentiles until the times of the Gentiles be fulfilled."—St. Luke* xxi. 24.

The Turks, however, must now very shortly surrender their possessions in Egypt to the Russians as representing the champions of the Jews, or to the English, French and other Anglo-Saxons now representing the Israelites, for in accordance with the reckoning of writers who put the date of the commencement of "Gentile times"—which period synchronises with that of Israel's "blindness in part"—at 606 BC and the termination thereof at 1914, the latter date, when considered in conjunction with all that happened in that year, and has happened since, may certainly be said to approximate the end of "Gentile times" and the lifting of Israel's yoke. More especially as we are clearly given to understand that the battle of God Almighty immediately precedes the restoration of the Israelites to the Holy Land. Apparently nearly all the Biblically prophesied signs which were to warn us of the approach of the present crisis have already been seen or heard; there have been wars and rumours of wars, earthquakes in divers places, pestilences, famines, signs and wonders in the sky, reappearance of the so-called "dead." Fire and brimstone and deadly hail storms from guns, poisonous gases, and bombs, have scorched, suffocated and mutilated humanity and piled its ghastly remains in heaps in town and street. It is true that we have yet to see "Jerusalem compassed with armies," although even before these pages reach the press we may have done so, and in this case it would seem that we should then watch diligently for the greatest sign of all, namely that of the appearance of the Son of Man in the sky, which sign was to warn us that the final wrench destined to sever the conditions of the old age from those of the new would be "even at our doors."[32]

In days of yore the Assyrians were the most dreaded enemies of the former house of Israel, and at that time the Israelites, although too cyclically advanced to be great fighters, had grown careless; and, as laggards on the material line of evolution, interested themselves in unprofitable material pursuits, loved flagons of wine (*Hosea* iii. 1), and were consequently "out of the way through strong drink" (*Isa.* xxviii. 7). On the other hand Assyria, immersed in militarism, and perfect in bowmanship, strategy and valour, was a constant source of terror to them and, as such, was used by Divinity over and over again as a material method of punishment calculated to sober Israel and imbue him with a keener sense of responsibility. And as the reader will find on perusal of other works on the Anglo-Israel subject that nearly all writers agree that Assyria is now represented by Germany, we find the Assyrians again in the time of the latter-day Israelites (now represented by England, France, and their Allies) still immersed in militarism, still advanced in material science and strategy, and still Divinely used as a chastening rod against Israel, even on the eve of the lifting of his yoke. To those among us, therefore, who raise no objection to the stigma of "perfidious" Albion, the following passage from the book of Isaiah applies equally to the former and the latter-day Israelites: *O, Assyrian, the rod of mine anger, and the staff in their hand is mine indignation. I will send him against an hypocritical nation, and against the people of my wrath will I give him a charge, to take the spoil, and to take the prey, and to tread them down like the mire of the streets (Isa. x. 5–6).* And it may be said in passing that the continuation of this chapter of Isaiah makes truly profitable reading at the present time.

Theosophically, the more perfect the militarism of a nation, the more backward is its moral development, and in the natural course of soul evolution those that are backward must be used as scourges to promote the development of the morally advanced; thus in the plan of evolution these younger souls represent the reverse side of good, otherwise evil; but in strict justice to all humanity we must remember that after the soul of man has "fallen" (as allegorised by the fall of Adam and Eve) into matter, or in theosophical parlance, has entered[33] upon the material line of evolution, the forces of good and evil are *both* necessary to its development in the material universe; therefore younger souls, whether racial or individual, do but fulfil their divinely appointed work in the scheme of evolution when, at given times, they are bound into the rod whereby the spiritual laggards (national or individual) are whipped into the paths of righteous living.[34]

In the divine plan of the return of the twelve tribes of Israel to their former inheritance in the Holy Land, it has already been said that the two tribes called Judah which represent the Jews were destined to repossess themselves of their patrimony before the lost ten tribes could be restored to theirs; although ultimately Judah and Israel would "walk together" in Egypt, this arrangement having been made by reason of a certain unfair severity which has, during the period of their separation, characterised the demeanour of Israel towards Judah and which, in the event of Israel's being the first to take possession of the land in Egypt would result in his unfair dealing with Judah. In other words, the Jews, as aforesaid, having retained throughout the whole duration of the curse, a clearer knowledge and appreciation of divinity than the lost tribes, are consequently, as a race, "older souls" and thus destined to work out their salvation first. Therefore we are told in the twelfth chapter and seventh verse of *Zech.*, that *"the Lord will save the tents of Judah first, so that the glory of the House of David do not magnify themselves against Judah."* Moreover Jesus of Nazareth said to the woman of Samaria: *"Ye worship ye know not what: we know what we worship: for salvation is of the Jews."*

Who then of all the peoples now taking part in the great battle of God Almighty do we particularly associate with the Jews? The answer is: Russia.

And again the question may arise, why so? During the present War Russia has strangely altered her tactics as regards the Jews; not only is she now fraternising with them at home, but she has also gathered them in their thousands into her armies, which are slowly but surely fighting their way to Judah's promised inheritance in the Holy Land. It is of course well known that the Jews have been rapidly returning to Palestine for many years and that they now form some 60 per cent, of the 80,000 inhabitants of the Holy City; if therefore the Russian Jews in the Tzar's forces should be added to this number Judah's elect remnant would be more than complete. It would seem that we should at the present time accept Russia as the latter-day champion of the Jews for the following reasons: the Jewish prophet Daniel was divinely shown in a vision what should befall his people in the latter days; he was given to understand that although, with Israel, the Jews had a terrible punishment to face, the spiritual significance of that punishment should be perceived by one only of all the princes fighting in the battle of God Almighty for the redemption of the whole united house of Israel. "*I will shew thee*" said Daniel's Angel informant, "*that which is noted in the Scripture of truth, and there is none that holdeth with me in these things, but Michael your prince.*"[35] Furthermore Daniel is informed that during the awful happenings of the latter days, St. Michael, the Guardian Angel of the Jews, should appear in the visible Universe. "*At that time*," said the Angel, "*shall Michael stand up, the great prince which standeth for the children of thy people: and there shall be a time of trouble, such as never was since there was a nation even to that same time: and at that time thy people shall be delivered, everyone that shall be found written in the book.*"[36]

Understanding then that God works in the material Universe with material tools and that therefore if St. Michael were appointed to inspire the army destined to bring about the restoration of the Jews to their lost inheritance, the inspiration of the angel must be materially reflected in the leader of that army, we realise that those who are able thus to reflect divinity in this visible world are they whose faith in deity is as strong, pure and simple as that of a little child. Such faith the Russians have, and the title of their princes having been formerly "kniaz" (prince), or "veliki kniaz" (great prince),[37] the Tzar is necessarily the "great Prince" of the Russians. At the very outset of the war he intuitively struck his first blow at Israel's ancient enemy, the false prophet of alcohol, thus purifying the armies which were destined to respond to the Divine call to arms, and at that time, *i.e.*, in the early days of the war, he intuitively turned his attention to the afflictions of the Russian Jews and promised his Jewish subjects equal citizen rights with the rest of his people; thus freeing them to travel after the war, and, presumably, if they would, to return to Palestine. In a deeply religious spirit which was reflected throughout his whole army, the Tsar then entered into the war; and the strong but simple faith in the Wisdom of Omnipotence which has enabled his soldiers to bear all their trials and reverses with a patience and long-suffering silence which is almost beyond material comprehension, has been a revelation of the depth and beauty of the soul of the Russian soldier which will linger in the memory of noble minds for evermore. We are told that the vision of St. Michael has appeared upon the battlefields in various theatres of the present war, both to the French and Russian soldiers, and as the Guardian Angel of the Jews, we understand that the Saint would naturally also represent the Spiritual "Great Prince" of the Israelites as now represented by the English, French, etc.— judging, however, by the information which comes from Russia, it has been oftener to the Russians that St. Michael has appeared. If then we accept Russia as Judah's liberator and ourselves as part of scattered Israel, we must not magnify ourselves against Russia though she may pass before us into the plain of Esdraelon and on to the field of Megiddo, where the Jews from Palestine may join her; and though it be she who shall there strike or parry the first blow in the final struggle for their emancipation. For the tents of Judah must be saved first. has been explained that units of the lost ten tribes of Israel may be found among Anglo-Saxons all over the world and therefore the elect remnant of these tribes destined ultimately to be received by Judah in the Holy Land may be gathered not only from the countries of the Allies but also from those of their enemies, or from neutrals.[38]

The natural law which theosophists call Karmic and whose action has been so aptly described by St. Paul in his well-remembered words, "whatsoever a man soweth that shall he also reap," ensures to the Turks, as modern representatives of Edom, such appalling losses in the closing scenes of this war as to amount almost to annihilation; for apart from the fact of the "times" during which, as Gentiles, they have been treading down Israel's inheritance in the Holy Land, being now on the point of fulfilment, Edom, as the fitting descendant of Jacob's wild and roving brother, has for long years hunted and destroyed his fellow men; torturing, plundering and murdering such countless thousands of Christian souls that the inevitable reaction of Karmic law which is identical with what theology describes as "Divine Justice," must ultimately result in wholesale destruction of his own people. If we realise that the words "Mount Seir" mean Edom country, otherwise Turkey, and remember the long years of terrible Turkish crimes which, formerly perpetrated in Armenia, have lately been extended in so inhuman a manner to Albania, we fully understand why Edom has come into the war "in dyed garments"[39] and the following words clearly indicate the unalterable action of Divine or Karmic law: *"As I live, saith the Lord, I will prepare thee unto blood, and blood shall pursue thee: since thou hast not hated blood, even blood shall pursue thee. Thus will I make Mount Seir most desolate, and cut off from it him that passeth out and him that returneth; and I will fill his mountains with his slain men."*

We see then that evil as well as good has always had its predestined place in what may reverently be described as the Divine Workshop of the soul; for everything has its reverse side and—*Demon est Deus Inversus*[40]—therefore, though Edom's garments are soaked in blood, as indeed have lately been those of Germany also, yet we are reminded that Edom is our brother[41]; and that Germany represents Assyria, the weapon Divinely chosen to effect Israel's "correction in measure."

In conclusion, the subject of the visions of Archers and Bowmen which we are told have been seen since the outbreak of this war, calls our attention to the twenty-seventh chapter of the book of the prophet Ezekiel, which deals with a certain matter concerning the former house of Israel. In a vision the prophet is shewn a valley strewn with the dried and whitened bones of representatives of the whole recognised house of Israel of former days, and he is told that though in life these Israelites were sceptical as to the possibility of the fulfilment of God's promise ultimately to restore Israel to his promised land; yet, notwithstanding their disbelief and the number of years that had whitened their bones, the prophet should see how, while gathering together the younger Israelites in the latter days, these former representatives of God's people should themselves be raised from the dead and should join their descendants in Egypt at the time appointed. Accordingly Ezekiel hears a noise and a shaking, the dried bones rise in the valley of death, fit themselves to their accustomed joints and stand upon their feet. Sinews and flesh are laid upon the bones, breath from the four winds of heaven fills their nostrils and finally they "form up" into "an exceeding great army." It is then but logical to argue thus, that if these be the latter days, these former Israelites are already in the superphysical plane of life which interpenetrates our own; that if they are to accompany elect Israel of to-day to his inheritance in Egypt, they must naturally take a personal interest in helping to win the battles which ultimately restore the whole house of Israel to his own. That having been described as an "exceeding great army" they were—when they stood upon their feet—apparently prepared for war; and having risen as soldiers, they must, according to an unalterable divine fundamental law, have fallen as such. And as they fell in the days when bows and arrows were used, with bows and arrows they would rise again; finally, having been spiritually raised instead of being born of the flesh, they would move on the lowest spiritual plane instead of upon the physical—and as this plane is represented by what we call the 'space' which lies about us, these bowmen could readily form behind or in front of the armies of the allies, and, by the same methods as have been fully described in the first part of this book, they would become visible to certain persons on the physical plane of life.

Finally, it should be pointed out that the visions seen by the soldiers of the allied armies on the various battlefields of the present war, were not the first warnings we received of its approach. In the autumn of the year 1913 some very remarkable visions were seen in the village of Alzonne in France, where Joan of Arc on horseback appeared in the sky, and also St. Michael, St. Margaret, and others[42]; while during the summer of the same year, many people in England spoke of a curious "thing" which was visible one night in the heavens, and which, by those who saw it, was said to resemble a golden fleece. If then all these signs and wonders which were Biblically prophesied should herald the approach of the latter days and the commencement of the battle of God Almighty, have come and have failed to awaken the materialist; we may be well assured that even though we see "Jerusalem compassed with armies" and "the sign of the Son of Man coming in the sky," even then the materialist will remain blind to the spiritual power which underlies the dead-letter rendering of the Gospel of Christianity which he professes to believe.

• TWELVE •

Charles Warr and "The Unseen Host"

First published: p. 19–31 in *The Unseen Host: Stories of The Great War*. Paisley: Alexander Gardner, 1916.

Of the writers who are represented here, Charles Laing Warr was perhaps the most successful in his life and career. He was born on 20 May 1892 in Rosneath, Dunbartonshire, the son of the Reverend Alfred Warr. He matriculated Glasgow Academy and in 1914 received from Edinburgh University his MA. Shortly thereafter, states his profile in the *Dictionary of National Biography*, he was "commissioned to the 9th Argyll and Sutherland Highlanders ... and dangerously wounded at Ypres in May 1915."[1] He evidently experienced a spiritual awakening, for he wrote *The Unseen Host* and began to take "divinity classes at Glagow and became assistant minister of the cathedral there (1917–18)."[2] He was steadily promoted, becoming Minister of St. Paul's Greenock (1918–1926), then minister of St. Giles's Edinburgh, and then was appointed "both dean of the Chapel Royal and of the Order of the Thistle in the same year [1926]."[3] He was a friend of George V, King of England, and became his chaplain in 1936, serving also as the chaplain to Edward VIII, George VI, and Queen Elizabeth II. He retired in 1962, and when he died in Edinburgh on 14 June 1969, Her Majesty was represented at the funeral.[4]

The stories in *The Unseen Host* were popular—the book was to go through ten editions—perhaps because they blended first-hand verisimilitude of the war with an agreeable and uncontroversial piety. They have few narrative surprises and are straightforward in presenting their combination of patriotism and faith. As Warr's preface makes clear, he strove for these effects, for he is forthright in hoping that the book "may afford a sense of security to a few who are going forth to take up the sword which has fallen from the hands of others. It may help them to trust in the presence of an 'Unseen Host' about their daily path." That the book was so popular indicates that Warr succeeded, but he is also far from being discreditable as a writer of fiction. He frames his story with capably drawn settings and characterizations, takes the time to create a sense of suspense, and does not make the mistake of being too overt in the presentation of the supernatural. Warr was to revisit the events and personalities of the Great War in *Echoes of Flanders:*[5] its stories, too, possess many of these virtues. Coincidentally, it was issued by the same publisher that was responsible for Arthur Machen's *The Bowmen*.

Preface

I feel that this volume requires a word of explanation, if only in view of the fact that the age in which we live has tended towards the development in many men of a condition of mind which forbids not only a belief in, but even toleration of the idea of the mere possibility of anything which cannot be explained in terms of materialistic experience. To those who cultivate this school of thought I offer but one word of advice—Do not read this book: it will only annoy you. But to those who are still old-fashioned enough to believe that "there are more things in heaven and earth than are dreamed of in our philosophy [sic],"[6] I give this little volume, knowing that from them it will receive at least sympathy, and from a few, credence.

I do not attempt to explain the occurrences set forth—I cannot explain them, nor can anyone else. I merely asseverate that to the best of my knowledge they are all true, and are in no case the figments of my own imagination.

This volume is not intended as an addition to the flood of controversial literature which has surged around the conception of "The Angelic Host at Mons." I feel that time is indeed too precious to waste in any such vain argument. It is only because I personally hold these stories to be true that they are given to the public. By "true" I would not for one minute contend that the spiritual can be seen by the eye of flesh—that idea seems to border on the grotesque. It is surely only spirit that could behold spirit, and therefor [sic] spiritual appearances, if seen or heard at all, can only be discernible spiritually, by some indefinable sympathy of soul with soul. We all know these strange moments of revelation—a passing glance in some one's eye, a flitting shadow on a face, revealing suddenly unfathomed depths—which might not that become if it were immeasurably intensified?

And so perhaps some of the pages in this book may afford a sense of security to a few who are going forth to take up the sword which has fallen from the hands of others. It may help them to trust in the presence of an "Unseen Host" about their daily path. It may assist those of them to whom the call shall come, to enter, like true British soldiers with level eyes and laughing lips, the valley of the shadow of death.

It is best to keep an open mind on things as to whose source or purpose or existence we cannot even guess. After all, as Dr. Johnson says, this is a question which, after five thousand years, is yet undecided[7]—a question which, whether in theology or philosophy, is one of the most important that can come before the human understanding.

And I so love to think that one day in the Isle of Dreams, far away through the gates of the west, we each and all of us will come to know whatever there is to be known of the eternal mystery which, in its immense and awful silence, surrounds with its darkness our throbbing little lives.

The Unseen Host

As one walks from the grand Place of Ypres down the Rue de Lille to the old hoary town-gateway and the deep broad moat where the white swans used to revel in the sunlight, there stands about half-way down on the left hand side—or rather stood, for nothing stands now in that once beautiful city—a little tavern, which up to the month of April last was much frequented by the British soldiery. It was a humble enough place—a little room with eight or nine tables and about twice as many chairs. Half a dozen faded prints hung on the walls, cheap muslin curtains were on the windows, and the decoration was completed by two blue china pots, each holding the remains of a dusty plant, long since dead. There was no oil-cloth on the floor, no mats: the girl who made the coffee said they used to have them before the October bombardment, but now—well, it was safer and more economical to have as few things as possible to be destroyed. And she would pout with her pretty lips and shrug her dainty shoulders.

One Sunday evening, as the sun was setting and the shadows were long in the white dusty streets, I heard in that room a queer story, a story the like of which I had never heard before—past man's understanding. Four of us sat at a table, the only occupants of the room at the time, and the air was thick with our tobacco smoke. The girl behind the bar was cleaning glasses and humming gaily to herself—they sang and laughed in Ypres to the last. Outside, the broad thoroughfare was thronged with soldiers and civilians walking in the evening light. Occasionally the windows would rattle as chance shells exploded in the town.

The man who told the tale was a private soldier, dirty, mud-stained, and unshaven. Yet from his lips fell a wonderful story, just as in strange places one lights on some rare flower. He told it with many an oath and many a blasphemy, as soldiers love to do, but with a fire in his eyes which bespoke a living soul. And those two friends who sat with me there and listened to him have passed into the clearer light where the secrets of the stars are disclosed and every tangled skein of earth is unraveled to the eye: and I am left alone, to grope in the darkness, to wonder, to hope, and again to wonder; until for me, too, all mists be rolled away. And as I tell this tale as I heard it a great sadness fills my heart—for I feel that I tell it to a world that will believe it not.

It was in the grey of the early morning that a sentry spotted something moving among the long grass beyond the barbed wire. He watched intently for a few minutes but could not be certain—the ground mist was heavy and was so deceptive. A few seconds later he again felt convinced that something moved near the same place. He raised his rifle and fired three rounds on the off chance of it being a prowling German. His shot seemed to be the signal for a perfect tornado of yells, and suddenly out of the mist there loomed hosts of phantom-like figures, armed with wire-cutters. In a moment they were on the wire, cutting as for their life—*snip* went strand after strand.

It was all sudden and unexpected, but in a minute the trench garrison lined the parapet, and a murderous fire poured in upon the attacking Germans. There is small chance of life when cutting wire ten yards from the enemy's trench, and the grey figures went down by scores, some hanging on the wire, others piled in heaps of dead and wounded. Yet on they came in dense masses, swarming through the mist like ghosts in the teeth of a sweeping storm of lead. Nothing seemed to be able to stop them, and, though falling by hundreds in doing it, the wire was being cut more and more each minute. And ever on they came, climbing over the heaps of their dead. Soon there would be a bridge of corpses over the entanglements.

The rifles of the defenders grew red-hot in their hands, but they kept up the fire. Through the rattle and din could be heard the shrill voices of the Cockney Tommies vieing [*sic*] with one another as to who should go into the jaws of death with the best joke on his lips.

And the Germans still swarmed over. At the right flank of the trench they were almost through the wire and would soon be scrambling over the big ditch and up the parapet; a few seconds more and the centre might fall.

"Keep it up lads, keep it up, for God's sake," yelled the platoon sergeant through the uproar; "when I gives the word, up and at 'em with the bayonet."

With their hands blistered and cut, and their faces filthy with powder and smoke, the dishevelled [*sic*] wild-eyed garrison fired on....

A shrill whistle suddenly sounded, and the Germans turned and retreated into the mist, leaving behind them their dead and wounded piled in heaps. A hoarse cheer went up from the British trenches. The enemy had retired when victory was almost within their grasp, had they but realised it.

"That was a near thing an' no mistake," said the platoon-sergeant, drawing the back of his hand across his cracked lips. "Gawd! I'm 'ot!" He pushed his cap back off his forehead and, sitting down on an ammunition box, began to pull through the barrel of his rifle.

"All the rifles cleaned at once, boys," he shouted along the trenches. "Come on there, Atkins, lift your carcase off that fire-step—you're not 'ere on a bloomin' pic-nic, are yer?"

The hot smoking rifles were cleaned and polished, ready for immediate use; the corroded barrels were oiled and shining.

"They'll be at us again before long," growled the sergeant, squirting tobacco juice from the corner of his mouth. "The wire's down now, and they've got a bloomin' Piccadilly over their pals' corpses. Double these sentries, gray."

His corporal walked along the trench and saw the order executed, then returned and sat down by the sergeant.

"Where's the orficer been all the while?" he asked, lighting a cigarette.

"Blow'd if I know—never seen him since the blighters attacked—well, my lad, what is it?"

The officer's orderly approached.

"Mr. Venables wants to speak to you, sergeant," he said; "I can't make out what's gone wrong with him. He slept in his dug-out all through the attack. I shook and shook him an' 'e wouldn't wake. I yells inter his ear and he wouldn't 'ear me. Then I pours the water out of 'is bottle over 'is face and down 'is neck—and damn'd if he'd open 'is bloomin' eyes. I thought 'e was dead but for 'is breathin'.... Never see'd anythin'—."

"Arnott!" shouted a voice from the officer's dug-out.

"There 'e is, sergeant, hollerin' for yer ... better look slippy."

Sergeant Arnott scrambled along to the dugout and crawled inside. The subaltern in charge of the trench sat on a biscuit box, his head in his hands. He sat in silence for a while, then looked up—his eyes were very bright and shining.

"When did that attack begin, Arnott?"

"About ten minutes after you had been round the trench, sir—it came on sudden-like."

"And how long did it last?"

"About 'arf an hour, sir. I thought the blighters were in on us—they would 'ave bin, too, if they'd only 'ad the sense to keep on. They'll be at us again soon, sir—the wire's mostly all cut."

The subaltern passed a hand wearily across his brow.

"It's so funny, Arnott, but I must have been asleep all the time they were attacking—."

"You was, sir," interposed the sergeant gravely, "sleepin' like a top.... Meredith 'e couldn't waken you, 'e says, although 'e poured the water from your water-bottle down your neck."

The subaltern smiled faintly.

"Yes? ... But I had a strange dream ... can't remember much of it, ... but a shining figure seemed to speak to me and to tell me we were going to be in for a deuced hot time of it—you see, Arnott, this part is the key to the British position—."

The sergeant nodded.

"But he said we were to stick it out no matter what happened and he

Twelve • Charles Warr and "The Unseen Host"

would help us—and then he went away.... I remember he had a sword in his hand—it looked like fire. He was awfully like a big fellow on the reredos in the church at home—an angel—Michael, I think they call him. But it was all rather strange, Arnott, wasn't it?" he added, smiling, and lit a cigarette.

"It was that, sir."

"Well, come round the trench with me and see that these fellows are all ready if they do attack us."

The words had scarcely left his lips when there was a wild shout from the sentries, and the rattle of rapid fire broke out. The officer and his sergeant raised their heads above the parapet. It was clear enough now to see the German lines, and the sight they saw was that which, when seen for the first time, brings a curious momentary flutter to even the stoutest heart—the German hordes attacking in close formation. They were already half over the no-man's-land between the two trenches, falling, falling, row after row, but still coming on. Over the British trench shrieked the shrapnel, and glancing backwards, the officer saw it bursting over the support trenches, and the intervening waste being smashed with high explosives. Few, if any supports would get up through that awful inferno. The reserves of grey troops seemed endless—would they never stop pouring over the distant parapets?

Step by step they gained ground, despite the steadiness and accuracy of our fire; little by little the ranks came nearer, mown down like grain, but always immediately replaced. On either side the British trenches poured in their enfilade fire, then ceased—it was getting too risky, as they might damage their own men.

"Keep that—machine-gun goin', men," yelled Sergeant Arnott, perspiration running in streams down his fiery face, "keep it goin'! ... what the 'ell are you waitin' for?"

"Machine gun's jammed!" came back the grim reply.

"God in 'eavin'!" muttered the sergeant, "our ticket's in" ... and seizing a rifle he commenced blazing away.

"'Ow's that for Bisley?" shouted a Tommy, as a bearded German fell fifteen yards from the parapet.

"First bull you ever made, sonny," jeered his neighbor; "'oly Moses, but they're gettin' close."

The little band prepared to face the end.

"'*We all go the same way 'ome*'"[8] blithely sang a young private, jamming his magazine full.

For five minutes they fired desperately.

"Bill! wot the 'ell's that?" yelled someone.

"Wot the 'ell's wot?"

The two men filled their magazines like lightning, and shouted as they fired:

"That there trampin'—I can 'ear it above the bloomin' row—there you are, at our back! like a bloomin' army."

Bill glanced hurriedly over the waste ground between the firing line and supports.

"There's no bloomin' army there," he said, grimly; "wish to Gawd there was."

But in a moment he heard it—so did the others—the sound as of a great host advancing in their rear. Glances were cast over their shoulders, but the fire never slackened. There was no one there, and the Germans drew nearer.

Tramp, tramp, tramp....

It sounded on their ears through the roar of the shells and the rattle of the musketry, like the marching of ten thousand men, steady, rhythmical, coming nearer, nearer....

Tramp, tramp ... like the surge of a great sea ... and the clatter of hoofs, loud and fierce, the clatter of squadrons of horsemen...

Tramp, tramp ... the unseen host drew closer, closer ... over the British trench swept something like the rush of a mighty wind, whirling them from their feet on to the ground.

The Germans who had reached the parapet stood as if turned to stone. One man had time to fire his bullet at the subaltern ... then the grey battalions turned and fled....

Tramp, tramp, tramp—and onward swept the unseen host....

"O, thank God! there he is," cried the subaltern, shot in the head, ere he fell back, "there he is—how like he is to the fellow on the reredos in the church at home—at home—."

As he fell back he pointed beyond their parapet, and those near him who heard him and followed his finger saw a great light, a radiant figure, something that flashed like a sword of flame—only for a moment—then nothing but the retreating Germans, rushing for the cover of their trenches.

"I 'ope I 'aven't tired you with my story, sirs," said the private when he was finished, "but as you was good enough to speak to me, I thought you would like to 'ear it ... good-night, sirs."

He saluted and went out.

That man, snatched in some mysterious way from the mouth of death, believed that on his side that day had fought Gabriel the captain of the hosts of heaven, Michael the archangel, and all angels, with the powers and principalities of light—had fought for him, and did smite and win the victory....

And I believe it too.

• THIRTEEN •

Arthur Machen and "The Angels of Mons: Absolutely My Last Word on the Subject"

First published: *The [London] Evening News*, 7 April 1916.

For a time, Arthur Machen responded to the additional claims of angelic apparitions in the pages of *The Evening News*. His responses tended to be repetitive, noting that the claimants provided unverifiable anecdotes, not verifiable fact, and that he was simply and reasonably asking for information that any genuine claimant should be able to provide.

On 7 April 1916 *The Evening News* published Machen's "The Angels of Mons: Absolutely My Last word on the Subject," a response that called to the attention of perhaps a wider audience than it deserved I. E. Taylor's *Angels, Saints & Bowmen of Mons*:

> There is a certain land—and it is a very pleasant land—called Gwent, or more commonly, Monmouthshire. This land, as my colleague, "The Londoner,"[1] reminds me, was the land of the longbow.
>
> Now I am proud to write this, for I am a man of Gwent, a citizen of Caerleon-on-Usk, which is no mean city, but I would almost say that the ancestral longbow may be too long and too strong. I pulled it as well as I could in the tale of "The Bowmen," which was printed in *The Evening News* about eighteen months ago. I do not think that I need tell again in detail the story of what happened. In brief, there was a widespread delusion—I still hold it to have been a delusion—that our soldiers were supernaturally assisted during the retreat from Mons; and there was a subsidiary delusion to the effect that a large mass of evidence was in existence proving the fact of this supernatural assistance. These are the main points of this very queer business. I cannot enter into the matter more minutely, lest this twice-cooked cabbage, to use Juvenal's phrase, should sicken my readers; and sicken me also. If there is anybody who wants to hear about it all over again, I would refer him to "The Bowmen," published by Messrs. Simpkin, Marshall, and Co.

Well, frankly, I thought that the whole thing was at last done with, that "The Bowmen" slept with the Russians in the grave of a common oblivion. The British Museum had applied to me with a puzzling request that I should furnish them with the information in my possession as to the "literature" on the subject; and with this, I thought, the whole story ends.

"Haro! Haro!"

"Instead of which": here, newly set forth by the Theosophical Publishing Company, comes "Angels, Saints & Bowmen of Mons: An Answer to Mr. Arthur Machen and Mr. Harold Begbie" by J. E. Taylor.

The arrow that I shot into the air is, evidently, still doing its deadly work. It is I that will soon be crying "Haro! haro! à mon aide, mon prince, ou me fait tort."[2]

Frankly, and without any intention of disrespect, I must say that I can make nothing of Mr. Taylor. He is angry both with Mr. Harold Begbie (the author of "On the Side of the Angels") and myself.

"From the point of view of the prophet, the theosophist and the occultist, the idea of the visions of our soldiers having resulted from the publication of Mr. Machen's story of 'The Bowmen' is almost incomprehensibly ridiculous; and the reproduction, by Mr. Harold Begbie, of statement after statement in a necessarily fruitless endeavour to prove a spiritual reality to material understanding, is, from the above point of view, a lamentable waste of time and energy which might have been profitably employed in answering the only vital question which arises, namely, What is the meaning of the visions which the soldiers saw?"

Curious Logic

Well: there you are. The man who says that he thinks that his story in *The Evening News* states that the legend of the apparitions is ridiculous, and the man who says that he can prove that there were apparitions is equally ridiculous. The matter stands thus: there must have been apparitions; so what did they mean?

Now from this very beginning, I cannot follow Mr. Taylor. I do not know how he is so certain that there were apparitions of saints, angels and bowmen during the retreat from Mons. He says that Mr. Begbie is quite out of court in bringing evidence—or, as I should put it, what Mr. Begbie thinks evidence—to prove that there was a supernatural intervention during the noble retreat of our Army; and yet he quotes freely from Mr. Begbie's book. I find allusions to the experience of "the German soldiers" quoted by Mr. Begbie, in the story "told by an English lady ... reported by Mr. Begbie," and so forth. I find alleged supernatural experiences on the battlefield introduced by the phrase "we are told that" or "our soldiers declare," quite in Mr. Begbie's own manner. So, I really think that Mr. Taylor has used Mr. Begbie harshly. He should not take Mr. Begbie's instances and Mr. Begbie's methods, and then tell Mr. Begbie that he has wasted his time and energy.

The Valley of Dry Bones

And as for Mr. Taylor's own exegesis of bowmen and saints and angels? Well, my longbow has, it seems, shot an arrow into strange regions indeed. Mr. Taylor discourses of the Hebrew prophets, of a mass of clotted Theosophy, of Judah and the Ten Tribes, of the Apocalypse, of the failure of ecclesiasticism, of the Turk; of I know not what. He has an open mind, I think, about those famous bowmen. They may be saints, or angels, or they may be dead English soldiers still fighting on for the good cause. Or finally, they may be, nay are, the terrible inhabitants of the Valley of Dry Bones, seen by the prophet Ezekiel in his vision.

That having been described as an "exceeding great army" they were—when they stood upon their feet—apparently prepared for war; and having risen as soldiers, they must, according to an unalterable divine fundamental law, have fallen as such. And as they fell in the days when bows and arrows were used, with bows and arrows they would rise again.

Very well; nay, prodigious; but I must say that I certainly invented the story of the Bowmen, whatever may be said of the stories of the angels; and so I really do not see what Ezekiel's vision has to do with it.

But there are many things in this treatise which I do not understand. I see that "the Turks ... must very shortly surrender their possessions in Egypt to the Russians as representing the champions of the Jews, or to the English, French and other Anglo-Saxons now representing the Israelites."

Really: the Turks have no possessions in Egypt. And, though all the Mahatmas of Tibet rise up against me, I will maintain that the French are not Anglo-Saxons.

Haro!

Nevertheless, Machen's last word turned out to be premature, for with "The Return of the Angels: This Time They Are at Ypres," published in *The Evening News* on 3 July 1916, Machen once again resumed his documentation of the legend:

The "Angels of Mons" are with us once more; and in my opinion, their latest appearance is by far their best.

Mrs. Margaret L. Woods[3] has a noble and eloquent poem in the current number of the *Fortnightly Review*. It is called "The First Battle of Ypres," and tells in heroic verse of the heroic resistance of the thin line of British with small French supports to the great push of the Germans for Calais.[4]

This was the battle of October-November 1914. The British line was weak, the cooks and service men were hurried up to hold it against the flower of the Prussian Army. How was it that the Prussian Guard was driven back?

> Why paused they and went backward,
> With never a foe before,

> Like a long wave dragging
> Down a level shore,
> Its fierce reluctant surges, that came triumphant storming
> The land, and powers invisible drive to Its deep returning?

And the answer is that we had Great Reserves; Reserves that were more than mortal.

> Marlborough's men, and Wellington's, the burghers of Courtrai,
> The warriors of Plantagenet, King Louis' Gants gláces—
> And the young, young dead from Mons and the Marne river.
> Old heroic fighting men
> Who fought for chivalry,
> Men who died for England,
> Mother of Liberty.
> In the world's dim heart, where the waiting spirits slumber,
> Sounded a roar when the walls were rent asunder
> That parted Earth from Hell, and summoning them away,
> Tremendous trumpets blew, as at the Judgment Day—
> And the dead came forth, each to his former banner.

Mrs. Woods, indeed, disclaims all connection between her poem and the legend which was originally in *The Evening News* under the title of "The Bowmen," and then begot that group of legends known conveniently by that generic name of "The Angels of Mons."

She says that the story was received from "a very competent witness," who relates that the Germans broke through our line at Ypres three times and then retired, for no apparent reason.

On each of these occasions prisoners, when asked the cause of their retirement, replied: "We saw your enormous Reserves." We had no Reserves. The story was incidentally confirmed by the remark of another officer on the curious conduct of the Germans in violently shelling certain empty fields behind our lines.[5]

It may be so, but I think I remember that the "enormous Reserves" story was told with respect to the retreat from Mons.

And I note another point of contact between Mrs. Wood's account and the accounts of "the Angels" that I was examining a year ago. That is, that the witnesses are anonymous. Now it is "a very competent witness" and "another officer." Then it was "a nurse," "a well-known baronet," "a clergyman in the west of England"—a somebody without a name or an address.

Let me guard myself by saying that I by no means deny the truth of the story which Mrs. Woods has so beautifully elaborated. I know nothing about its truth or falsity; I simply suspend my judgment pending the production of first hand, testable evidence. I do not think that we should be called upon to accept the story of a specific miraculous occurrence on evidence which is not evidence, but merely rumour and gossip.

And, pending the production of real testimony, I am strongly inclined to think that this brave poem of dead warriors rising in dreadful array and gathering again to their ancient banners is the most worthy and valiant offspring of an unworthy father: "The Bowmen."

Machen continued to respond publicly to reports and stories of the Angels until late 1917 when either he or his readership at last had enough and published no more of his columns on the subject. His letters to Vincent Starrett reveal that he responded to questions about his authorship and responsibility for many years thereafter and had strong opinions about those who exploited his vision for personal ends.

One would like to believe that Arthur Machen would have approved of this volume. Certainly he would have appreciated being permitted the final word on the subject. Nevertheless, one regrets that this final word is given posthumously and that during his lifetime Machen never learned he reasons for the success of his simple and patriotic story and even had to fight to be acknowledged as its creator. Had he known of John Charteris's and Harold Begbie's probable roles in publicizing the story of the Angelic Bowmen, Machen might have been able to accept its success and to recognize how he had, inadvertently yet genuinely, filled a crucial need at a critical time.

Chapter Notes

Chapter One

1. Arthur Machen. "The Bowmen: The Angels of Mons." *The* [London] *Evening News* (29 September 1914) 3. This piece is often referred to by, and printed under, its subtitle. Machen himself referred to it simply as "The Bowmen" in his accounts given in its first book appearance (*The Bowmen and Other Legends of the War*. London: Simpkin, Marshall, Hamilton, Kent, 1915) and in the autobiographical notes given in *Arthur Machen: A Bibliography*, by Henry Danielson (London: Henry Danielson, 1923).

A few words must be said about the pronunciation of Machen's last name. Machen himself stated that "Mackin is the right pronunciation; though there are tribes who spell it the same way and call it Maytchen." *Starrett vs. Machen: A Record of Discovery and Correspondence*, ed. by Michael Murphy (St. Louis, MO: Autolycus Press, 1977). 46. My father once wrote that the name was to be pronounced "match-en." (E. F. Bleiler. "Arthur Machen." *Supernatural Fiction Writers: Fantasy and Horror*, ed. E. F. Bleiler. New York: Scribner's, 1985. 351). Having learned of Machen's preferred pronunciation, I asked him why he had stated "match-en." His response was that this was how Vincent Starrett (an old friend) said it.

2. I. F. Clarke. *Voices Prophesying War: Future Wars, 1763–3749* (Oxford: Oxford University Press, 1992). 35.

3. G. K. Chesterton. *The Crimes of England* (London: Cecil Palmer & Hayward, 1915). 121.

4. C. S. Lewis. *The Collected Letters of C. S. Lewis. Volume I: Family Letters 1905–1931*, ed. by Walter Hooper (New York: Harper San Francisco, 2004). 150.

5. C. S. Lewis. *The Collected Letters of C. S. Lewis. Volume II: Books, Broadcasts, and the War, 1931–1949*, ed. by Walter Hooper (New York: Harper San Francisco, 2004). 337.

6. Walter Hooper. "Note." *The Collected Letters of C. S. Lewis: Volume II: Books, Broadcasts, and the War, 1931–1949* (New York: Harper San Francisco, 2004). 337n.

7. Arthur Conan Doyle. *The History of Spiritualism*. Vol. II (New York: Arno Press, 1975; 1926). 243.

8. Arthur Conan Doyle. *The British Campaign in France and Flanders, 1914* (London: Hodder and Stoughton, 1916).

9. Alfred Dodd. *The Ballad of the Iron Cross* (London: Erskine Macdonald, 1918). 33.

10. Sydney C. Baldock. Angels of Mons (*Rêve Mystique*) (London: Gould & Bottler, 1915).

11. Paul Paree. Angel of Mons Waltz (London: Lawrence Wright Music, 1916).

12. Tim Crook. "Vocalizing the Angels of Mons: Audio Dramas as Propaganda in the Great War of 1914 to 1918." *Societies* 4 (2014): 180–221. Doi: 10.3390/soc4020180. Accessed 1 September 2014.

13. "The Angels of Mons" (1915). http://www.imdb.com/title/tt2361469/?ref_=fn_tt_tt_1. Accessed 22 October 2014.

14. "Thomas William Hodgson Crosland." *Wikipedia*. http://en.wikipedia.org/wiki/Thomas_William_Hodgson_Crosland. Accessed 24 June 2014.

15. The British Museum held exhibition cases containing such objects as "ground stone axes from German, Austria-Hungary, the Netherlands and Belgium. From the last

comes a broken pick made from an antler of a red deer, and roughly chipped unground flint tools, found at Spiennes near Mons, where mines for working flint tools were discovered." British Museum. *A Guide to the Antiquities of the Stone Age in the Department of British and Mediaeval Antiquities* (London: Printed by Order of the Trustees, 1902). 85–86.

16. See, for example, *The [London] Times* of 17 April 1893 ("The Franchise Agitation in Belgium"); 18 April 1893 ("The Agitation in Belgium"); 19 April 1893 ("The Belgian Agitation and Franchise Reform"); 14 September 1893 ("The French and Belgian Miners"). News of the strike was likewise reported in a variety of sources in the United States in a variety of sources; e.g., the 12 April 1893 *New York Times* ("Many Riots in Belgium"); the 22 April 1893 *Christian Union* ("The Outlook"); the 29 September 1893 *Chicago Daily Tribune* ("Strikers Hold a Mass-Meeting").

17. "It is well to see portions of Belgium, Holland, and Germany before visiting Switzerland and Italy ... Mons (*Hôtel Couronne*) had a castle built by Julius Caesar. It is the centre of a great coal-mining country. Splendid interior of the *Cathedral of St. Waudru* (1450–1589) and *Hôtel de Ville* (1458). Belfry built in 1662 by the Spaniards. At *Malplaquet*, 3 M S.E., Marlborough defeated the French in 1700, and lost 20,000 men." Edward King. *Cassell's Complete Pocket-Guide to Europe*. Revised and Enlarged (London: Cassell, 1897). 201.

18. Nathaniel Newnham-Davis. *The Gourmet's Guide to Europe*. Second edition (New York: Brentano's, 1908). 105.

19. *Black's Shilling Guide to Scotland*. Thirteenth edition (London: Adam and Charles Black, 1906). 24. It should perhaps be mentioned that the other story provided is that Mons Meg was "forged by a Galloway blacksmith and his sons."

20. John French. *1914* (Boston and New York: Houghton Mifflin, 1919). 53–54.

21. "British Army's Stern Fight. Official Report. Casualties Not Heavy." *The Times* 25 August 1914: 6.

22. "On the Defensive. The Importance of Namur." *The Times* 25 August 1914: 7.

23. "The War Day by Day. Position in Belgium." *The Times* 26 August 1914: 6.

24. http://spartacus-educational.com/FWWtimes.htm. Accessed 24 June 2014.

25. *The Parliamentary Debates (Official Report). Fifth Series—Volume LXXV. Fifth Session of the Thirtieth Parliament of the United Kingdom of Great Britain & Ireland 6 George V. House of Commons. Eighth Volume of Session 1914–1915* (London: HMSO, 1915).

26. James Myles Hogge. "Remarks." *The Parliamentary Debates (Official Report). Fifth Series—Volume LXXV. Fifth Session of the Thirtieth Parliament of the United Kingdom of Great Britain & Ireland 6 George V. House of Commons. Eighth Volume of Session 1914–1915* (London: HMSO, 1915). 1395. A liberal politician, he was elected to Parliament as representative of Edinburgh East in the by-election of February 1912.

27. H. G. Wells. *Mr. Britling Sees It Through* (London: Cassell, 1916). 223.

28. Brigadier-General Sir James E. Edmonds. *A Short History of World War I* (Oxford: Oxford University Press, 1951). 29.

29. John Mosier. *The Myth of the Great War: A New Military History of World War I* (New York: HarperCollins, 2001). 75.

30. Mark Valentine. *Arthur Machen* (Mid Glamorgan, Wales: Seren, 1995). 9.

31. Arthur Machen. *A Few Letters from Arthur Machen. Letters to Munson Havens*, with an introduction by Roger Dobson (Wirral, Cheshire: Aylesford Press, 1993). 20.

32. Arthur Machen. *Selected Letters: The Private Writings of the Master of the Macabre*, ed. by Roger Dobson, Godfrey Brangham, and R. A. Gilbert (Northamptonshire, England: Aquarian Press, 1988).

33. Valentine. *Machen*, 12.

34. Valentine, *Machen*, 13.

35. Arthur Machen. "Note." *Arthur Machen: A Bibliography*, by Henry Danielson, with notes, biographical and critical, by Arthur Machen, and an introduction by Henry Savage (New York: Haskell House, 1970; 1923). 1–2.

36. Machen. "Note." *Arthur Machen*, 3.

37. Machen. "Note." *Arthur Machen*, 4.

38. Marguerite, Queen of Navarre. *The Heptameron or Tales and Novels of Marguerite, Queen of Navarre, now first completely done into English Prose and Verse from the Original French by Arthur Machen*. London: Privately Printed [i.e., London: Dryden Press], 1886.

39. Machen. "Note." *Arthur Machen*, 7–8.

40. Arthur Machen. *The Chronicle of Clemendy; or, the History of the IX Joyous Journeys. In which are Contained the Amo-*

rous *Inventions and Facetious tales of Master Gervase Perrot, Gent., now for the first time done into English, by Arthur Machen, Translator of the Heptameron of Margaret of Navarre* (Carbonnek: Privately Printed for the Society of Pantagruelists, 1888).
41. Machen, *The Chronicle of Clemendy*, viii.
42. Valentine, *Machen*, 17.
43. Valentine, *Machen*, 18.
44. Jacques Casanova. *The Memoirs of Jacques Casanova Written by Himself*, now for the first time translated into English [by Arthur Machen]. London: Privately Printed, 1894. Mark Valentine states that "his translation proved popular, and has been reprinted over seventeen times. Machen remained quietly proud of his achievement, supplying new prefaces to three subsequent editions." Valentine, *Machen*, 19.
45. Arthur Machen. *The Great God Pan and The Inmost Light* (London: John Lane, 1894).
46. Arthur Machen. *The Three Imposters* (London: John Lane, 1895).
47. Arthur Machen. *The House of Souls* (London: Grant Richards, 1906).
48. Arthur Machen. *The Hill of Dreams* (London: Grant Richards, 1907).
49. E. F. Bleiler. "Arthur Machen." *Supernatural Fiction Writers: Fantasy and Horror*, ed. E. F. Bleiler (New York: Scribner's, 1985). 351.
50. S. T. Joshi. "Arthur Machen." *Supernatural Literature of the World; An Encyclopedia*, ed. S. T. Joshi and Stefan Dziemianowicz (Westport, CT: Greenwood, 2005). 754.
51. Machen. "Note." *Arthur Machen*, 39–40.
52. Machen. "Note." *Arthur Machen*, 42.
53. Machen, *Hill of Dreams*, 231.
54. Valentine, *Machen*, 18.
55. Valentine, *Machen*, 75.
56. Lord Alfred Douglas. *The Autobiography of Lord Alfred Douglas* (London: Martin Secker, 1929). 245.
57. *Starrett vs. Machen: A Record of Discovery and Correspondence*, ed. by Michael Murphy (St. Louis, MO: Autolycus Press, 1977). 27–28.
58. Douglas, *Autobiography*, 245.
59. Valentine, *Machen*, 111.
60. Vincent Starrett. *Arthur Machen: A Novelist of Ecstasy and Sin* (Chicago: Walter M. Hill, 1918). 5. This appeared first in *Reedy's Mirror* (5 October 1917); it has since been reprinted in *Buried Caesars* (Chicago: Covici McGee, 1923).
61. Starrett vs. Machen. 16.
62. Starrett vs. Machen. 9.
63. S. T. Joshi. *Lovecraft's Library: A Catalogue*. Revised and enlarged (New York: Hippocampus Press, 2002). Oddly, *The Bowmen* does not appear in this catalogue.
64. H. P. Lovecraft. *Supernatural Horror in Literature*, ed. by E. F. Bleiler (New York: Dover Publications, 1973). 88. Also, H. P. Lovecraft. *The Annotated Supernatural Horror in Literature*, ed. by S. T. Joshi (New York: Hippocampus Press, 2000). 61. A slight discrepancy exists between the texts given in these two volumes.
65. Lovecraft, *Supernatural Horror*, ed. Bleiler. 95. Also: Lovecraft, *Annotated Supernatural Horror*, ed. Joshi. Again, there are slight discrepancies between the texts given.
66. On this occasion, Starrett wrote:
One of the finest British writers of our time celebrated his eightieth birthday anniversary on March 3 [1943], if celebrated is the word. Almost simultaneously, an appeal was made on his behalf, thru the London *Times*, asking assistance for the distinguished author in his old age....
Few personal disasters could have been more accurately predicted than this one. There are only two possible attitudes a writer may adopt toward his profession: He may elect to serve literature or to make literature serve him. It is Machen's triumph and lasting honor that he chose the first course and never wavered from it. He was never for a moment popular; yet for fifty years the distinction of his style and thought has been one of the most unmistakable of literary phenomenons. He never really knew economic security; yet he had written some of the most extraordinary stories in the whole range of English literature, including at least one masterpiece, *The Hill of Dreams*. He began his career in the traditional poverty of genius and he is ending it, it would appear, in much the same way. It was inevitable, no doubt, the world being what it is; but one feels no obligation to think better of the world on that account." Vincent Starrett. "Books Alive." *Chicago Daily Tribune*. 28 March 1943. E15.
The version of this encomium that appears in *Starrett vs. Machen* (p. 22–23) differs somewhat as to spelling and punctuation, and it is not known which version Starrett would have preferred.
67. "Arthur Machen." *Chicago Daily Tribune*. 16 December 1947. 27.

68. "Arthur Machen, Novelist, Dies: Author of the Story That Led to 'Angel of Mons' Legend—Won Fame in His Fifties." *The New York Times*. 16 December 1947. 34.
69. "Mr. Arthur Machen: Literature of Awe." *The Times*. 16 December 1947. 6.
70. Vincent Starrett. "Books Alive." *Chicago Daily Tribune*. 28 December 1947. G2.
71. Richard Simms. http://eveningnews.atwebpages.com/index.htm. Accessed 18 June 2014.
72. "During his journalistic period (roughly 1907–1921) he produced something like 1,500 attributable pieces on daily events, antiquities, folklore, London, historical crimes, literature—all written with a facility that became legendary on the Street." E. F. Bleiler. "Arthur Machen." *Supernatural Fiction Writers*, 356.
73. Alexander Crawford was the name used by the fantasist David Lindsay's older brother (1869–1915).
74. This is not meant to denigrate such scholars as Phillip Ellis, whose "Spectral Soldiers: Possible Literary Antecedents for 'The Bowmen'" (*Studies in Weird Fiction* No. 24: 5–8. Winter 1999) links it to Herodotus's *Histories*. One can if inclined find mentions of St. George, bowmen, and battles in hundreds of previous works of literature, including ballads and verse. The Greek historians do not need to be evoked.
75. Arthur Machen. "The Mons Angels: The Growth of a Miracle Fiction." *The Daily Mail*. 28 July 1915. This article, bylined Arthur Machen, is not listed in Adrian Goldstone and Wesley D. Sweetser's *A Bibliography of Arthur Machen* (Austin, TX: University of Texas Press, 1965) but is available online at http://www.warrelics.eu/forum/ww1-allies-greatbritain-france-usa-etc-1914-1918/angelsmons-372136-3/. Accessed 22 October 2014.
76. One wonders if Machen ever realized that the versions of his story present folklore from the beginning and the end of the first battle of the First World War.
77. Arthur Machen. *The Angels of Mons: The Bowmen and Other Legends of the War* (New York: Putnam's, 1915).
78. Machen. "Note." *Arthur Machen*, 43.
79. I.e., "I don't think anything about Harold Begbie or his books. "On the Side of the Angels" was a publisher's commission; I don't think that Harold believes in a word of it. I don't think he's fool enough to do so." *Starrett vs. Machen*. 51.
80. J. M. Bourne. "Charteris, John." *Dictionary of National Biography*. Oxford University Press, 2004. Online ed, October 2008. Accessed 20 June 2014.
81. John Charteris. *At G. H. Q.* (London: Cassell, 1931).
82. Charteris, *At G. H. Q.*, 25–26.
83. Charteris, *At G. H. Q.*, 75.
84. David Clarke. *The Angel of Mons; Phantom Soldiers and Ghostly Guardians* (London: John Wiley, 2004). 218.
85. Charteris, *At G. H. Q.*, 75–76.
86. Sir Almeric Fitzroy. *Memoirs*. Vol. II (New York: George H. Doran, 1925). 569–570.
87. Clarke, *The Angel of Mons*, 216.
88. Clarke, op. cit.
89. Charteris, *At G. H. Q.*, 4.
90. Published first in *The Daily Chronicle* on the day after the appearance of the Amiens Dispatch, its conclusion remains powerful: "Will you slink away, as it were from a blow, / Your old head shamed and bent? / Or say—I was not the first to go, / But I went, thank God, I went?"

Chapter Two

1. "Turpenite." *The New York Times*. 1 October 1914. 10.
2. ["Turpenite."] *Popular Electricity and Modern Mechanics*. November 1914. 558. "A recent report has it that the French army is using shells filed with a deadly gas they term as 'Turpenite.' It is said that all living creatures in the vicinity such an exploding shell are killed." See also "Gas Bombs Used by English and French." *The Fatherland*. 2 June 1915. 11. "In the vicinity of Epernay I saw a German trench in which every soldier was dead, still in the position of firing and with no wounds. Was this the effect of turpenite? I cannot say definitely, but death seemed the result of asphyxiation."
3. Presumably Sir John Stainer (1840–1901), organist, composer, and chorister of St. Paul's Cathedral.
4. Literally "praise the eternal banquet." The term does not appear to be a literary reference.
5. Greek lyric poet who lived during the sixth century BCE on the island of Lesbos.
6. English writer (Joseph) Rudyard Kipling (1865–1936) was in 1907 the first English language writer to be awarded the Nobel Prize for Literature. Machen could be referencing "The Drums of the Fore and Aft"

(written 1888 but first published in *Soldier Tales* [1896]) or "The Lost Legion" (*The Strand*, May 1892), both of which share this theme. However, in "The Mons Angels: The Growth of a Miracle Fiction," *The Daily Mail*, 28 July 1915, Machen writes "I think that Kipling's story called, if I remember, "The Dead Rissala" had something to do with its conception; but, of course, the main idea of spiritual interpolation in an earthly battle is age-old and common, I should suppose, to all people and all mythologies." No such work by this title appears to exist, but the phrase occurs within "The Lost Legion."

7. Scholar and journalist Arthur Oswald Barron (1868–1939) had a daily column for *The Evening News* which he signed "The Londoner."

8. The Welsh form of the Archangel Michael's name.

9. Probably Welsh Saint Teilo (500?–560).

10. Machen may have in mind the fifth century Welsh saint whose name is now variously spelled as Illtud or Eltud.

11. The Welsh form of the name of the sixth century Bishop who became the Patron Saint of Wales following his death, Saint David (500?–589).

12. A variant spelling of the name now more commonly given as Cadwaladr ap Cadwallon, the King of Gwynedd (died 682).

13. Sir Ralph Shirley. For more information on him see the biography given in Chapter 10, *The Angel Warriors at Mons*.

14. The editor of *The Evening News* at this time was Walter J. Evans, but it is not known if this is the person to whom Machen refers.

15. None of these pamphlets has been seen, but one was evidently encountered by Mrs. St. John Mildmay, who used chunks of it in "Phantom Armies Seen in France," *The North American Review*, August 1915. 207–212. The text of "The Bowmen" given here is that which appeared in *The Evening News* of 29 September 1914, for it mentions turpenite. Mildmay's article was then encountered by British occult researcher Hereward Carrington, who used it in *Psychical Phenomena and the War* (New York: Dodd, Mead, 1918) and accounts such as that published in *The Best Psychic Stories*, ed. Joseph Lewis French (New York: Boni and Liveright, 1920).

16. Author and Theosophist Alfred Percy Sinnett (1840–1921).

17. Presumably Bishop of Calcutta James Edward Cowell Welldon (1854–1937).

18. Presumably Bishop of Durham, Dean Herbert Hensley Henson (1863–1947).

19. John Taylor Smith, KCB, CVO, DD (1860–1928), Bishop of Sierra Leone and Chaplain-General to the British Armed Forces from 1901–1925.

20. Presumably Robert Forman Horton (1855–1934).

21. Liberal Politician Joseph Compton-Rickett (1847–1919) was MP for Osgoldcross at the time Machen wrote this.

22. Loyal and devoted servant to Mr. Pickwick in Charles Dickens's *The Pickwick Papers* (serial 1836–1837; book, 1837).

23. Helena Petrovna Blavatsky (1831–1891), Russian-born occultist and establisher of the original Theosophical Society.

24. William Quan Judge (1851–1896), Irish-born co-founder of the original Theosophical Society along with Helena Petrovna Blavatsky, Henry Steel Olcott, and others. Following Blavatsky's death, letters were found supposedly from Mahatmas endorsing Judge's leadership.

25. William Leonard Courtney (1850–1928), prolific scholar, author, and editor of the *Fortnightly Review* from 1894–1928. The work being referenced is apparently Courtney's *The Meaning of Life* (1914), though *Armageddon—and After* (1914) may also qualify.

26. The newspaper has a lower-case *c* for Censorship.

27. The newspaper has, "as if the agonies of their brothers in the battlefield," etc.

28. The newspaper has a lower-case *c* for Censorship.

29. The newspaper has, "terrible cannonade."

30. The newspaper has, "rent them and destroyed them."

31. The newspaper has, "goodbye to Tipperary." The reference is to a song from 1912 that became enormously popular in 1914 and thereafter, "It's a Long, Long Way to Tipperary" was written by Jack Judge and Harry Williams. Several versions exist.

32. The newspaper has, "an opportunity for fancy shooting might never occur again."

33. The newspaper has, "and the few machine guns did their best."

34. The newspaper has, "but others came on and on and on."

35. Ephesians 3.21.

36. The newspaper puts a comma after soldiers.

37. This aside is not present in the newspaper.
38. The newspaper has, "queer dishes."
39. The newspaper has, "may St. George be a present help to the English."
40. The newspaper puts a comma after money.
41. The newspaper puts a comma after for.
42. The newspaper has, "this summons."
43. The newspaper does not have a comma after "hear."
44. The newspaper has, "Knight of Heaven, aid us."
45. The newspaper has, "German host."
46. The newspaper has, "in plain English."
47. The newspaper has, "what are ye talking about?"
48. The newspaper has, "guttural screams."
49. The newspaper has, monseigneur.
50. This line is not present in the newspaper.
51. The newspaper has, "the singing arrows darkened the air; the heathen horde melted from before them."
52. The newspaper has, "Don't hear them," Tom yelled back; "but, thank God, anyway, they've got it in the neck."
53. The newspaper has, "the contemptible English must have employed turpenite shells, as no wounds were discernible on the bodies of the dead German soldiers." One wonders if John Charteris was behind the brief existence of turpenite.
54. The newspaper puts a comma after steak.
55. See note 13, above.
56. For more information on Phyllis Campbell see the biography given in Chapter 4, *Back of the Front*.
57. The short, fat, and perpetually irascible Mr. Justice Stareleigh presides over the case of *Bardell v. Pickwick* in Charles Dickens's *The Pickwick Papers* (serial 1836–1837; book, 1837).

Chapter Three

1. Harold Begbie. "Fall In!" *The Daily Chronicle* 31 August 1914.
2. *Starrett vs. Machen: A Record of Discovery and Correspondence*, ed. by Michael Murphy. (St. Louis, MO: Autolycus Press, 1977). 50.
3. Harold Begbie, *On the Side of the Angels: The Story of the Angels at Mons. An Answer to the Bowmen*. Second edition. London: Hodder & Stoughton, 1915. 48–49. This statement remains in the fourth edition of *On the Side of the Angels*, perhaps inadvertently causing confusion.
4. Begbie, *On the Side of the Angels*. Second edition. 61–62
5. Phyllis Campbell ... became involved a little later in a scandal in which an officer was also concerned; I believe her to have become a conscious liar in the matter." *Starrett vs. Machen: A Record of Discovery and Correspondence*. St. Louis, MO: Autolycus Press, 1977. 51.
6. W. H. Salter. "An Inquiry Concerning the Angels at Mons." *Journal of the Society for Psychical Research*. December 1915.
7. Loyal and devoted servant to Mr. Pickwick in Charles Dickens's *The Pickwick Papers* (serial 1836–1837; book, 1837).
8. It is not known which superficial German philosophers Mr. Begbie had in mind.
9. Playful or frolicsome.
10. Scholar and journalist Arthur Oswald Barron (1868–1939) had a daily column for *The Evening News* which he signed "The Londoner."
11. Charles Augustin Sainte-Beuve (1804–1869), a French literary critic.
12. Joseph Joubert (1754–1824), French Essayist and Moralist. It is not known where Begbie encountered this statement but a likely possibility is on p. 76 of "Joubert," appearing in *Sainte-Beuve: On Men and Women*, ed. by William Sharp. London: Gibbings; Philadelphia: J. B. Lippincott, 1901. Begbie also quoted it in *The Bed-Book of Happiness: Being a Colligation or Assemblage of Cheerful Writings Brought Together from Many Quarters into This One Compass for the Diversion, Distraction and Delight of Those Who Lie Abed—A Friend to the Invalid, a Companion to the Sleepless, an Excuse to the Tired*. London: Hodder and Stoughton, 1914. 270.
13. Hawley Harvey Crippen (1862–1910), American homeopath resident in England accused, convicted, and executed for killing his wife. Crippen fled with his mistress Ethel "Le Neve" Neave but was caught, the apprehension involving the first use of wireless communication for this purpose. It is not known to which novelist Begbie alludes, but William Le Queux (1864–1927) did write about the case.
14. I.e., "There are more things in heaven and earth, Horatio, / Than are dreamt of in

your philosophy." Shakespeare. *Hamlet* (Act 1, Scene 5, lines 167–168).
15. Biographical information has not been available on either this name or the later spelling of "Courtenay Wilson."
16. In the late nineteenth century, this term was used interchangeably among soldiers and sailors as a slang term for the First Lieutenant.
17. The soldiers from the Royal Munster Fusiliers.
18. One of the Foot Guard regiments of the British Army.
19. The Polish Light Cavalry, some 26 regiments of which were in the Imperial German Army.
20. I.e., Ypres.
21. Private Cleaver was rapidly revealed to be a liar, his statement shown to be demonstrably false. These paragraphs were removed from later printings.
22. For more information on Phyllis Campbell see Chapter 4: Phyllis Campbell: *Back of the Front*.
23. Although one may find references to a Welsh private (1895?–1915) of this name, a chaplain name has not been located.
24. Ralph Shirley. For more information on him see Chapter 10: Ralph Shirley: *The Angel Warriors at Mons*.
25. Noted English poet and critic (1822–1888).
26. In 1901 the Reverend George Gustavus Monck was appointed Rector of Closworth, Sherborne, Dorset, but he does not seem to have become the Prebendary of Wells and the Rural Dean of Martock. "Additions and Corrections." College of Arms, Great Britain. *Visitation of England and Wales*, vol. 12, ed. by Frederick A. Crisp. Privately Printed, 1904. 43.
27. I.e., Alexander Alfred Boddy (1854–1930), Anglican vicar and one of the co-founders of British Pentacostalism.
28. I.e., Richard I, King of England (1157–1199).
29. Also given as Geoffroy de Bouillon and Godfrey of Bouillon (1060–1100). He led the troops that entered Jerusalem in 1099 and ruled for but one year before his death.
30. Frances Helen, Mrs. FitzGerald Beale, was a member of the Queen's County Local War Pensions Committee.
31. I.e., nonconformist divine Robert Forman Horton (1855–1934).

32. [Harold Begbie]: I have myself seen the written account of a similar incident sent home by a distinguished British officer, who took it down from the soldier's own lips, a man named Casey. The officer was holding a Court appointment at the outbreak of hostilities.
33. For more information on this story see Chapter 8: W. H. Leathem and *The Comrade in White*.
34. Probably the vicar of the church of St. Paul, Mill-Hill.
35. Presumably the English romantic novelist, Edith Noel Danielle (1872–?), who signed herself Mrs. Hubert Barclay.
36. Scottish writer Annie Shepherd Swan (1859–1943) also used the names David Lyall and wrote under her married name as Mrs. Burnett Smith.
37. [Harold Begbie]: A friend of mine told me that a young officer in the Guards, home on a few days' leave, arrived to find his mother and a party of friends playing Bridge. After their greetings, the mother spoke about the inconveniences in social life which have flowed from this War. The young soldier said, "Don't talk like that, Mother. This War has, taught me that *there is only one thing that really matters and that is God.*" My friend tells me that before the War he was the last man in the world to have spoken in this fashion.
38. I.e., Major English scholar, lecturer, evolutionary proponent, and man of science Thomas Henry Huxley (1825–1895).
39. I.e., Major English naturalist and evolutionary proponent Charles Robert Darwin (1809–1882).
40. I.e., Major French chemist, microbiologist, and discoverer of the principles of vaccination Louis Pasteur (1822–1895).
41. Major English naturalist, biologist, explorer, anthropologist (1823–1913) perhaps best known for postulating the theory of evolution through natural selection.
42. I.e., Alfred Russel Wallace. "Miracles and Modern Spiritualism." Three essays serialized in 1874; first book publication as *On Miracles and Modern Spiritualism: Three Essays*. London: James Burns, 1875.
43. I.e., noted French philosopher Henry Louis Bergson (1859–1941), awarded the Nobel Prize (for Literature) in 1927.

Chapter Four

1. Although there are intriguing similarities in their lives, she is not to be confused with the Welsh-born Australian composer and Theosophist of the same name (1891–1974).
2. Almost certainly English scholar and editor William Leonard Courtney (1850–1928).
3. E. W. Walters. *Heroines of the World-War* (London: Charles H. Kelly, 1916). 144.
4. Like so much associated with Ms. Campbell, this relationship is up for dispute. Douglas Sladen. *Twenty Years of My Life*. New York: E. P. Dutton, 1913, states that Frances Campbell "married a cousin of the late Duke of Argyll, who was out in Queensland" (243). Other sources state he was the brother. *The Gundagai Times and Tumut, Adelong and Murrumbidgee District Advisor* of 16 August 1912 avoids taking a stand and sates simply that he was "a relative of the Duke of Argyll." http://nla.gov.au/nla.news-article12223661. Accessed 22 September 2014.
5. Indian Cemeteries. "Howard Douglas Campbell. Monument of Howard Douglas Campbell at All Souls Church, Cawnpore." http://www.indian-cemeteries.org/viewimage.asp?ID=130. Accessed 22 September 2014.
6. *Myrtleford Mail and Whorouly Witness*, 16 September 1915, 4. This article is a reprint of an article appearing first in *The Evening News* on an unspecified date.
7. "Duke's Relative a Suicide?" *New York Times*. 27 March 1901. 5.
8. "Items of Interest." *The Maitland Weekly Mercury*. 18 May 1901. 11. http://nla.gov.au/nla.news-article126796351. Accessed 22 September 2014.
9. "She was employed upon many of the most important papers in this country and in America. Amongst others, she regularly contributed signed articles to the *Westminster Gazette* and also wrote for *Vanity Fair* and *Country Life*. She had been employed on one occasion by the *Daily Mail* at a salary of £50 a week to write accounts of the disturbance in Morocco in 1906. The plaintiff was also a great personal friend of the late Mr. W. T. Stead and was employed by him on the *Review of Reviews*." "A Voyage in the Mediterranean." *Times* (London) 13 June 1912: 3. The Times Digital Archive, Web. 22 Sept. 2014.
10. "Dispute Over a Sea Trip." *The Standard*. 19 June 1912. 5. http://newspaperarchive.com/uk/middlesex/london/london-standard/1912/06-19/page-5. Accessed 22 September 2014.
11. William Thomas Stead died aboard the RMS *Titanic* on 15 April 1912.
12. "Dispute Over a Sea Trip," op. cit.
13. "Sea Trip Dispute: Mystery of a Package for Mr. W. T. Stead." *The Standard* 25 June 1912.
14. King's Bench Division. "A Voyage in the Mediterranean: Campbell v. The Prince Line (Limited)." *Times* (London, England) 26 June 1912: 3. The Times Digital Archive. Web. 22 Sept. 2014.
15. David Clarke. *The Angel of Mons: Phantom Soldiers and Ghostly Guardians*. West Sussex, England: John Wiley, 2004. 137.
16. W. H. Salter. "An Inquiry Concerning the Angels at Mons." *Journal of the Society for Psychical Research*. December 1915.
17. "Broadcasting: Home Stations." *Times* (London, England) 23 December 1937: 4. The Times Digital Archive. Web. 22 Sept. 2014. Although *The White Hen* is apparently set in France, the authorship cannot be definitely linked to the author of *Back of the Front*. "The Hand of Thais" has been neither heard nor read and does not appear to be available. Furthermore, Phyllis Campbell is hardly an uncommon name.
18. *Starrett vs. Machen: A Record of Discovery and Correspondence* (St. Louis, MO: Autolycus Press, 1977). 51.
19. Perhaps best translated as "ulterior motive."
20. A mis-statement: the soldier sees the motto, not St. George. One wonders if this was an intentional error.
21. A slang term used to refer to the Germans and the German soldiers, particularly during the First World War.
22. The Polish Light Cavalry, some 26 regiments of which were in the Imperial German Army.

Chapter Five

1. *An Invention for Conveying Invalids and Others by Rail or Road in a Recumbent Position* (GBD190413506; 190413506 [A]) ; *Improvements Relating to Stands for Hammocks* (GBD190517244; 190517244 [A]); *An Improved Medicated Pillow, Cushion or the Like* (GBD190802310; 190802310 [A]) ; *Improvements in or Relating to Bath Chairs & Hammocks* (GBD190317148; 190317148 [A]).

2. *Oreiller hygiénique* (FRD386674; 3866 74 [A]).
3. 29 September.
4. A village in Surrey, England, which hosts shooting ranges owned by the Ministry of Defence. In the Olympics of 1908, Bisley was the host of the majority of the shooting events.
5. This street is present in neither the newspaper nor the published versions of 1915.
6. Machen gives the meaning as "May St. George be a present help to the English."
7. See Chapter 3: Harold Begbie: *On the Side of the Angels*.
8. See Chapter 10: Ralph Shirley: *The Angel Warriors at Mons*.
9. Louis of Nassau (1538–1574), the third son of William of Nassau and Juliana of Stolberg, was important in the revolt of the Netherlands against Spain. He perished in combat against the Spanish in the Battle of Mookerheyde.

Chapter Six

1. Alfred Douglas. *Oscar Wilde and Myself* (London: John Long, 1914).
2. Merlin Holland. "Biography and the Art of Lying." *The Cambridge Companion to Oscar Wilde*, ed. Peter Raby (Cambridge, UK: Cambridge University Press, 1997). 8.
3. "I withdraw what I said about Oscar in that book. What I said does not, on the whole, represent the real truth, either about the facts of our friendship or my feelings for him. The whole book is distorted and wrenched out of focus by the bewildered resentment and indignation which overcame me when I first read the "unpublished portion" of *De Produndis* in the year 1913 or 1912," Alfred Douglas. *The Autobiography of Lord Alfred Douglas* (London: Martin Secker, 1929). 136.
4. Karl Beckson. *The Oscar Wilde Encyclopedia* (New York: AMS Press, 1998). 80.
5. W. T. H. Crosland. *The First Stone: On Reading the Unpublished Portions of 'De Profundis'* (London: The Author, 1912). 9.
6. Alfred Douglas. *The Autobiography of Lord Alfred Douglas* (London: Martin Secker, 1929). 136.
7. W. Sorley Brown. "The Life and Genius of T. W. H. Crosland." *The Flying Horse* 1.1 New Series (1927). 2.
8. "Mr. T. W. H. Crosland." *The Times* (London, England). 24 December 1924. 12. Accessed 23 September 2014.
9. W. Sorley Brown. *The Life and Genius of T. W. H. Crosland* (London: Cecil Palmer, 1928). 38–39.
10. Brown. *The Life and Genius*. 40.
11. "Mr. T. W. H. Crosland." *The Times* (London England). *Op cit.*
12. "Mr. Machen—or 'Mr. Mac Hen,' as Crosland used to call him in friendly intercourse—'a name that's worth more than we can possibly pay you'—was made the target of humour and delicate satire in Crosland's dainty volume, which recounted the wonderful experiences of Privates Sweets and Cheese, who end by being kept in custody till the state of their minds is inquired into." Brown. *The Life and Genius*. 349–350.
13. Brown. *The Life and Genius*. 350. Crosland was to lose a son, W. P. Crosland, in action on 16 August 1917. His reaction to the news is unknown.
14. Horatio Herbert Kitchener, First Earl Kitchener of Khartoum and of Broome, (1850–1916), was a senior British army officer, colonel administrator, and cabinet minister. Along with about 600 others he was drowned off the Orkney Islands when his ship, *HMS Hampshire*, struck a German mine.
15. Charles Garvice (1850–1920) was a prolific British writer of romance novels.
16. I.e., English writer (Joseph) Rudyard Kipling (1865–1936) was in 1907 the first English language writer to be awarded the Nobel Prize for Literature.
17. I.e., Irish writer Henry De Vere Stacpoole (1863–1951), prolific author, probably best known for *The Blue Lagoon* (1951). The origin of this phrase has not been located.
18. English Romantic poet, painter, and printmaker (1757–1827).
19. The origin of this phrase has not been located.
20. I.e., English Liberal politician and statesman David Lloyd George (1863–1945), First Earl Lloyd-George of Dwyfor, who from 1908–1915 was Chancellor of the Exchequer. He was later to serve as Secretary of State for War (1916) and as Prime Minister (1916–1922).
21. A song popular during the First World War, composer unknown. The lyrics vary, the third line occasionally making reference to a Colonel's daughter.
22. I.e., Royal Army Medical Corps.
23. I.e., French writer Henri René Albert

Guy de Maupassant (1850–1893) famed for his short stories.

24. See note 16.

25. Probably composer and writer Lewis Sydney (dates unknown).

26. I.e., English actor, playwright, journalist, and author Charles Hallam Elton Brookfield (1857–1913).

27. "The sale, I believe, was a very large one, but for reasons into which I need not enter, the book was not highly remunerative to me. However, it is always a satisfaction to find that one has put a little money into the pockets of good men." Machen. "Note." *Arthur Machen: A Bibliography*, by Henry Danielson, with notes, biographical and critical, by Arthur Machen, and an introduction by Henry Savage (New York: Haskell House, 1970; 1923). 43.

28. W. A. Eaton, a popular poet—a penny poet—and performer, dates unknown.

29. C.K.S. was British critic and journalist Clement King Shorter (1857–1926). He founded *Sphere* in 1900 and edited it until his death; it ceased in 1964.

30. Machen wrote no articles of this title, and *The Evening News* was in 1914 located in Carmelite House on Carmelite Street, not far from the Thames Embankment.

31. "The *Erewhon* man" was English author, scholar, and critic Samuel Butler (1835–1902).

32. Probably English theologian, apologist, and philosopher Bishop Joseph Butler (1692–1752).

33. Although Julius Caesar is also credited with this apothegm, it would appear to be a paraphrase originating in Joseph Butler's *Fifteen Sermons Preached at the Rolls Chapel* (1726).

34. Probably English theologian and apologist William Paley (1743–1805).

35. Classical Greek philosopher and mathematician who lived between about 428–347 BCE.

36. A song popular during the First World War, composed in 1914 by Ivor Novello.

37. Derived from American poet Ella Wheeler Wilcox's (1850–1919) "Solitude." Her original lines are "Laugh, and the world laughs with you / Weep, and you weep alone."

38. This poet has not been identified.

39. Free on board; i.e., the buyer pays for the transportation.

40. The opening lines of "Violets," a popular song from 1900, words by Julian Fane and music by Ellen Wright.

41. A popular song from 1914, words by P. Gilpin and music by Paul Williams.

42. See note 17.

43. I.e., prolific Anglo-French writer Joseph Hilaire Pierre René Belloc (1870–1953), who wrote as Hilaire Belloc. Crosland probably had in mind such articles as "The Geography of the War" (*Geographical Journal*, vol. 45, no. 1, 1915) and "The Economics of the War" (*The Dublin Review*, vol. 151, no. 312–313, January–April, 1915).

44. I.e., English poet, artist, and publisher Claud Lovat Fraser (1890–1921).

45. A song from 1912 that became enormously popular in 1914 and thereafter, "It's a Long, Long Way to Tipperary" was written by Jack Judge and Harry Williams. Several versions exist.

46. *Proverbs* 30: 19: The way of an eagle in the air; the way of a serpent upon a rock; the way of a ship in the midst of the sea; and the way of a man with a maid.

47. I.e., English performer, actor, comedian, and cultural figure Charles Spencer Chaplin (1889–1977).

48. I.e., English actor and theatrical manager Charles Blake Cochran (1872–1951).

49. See note 20.

50. I.e., British composer and conductor Herman Finck (1872–1939), who during the First World War wrote such popular music as "Gilbert the Filbert."

51. I.e., British man of letters, author, and journalist Edward Verrall Lucas (1868–1938), on the staff of *Punch* from 1904 until his death.

52. I.e., English theatrical director (1887–1960), who later became a director of motion pictures.

53. I.e., Anglo-Irish writer, publisher, journalist, and editor (1856–1931). At the time of this writing, he had written much journalism and a number of novels but had not yet written his multivolume *My Life and Loves*, the first volume of which was published in 1922, perhaps the only work for which he is remembered. It is fairly certain that if he had, Crosland would not have cited him so flippantly.

54. See note 14.

55. First published in *The Daily Chronicle* on 31 August 1914, Begbie's poem "Fall In!" was enormously popular as a recruitment item. These lines appeared in the conclusion

of its third (of four) eight-line stanzas, and Crosland does not quote them quite correctly. "Will you slink away, as it were from a blow, / Your old head shamed and bent? / Or say—I was not the first to go, / But I went, thank God, I went?"

56. I.e., Anglo-Irish soldier and statesman Arthur Wellesley, First Duke of Wellington (1769–1852), whose military exploits and victories, particularly over Napoleon at Waterloo in 1815, would have been familiar to all English.

57. I.e., English officer Horatio Nelson, First Viscount Nelson 1758–1805), whose 1805 naval victory at Trafalgar and dying words would have been familiar to all English.

58. I.e., Emperor of Austria, Apostolic King of Hungary, and President of the German Confederation, Kaiser Franz Joseph I (1830–1916).

59. A reference to and adaptation of the opening line of William Wordsworth's "London, 1802": "Milton! thou should'st be living at this hour."

60. A reference to the Duke of Wellington, in particular an iron equestrian statue cast by Sir John Steell in 1852.

61. If Kitchener said this, the source has not been located. "Good-bye, Piccadilly; Good-bye, Leicester Square" are lines from "Tipperary" (see note 45).

62. See note 16.

63. The question of whether Crosland—a newspaperman such as Begbie and Machen—was unaware that Begbie appears to have falsified much of his evidence remains unanswered, but these seemingly laudatory passages may have been meant ironically, particularly when Crosland later writes of much of Begbie's testimony being "spoilt."

64. The fifth line of George Herbert's poem "The Church Porch."

65. Probably translated as *condescending*.

Chapter Seven

1. A. E. Garnier. *The Chronicles of the Garniers of Hampshire During Four Centuries (1530–1900)*. (Norwich and London: Jarrold and Sons, the Empire Press, 1900). 93.

2. John Garnier. *Israel in Britain: A Brief Statement of the Evidences in Proof of the Israelite Origin of the British Race* (London: Robert Banks, 1890).

3. John Garnier. *The Great Pyramid: Its Builder and Its Prophecy. With a Review of the Corresponding Prophecies of Scripture Relating to Coming Events and the Approaching End of the Age* (London: Robert Banks, 1905). This went through many revisions and expansions.

4. "Biography and Roots of Colonel John Garnier—Breeder of Governor' Sire Lion." http://the-mastiff-by-marcel-wynants.com/garnier.html. Accessed 2 October 2014.

5. "The British Israelites." www.badarchaeology.com. Accessed 2 October 2014.

6. [John Garnier]: *The Angel Warriors of Mons*, by Ralph Shirley, published by The Newspaper Publicity Co., 61, Fleet Street, E.C., price 1d; *On the Side of the Angels*, by Harold Begbie; Hodder & Stoughton, price 1s.

7. Royal Field Artillery.

8. The Polish Light Cavalry, some 26 regiments of which were in the Imperial German Army.

9. Cleaver was, however, rapidly revealed as a liar.

10. In 1901 the Reverend George Gustavus Monck was appointed Rector of Closworth, Sherborne, Dorset, but he does not seem to have become the Prebendary of Wells and the Rural Dean of Martock. "Additions and Corrections." College of Arms, Great Britain. *Visitation of England and Wales*, vol. 12, ed. by Frederick A. Crisp (Privately Printed, 1904). 43.

11. Alexander Alfred Boddy (1854–1930), Anglican vicar and one of the co-founders of British Pentecostalism.

12. The Boxer Rebellion of 1898–1900 in Beijing.

13. I.e., Russian General Michael Dimitrievitch Skobeloff (1843?–1882).

14. I.e., French Marshal Joseph Jacques Césaire Joffre (1852–1931), who was instrumental in defeating the Germans at the First Battle of the Marne in 1914.

15. I.e., Anglo-Irish Field Marshal John Denton Pinkstone French, First Earl of Ypres (1852–1925), who served as Commander in Chief of the B. E. F. for the first two years of the war.

16. I.e., General Sir Horace Lockwood Smith Dorrien (1858–1930), one of the senior B.E.F. commanders during the war, a courageous man unjustly dismissed and unfairly dealt with by Sir John French in his memoirs.

17. [John Garnier]: Mr. Machen is an extreme Ritualist, and it is stated that he is about to join the Church of Rome. The Cath-

olic Herald, Sept. 1915. *National Protestant Federation*, Sept., 1915, p. 158.
   18. Commander of the Canaanite army of King Jabin of Hazor who oppressed the Hebrews.
   19. I.e., Roman emperor who lived from approximately CE 272–337 and who reigned from 306 until his death.
   20. [John Garnier]: It will be noted that in other visions the appearance of angels only do not produce the overwhelming physical effect as in the two cases mentioned above.
   21. I.e., Anglo-Irish Protestant clergyman Michael Hobart Seymour (1800–1874).
   22. [John Garnier]: *Evenings with the Romanists*, p. 239. [JG].
   23. The Battle of Augustovo occurred in early October, 1914; German losses were estimated at about 60,000.

Chapter Eight

   1. Neither early appearance has been located. They are described in R. Thurston Hopkins's *War and the Weird* (London: Simpkin, Marshall, Hamilton, Kent, 1916), which reprints without attribution the majority of Reverend Leathem's text.
   2. A. Donald MacLeod. "The Dominie: Herbert S. Mekeel, His Clergy Conscripts, and Their Impact on the Presbyterian Church in Canada, 1935–1979." A Paper Presented to the Canadian Society of Presbyterian History, 29 September 2007. http://adonaldmacleod.com/papers/the-dominie-herbert-s-mekeel-his-clergy-conscripts-and-their-impact-on-the-presbyterian-church-in-canada-1935-1979/. Accessed 2 October 2014.
   3. The other titles are *The House with the Two Gardens, and Other Parables and Addresses for Children* (London: H. R. Allen, 1913) and *Life of St. Francis of Assisi* (London: James Clarke, 1926). He is not to be confused with the William Harvey Leathem who authored such works as *John Wesley, 1703–1791: A Study in Sainthood and Genius* (London: Church Book Room Press, 1947).
   4. From *Come Ye Disconsolate*, a Presbyterian hymn, words by Thomas Moore and Thomas Hastings.
   5. Luke 19: 42.

Chapter Nine

   1. C. Conway Plumbe. "A Canadian to His Parents." *Poems from Punch 1909–1920*, ed. Walter Brooks Drayton Henderson (London: Macmillan, 1922). 205–206.
   2. C. Conway Plumbe. "My American Cousins." *Voices of Silence: The Alternative Book of First World War Poetry*, ed. Vivien Noakes (Stroud, Gloucestershire: History Press, 2006). This verse speaks of "our English songs."
   3. "Review." *Nature*, 119 (Issue 3002, 1927), 714–715.
   4. C. Conway Plumbe. *Factory Well-Being* (London: Seven Oaks, 1949).
   5. C. Conway Plumbe. *Factory Health Safety and Welfare Encyclopaedia* (London: National Trade Press, 1953).
   6. C. Conway Plumbe. *Release from Time* (London: Hodder, 1950).

Chapter Ten

   1. "University Intelligence." *The Times* (London, England): 28 February 1890. 8. The Times Digital Archive, Web. 12 October 2014.
   2. Elliott O'Donnell. *Animal Ghosts, or Animal Hauntings and the Hereafter* (London: William Rider, 1913).
   3. Arthur Edward Waite. *Raymond Lully: Illuminated Doctor, Alchemist and Christian Mystic* (London: William Rider, 1922).
   4. H. Stanley Redgrove. *Joseph Glanville and Psychical Research in the Seventeenth Century* (London: William Rider, 1921) and *Alchemy: Ancient and Modern* (London: William Rider, 1922).
   5. Hereward Carrington. *Death: Its Causes and Phenomena, with Special Reference to Immortality* (London: William Rider, 1911) and *The Problems of Psychical Research: Experiments and Theories in the Realm of the Supernormal* (London: William Rider, 1914).
   6. John Cowper Powys. *Odes and Other Poems* (London: William Rider, 1896); *Poems* (William Rider, 1899); *Visions and Revisions: A Book of Literary Devotions* (London: William Rider, 1915).
   7. Theodore Powys. *The Soliloquy of a Hermit* (London: William Rider, 1916).
   8. "Obituary." *The Times* (London, England): 31 December 1946. 4. The Times Digital Archive, Web. 12 October 2014.
   9. W. H. Salter. "An Inquiry Concerning the Angels at Mons." *Journal of the Society for Psychical Research*. December 1915.
   10. The cost of *The Angel Warriors at Mons* was one penny.

11. I.e., French Marshal Joseph Jacques Césaire Joffre (1852–1931), who was instrumental in defeating the Germans at the First Battle of the Marne in 1914.

12. I.e., Anglo-Irish Field Marshal John Denton Pinkstone French, First Earl of Ypres (1852–1925), who served as Commander in Chief of the B. E. F. for the first two years of the war.

13. I.e., British politician, historian, reviewer, and poet Thomas Babington Macaulay, First Baron Macaulay (1800–1859).

14. Macaulay's poem celebrating a legendary Roman victory over the Latin League, in which the Tarquins attempted to take the Roman throne. Castor and Pollux fought for the Romans.

15. 2 Kings 6: 16. The servant is told, "Fear not, for they that be with us are more than they that be with them."

16. I.e., leader of the Maccabean revolt against the Seleucid Empire in 167–160 BCE.

17. I.e., Antiochus IV Epiphanes, Greek king of the Seleucid Empire and opponent of Judas Maccabeus until his death in 164 BCE.

18. [Ralph Shirley]: II Maccabeus, xi, 8, 9, 10.

19. [Ralph Shirley]: Reprinted in the September number.

20. I.e., English Theosophist Mabel Collins (1851–1927). *The Crucible* (London: Theosophical Publishing Society, 1915).

21. Collins, *The Crucible*.

22. I.e., Alexander Alfred Boddy (1854–1930), Anglican vicar and one of the co-founders of British Pentecostalism.

23. [Ralph Shirley]: From an address at an open-air meeting reported in the *Sunderland Echo* of August 16.

24. I.e., Alice May Callow, secretary of the Higher Thought Centre from 1900. She might have been born c. 1858 and was apparently still living in 1944 per Dr. Emmet Fox, "A History of New Thought" *The New Thought Bulletin* (January 1944).

25. The New Thought / Higher Thought movement was a spiritual movement originating in the United States, with many of its tenets derived from Christian Science.

26. I.e., Russian General Michael Dimitrievitch Skobeloff (1843?–1882).

27. I.e., Irish politician George-Nugent Grenville, Second Baron Nugent of Carlanstown (1788–1850).

28. Shirley misquotes slightly. "The world abounds with histories of praeternatural appearances the most utterly incredible, supported by testimony the most undeniable." Lord Nugent. *Some Memorials of John Hampden, His Party, and His Times*. Vol. 2 (London: John Murray, 1832). 302–303.

29. Again, Shirley misquotes slightly. "Yet is this story attested upon the oath of three officers, men of honour and discretion, and of 'three other gentlemen of credit,' selected by the King as commissioners to report upon these prodigies, and to tranquillize and disabuse the alarms of a country town...." Lord Nugent. *Some Memorials of John Hampden*. Vol. 2. 303.

30. Shirley incorrectly transcribes the sixth word of the title: *shewing* rather than *showing*.

31. I.e., English cavalier, politician, soldier, and poet Sir Edmund Verney (1596–1642).

32. *A Great Wonder in Heaven Shewing the Late Apparitions and Prodigious Noyses of War and Battels Seen on Edge-Hill neere Keinton in Northampton-shire: Certified Under the Hands of William Wood Esquire and Justice for the Peace in the Said Countie, Samuel Marshall, Preacher of Gods Word in Keinton and Other Persons of Qualitie* (London: Printed for Tho. Iackson, Ian. 23, 1642).

5–7. Shirley's transcription is essentially correct, though some spellings have been perhaps unintentionally modernized.

33. I.e., American historian John Lothrop Motley (1814–1877). *The Rise of the Dutch Republic* (New York: Harper, 1856).

34. I.e., Psalm 551. "Christian, seek not yet repose; / Hear thy guardian angel say: / Thou art in the midst of foes; / Watch and pray: / Principalities and powers, / Mustering their unseen array."

Chapter Eleven

1. *Essays on Theosophy* (London: Swann Sonnenschein, 1908); *The Suffrage Movement from Its Evolutionary Aspect* (London: Swann Sonnenschein, 1910); *The Latter Days* (H. R. Allenson, 1914); and *Concerning Airmen or the Superphysical Plane* (London: Theosophical Publishing House, 1916).

2. Barry Thompson. Personal correspondence. 7 May 2014.

3. "Theosophy." *Encyclopedia of Occultism & Parapsychology: A Compendium of Information on the Occult Sciences, Magic,*

Demonology, Superstitions, Spiritism, Mysticism, Metaphysics, Psychical Science, and Parapsychology, with Biographical and Bibliographical Notes and Comprehensive Indexes, ed. J. Gordon Melton. 4th ed. (Detroit: Gale, 1996). 1307.

4. "Theosophical Society." *Encyclopedia of Occultism & Parapsychology*. 1305.

5. [Isabelle E. Taylor]: Armageddon, otherwise Megiddo, lies in the plain of Esdraelon, a broad valley of Northern Palastine, constituting the Valley of Kishon and extending westwards from Mount Hermon to the slopes of the Carmel Range. See Chambers' *Encyclopaedia*, etc.

6. [Isabelle E. Taylor]: See *Hosea* iii. I, and *Isa*, xxviii. I to 7.

7. [Isabelle E. Taylor]: The condition Biblically described as " void."

8. [Isabelle E. Taylor]: Be not deceived; God is not mocked: for whatsoever a man soweth that shall he also reap. St. Paul to Gal. vi. 7.

9. [Isabelle E. Taylor]: What is true of the sinner is also true of the Saint.—Author.

10. Ms. Taylor's text has connecthim, an obvious error.

11. [Isabelle E. Taylor]: See *The Latter Days*, by I. E. Taylor.

12. [Isabelle E. Taylor]: See *Essays on Theosophy*, by I. E. Taylor.

13. [Isabelle E. Taylor]: "Think not that I am come to destroy the law or the prophets: I am not come to destroy but to fulfil." *St. Matt.* v. 17.

14 [Isabelle E. Taylor]: "Till heaven and earth pass, one jot or one tittle shall in no wise pass from the law till all be fulfilled." *St. Matt.* v. 18.

15. [Isabelle E. Taylor]: "Ye worship ye know not what; we know what we worship: for salvation is of the Jews." *St. John* iv. 22.

16. [Isabelle E. Taylor]: "The Lord shall save the tents of Judah first." *Zech.* xii. 7.

17. [Isabelle E. Taylor]: The wrath of God signifies the obscuration of Spiritual "light" or understanding form man while he is evolving on the material line.

18. Ms. Taylor's text has inherittance, an obvious error.

19. Ms. Taylor's text has a colon (:) rather than the quotation marks ("), an obvious error.

20. Ms. Taylor's text has qeestions, an obvious error.

21. I.e., William A. Redding. *Our Near Future: A Message to All the Governments and People of Earth*. Peekskill-on-Hudson, NY: Loomis, 1896.

22. [Isabelle E. Taylor]: *St. Matt.* xxiv. 21.

23. Matthew: 24:6.

24. [Isabelle E. Taylor]: *Dan.* xi. 13.

25. [Isabelle E. Taylor]: Wait ye upon me, saith the Lord, until the day that I rise up to the prey; for my determination is to gather the nations, that I may assemble the kingdoms, to pour upon them mine indignation. *Zept.* iii. 8.

26. [Isabelle E. Taylor]: *Dan.* xi. 34.

27. [Isabelle E. Taylor]: "The Priests shall have no part nor inheritance with Israel." *Deut.* xviii. I.

28. [Isabelle E. Taylor]: "And at that time shall Michael stand up, the great prince which standeth for thy people; and there shall be a time of trouble such as never was since there was a nation even to that same time." *Dan.* xi. I.

29. [Isabelle E. Taylor]: "So shall it be at the end of the world: the angels shall come forth, and sever the wicked from among the just." *St. Matt.* xxiii. 49.

30. [Isabelle E. Taylor]: "For my people is foolish, they have not known me; they are wise to do evil but to do good they have no knowledge." *Jer.* Iv. 22. "I am with thee, saith the Lord, to save thee: though I make a full end of all nations whither I have scattered thee, yet will I not make a full end of thee but I will correct thee in measure, and will not leave thee altogether unpunished." *Jer.* xxx. II.

31. [Isabelle E. Taylor]: *St. Paul to Rom.* ix 6. See *The Latter Days*, I.E. Taylor.

32. [Isabelle E. Taylor]: *St. Matt.* xxiv.

33. Ms. Taylor's text has eutered, an obvious error.

34. [Isabelle E. Taylor]: Behold I have created the smith that bloweth the coals in the fire, and that bringeth forth an instrument for his work; and I have created the waster to destroy." *Isa.* liv. 16.

35. [Isabelle E. Taylor]: *Dan.* x. 21.

36. [Isabelle E. Taylor]: *Dan.* xii. 1.

37. [Isabelle E. Taylor]: Czar, more properly Tsar. The title of the Russian princes was "kiiaz" (prince) or "veliki kniaz" (great prince). *Chambers' Encyclopedia*.

38. [Isabelle E. Taylor]: "I will gather the remnant of my flock out of all countries whither I have driven them and I will bring them again to their fold." *Jer.* xxiii. 3.

39. [Isabelle E. Taylor]: "Who is this that cometh from Edom with dyed garments?"

40. "An old kabbalistic motto holds that *Demon est Deus inversus,* 'The devil is God upside down,' or 'The devil is God's complement.'" John Algeo. "The Dark Side of Light." *Quest* 93.2 (March–April 2005): 65–69. https://www.theosophical.org/publications/1375. Accessed 25 October 2014.
41. [Isabelle E. Taylor]: *Exe.* xxxi. 6. "Thou shalt not abhor an Edomite; for he is thy brother." *Dieut.* xxiii. 7.
42. [Isabelle E. Taylor]: See *The Latter Days.*

Chapter Twelve

1. Ronald Selby Wright. "Charles Laing Warr." *Dictionary of National Biography.* http://www.oxforddnb.com/view/article/36750. Accessed 14 October 2014.
2. Ibid.
3. Ibid.
4. "Court Circular." *Times* [London England] 19 June 1969. 10. The Times Digital Archive. Web. 14 October 2014.
5. Charles Laing Warr. *Echoes of Flanders* (London: Simpkin, Marshall, Hamilton, Kent, 1916).
6. I.e., "There are more things in heaven and earth, Horatio, / Than are dreamt of in your philosophy." Shakespeare. *Hamlet* (Act 1, Scene 5, lines 167–168).
7. I.e., James Boswell. *The Life of Johnson: Including a Tour of the Hebrides,* ed. John W. Croker (London: John Murray, 1876). 596. "Miss Seward (with an incredulous smile). 'What, Sir! about a ghost!'" Johnson (with solemn vehemence). "Yes, Madam; this is a question which, after five thousand years, is yet undecided; a question, whether in theology or philosophy, one of the most important that can come before human understanding."

8. A 1912 quick march by J. Ord Hume, "We All Go the Same Way Home" was given lyrics by C. W. Murphy and Peter Dalton.

Chapter Thirteen

1. Scholar and journalist Arthur Oswald Barron (1868–1939) had a daily column for *The Evening News* which he signed "The Londoner."
2. The Clameur de Haro of Sark. Literally, "Haro! Haro! To my aid, my Prince, I am being wronged." The Clameur de Haro is one of the governing laws of the channel Isle of Sark, holding that in any dispute, a person feeling his rights are being violated can obtain immediate cessation of actions until a court adjudicates them. Where Machen learned of the Clameur de Haro is not known, but it is worth mentioning that the Clameur de Haro is apparently accorded an entry in the 1911 *Encyclopaedia Britannica.*
3. I.e., English poet and novelist Margaret Louisa Woods (1856–1945).
4. Collected in *The Return and Other Poems* (London: John Lane, the Bodley Head; New York: John Lane, 1921). 43–48.
5. A somewhat different story concludes Ms. Woods's preface to *The Return and Other Poems.* "The poem on the first battle of Ypres, was not in any way suggested by the Angel of Mons fable, but by a private letter. / The writer, a young man of high character and intelligence, was acting as interpreter at the time of the battle. He questioned a considerable number of prisoners as to the cause of the apparently inexplicable withdrawal of the Germans on three occasions. The reply was always the same, 'We dared not advance when we saw your immense reserves.' / We had, in fact, no reserves." Woods, *The Return,* vii.

Bibliography

Adam and Charles Black (Firm). *Black's Shilling Guide to Scotland*. London: Adam and Charles Black, 1906.
Algeo, John. "The Dark Side of Light." *Quest* 93.2 (March–April 2005):65–69. https://www.theosophical.org/publications/1375. Accessed 25 October 2014.
"The Angels of Mons" (1915). IMDB. http://www.imdb.com. Accessed 22 October 2014.
"Arthur Machen." *Chicago Daily Tribune*. 16 December 1947. 27.
"Arthur Machen, Novelist, Dies: Author of the Story That Led to 'Angel of Mons' Legend—Won Fame in His Fifties." *The New York Times*. 16 December 1947. 34.
Baldock, Sydney C. "Angels of Mons *(Rêve Mystique)*." London: Gould & Bottler, 1915.
Beckson, Karl. *The Oscar Wilde Encyclopedia*. New York: AMS Press, 1998.
Begbie, Harold. *The Bed-Book of Happiness: Being a Colligation or Assemblage of Cheerful Writings Brought Together from Many Quarters into This One Compass for the Diversion, Distraction and Delight of Those Who Lie Abed—A Friend to the Invalid, a Companion to the Sleepless, an Excuse to the Tired*. London: Hodder and Stoughton, 1914.
_____. "Fall In!" *The Daily Chronicle*. 31 August 1915. http://www.europeana1914-1918.eu/. Accessed 25 October 2014.
_____. *On the Side of the Angels: The Story of the Angels at Mons. An Answer to the Bowmen*. Second edition. London: Hodder & Stoughton, 1915.
_____. *On the Side of the Angels: The Story of the Angels at Mons. An Answer to the Bowmen*. Third edition. London: Hodder & Stoughton, 1915.
_____. *On the Side of the Angels: The Story of the Angels at Mons. An Answer to the Bowmen*. Fourth edition. London: Hodder & Stoughton, 1915.
"Biography and Roots of Colonel John Garnier—Breeder of Governor' Sire Lion." http://the-mastiff-by-marcel-wynants.com/garnier.html. Accessed 2 October 2014.
Bleiler, E. F. "Arthur Machen." *Supernatural Fiction Writers: Fantasy and Horror*, ed. E. F. Bleiler. New York: Scribner's, 1985.
Boswell, James. *The Life of Johnson: Including a Tour of the Hebrides*, ed. John W. Croker. London: John Murray, 1876.
Bourne, J. M. "Charteris, John." *Dictionary of National Biography*. Oxford University Press, 2004. Online ed, October 2008. Accessed 20 June 2014.
"The British Israelites." www.badarchaeology.com. Accessed 2 October 2014.
British Museum. *A Guide to the Antiquities of the Stone Age in the Department of British and Mediaeval Antiquities*. London: Printed by Order of the Trustees, 1902.
Brown, W. Sorley. *The Life and Genius of T. W. H. Crosland*. London: Cecil Palmer, 1928.
_____. "The Life and Genius of T. W. H. Crosland." *The Flying Horse* 1.1 New Series. 1927.
Campbell, Phyllis. *Back of the Front*, with an introduction by W. L. Courtney. London: G. Newnes, 1915.
Carrington, Hereward. *Death: Its Causes and Phenomena, with Special Reference to Immortality*. London: William Rider, 1911.

Bibliography 219

_____. "The Phantom Armies Seen in France." *The Best Psychic Stories*, ed. Joseph Lewis French. New York: Boni and Liveright, 1920.
_____. *The Problems of Psychical Research: Experiments and Theories in the Realm of the Supernormal*. London: William Rider, 1914.
_____. *Psychical Phenomena and the War*. New York: Dodd, Mead, 1918.
Casanova, Jacques. *The Memoirs of Jacques Casanova Written by Himself*, now for the first time translated into English [by Arthur Machen]. London: Privately Printed, 1894.
Charteris, John. *At G. H. Q.* London: Cassell, 1931.
Chesterton, G. K. *The Crimes of England*. London: Cecil Palmer & Hayward, 1915.
Churchwoman, A. [i.e., Mary Coultman Horne.] *The Chariots of God*, illustrated by Alfred Pearse. London: Arthur H. Stockwell, 1916?
Clarke, David. *The Angel of Mons; Phantom Soldiers and Ghostly Guardians*. London: John Wiley, 2004.
Clarke, I. F. *Voices Prophesying War: Future Wars, 1763–3749*. Oxford: Oxford University Press, 1992.
Collins, Mabel. *The Crucible*. London: Theosophical Publishing Society, 1915.
Conan Doyle, Arthur. *The British Campaign in France and Flanders, 1914*. London: Hodder and Stoughton, 1916.
_____. *The History of Spiritualism*. Vol. II. New York: Arno Press, 1975.
"Court Circular." *The Times*. 19 June 1969. 10.
Crisp, Frederick A., ed. *Visitation of England and Wales*. Vol. 12. Privately Printed, 1904.
Crook, Tim. "Vocalizing the Angels of Mons: Audio Dramas as Propaganda in the Great War of 1914 to 1918." *Societies* 4 (2014): 180–221. Accessed 1 September 2014.
Crosland, T. W. H. *Find the Angels: The Showmen: A Legend of the War*. London: T. Werner Laurie, 1915.
_____. *The First Stone: On Reading the Unpublished Portions of 'De Profundis.'* London: The Author, 1912.
"Crosland, Thomas William Hodgson." *Wikipedia*. http://en.wikipedia.org. Accessed 24 June 2014.
Danielson, Henry. *Arthur Machen: A Bibliography*. London: Henry Danielson, 1923.
Dickens, Charles. *The Posthumous Papers of the Pickwick Club*. [i.e., *The Pickwick Papers*.] London: Chapman and Hall, 1837. Published monthly, April 1836–November 1837.
"Dispute Over a Sea Trip." *The Standard*. 19 June 1912. 5. http://newspaperarchive.com/uk/middlesex/london/london-standard/1912/06-19/page-5. Accessed 22 September 2014.
Dodd, Alfred. *The Ballad of the Iron Cross*. London: Erskine Macdonald, 1918.
Douglas, Lord Alfred. *The Autobiography of Lord Alfred Douglas*. London: Martin Secker, 1929.
_____, [and T. W. H. Crosland]. *Oscar Wilde and Myself*. London: J. Long, 1914.
Edmonds, Brigadier-General Sir James E. *A Short History of World War I*. Oxford: Oxford University Press, 1951.
Ellis, Phillip. "Spectral Soldiers: Possible Literary Antecedents for 'The Bowmen.'" *Studies in Weird Fiction* (Winter 1999) No. 24: 5–8.
Fitzroy, Sir Almeric. *Memoirs*. Vol. II. New York: George H. Doran, 1925.
Fox, Emmet. "A History of New Thought." *The New Thought Bulletin*. January 1944.
French, John. *1914*. Boston and New York: Houghton Mifflin, 1919.
Garnier, A. E. *The Chronicles of the Garniers of Hampshire During Four Centuries (1530–1900)*. Norwich and London: Jarrold and Sons, the Empire Press, 1900.
_____. *The Great Pyramid: Its Builder and Its Prophecy. With a Review of the Corresponding Prophecies of Scripture Relating to Coming Events and the Approaching End of the Age*. London: Robert Banks, 1905.
_____. *Israel in Britain: A Brief Statement of the Evidences in Proof of the Israelite Origin of the British Race*. London: Robert Banks, 1890.
_____. *The Visions of Mons and Ypres: Their Meaning and Purpose*. By the author of "The Great Pyramid," etc. London: Robert Banks, 1915.
"Gas Bombs Used by English and French." *The Fatherland*. 2 June 1915. 11.
Goldstone, Adrian, and Wesley D. Sweetser. *A Bibliography of Arthur Machen*. Austin: University of Texas Press, 1965.

Bibliography

The Gundagai Times and Tumut, Adelong and Murrumbidgee District Advisor. http://trove.nla.gov.au/ndp/del/title/487. Accessed 22 September 2014.
Holland, Merlin. "Biography and the Art of Lying." The Cambridge Companion to Oscar Wilde, ed. Peter Raby. Cambridge, UK: Cambridge University Press, 1997.
Hopkins, R. Thurston. War and the Weird. London: Simpkin, Marshall, Hamilton, Kent, 1916.
Horne, Mary Coultman. An Improved Medicated Pillow, Cushion or the Like. http://www.directorypatent.com/GB/190802310-a.html.
_____. Improvements in or Relating to Bath Chairs & Hammocks. http://www.directorypatent.com/GB/190317148-a.html.
_____. Improvements Relating to Stands for Hammocks. http://www.directorypatent.com/GB/190517244-a.html.
_____. An Invention for Conveying Invalids and Others by Rail or Road in a Recumbent Position. http://www.directorypatent.com/GB/190413506-a.html.
_____. Oreiller Hygenique. http://www.directorypatent.com/FR/386674-a.html.
Indian Cemeteries. "Howard Douglas Campbell. Monument of Howard Douglas Campbell at All Souls Church, Cawnpore." http://www.indian-cemeteries.org/viewimage.asp?ID=130. Accessed 22 September 2014.
Joshi, S. T. "Arthur Machen." Supernatural Literature of the World; An Encyclopedia, ed. S. T. Joshi and Stefan Dziemianowicz. Westport, CT: Greenwood, 2005.
_____. Lovecraft's Library: A Catalogue. Revised and enlarged. New York: Hippocampus Press, 2002.
_____. Unutterable Horror: A History of Supernatural Fiction. Hornsea, England: PS Publications, 2012.
_____. The Weird Tale. Austin: University of Texas Press, 1990.
King, Edward. Cassell's Complete Pocket-Guide to Europe. Revised and Enlarged. London: Cassell, 1897.
Kipling, Rudyard. "The Drums of the Fore and Aft." Wee Willie Winkie and Other Child Stories. India: A. H. Wheeler, 1888.
_____. "The Lost Legion." The Strand, May 1892. 476–483.
Leathem, W. H. The Comrade in White, introduction by Hugh Black. New York: Fleming H. Revell, 1916.
_____. The House with the Two Gardens, and Other Parables and Addresses for Children London: H. R. Allen, 1913.
_____. John Wesley, 1703–1791: A Study in Sainthood and Genius. London: Church Book Room Press, 1947.
_____. Life of St. Francis of Assisi. London: James Clarke, 1926.
Lewis, C. S. The Collected Letters of C. S. Lewis. Volume I: Family Letters 1905–1931, ed. by Walter Hooper. New York: Harper San Francisco, 2004.
_____. The Collected Letters of C. S. Lewis. Volume II: Books, Broadcasts, and the War, 1931–1949, ed. by Walter Hooper. New York: Harper San Francisco, 2004.
Lovecraft, H. P. The Annotated Supernatural Horror in Literature, ed. by S. T. Joshi. New York: Hippocampus Press, 2000.
_____. Supernatural Horror in Literature, ed. by E. F. Bleiler. New York: Dover Publications, 1973. 88.
MacLeod, A. Donald. "The Dominie: Herbert S. Mekeel, His Clergy Conscripts, and Their Impact on the Presbyterian Church in Canada, 1935–1979." A Paper Presented to the Canadian Society of Presbyterian History, 29 September 2007. http://adonaldmacleod.com/papers/the-dominie-herbert-s-mekeel-his-clergy-conscripts-and-their-impact-on-the-presbyterian-church-in-canada-1935i1979/. Accessed 2 October 2014.
Machen, Arthur. "The Angels of Mons: Absolutely My Last Word on the Subject." The [London] Evening News (7 April 1916) 2.
_____. The Angels of Mons: The Bowmen and Other Legends of the War. New York: Putnam's, 1915.
_____. "The Bowmen: The Angels of Mons." The [London] Evening News (29 September 1914) 3.
_____. The Bowmen and Other Legends of the War. London: Simpkin, Marshall, Hamilton, Kent, 1915.

Bibliography

_____. *A Chapter from the Book Called the Ingenious Gentleman Don Quijote de la Mancha, Which by Some Mischance Has Not Till Now Been Printed*. London: George Redway, 1887.

_____. *The Chronicle of Clemendy; or, The History of the IX. Joyous Journeys. In Which Are Contained the Amorous Inventions and Facetious Tales of Master Gervase Perrot, Gent., Now for the First Time Done into English by Arthur Machen*. London: Privately Printed for the Society of Pantagruelists, 1888.

_____. *Eleusinia. By a Former Member of H.C.S.* Hereford: Joseph Jones, 1881.

_____. *A Few Letters from Arthur Machen. Letters to Munson Havens*, with an introduction by Roger Dobson. Wirral, Cheshire: Aylesford Press, 1993.

_____. *The Great God Pan and the Inmost Light*. London: John Lane, 1894.

_____. *The Hill of Dreams*. London: Grant Richards, 1907.

_____. *The House of Souls*. London: Grant Richards, 1906.

_____. "The Mons Angels: The Growth of a Miracle Fiction." *The Daily Mail*. 28 July 1915. http://www.warrelics.eu/forum/ww1-allies-great-britain-france-usa-etc-1914-1918/angels-mons-372136-3/. Accessed 22 October 2014.

_____. ["Notes"]. *Arthur Machen: A Bibliography*, by Henry Danielson. London: Henry Danielson, 1923.

_____. "The Return of the Angels: This Time They Are at Ypres." *The* [London] *Evening News* (3 July 1916) 2.

_____. *Selected Letters: The Private Writings of the Master of the Macabre*, ed. by Roger Dobson, Godfrey Brangham, and R. A. Gilbert. Northamptonshire, England: Aquarian Press, 1988.

_____. *The Three Imposters*. London: John Lane, 1895.

Maitland Weekly Mercury. trove.nla.gov.au/ndp/del/title/492. Accessed 4 September 2014.

Marguerite, Queen of Navarre. *The Heptameron or Tales and Novels of Marguerite, Queen of Navarre, Now First Completely Done into English Prose and Verse from the Original French by Arthur Machen*. London: Privately Printed [i.e., London: Dryden Press], 1886.

Mildmay, Mrs. St. John. "Phantom Armies Seen in France." *The North American Review*. August 1915. 207–212.

"Mr. Arthur Machen: Literature of Awe." *The Times*. 16 December 1947. 6.

"Mr. T. W. H. Crosland." *The Times*. 24 December 1924. 12.

Mosier, John. *The Myth of the Great War: A New Military History of World War I*. New York: HarperCollins, 2001.

Motley, John Lothrop Motley. *The Rise of the Dutch Republic*. New York: Harper, 1856.

Murphy, Michael, ed. *Starrett vs. Machen: A Record of Discovery and Correspondence*. St. Louis, MO: Autolycus Press, 1977.

Myrtleford Mail and Whorouly Witness. http://trove.nla.gov.au/ndp/del/title/584. Accessed 18 September 2014.

Newnham-Davis, Nathaniel. *The Gourmet's Guide to Europe*. Second edition. New York: Brentano's, 1908.

Nugent, Lord. *Some Memorials of John Hampden, His Party, and His Times*. Vol. 2. London: John Murray, 1832.

"Obituary." *The Times*. 31 December 1946. 4.

O'Donnell, Elliott. *Animal Ghosts, or Animal Hauntings and the Hereafter*. London: William Rider, 1913.

Paree, Paul. "Angel of Mons Waltz." London: Lawrence Wright Music, 1916.

The Parliamentary Debates (Official Report). Fifth Series—Volume LXXV. Fifth Session of the Thirtieth Parliament of the United Kingdom of Great Britain & Ireland 6 George V. House of Commons. Eighth Volume of Session 1914–1915. London: HMSO, 1915.

Plumbe, C. Conway. "The Angels of Mons." *Punch, or the London Charivari*. 6 October 1915. 293.

_____. "A Canadian to His Parents." *Poems from Punch 1909–1920*, ed. Walter Brooks Drayton Henderson. London: Macmillan, 1922.

_____. *Factory Health Safety and Welfare Encyclopaedia*. London: National Trade Press, 1953.

_____. *Factory Well-Being*. London: Seven Oaks, 1949.

———. "My American Cousins." *Voices of Silence: The Alternative Book of First World War Poetry*, ed. Vivien Noakes. Stroud, Gloucestershire: History Press, 2006.
———. *Release from Time*. London: Hodder, 1950.
Powys, John Cowper. *Odes and Other Poems*. London: William Rider, 1896.
———. *Poems*. William Rider, 1899;
———. *Visions and Revisions: A Book of Literary Devotions*. London: William Rider, 1915.
Powys, Theodore Powys. *The Soliloquy of a Hermit*. London: William Rider, 1916.
Redding, William A. *Our Near Future: A Message to All the Governments and People of Earth*. Peekskill-on-Hudson, NY: Loomis, 1896.
Redgrove, H. Stanley. *Alchemy: Ancient and Modern*. London: William Rider, 1922.
———. *Joseph Glanville and Psychical Research in the Seventeenth Century*. London: William Rider, 1921.
"Review." *Nature*, 119 (Issue 3002, 1927), 714–715.
Salter, W. H. "An Inquiry Concerning the Angels at Mons." *Journal of the Society for Psychical Research*. December 1915.
Sharp, William, ed. *Sainte-Beuve: On Men and Women*. London: Gibbings; Philadelphia: J. B. Lippincott, 1901.
Shirley, Ralph. *The Angel Warriors at Mons Including Numerous Confirmatory Testimonies, Evidence of the Wounded, and Certain Curious Historical Parallels. An Authentic Record*. London: Newspaper Publicity, 1915.
Simms, Richard. "The Evening News Short Story Index." http://eveningnews.atwebpages.com/index.htm. Accessed 18 June 2014.
Sladen, Douglas. *Twenty Years of My Life*. New York: E. P. Dutton, 1913.
Starrett, Vincent. *Arthur Machen: A Novelist of Ecstasy and Sin*. Chicago: Walter M. Hill, 1918.
———. "Arthur Machen: A Novelist of Ecstasy and Sin." *Reedy's Mirror*. 5 October 1917.
———. "Books Alive." *Chicago Daily Tribune*. 28 March 1943. E15.
———. "Books Alive." *Chicago Daily Tribune*. 28 December 1947. G2.
———. *Buried Caesars: Essays in Literary Appreciation*. [Chicago]: [Covici-McGee], 1923.
Taylor, Isabelle E. *Angels, Saints & Bowmen of Mons: An Answer to Mr. Arthur Machen and Mr. Harold Begbie*. London: Theosophical Publishing Society, 1916.
———. *Concerning Airmen or the Superphysical Plane*. London: Theosophical Publishing House, 1916.
———. *Essays on Theosophy*. London: Swann Sonnenschein, 1908.
———. *The Latter Days*. London: H. R. Allenson, 1914.
———. *The Suffrage Movement from Its Evolutionary Aspect*. London: Swann Sonnenschein, 1910.
"Theosophy." *Encyclopedia of Occultism & Parapsychology: A Compendium of Information on the Occult Sciences, Magic, Demonology, Superstitions, Spiritism, Mysticism, Metaphysics, Psychical Science, and Parapsychology, with Biographical and Bibliographical Notes and Comprehensive Indexes*, ed. J. Gordon Melton. Fourth edition. Detroit: Gale, 1996. 1307.
Thompson, Barry. [Personal correspondence.] 7 May 2014.
"The Times and the First World War." http://spartacus-educational.com/FWWtimes.htm. Accessed 24 June 2014.
The Times Digital Archive, 1785–2006. Gale Digital Collections.
"Turpenite." *The New York Times*. 1 October 1914. 10.
["Turpenite."] *Popular Electricity and Modern Mechanics*. November 1914. 558.
"University Intelligence." *The Times*. 28 February 1890. 8.
Valentine, Mark. *Arthur Machen*. Mid Glamorgan, Wales: Seren, 1995.
Waite, Arthur Edward. *Raymond Lully: Illuminated Doctor, Alchemist and Christian Mystic*. London: William Rider, 1922.
Wallace, Alfred Russel. *On Miracles and Modern Spiritualism: Three Essays*. London: James Burns, 1875.
Walters, E. W. *Heroines of the World-War*. London: Charles H. Kelly, 1916.
Warr, Charles Laing. *Echoes of Flanders*. London: Simpkin, Marshall, Hamilton, Kent, 1916.

———. *The Unseen Host: Stories of the Great War*. Paisley: Alexander Gardner, 1916.
Wells, H. G. *Mr. Britling Sees It Through*. London: Cassell, 1916.
Woods, Margaret L. *The Return and Other Poems*. London: John Lane, 1921.
Wright, Ronald Selby. "Warr, Charles Laing." *Dictionary of National Biography*. http://www.oxforddnb.com/view/article/36750. Accessed 14 October 2014.

Index

Aberdeen (Scotland) 16
Academy (periodical) 9, 103
Adam 185
Adam and Charles Black (publisher) 204*n*
Adelong (Australia) 210*n*
Adsit Anglis Sanctus Georgius 12, 27, 95
Agincourt (France) 11, 13, 22, 28
"Agitation in Belgium" 204*n*
Aisne (France) 139, 140
Albert, 4th Earl Grey 31
Alchemy: Ancient and Modern (Redgrove) 214*n*
Alexander Gardner (publisher) 190
Algeo, John 217*n*
All Souls Church (Cawnpore) 210*n*
Alzonne (France) 189
Amiens Dispatch (Moore) 5, 6, 12, 13, 20
AMS Press (publisher) 211*n*
Anatomy of Melancholy (Burton) 8
Anatomy of Tobacco (Machen) 8
Anderson, Paul 71
Angel of Islington 115
"Angel of Mons" (*Rêve Mystique*) (Baldock) 3, 203*n*
Angel of Mons: Phantom Soldiers and Ghostly Guardians (Clarke) 206*n*, 210*n*
"Angel of Mons Waltz" (Paree) 3, 203*n*
"Angel of the Covenant" 60
Angel Warriors at Mons (Shirley) 153–164, 209*n*, 211*n*, 213*n*
"Angelic Leaders" (Campbell) 28
"Angels of Mons" (film) 3
"Angels of Mons" (Plumbe) 151–152
"Angels of Mons: Absolutely My Last Word on the Subject" (Machen) 197–199
Angels, Saints & Bowmen of Mons: An Answer to Mr. Arthur Machen & Mr. Harold Begbie (Taylor) 165–189, 197
Angustovo *see* Augustovo
Animal Ghosts, or Animal Hauntings and the Hereafter (O'Donnell) 214*n*

Antioch and Antiochus 28, 157, 209*n*, 215*n*
Aquarian Press (publisher) 204*n*
Arabian Nights 7
Archangel (Russia) 16
Argonne (France) 148
Argyll (Scotland) 210*n*
Armageddon (Middle East) 166, 121, 207*n*, 216*n*
Armageddon—and After (Courtney) 207*n*
Arno Press (publisher) 203*n*
Arnold, Matthew 53
Arthur H. Stockwell (publisher) 93
"Arthur Machen" (Bleiler) 203*n*, 205*n*, 206*n*
Arthur Machen (Valentine) 7, 8, 204*n*
Arthur Machen: A Bibliography (Danielson) 204*n*, 212*n*
Arthur Machen: A Novelist of Ecstasy and Sin (Starrett) 10, 205*n*
"Arthur Machen, Novelist, Dies" 206*n*
artists 151
Assyria 156, 184, 185
At G.H.Q. (Charteris) 15, 17, 206*n*
"Atalanta in Calydon" (Swinburne) 2
Augustovo (Poland) 146, 160, 161, 214*n*
Australia and Australians 77, 78, 136, 210*n*
Auteil (France) 104
Autobiography of Lord Alfred Douglas (Douglas) 10, 205*n*, 211*n*
Autolycus Press (publisher) 203*n*, 205*n*, 208*n*, 210*n*
Avory, Justice 79
Aylesford Press (publisher) 204*n*

B., A.M. 55, 137, 173
Babylon 144
Back of the Front (Campbell) 77–92, 208*n*, 209*n*, 210*n*
Bad Archaeology 129
Balaam and his ass 173, 174
Baldock, Sydney C. 3, 203*n*
Ballad of the Iron Cross (Dodd) 203*n*

225

Barclay, Mrs. Hubert *see* Daniel, Edith Noelle
Bardell v. Pickwick (Dickens) 208*n*
Barron, Arthur Oswald 22, 37, 207*n*, 208*n*, 217*n*
Basil, Father 74
Basque language 106
Bath (England) 16
Battle of Dorking (Chesney) 2, 18
"Battle of Lake Regillus" (Macaulay) 156
"Battle Weary Finns See Angels" 3
BBC *see* British Broadcasting Corporation
Beaconsfield (England) 46
Beale, Frances Helen (Mrs. Fitzgerald) 58, 209*n*
Becker, Karl 211*n*
Bed-Book of Happiness: Being a Collation or Assemblage of Cheerful Writings Brought Together from Many Quarters into This One Compass (etc.) (Begbie) 208*n*
Bedlam (London) 79
B.E.F. *see* British Expeditionary Force
Begbie, Harold 17, 18, 31-76, 79, 96, 121, 123, 124, 127, 129, 142, 147, 165, 166, 173, 174, 198, 201, 206*n*, 208*n*, 211*n*, 212*n*, 213*n*
Begbie, Mars Hamilton 31
Beijing (China) *see* Pekin (China)
Belfast (Ireland) 147
"Belgian Agitation and Franchise Reform" 204*n*
Belgians and Belgium 47, 85, 93, 104, 108, 200, 204*n*
Belloc, Hilaire Pierre René 121, 212*n*
Benson, Frank 9
Bergson, Henri 74, 209*n*
Berlin (Germany) 55, 120, 126
Best Psychic Stories (French) 207*n*
Bexhill (England) 104
Bibliography of Arthur Machen (Goldstone & Sweetser) 206*n*
Binche (Belgium) 4
"Biography and Roots of Colonel John Garnier—Breeder of Governor' Sire Lion" 213*n*
"Biography and the Art of Lying" (Holland) 211*n*
Birkenhead (England) 46
Bisley (England) 27, 95, 195, 211*n*
Bitterne (England) 41
Black, Hugh 147
Black propaganda 17
Blackpool (England) 109
Black's Shilling Guide to Scotland 4, 204*n*
Blackwood's Magazine 2
Blake, William 108, 211*n*
Blavatsky, Helena Petrovna 25, 165, 207*n*
Bleiler, E.F. 9, 203*n*, 205*n*, 206*n*
Blue Lagoon (Stacpoole) 211*n*

Boddy, Alexander Alfred 55, 135, 158, 159, 209*n*, 213*n*, 215*n*
Bomb Battery 4
Bonaparte, Napoleon 213*n*
Boni and Liveright (publisher) 207*n*
Book of Genesis 53
Book of Numbers 173
"Books Alive" (Starrett) 205*n*
Booth, William 31, 32
Borrow, George 7
Boswell, James 217*n*
Boulogne (France) 104
Bourne, J.M. 206*n*
"The Bowmen: The Angels of Mons" (Machen) 19-30
Boxer Rebellion and Boxers 135, 213*n*
Brangham, Godfrey 204*n*
Brentano's (publisher) 204*n*
"British Army's Stern Fight" 204*n*
British Broadcasting Corporation 210*n*
British Campaign in France and Flanders, 1914 (Doyle) 3, 203*n*
British Expeditionary Force (BEF) 5, 6, 20, 213*n*, 215*n*
British Israelites (Garnier) 213*n*
British Library 93, 165
British Museum 203*n*
British Race 129
"Broadcasting: Home Stations" (BBC) 210*n*
"Broken British Regiments Battling Against the Odds" 5
Brookfield, Charles (Hallam Elton) 112, 212*n*
Broome (England) 211*n*
Brown, W. Sorley 103, 211*n*
Browndown Range (England) 100
Brussels (Belgium) 4
Bucks (England) 58
Buffalo County (United States) 120
Bulgarian language 106
Buried Caesars (Starrett) 205*n*
Burleigh, Bertram 3
Burton, Robert 8
Butler, Joseph 113, 212*n*
Butler, Samuel 113, 212*n*

C, Doctor 70
cabbage 197
Cadwaladyr Vendigeid (Saint) 22, 207*n*
Caerleon-on-Usk (Wales) 7, 197
Caesar *see* Julius Caesar
Calais (France) 199
Callow, Miss Alice May 134, 159, 215*n*
Cambridge Companion to Oscar Wilde (Raby, ed.) 211*n*
Cambridge University Press (publisher) 211*n*
Campbell, Lady Archibald 46, 129

Campbell, Frances 210n
Campbell, Francis [sic] 46
Campbell, Howard Douglas 77, 78, 210n
Campbell, Phil 79
Campbell, Phyllis (composer) 210n
Campbell, Phyllis Frances 28, 29, 33, 46- 53, 77–92, 129–133, 137–139, 154, 157, 158, 163, 208n, 209n
Campbell, Phyllis Vivian 77, 78, 79
Campbell v. the Prince Line (Limited) 78, 210n
Canaanites 214n
Canada and Canadians 91, 135, 147, 151
"Canadian to His Parent" (Plumbe) 214n
Canal du Centre (Belgium) 5
Cape (no location) 128
Cape Breton (Canada) 71
Carib Prince (liner) 78
Carmel Range (Middle East) 216n
Carrington, Hereward 153, 207n, 214n
Casanova, Jacques 8, 205n
Cassell (publisher) 204n
Cassell's Complete Pocket-Guide to Europe (King) 204n
Castor 156, 215n
Catholic Herald (periodical) 214n
Catholics 130, 131, 143–146, 156, 213–214n
Cawnpore (India) 77, 210n
Cecil Palmer (publisher) 211n
Cecil Palmer & Hayward (publisher) 203n
Celts 7
Cerizy (France) 139, 140
Cervantes, Miguel de 7
Chambers' Encyclopaedia 216n
Chantilly (France) 91
Chapel Royal (England) 190
Chaplin, Charlie (Charles Spencer) 121, 212n
Charing Cross (England) 105
Chariots of God (Horne) 93–101
Charleroi (Belgium) 4
Charleroi Canal (Belgium) 5
Charles H. Kelly (publisher) 210n
Charteris, John 15–17, 201, 206n, 208n
Chatham (England) 128
Chaudfontein (Chaudfontaine) (Belgium) 104
Chelsea Barracks (England) 46
Cheshire (England) 46
Chesney, George Tomkyns 2
Chesterton, G.K. (Gilbert Keith) 2–3, 37, 203n
Chicago Daily Tribune (newspaper) 11, 204–206n
China and Chinese 135, 159
Chinese language 106
Chobham Heights (England) 123
Choctaw language 106

Christian Union (newspaper) 204n
Chronicle of Clemendy (Machen) 8, 11, 204n, 205n
Chronicles of the Garniers of Hampshire During Four Centuries (Garnier) 128, 213n
Church Book Room Press (publisher) 214n
Church Family Newspaper (newspaper) 59
"Church Porch" (Herbert) 125
Church Times (periodical) 23, 33, 55, 93, 96, 137, 173
churchwoman see Horne, Mary Coultman
Clameur de Haro of Sark 198, 217n
Clarke, David 16, 17, 206n, 210n
Clarke, I.F. 203n
Cleaver, Private 33, 46, 134, 209n, 213n
Closworth (England) 33
Cochran, Charles Blake 121, 212n
Collected Letters of C.S. Lewis vols. 1 & 2 (Lewis) 203n
Collins, Mabel 158, 215n
Come Ye Disconsolate (Moore/Hastings) 214n
Compton-Rickett, Joseph 24, 207n
"Comrade in White" 60
Comrade in White (Leathem) 60, 147–150
Conan Doyle, Arthur 2–3, 203n
Concerning Airmen or the Superphysical Plain (Taylor) 215n
Conde (Belgium) 5
"Conscription and Sleeping Out" 112
Constantine 144, 214n
Constantine the Great 144
Contemporary Review (periodical) 154
Cornhill (periodical) 154
Corpse Factory 17
"Court Circular" 217n
Courtney, William Leonard 25, 77, 80, 207n, 210n
Courtrai (Belgium) 200
Courville, Albert de 121, 212n
Covici McGee (publisher) 205n
Cox, Dr. 71
Crawford, Alexander 12, 206n
Crecy (France) 11
Crimes of England (Chesterton) 2, 203n
Crippen, Hawley Harvey 38, 208n
Crisp, Frederick A. 209n, 213n
Croker, John W. 217n
Crook, Tim 203n
Crooks, William 31
Crosland, T.W.H. (Thomas William Hodgson) 4, 102–127, 203n, 211n
Crosland, W.P. 211n
Crucible (Collins) 158, 215n

Daily Chronicle (newspaper) 24, 32, 206n, 208n, 212n
Daily Express (newspaper) 10

228   INDEX

Daily Mail (newspaper) 13, 33, 46, 97, 134, 206n, 207n, 210n
Daily News (newspaper) 3
Dalton, Peter 217n
Daniel 166, 186, 216n
Daniel, Edith Noelle 60, 209n
Danielson, Henry 204n, 212n
Danish language 106
Dardanelles (France) 59, 61, 136
"Dark Side of Light" (Algeo) 217n
Darwin, Charles 65, 209n
David 185
De Profundis (Wilde) 211n
"Dead Rissala" (Kipling) 207
Dean of Lincoln (England) 128
Dean of Winchester (England) 128
Death: Its Causes and Phenomena (Carrington) 214n
Demon est Deus Inversus 188, 217n
Desdemona (Shakespeare/Othello) 105
Deuteronomy 145, 216n, 217n
Devereux, Robert 153
Devon (England) 31
Devonshire Place (England) 46
Dewi (Saint) 22, 207n
Dickens, Charles 7, 25, 29, 207n, 208n
Dictionary of National Biography 15, 31, 190, 206n, 217n
"Dispute Over a Sea Trip" 210n
Dix (soldier) 51
Dobson, Roger 204n
Dodd, Alfred 3, 203n
Dodd Mead (publisher) 207n
Dogs of the British Islands ("Stonehenge") 128
Dominie: Herbert S. McKeel, His Clergy Conscripts, etc. (MacLeod) 214n
Domrémy (France) 81, 90, 132, 158
Don Quixote (Cervantes) 7, 8
Dorien see Dorrien, Horace Lockwood Smith
Dorrien, Horace Lockwood Smith 140, 213n
Dorset (England) 33, 209n, 213n
Dothan (Mevo Dotan; Middle East) 156
Douglas, Lord Alfred 4, 9, 10, 102, 205n, 211n
Dover Publications (publisher) 205n
Driesden, Basil Feodorovitch von 73, 74
"Drums of the Fore and Aft" (Kipling) 206
Dryden Press (publisher) 204n
Dublin Fusiliers 58, 135, 155
Dublin Review (periodical) 212n
Dudley, Captain 162
Duke of Wellington see Wellesley, Arthur
"Duke's Relative a Suicide?" 210n
Dumfrieshire (Scotland) 15
Dziemianowicz, Stefan 205n

Earl Ferrers 153
Earl of Essex 153
Easy, Private J. 99
Eaton, W.A. 212n
Echoes of Flanders (Warr) 191, 217n
"Economics of the War" (Belloc) 212n
Edge Hill/Edgehill (England) 96, 161, 162, 163
Edinburgh (Scotland) 147, 190
Edinburgh University 190
Edmonds, James E. 6, 204n
Edom (Middle East) and Edomites 183, 187, 216n
Edward VIII, King of England 190
Egypt 128, 183-185, 188, 199
Elephant and Castle (omnibus) 115
Eleusinia (Machen) 7
Elisha 144, 145
Elizabeth I, Queen of England 153
Elizabeth II, Queen of England 190
Elliot Stock (publisher) 129
Ellis, Phillip 206n
Embankment Times (imaginary newspaper) 112
Empire Press (publisher) 213n
Encyclopaedia Britannica 217n
Encyclopedia of Occultism & Parapsychology (Melton, ed.) 215n
English Channel (England) 154, 160
English Civil War 161
E.P. Dutton (publisher) 210n
Epernay (France) 206n
Ephesians 97, 207n
Epiphanes 157, 215n
Epistle to the Ephesians (Paul) 97
Epistle to the Romans (Paul) 180
"Erectheus" (Swinburne) 2
Erewhon (Butler) 113, 212n
Erskine Macdonald (publisher) 203n
Esaias 180
Esau 183
Essays on Theosophy (Taylor) 215n, 216n
Essex (England) 77
Essex, Earl 153
Evans, Walter 22, 207
Eve 185
Evening News (newspaper) 7, 10-14, 19, 21, 24, 25, 34, 36, 49, 50, 54, 56, 57, 60, 61, 63, 93, 98, 99, 112, 123-125, 155, 163, 197-200, 203n, 207n, 208n, 212n, 217n
Evenings with the Romanists 146, 214n
Ezekiel 166, 188, 199, 217n

Factory Health Safety and Welfare Encyclopaedia (Plumbe) 151, 214n
Factory Well-Being (Plumbe) 151, 214n
"Fall In!" (Begbie) 17, 122, 206n, 208n, 212n
Fane, Julian 212n

Index 229

Fatherland (periodical) 206*n*
Feakes, Paul 12
Feast of St. Michael and All Angels 93
Ferrers, Earl 153
Few Letters from Arthur Machen (Machen) 204*n*
Fifteen Sermons Preached at the Rolls Chapel (Butler) 113, 212*n*
Finck, Herman 121, 212*n*
Find the Angels: The Showmen: A Legend of the War (Crosland) 102–127
"Fireman's Wedding" 112
"First Battle of Ypres" (Woods) 199–200
First (1st) Cheshire Regiment 46
First Stone: On Reading the Unpublished Portions of "De Profundis" (Crosland) 102, 211*n*
Fitzroy, Almeric 16, 206*n*
Fitzroy, Ernest J.A. 60, 209*n*
Flanders (Belgium) 24, 36, 108
Fleming H. Revell Company (publisher) 147
Flintshire (England) 46, 134
Flying Horse (periodical) 211*n*
Foreign Office (England) 17
Fortnightly Review (periodical) 199, 207*n*
Fox, Emmet 215*n*
France and the French *see* individual names and regions
"Franchise Agitation in Belgium" 204*n*
Fraser, (Claud) Lovat 121, 212*n*
French, John Denton Pinkstone 5, 139, 140, 155, 204*n*, 213*n*, 215*n*
French, Joseph Lewis 207*n*
"French and Belgian Miners" 204*n*
French Army 5, 42
French language 106
Furnes (Belgium) 104

Gaelic 16
Gale (publisher) 216*n*
Gants gláces 200
"Garden of Avallaunius" (Machen) 9
Gare du Nord (France) 107
Garnier, A.E. 128, 213*n*
Garnier, Caroline 128
Garnier, John 128–146, 213–214*n*
Garnier, Thomas 128
Garvice, Charles 107, 211*n*
"Gas Bombs Used by English and French" 206*n*
G.B. Samuelson Productions Company 3
"Gentleman with a Duster" (Begbie) 32
Geoffroi de Bouillon 58, 209*n*
Geoffroy de Bouillon *see* Geoffroi de Bouillon
Geographical Journal (periodical) 212*n*
"Geography of the War" (Belloc) 212*n*
George V, King of England 190

George VI, King of England 190
George H. Doran (publisher) 206*n*
George Newnes (publisher) 77
George Redway (publisher) 8
Germans and Germany *see* individual names and regions
Gibbings (publisher) 208*n*
Gilbert, R.A. 204*n*
"Gilbert the Filbert" (Finck) 212*n*
Giles-Puller, Christopher William 128
Giles-Puller, Mary Caroline 128
Gilpin, P. 212*n*
Glasgow Academy 190
Globe (newspaper) 6, 32
gloves 200
Godfrey of Bouillon *see* Geoffroi de Bouillon
Golden Dawn 9
Goldstone, Adrian 206*n*
Gordon Highlanders 147
Gore, Lieutenant 71
Gospel of St. John 169
Gospel of St. Mark 53
Gospel of St. Matthew 181
Gould & Bottler (publisher) 203*n*
Gourmet's Guide to Europe (Newnham-Davis) 4, 204*n*
Governor (mastiff) 128, 213*n*
Grant Richards (publisher) 9, 205*n*
Great God Pan (Machen) 9, 205*n*
Great Pyramid (Egypt) 128, 129
Great Pyramid: Its Builder and Its Prophecy (Garnier) 129, 213*n*
Great Wonder in Heaven (Jackson) 161, 215*n*
Greenwood (publisher) 205*n*
Grenville, George-Nugent 215*n*
Guernsey (England) 128
Guest, Mrs. 136
Guide to the Antiquities of the Stone Age in the Department of British and Medieval Antiquities (British Museum) 204*n*
Gundagai (Australia) 210*n*
Gundagai Times and Tumut, Adelon and Murrumbridgee District Advisor (newspaper) 210*n*
Gurney, Edmund 70
Gwent (Wales) 7, 22, 197, 207*n*
Gwynedd, King 207*n*

H, Colonel 70
Haig, Douglas 15
Hamilton, W.K. 128
Hamlet and *Hamlet* (Shakespeare) 40, 112, 208–209*n*, 217*n*
Hampshire (England) 57
HMS Hampshire 211*n*
"Hand of Thais" (Campbell) 80, 210*n*
Harmsworth, Alfred 10

Harmsworth, Harold 10
Harper (publisher) 215n
Harper San Francisco (publisher) 203n
Harris, Frank 121, 212n
Harvey, John 71
Haskell House (publisher) 204n, 212n
Hastings, Thomas 214n
Havens, Munson 204n
Haversham, Lord (Arthur Divett Hayter; Baron Haversham) 17
Hazlehurst, George S. 46, 134
Hebrew prophets 199; *see also* Israel and Israelites
Henderson, Walter Brooks Drayton 214n
Henry Danielson (publisher) 203n
Henson, (Herbert) Hensley 24, 207n
Heptameron (Marguerite, Queen of Navarre) 8, 204n
Herbert, George 125, 213n
Hereford Cathedral School 7
Herodotus 8, 206n
Heroines of the World-War (Walter) 77, 210n
Hertfordshire (England) 71, 128
Highbury (England) 115
Higher Thought Centre (England) 134, 159, 215n
Hill of Dreams (Machen) 9, 11, 205n
Hindustani language 106
Hippocampus Press (publisher) 205n
"History of New Thought" (Fox) 215n
History of Spiritualism (Conan Doyle) 3, 203n
History Press (publisher) 214n
Hodder, and Hodder and Stoughton (publisher) 31, 203n, 208n, 213n, 214n
Hogg, Amy 9
Hogge, James Myle 6, 204n
Holland, Merlin 211n
Holy Grail 7
Hooper, Walter 203n
Hopkins, R. Thurston 214n
Horne, Mary Coultman 93–101
Horton, Robert Forman 24, 58, 59, 207n, 209n
Hosea 184
Houghton Mifflin (publisher) 204n
House of Souls (Machen) 9, 205n
House with Two Gardens (Leathem) 214n
Hoxton (England) 45
H.R. Allen (publisher) 214n
Hudleston, Dorothy Purefoy 9, 11
Huxley, Thomas Henry 65, 209n
Hyland, Peggy 3

Iltyd (Saint) 22, 207n
Improved Medicated Pillow, Cushion or the Like (Horne) 210n

Improvements in or Relating to Bath Chairs & Hammocks (Horne) 210n
Improvements Relating to Stands for Hammocks (Horne) 210n
"In the Shadows" (Finck) 121, 212n
"In the Trenches" (Leathem) 147–150
Indian Cemeteries 210n
"Inquiry Concerning the Angels of Mons" (Salter) 33, 208n, 210n, 214n
Intention for Conveying Invalids and Others by Rail or Road in a Recumbent Position (Horne) 210n
Ireland and Irish 147, 215n
Irish Guard 50, 90, 130, 132, 158, 163
Isaiah 166, 184, 185
Isle of Man (England) 109
Isle of Wight (England) 128
Islington (England) 104, 115
Israel and Israelites 119–120, 129, 156, 171–174, 177, 179, 180, 181, 183, 185, 186, 188, 199, 213n, 214n
Israel in Britain: A Brief Statement of the Evidences in Proof of the Israelite Origin of the British Race (Garnier) 213n
Italian language 106
Italy 204n
"Items of Interest" 210n
"It's a Long, Long Way to Tipperary" (Judge and Williams) 12, 26, 121, 207n, 212n, 213n

Jabin 214n
Jackson, Thomas 161, 215n
Jacob 187
James Burns (publisher) 209n
James Clarke (publisher) 214n
Jarrold and Sons (publisher) 213n
J.B. Lippincott (publisher) 208n
Jeanne d'Arc *see* Joan of Arc
Jennings, Hargrave 8
Jeremiah 166, 216n
Jerusalem (Israel) 189
Jesuit College 71
Jesuit Order 71
Jesus Christ 35, 36, 58, 144–146, 147–150, 160, 181, 182, 185
Jews *see* Israel and Israelites
Joan of Arc 29, 47, 49, 81, 83, 89, 90, 130, 138, 155, 158, 163, 164, 189
Joffre, Joseph Jacques Césaire 6, 138, 155, 213n, 215n
John Bull (periodical) 23
John Lane (publisher) 205n, 217n
John Long (publisher) 211n
John Murray (publisher) 215n, 217n
John Wesley, 1703–1791 (Leathem) 214n
John Wiley (publisher) 205n, 210n
Johnson, Samuel 191, 217n

Jones, Arthur Llewellyn 7
Jones, Janet 7
Jones, John Edward 7
Joseph Glanville and Psychical Research in the Seventeenth century (Redgrove) 214*n*
Joseph Jones (publisher) 204*n*
Joshi, S.T. 9, 205*n*
Joubert, Joseph 37, 208*n*
Journal of the Society for Psychical Research (periodical) 208*n*, 210*n*, 214*n*
Judah 180, 181, 185, 186, 199
Judea 24, 35
Judge, Jack 207*n*, 212*n*
Judge, William Quan 25, 165, 207*n*
Judges 144
Juliana of Stolberg 211*n*
Julius Caesar 204*n*, 212*n*
Julius Caesar and *Julius Caesar* (Shakespeare) 113, 212*n*
Juvenal 197

Kaiser (Franz Joseph I) 23, 126, 213*n*
Kashin (Russia) 74
"Keep the Home Fires Burning" (Novello) 113, 212*n*
Keinton (England) 161, 162
Kensington (England) 117, 134, 159
Khartoum (Sudan) 211*n*
King, Edward 204*n*
Kipling, (Joseph) Rudyard 21, 107, 111, 123, 125, 206–207*n*, 211*n*
Kirke, Lewis 162
Kishon (Middle East) 216*n*
Kitchener, Lord Horatio Herbert 105, 121, 127, 143, 211*n*, 212*n*, 213*n*
Koi (Russia) 74

La Fere (France) 140
Lancashire 71
Lancashire Fusiliers 28, 48, 54, 131
Lancaster, Mr. 101, 136, 156
Landrecies (France) 139, 140
Lang's Neck (England) 70
Latin language 27, 28
Latter Days (Taylor) 215*n*, 217*n*
Lawrence Wright Music (publisher) 203*n*
Leatham, W.H. (William Harvey) 60, 147–150
Le Cateau (France) 98, 139, 140
Leeds (England) 103, 107
Leeds Mercury Weekly Supplement (newspaper) 103
Le Queux, William 208*n*
Lewis, C.S. (Clive Staples) 2–3, 203*n*
Lewknor Rectory (England) 128
Liège (Belgium) 4
"Life and Genius of T.W.H. Crosland" (Brown) 211*n*

Life and Genius of T.W.H. Crosland (Brown) 211*n*
Life of Johnson: Including a Tour of the Hebrides (Boswell) 217*n*
Life of St. Francis of Assisi (Leathem) 214*n*
Light (periodical) 22, 56, 58
Lincoln (England) 128
Lindsay, David 206*n*
Lined with Rags (Campbell) 80
Lion (mastiff) 128, 213*n*
Living Church (periodical) 147
Llanddewi Fach (Wales) 7
Lloyd George, David 109, 121, 211*n*, 212*n*
Lodge, Oliver 31
London (England) 7, 12, 32, 61, 77, 103, 115
"London, 1802" (Wordsworth) 213*n*
London Evening News see *Evening News*
London Times see *Times*
"Londoner" 22, 37, 197, 207*n*, 208*n*, 217*n*
Loomis (publisher) 216*n*
"Lost Legion" (Kipling) 207*n*
Louis of Nassau 96, 211*n*
Louis XIV (France) 200
Lovat Scouts 16
Lovecraft, H.P. 11, 205*n*
Lovecraft's Library (Joshi) 205*n*
Low Moor (England) 109
Lucas, E.V. (Edward Verrall) 121, 212*n*
Ludgate Circus (England) 115
Luke 149, 184, 214*n*
Lyall, David see Swan, Annie S.

Macaulay, Thomas Babington 156, 215*n*
Maccabeaus 157, 215*n*
Machen, Arthur Hilary 9
Machen, Arthur Llewellyn Jones 19–30, 197–201, and throughout
Machen, Janet Frances 9
MacLeod, A. Donald 214*n*
Macmillan (publisher) 214*n*
Mahatmas 164, 166, 199, 207*n*
Maitland (Australia) 210*n*
Maitland Weekly Mercury (newspaper) 210*n*
Malplaquet (France) 204*n*
Malta 72, 128
Manchester Guardian (newspaper) 58
"Many Riots in Belgium" 204*n*
March, Miss 58
Marguerite, Queen of Navarre 8, 204*n*
Marlborough (England) 204*n*
Marlborough (John Churchill, First Duke of Marlborough) 200
Marne (France) 138, 139, 140, 154, 200, 213*n*, 215*n*
Marshall, Samuel 161, 162
Martin Secker (publisher) 205*n*, 211*n*
Martock (England) 33, 54, 134, 209*n*
Marylebone (England) 77, 128

Massingham, H.W. (Henry William) 32
Mastiffs 128, 213n
Matthew 145
Maubeuge (Belgium) 4
Maupassant, Henry René Guy de 111, 211–212n
McKeel, Herbert S. 214n
Meadow Lane, Leeds (England) 107
Meaning of Life (Courtney) 207n
Mediterranean Sea 78
Megiddo (Middle East) 187, 216n
Melton, J. Gordon 215–216n
Memoirs (Fitzroy) 16, 206n
Memoirs of Jacques Casanova (Casanova) 8
Memorials of John Hampden, His Party and Times (Nugent) 163
Merchant Taylor's School 31
Meuse (Belgium) 6
Middle East *see* Israel and Israelites; specific location (i.e., Edom)
Mihangel (Saint) 22, 207n
Mildmay, Mrs. St. John 207n
Mills & Boon (publisher) 32, 80, 210n
Milton, John 33, 213n
"Miracles and Modern Spiritualism" (Wallace) 70, 209n
Mirrors of Downing Street (Begbie) 32
"Mr. Arthur Machen: Literature of Awe" 206n
Mr. Britling Sees It Through (Wells) 6, 204n
"Mr. T.W.H. Crosland" 211n
Monck, G.G. (George Gustavus) 33, 54, 134, 209n, 213n
Monkwearmouth (England) 101, 135, 158
Monmouthshire (Wales) 197
Mons (Belgium) 1, 4–7
"Mons Angels: The Growth of a Miracle Fiction" (Machen) 13, 206n, 207n
Mons Meg 4
Monument of Howard Douglas Campbell 210n
Mook Heath (England) 163
Mookerheyde (Netherlands) 211n
Moorcum (probably Moorcambe, England) 109
Moore, Arthur 5
Moore, Thoams 214n
Moorlands (England) 41
Morocco 210n
Mosier, John 7, 204n
Motley, John Lothrop 163, 215n
Motley's Rise of the Dutch Republic [sic] (Motley) 163, 215n
Mount Hermon (Middle East) 187, 216n
Mount Seir (Middle East) 187, 216n
Munsters (England) 98, 140, 209n
Murphy, C.W. 217n
Murphy, Michael 204n, 205n, 208n, 210n

Murrumbidgee District (Australia) 210n
"My American Cousins" (Plumbe) 214n
My Life and Loves (Harris) 212n
Myrtleford (Australia) 210n
Myrtleford Mail and Whorouly Witness (newspaper) 210n
Myth of the Great War (Mosier) 7, 204n

Namur (France) 204n
Nancy (France) 148
Napoleon *see* Bonaparte, Napoleon
National Federation of Free Church Councils 24
National Protestant Federation (periodical) 214n
National Trade Press (publisher) 214n
Nature (periodical) 214n
Naumer (Belgium) 6
Neave, Ethel 208n
Nelson, Horatio, First Viscount Nelson 213n
Nephilim (Garnier) 129
Netherlands 211n
Netley Hospital (England) 45, 134
Neuve-Chapelle (France) 54, 58, 134, 135
New Church Weekly (periodical) 23
New College (Edinburgh) 147
New Thought 157, 215n
New Thought Bulletin (periodical) 215n
New York (United States) 120
New York Times (newspaper) 11, 13, 19, 77, 204n, 206n, 210n
Newcastle-on-Tyne (England) 78
Newnham-Davis, Lieutenant Colonel 4, 204n
Newspaper Publicity Co. (publisher) 153, 154, 213n
1914 (French) 204n
Nineteenth-Century (periodical) 97
Ninth (9th) Argyll 190
Ninth (9th) Lincolns 99
Noah 178
Noakes, Vivien 214n
North American Review (periodical) 207n
Northampton (England) 16
Northamptonshire (England) 161
Nova Scotia (Canada) 71
Novello, Ivor 113, 212n
Noyon (France) 140
Nugent, George-Nugent Grenville 161, 163, 215n

"Obituary" (Shirley) 214n
Observer (newspaper) 54
Occult Review (periodical) 22, 28, 46, 51, 52, 54, 56, 77, 79, 153, 154, 157
Odes and Other Poems (Powys, J.C.) 214n
O'Donnell, Elliott 153, 214n
Oise (France) 139, 140

Index

Olcott, Henry Steel 165, 207n
"Old Contemptibles" 11
On Miracles and Modern Spiritualism (Wallace) 209n
"On the Defensive" 204n
On the Side of the Angels (Begbie) 18, 31–76, 93, 96, 121, 166, 173, 198, 208n, 210n, 213n
Ongar (England) 77
Order of the Thistle 190
Oreiller hygiénique (Horne) 211n
Orkney Islands (Scotland) 211n
Oscar Wilde and Myself (Douglas) 4, 102, 211n
Oscar Wilde Encyclopedia (Beckson) 211n
Osgoldcross (England) 207n
Othello and *Othello* (Shakespeare) 105
"Other Side of the Angels" (Crosland) 123
Our Near Future (Redding) 181, 216n
"Our Unseen Enemies and Allies" (Sinnett) 97
Outlook (periodical) 103
Owen, Mr. 71
Oxford (England) 54, 134, 153, 162
Oxford University Press (publisher) 203n, 204n
Oxfordshire (England) 128
oysters 4

Paisley (Scotland) 190
Palestine 186, 216n
Paley, William 113, 212n
Pall Mall (periodical) 24
Pall Mall Gazette (periodical) 137
Paree, Paul 3, 203n
Paris *see* France
Parliamentary Debates (Official Report) (HMSO) 204n
Parry, Lady 128
Pasteur, Louis 65, 209n
patents 93, 210–211n
"Pax" 55
Pekin (China) 135, 159, 213n
Pentacostals (British) 213n, 215n
Perrot, Gervase 8
Persia and Persians 144
Petrograd (Russia) 137
Petrovo-Solovoro, M. 73
"Phantom Armies Seen in France" (Mildmay) 207
Pharisees 102
Piccadilly Circus (England) 104, 120
Pickwick Papers (Dickens) 25, 29, 207n, 208n
P.I.P. (periodical) 103
Plantagenets 200
Plato 113, 212n
Plevna (Turkey) 160
Plumbe, C. Conway 151–152, 214n

Plymouth (Canada) 128
Poems (Powys, J.C.) 214n
Poems from Punch 1909–1920 (Henderson) 214n
poets 3, 151
Poland 146, 160, 161, 209n, 210n, 213n, 214n
Political Struwwelpeter (Begbie) 32
Pollux 156, 215n
Ponomareff, Nicolas Ivanovitch 73, 74
Poole, Major 70
Popular Electricity and Modern Mechanics (periodical) 206n
Powys, John Cowper 153, 214n
Powys, Theodore 153, 214n
Presbyterians 147
Prince Line (business) 78
Problems of Psychical Research (Carrington) 214n
Proceedings (Psychical Research Society) 70
Proceedings (Society for Psychical Research) 33, 73
Proverbs 212n
Psalms 215n
Psychical Phenomena and the War (Carrington) 207n
Psychical Research Society 25, 70, 74
Punch, or the London Charivari (periodical) 151
Pyramid of Cheops (Egypt) 128, 129, 213n
Pyramid of Khufu (Egypt) 128, 129, 213n
Pythagoras 76

Queen's College/University 147
Queensland (Australia) 78
Quest, Mrs. 61

Rabbis 119–120
Raby, Peter 211n
R.A.M.C. *see* Royal Army Medical Corps
Raymund Lully: Illuminated Doctor, Alchemist and Christian Mystic (Waite) 214n
Reading (England) 16
Red Cross 41, 43, 80
Redding, William A. 181, 216n
Redgrove, H. Stanley 153, 214n
Reedy's Mirror (periodical) 205n
Regal Company 3
Regent Street (London) 36
Release from Time (Plumbe) 151, 214n
Return and Other Poems (Woods) 217n
"Return of the Angels: This Time They Are at Ypres" (Machen) 199–201
Revelation of St. John 145, 166
"Review" 214n
Review of Reviews (periodical) 210n
R.F.A. *see* Royal Field Artillery
R.H. Allenson (publisher) 215n

Rheims (France) 106
Rhine river (Germany) 108
Richard Coeur de Lion 57
Richard I, King of England *see* Richard Coeur de Lion
Richardson, Dr. 60, 61, 136
Rider & Company (publisher) 153
Rise of the Dutch Republic (Motley) 163, 215*n*
Robert Banks and Son (publisher) 128, 213*n*
"Robinson Crusoe of the soul" 9
Roman Catholics *see* Catholics
Rome and Romans (Italy) 143, 156, 215*n*
Rosicrucians (Jennings) 8
Rosneath (Scotland) 190
Royal Academy (England) 151
Royal Army Medical Corps (England) 110, 118, 211*n*
Royal Engineers (England) 128
Royal Field Artillery (England) 90, 130, 157, 213*n*
Royal Military Academy (England) 15
Royal Munster Fusiliers *see* Munsters (England)
Russell, G.W.E. (George William Erskine) 32
Russia and Russians 16, 39, 49, 73, 74, 96, 137, 138, 143, 154, 160, 164, 184–187, 198, 207*n*, 213*n*, 215*n*
Russo Turkish War 137, 160
Rynde (laundress) 106

S., C.K. *see* Shorter, Clement King
Sabbath *see* Shaboth
Saffron Walden (England) 59–60
St. Andrew's Presbyterian Church (Canada) 147
St. Cadwaladyr Vendigeid 22, 207*n*
St. Dewi 22, 207*n*
St. George 1, 12, 13, 22, 23, 27–29, 36, 48, 49, 53, 57, 58, 81, 84, 89, 90, 95, 130–132, 134, 138, 152, 155, 157, 159, 163, 164, 206*n*, 210*n*
St. Germain-en-Laye (France) 56, 137
St. Giles Edinburgh 190
St. Iltyd 22, 207*n*
St. James 24
St. Joan *see* Joan of Arc
St. John 166, 169, 216*n*
St. Leonards-on-Sea (England) 61, 136
St. Luke 149, 184, 214*n*
St. Margaret 189
St. Mark 53
St. Martin's Lane (London) 95
St. Mary-at-Hill (England) 60, 61
St. Marylebone (England) 77, 128
St. Matthew 181, 216*n*
St. Michael 29, 47, 49, 81, 83, 84, 89, 90, 93, 130, 132, 137, 138, 144, 155, 157, 158, 163, 183, 186, 187, 189, 207*n*

St. Mihangel 22
St. Paul 97, 171, 180, 181, 187
St. Paul's Cathedral (England) 10, 100, 206*n*
St. Paul's Greenock (Scotland) 190
St. Quentin (France) 139, 140
St. Stanislaus Kotska 71
St. Teilo 22, 207*n*
St. Waudru 204*n*
Sainte-Beuve, Charles Augustin 37, 38, 208*n*
Sainte-Beauve: On Men and Women (Sharp) 208*n*
Salter, W.H. 33, 208*n*, 210*n*, 214*n*
Samaritans 115
Sambre (Belgium) 5, 6
Sandown Park (England) 104
Sappho 21, 206*n*
Sark (England) 198, 217*n*
Savage, Henry 204*n*, 212*n*
Schopenhauer, Arthur 2
Scots and Scotland 77, 80, 84, 147, 190, 210*n*, 211*n*
Scots Guards 134, 140
Scott, Henry 71
Scott, Walter 7
"Scrap of Paper" (Crawford) 12
Scribner's (publisher) 203*n*, 205*n*
"Sea Trip Dispute" 210*n*
Seale, Gertrude 31
Sedan (France) 26
Selected Letters (Machen) 204*n*
Seleucids 215*n*
Seren (publisher) 204*n*
Seven Oaks (publisher) 214*n*
Seward, Miss Anna 217*n*
Seymour, Michael Hobart 146, 214*n*
Shaboth 119
Shakespeare, William 40, 105, 111, 127, 208–209*n*, 212*n*, 217*n*
Sharp, William 208*n*
Sherborne (England) 209*n*, 213*n*
Sherbroke, John 71
Shipley Glen (England) 104
Shirley, Ralph 22, 28, 51, 52, 54, 56, 96, 129, 137, 153–164, 207*n*, 209*n*, 211*n*, 213*n*, 215*n*
Short History of World War I (Edmonds) 6, 204*n*
Shorter, Clement King 112, 212*n*
Sidney Street (London) 26
Sierra Leone (Africa) 207*n*
Silima (Malta) 72
Simms, Richard 206*n*
Simpkins, Marshall, Hamilton, Kent and Co. (publisher) 14, 19, 197, 203*n*, 214*n*, 217*n*
Sin and Redemption (Garnier) 129
Sinnett, Alfred Percy 23, 56, 97, 207*n*
Sisera 144, 214*n*
Skobeloff, Michael Dimitrievitch 137, 138, 160, 164, 213*n*, 215*n*

Sladen, Douglas 210n
Smith, Mrs. Burnett see Swan, Annie S.
Smith, F.K. 78
Smith, John Taylor 24, 207n
Smith, William 7
Smith's Classical Dictionary (Smith, W.) 7
Societies (periodical) 203n
Society for Psychical Research 33, 73, 79, 154
Society of Pantagruelists (publisher) 205n
Soissons (France) 148
Soldier Tales (Kipling) 207n
"Soldier's Rest" (Machen) 20, 21
Soliloquy of a Hermit (Powys, T.) 214n
"Solitude" (Wilcox) 117, 212n
Solomon 120
Some Memorials of John Hampden, His Party, and His Times (Nugent) 215n
Somme (France) 139
South African War 38
South Kensington (England) 159
Southampton (England) 71
Southsea (England) 58
Spain 213n
Spanish Armada 76
"Spectral Soldiers: Possible Literary Antecedents for 'The Bowmen'" (Ellis) 206n
Spenser, Edmund 2
Sphere (periodical) 112, 212n
Stacpoole, Henry De Vere 108, 120, 121, 211n
Stainer, John 21, 206n
Standard (newspaper) 79, 210n
Starrett, (Charles Emerson) Vincent 10, 32, 201, 205n, 206n, 208n
Starrett vs. Machen: A Record of Discovery and Correspondence (Murphy, ed.) 203n, 205n, 206n, 208n, 210n
Stead, W.T. (William Thomas) 78, 79, 210n
Steell, John 213n
Stilwell-Taylor see Taylor, Isabelle E.
"Stonehenge" 128
Stonyhurst (England) 71
Stoughton, Miss 59, 60
Strand (periodical) 207n
"Strikers Hold a Mass-Meeting" 204n
Studies in Weird Fiction (periodical) 206n
Suffolk (England) 31
Suffrage Movement from Its Evolutionary Aspect (Taylor) 215n
suicide 77
Sunderland (England) 55
Sunderland Echo (newspaper) 215n
Supernatural Fiction Writers: Fantasy and Horror (Bleiler, ed.) 203n, 205n, 206n
Supernatural Horror in Literature (Lovecraft) 11, 205n
Supernatural Literature in the World (Joshi) 205n

Surrey (England) 165
Sutherland Highlanders 190
Suwalki (Poland) 160
Swan, Annie S. 60, 209n
Swan Sonnenschein (publisher) 165, 215n
Sweetser, Wesley D. 206n
Swift, Jonathan 33
Swinburne, Algernon Charles 2
Switzerland 148, 204n
Sydney (Canada) 71
Sydney, Lewis 111, 212n
Syria 144

T. Werner Laurie, Ltd. (publisher) 102
Tarquins 215n
Taylor, Isabelle E. 165–189, 198, 199
Taylor, Lucian 9
Teilo (Saint) 22, 207n
Tekleton (England) 59
telepathy 38, 123, 142
Ten Tribes of Israel 129, 199
Tennant, Edward 9
Tennyson, Alfred 7
Theosophical Publishing Company (publisher) 198
Theosophical Publishing House (publisher) 215n
Theosophical Publishing Society (publisher) 165, 215n
Theosophical Society (England) 165, 216n
"Theosophy" 215n
theosophy and theosophists 25, 164, 165–189, 199, 207n, 210n, 215–217n
Third (or 3rd) Canadians (Canada) 135, 159
Thompson, Barry 215n
Three Imposters (Machen) 9, 205n
Tibet 166, 199
Times (aka *London Times*; newspaper) 5, 11, 14, 36, 78, 103, 204n, 206n, 210n, 211n, 214n, 217n
Tipperary see "It's a Long, Long Way to Tipperary"
Toothill (England) 77
Toronto (Canada) 10
Town Topics (periodical) 23
Trafalgar (Spain) 213n
Trinity Church (England) 128
True Christ and the False Christ (Garnier) 129
Truth (periodical) 23
Tumut (Australia) 210n
Turks and Turkey 137, 160, 183, 184, 187, 199
Turpenite 13, 16, 19, 206n, 207n, 208n
Twenty Years of My Life (Sladen) 210n

Uhlans 43, 86, 89, 98, 133, 210n
Universe (periodical) 57, 156
"University Intelligence" 214n

University of Texas Press (publisher) 206n
"Unseen Host" (Warr) 190-196

Valenciennes (Belgium) 4
Valentine, Mark 7, 8, 204n, 205n
Valley of Dry Bones 188-189, 199
Vanity Fair (periodical) 103, 210n
Varney, Edmund *see* Verney, Edmund
Verney, Edmund 162, 215n
Views and Opinions of the Revd. Dr. Stiggins (Machen) 9-10
"Violets" (Fane and Wright) 212n
Virgin Mary 49, 160
Visions and Revisions (Powys, J.C.) 214n
Visions of Mons and Ypres: Their Meaning and Purpose (Garnier) 128-146
Visitation of England and Wales (Crisp, ed.) 209n, 213n
Vitry-le-François (France) 28, 48, 51, 53, 90, 131, 138, 141, 157
"Vocalizing the Angels of Mons" (Crook) 203n
Voices of Silence: The Alternative Book of First World War Poetry (Noakes) 214n
Voices Prophesying War: Future Wars, 1763-3749 (Clarke) 203n
"Voyage in the Mediterranean" 210n

Wainsman, Captain 162
Waite, A.E. (Arthur Edward) 153, 214n
Wales and the Welsh 7, 153
Wallace, Alfred Russel 66, 70, 209n
Walter M. Hill (publisher) 205n
Walters, E.W. 77, 210n
War and the Weird (Hopkins) 214n
"War Day by Day" 204n
War Office (England) 16, 17
Ware (England) 71, 128
Warr, Alfred 190
Warr, Charles Laing 190-196, 217n
Waterloo (Belgium) 213n
Waterloo Platform (England) 104, 114
Watkins, Oswald 49
"We All Go the Same Way Home" (Hume and Murphy) 217n
Weekly Dispatch (newspaper) 20, 93, 159
Weld, Philip 71
Welldon, James Edward Cowell 24, 207n
Weller, Sam (Dickens) 25, 34, 35, 207n

Wellesley, Arthur, First Duke of Wellington 200, 213n
Wells (England) 33, 54, 134, 209n
Wells, H.G. (Herbert George) 6, 204n
Welsh language 106
Wesleyan Methodist 28, 48, 131, 157
West Riding (England) 101, 135, 159
Westminster Gazette (periodical) 210n
Weymouth (England) 101, 136
W.H. Russell & Co. (publisher) 129
"White Feather Legion" (Crosland) 125
White Hen (Campbell) 80, 210n
"Whiter Than the Whitewash on the Wall" 109, 117
Whorouly (Australia) 210n
Wilcox, Ella Wheeler 37, 212n
Wilde, Oscar 4, 10, 102, 211n
"Will and Idea" (Schopenhauer) 2
William of Nassau 211n
William Rider & Son (publisher) 153, 154, 214n
Williams, Harry 207n, 212n
Williams, Paul 212n
Wilson, M. Courtney (Courtenay) 33, 41, 42, 43, 45, 132, 140, 155, 209n
Wipers *see* Ypres (France)
Witley (England) 60
Woking (England) 123
Wood, William 161, 162, 215n
Woodcocks 4
Woods, Margaret 199-200, 217n
Woolwich (England) 15
Wordsworth, William 213n
Work and Life (periodical) 147
Wright, Ellen 212n
Wright, Ronald Selby 217n
Wynard, George 71

XYZ Division (imaginary police) 114

Yiddish language 119
Yorkshire (England) 105, 106, 108, 109, 118
Youngsbury (England) 128
Ypres (France) 29, 39, 44, 49, 52, 101, 133, 135, 141, 146, 148, 159, 190, 192, 199, 200, 209n, 215n, 217n
Yriarte, Charles 2

Zechariah 185, 216n

www.ingramcontent.com/pod-product-compliance
Ingram Content Group UK Ltd.
Pitfield, Milton Keynes, MK11 3LW, UK
UKHW041942140426
5217IPUK00014B/620